THE NEXT

THE NEXT

DAN VINING

BERKLEY PRIME CRIME, NEW YORK

THE BERKLEY PUBLISHING GROUP
Published by the Penguin Group
Penguin Group (USA) Inc.
375 Hudson Street, New York, New York 10014, USA
Penguin Group (Canada), 90 Eglinton Avenue East, Suite 700, Toronto, Ontario M4P 2Y3, Canada
(a division of Pearson Penguin Canada Inc.)
Penguin Books Ltd., 80 Strand, London WC2R 0RL, England
Penguin Group Ireland, 25 St. Stephen's Green, Dublin 2, Ireland (a division of Penguin Books Ltd.)
Penguin Group (Australia), 250 Camberwell Road, Camberwell, Victoria 3124, Australia
(a division of Pearson Australia Group Pty. Ltd.)
Penguin Books India Pvt. Ltd., 11 Community Centre, Panchsheel Park, New Delhi—110 017, India
Penguin Group (NZ), Cnr. Airborne and Rosedale Roads, Albany, Auckland 1310, New Zealand
(a division of Pearson New Zealand Ltd.)
Penguin Books (South Africa) (Pty.) Ltd., 24 Sturdee Avenue, Rosebank, Johannesburg 2196,
South Africa

Penguin Books Ltd., Registered Offices: 80 Strand, London WC2R 0RL, England

This is an original publication of The Berkley Publishing Group.

This is a work of fiction. Names, characters, places, and incidents either are the product of the author's imagination or are used fictitiously, and any resemblance to actual persons, living or dead, business establishments, events, or locales is entirely coincidental.

First edition: August 2006

Library of Congress Cataloging-in-Publication Data

Vining, Dan.
   The next / by Dan Vining. — Berkley Prime Crime hardcover ed.
      p. cm.
   ISBN 0-425-20943-1
   1. Private investigators—Fiction. 2. Supernatural—Fiction. 3. Los Angeles (Calif.)—Fiction. I. Title.

PS3622.I56N49 2006
813'.6—dc22
                                        2006010803

PRINTED IN THE UNITED STATES OF AMERICA

10 9 8 7 6 5 4 3 2 1

THE NEXT

C H A P T E R O N E

Would you like a side of *Death* with that?

It was the Saugus Café, thirty miles north of downtown L.A., off Old 99, the Newhall Road, one of three or four spots claiming to have laid the table for James Dean's last meal, a slice of apple pie and a glass of milk if the legend had it right, before he drove his Spyder 550 on north over the Grapevine to Cholame and the Y intersection of the 41 and 46 highways where a Cal Poly kid in a black-and-white Ford turned in front of him. The diner was borderline shrine. There were pictures of Dean all along the wall above the long counter, the one from *Giant* with his arms draped over the rifle across his shoulders like it was the top bar of the cross or something, the other famous one that everybody's seen, Dean's hand at his waist, middle finger and thumb curled to touch, index finger pointing off camera. Above the register was one of Dean leaning against the silver Porsche roadster in front of a gas station down in L.A. where he had picked up his mechanic that morning. That *fateful* morning . . . Isn't that what they say? The two were on their way to a pro-am race up at Salinas when they bought it, when Mr. D waved the black flag. It was like they always said over the PA out at the old Saugus Speedway on hot Saturday nights, "The most dangerous miles driven tonight will be your trip here and home . . ."

But then again, as the racers like to say, it's not the going fast that kills you . . . It's the sudden stop.

The waitress waited. "Would you like a side of beans with that?" she said again.

"What kind of beans?" Jimmy Miles said. The place wasn't crowded. It was early afternoon. He could play with her a little.

"Ranchero beans," she said.

"Pot beans," Jimmy said.

"Uh-huh."

"Maybe cooked with a little bacon."

"Uh-huh."

There was a fly, big and blue and buzzing, the size of a jelly bean, flying in wack circles over the booth, slamming itself into the same spot on the plate glass window every half minute, trying to get out of there but not learning a damn thing from previous experience.

Jimmy knew a thing or two about that.

The waitress snatched it out of the air and snuffed it, dropped it onto the linoleum floor and flipped it under the table with the toe of her waitress shoe all in one seamless little . . . what would you call it? Dance?

"I guess I'd better," Jimmy said. "And a beer. Whatever you drink."

"I drink cherry Cokes," she said.

She was the kind of waitress who didn't write anything down, and he was the kind of customer who hadn't needed a menu, so she just tapped the Formica twice with her short, unpainted nails and stepped away.

"And pie," Jimmy said after her. "Apple. And milk."

"Why not?" she said without turning.

Jimmy looked out the window, across the street, at the old clapboard train station. It used to be across two lanes; now there were four and clotted with traffic. A hundred years ago, it had been a stagecoach trail. Two hundred, a mission trail, friars and priests. Five hundred, five *thousand*, and it would be indigenes with leathery feet, breaking the dirt down to dust.

The girl came back from the bathroom. Her eyes were red, but she wasn't crying anymore. She had a folded brown washroom towel in her hand, too rough to put to your eyes. She was maybe twenty-five, a Latina, but one who'd probably never been south of San Diego. Or maybe even Long Beach. She was wearing a rayon dress, like this was the forties. Or *The Postman Always Rings Twice*.

She hadn't looked at Jimmy once since he'd come in, or at anyone else in the place, off on her own trip. As soon as she sat back down in the banquette, her food came, a tuna melt and a side of fries from what Jimmy could see. She smiled up at the waitress, an open-eyed look that almost asked the woman to sit down and talk about it, femme to femme. Almost. There was a lot of *almost* in the young woman's story, from what Jimmy could already see.

"Anything else, hon?" the waitress said to her, like a nurse.

The girl shook her head. When the waitress was gone, the forced smile fell off the girl's face. She arranged the two plates so it suited her, pushed the ketchup bottle forward an inch, and then picked up half the sandwich and took a bite. A big bite, like a teenager, like a teenager on a date. They usually didn't eat, not like this, when they were sad or shaken and running like this. She reminded Jimmy of someone, though she didn't look anything like the other one, a woman out of his past—a face, a pair of eyes, a mouth, a shape still waiting in a room inside him anytime he opened the door. Maybe it was this girl's appetite. She ate like the date she was on was the tenth date or the twentieth or some number past counting, as if she didn't have to prove she was "ladylike" anymore. Like she loved you and knew you loved her, had seen her all kinds of ways.

Like that other one.

Or maybe it was just that her dress was soft light blue, like the feeling she brought over you.

She never finished her food, stopped after those first big bites. She bothered the fries another minute, then gave up, pushing the oval plate away so she could put her hands on the table in front of her. She wasn't married, or at least didn't wear a ring. She didn't wave for the bill, didn't seem in much of a hurry to get back on the road, just sat looking out the window right past Jimmy at her car, a baby-blue '70s Buick Skylark convertible that had been lowered a bit. A couple of minutes slid by like that, with her looking past Jimmy at the car, then the waitress appeared and pushed the ticket across the table to her. She looked at the slip of paper and took in a breath and slid out of the booth, as if it had been a note from the older woman that said, *Honey, you're just going to have to go on and deal with it.*

Her eyes were leaking again before she reached the door.

Jimmy waited a minute or two and then left a twenty on the table and stepped out into the dust and the truck stink from the highway. The Skylark was already gone out of sight, but it didn't matter. He knew she wasn't going anywhere but north. She wasn't going to turn around and head back to Los Angeles, he knew that. She was *hard-running* and that meant north and there was really only one way to go.

The sun was bright; the light had a kind of aluminum sheen to it. It had been hot the last few days. Hot and dry. Jimmy reached in and opened the glove box and found a pair of beat-up Ray-Bans. Tortoiseshell, almost red. He had brought the Porsche, the '64 Cabriolet, the ragtop, and the top was down. It wasn't the best car for this kind of thing, too showy, too one-of-a-kind, but something had made him pick it. He opened the door and let the wind blow through it a minute, cool off the seats before he got in it. It was September.

Dean died in September, didn't he?

Because he knew he could catch up to her, Jimmy didn't get back on the 5, took a right off Newhall Road instead, and drove out past what was left of the old speedway. A little memory jag. There were the wooden stands, red and white, peeling a little but looking permanent. The track was a dead flat third-of-a-mile asphalt oval, a "bullring" racetrack that had started out as a rodeo arena. A subdivision had built up around it now, plain-Jane two-story stucco houses with saplings staked in the yards, blank-faced houses, sand colored, looking like the boxes real houses would come in. The last races had been run ten years ago, but the owners had kept it up, rented out the facility for Sunday morning swap meets. A couple thousand people would come, even driving up from Los Angeles, church for believers in bargains.

But it was empty now, about as empty as empty gets. Where was the tumbleweed blowing through? Jimmy jumped a low chain-link fence on what they called the back chute and walked out to the center. It was paved from one side to the other, cracking and not as black as it used to be but so hot his shoes smacked.

He looked up at the stands, found the row where he used to like to sit. The top row.

Where *they* used to sit.

It looked bad in the daytime. In the present.

SO maybe it wasn't about James Dean after all . . .

The Skylark girl (he'd learn in a minute her name was Lucy, *Lucille*) had taken the exit off the 5 onto California 46, headed west toward Lost Hills and Paso Robles, and now she blew right by the intersection where Dean had died and then on past the memorial, a granite marker and a bend of stainless steel wrapped around an oak next to a café six miles along at Cholame.

Jimmy didn't stop either, just hung back a mile. A little two-car caravan traversing central Cal. There was enough rise and fall on the highway to give him a good look down at her every minute or so, to keep her in front of him without her seeing him.

He pulled off after ten or twelve miles of that.

"Did you do the Skylark?"

He was on the shoulder, directly under a whistling cell tower "camouflaged" to look like a spindly evergreen, which was particularly stupid given that this was in the middle of bare brown rolling hills, it the only "tree" for miles. Unless you counted the occasional oil derrick.

But the reception was good.

"I painted it for her," Angel said. "For her boyfriend, actually. He give it to her."

"Is he the problem?"

"You really *are* a detective."

"So he let her keep it when he left?"

"I guess. She kept it."

"I don't know, bud," Jimmy said, "I might be on *his* side, taking a man's car."

"He's dead."

"What's her name?"

When Angel told him, Jimmy sang, "You picked a fine time to leave me, Lucille . . ."

"Loose *wheel*," Angel said.

Back in the day on those Saturday nights at Saugus Speedway, when one of the old clunker stockers would kick loose a wheel, send it bouncing across the infield, the announcer—Jimmy remembered his name, Virgil Kirkpatrick—would wait a beat and then say the line: "You picked a fine time to leave me, loose wheel . . ." And the crowd would laugh, like he was Jay Leno.

"I drove on out there," Jimmy said. "The speedway. Jumped the fence."

"And it was sad," Angel said back to him.

"I can take sad," Jimmy said.

"Not so much as you think," Angel said.

"She's headed toward Paso Robles, unless she just wanted to cut over to the 101 or the coast. Any idea why?"

"That's why I'm paying you the big dollar," Angel said.

"I haven't been out of town in awhile," Jimmy said. "It's nice out here." A wind had blown over the hill, and the air smelled good, like the inside of a wooden box.

"Where did you pick her up?"

"She was right where you said she'd be, bright and early."

"Eagle Rock."

"Eagle Rock," Jimmy repeated. "She took a long time to pack the car, like she was waiting for me."

Nothing whistled down the line for a second or two.

"How does she look?" Angel said.

"Like they all do," Jimmy said. "One kind of them."

"Lost."

"Spooked. Alone. Running," Jimmy said. "Trying to get from what was to what's next. Way young to be so hurt. Or maybe I've just seen too many of them."

"Or maybe you're getting old in the soul," Angel said.

"It's about time."

"She's good-looking, huh?"

"She's not a Sailor," Jimmy said, almost a question.

"No."

"Tell me who she is to you," Jimmy said.

"Nobody," Angel lied. "Just a kid I wish wasn't so down."

LUCY in the Skylark stopped in Paso Robles all right, parked on the street, the main street, beside a pay phone. Pas was a pretty little town, out of the way enough to have slept through most of the booster efforts to improve it. There were a lot of Victorian B and Bs, ten thousand oaks, more brown grass hills ringing it. They'd all flush green in another month or so when the rain started. Father Junipero Serra had stopped here, planted the flag a few miles north, Mission San Miguel Archangel.

But nobody was going out by the mission today.

Lucy made a call and then got back behind the wheel and waited.

She seemed a little fidgety. She put the top down, out of nervousness, the way a girl straightens her skirt as the boy is coming back to the car. Or the way girls did when they still wore skirts, when the baby-blue Skylark was new. She kept her eyes straight ahead, except for looking up in the mirror every once in awhile.

Jimmy was out of the Porsche, up the street a half block and on the other side. He'd gone into a wood-front store and bought a pack of cigarettes. He hadn't smoked in ten years. A pack cost what it used to cost to go to the movies. He sat on a bus bench, sat up on the back of it like a hawk on a perch, and pulled the red ribbon and opened the pack. He tapped one out and put it between his fingers and struck the match.

So I'm one of those, he thought, *a guy a memory makes start smoking again.*

The first drag almost took off the top of his head.

A kid came walking up to the Skylark, walking in from a side street, thirteen, fourteen, on the out end of a growth spurt. (He'd probably been three inches shorter at the beginning of summer, when school let out.) He wore a Cake T-shirt and plaid "old man" polyester pants and red Converse lowboys. And a black porkpie hat. He carried a hardshell guitar case, a Les Paul from the shape and size of it.

Jimmy liked him right away, pretty much everything about him.

Les put the guitar in the backseat before he even really looked at Lucy behind the wheel. He stood there. She got out from behind the wheel to come around to him. He dropped his head and sent his eyes sideways. She was about to hug and kiss him, standing there beside the car, but thought better of it, just smiled a big, real smile and touched the brim of his little hat with a finger and said something that made him pull his head away and pretend to be irritated.

Fourteen.

He had a school backpack over his shoulder, his luggage. He threw it into the backseat with the guitar and got in up front. Lucy started the car and said something to him. He nodded. She threw the Skylark into an incautious U-turn and whipped around and came in right in front of Jimmy on the back of the bus bench and stopped. Big as hell.

She pushed it up into park and got out. She walked right past him without even half a look. She was either on to him or unnaturally oblivious.

Jimmy stayed put, ten feet away from the car. Les Paul fiddled with the radio controls, opened the glove box and dug around in it, but nothing seemed to catch his eye. He put his head back against the headrest, like he was half asleep. Or jazzbo cool.

Lucy came out with the goods, unbagged, a plastic bottle of Dr Pepper for the boy and a bag of Flamin' Cheetos. She had a Diet Coke for herself and a limp length of Red Vines hanging off of her lip. She got back behind the wheel. She snatched one of his Cheetos and popped it in her mouth and started the engine. She seemed, at least for that moment, almost happy. She drove off, still somehow managing never to acknowledge Jimmy's existence, just as the boy never had.

They were brother and sister.

Les Paul and Lucy in the Sky with Diamonds.

Jimmy had found a CD in the glove box he didn't remember ever buying, a double disk of Beatles outtakes and song demos from the time of *The White Album* and a few even back to *Sgt. Pepper's*. It seemed just right for this trip, loose, clean, unpredictable, underproduced, each song stripped down to its essence, sometimes with lyrics that had gotten dropped before the slick, finished versions. Just now, with Paso Robles in the rearview mirror and the Skylark a quarter mile ahead, it was "While My Guitar Gently Weeps," and a new verse . . .

> *I look from the wings at the play you are staging,*
> *While my guitar gently weeps . . .*

Jimmy sang out loud, riding along in the wind, sang the verses he knew, that everybody knew, and smiled all the way through the new verse, digging it.

THERE was no wrong way to come into San Francisco. No wrong time of day. No wrong time of year. Here was one place, changed as it was, that didn't make you wish it was twenty years ago. Or fifty. Or even make you wish that you were that younger version of yourself, before everything happened that had happened, as some places do. As L.A. did.

You were you, now was now.

San Francisco was San Francisco.

It was eight or nine at night when the two-car caravan blew in from SoCal. Since it was just past summer, there was still some light in the blue to the west, Bombay-Sapphire-gin-bottle blue. Of course, it was twenty degrees cooler than it had been down south. Just right. The Skylark was five cars ahead of Jimmy, top up now. The top on the Porsche was still down. There was traffic around him, but Jimmy still heard the pop, the click of the Porsche's lighter and reached for it, turned the orange circle to him and lit another cigarette. He had stopped a ways back and bought a couple of bottles of beer. What was next, torching up a joint? He was enjoying himself a little too much, like that early part of a night (that later turns out bad) when you first taste that first drink in the first place you stop and she for a minute lets down her resistance and looks at you, just in the moment, forgetting for a moment what you both know, that you were both there to talk the other out of or into something.

So Jimmy was still thinking about *her*. And they'd never even been to San Francisco together.

Lucy and Les had come all the way up the Central Valley on the 101, staying at the limit. The sister and brother had talked a little, then had fallen silent, at least from what Jimmy could see ten car lengths back. A bit below San Jose, in the last stretch of farmland, as the sun was dropping, Lucy had pulled into a rest area and gone to the ladies' room, leaving the boy in the car. She stayed long enough to make Jimmy wonder if she'd fallen back into her gloom. Or something worse. Maybe she'd just made a call from the pay phone. She didn't seem to have a cell. When she came back to the car, that's when she'd put up the top. And she drove faster after that. She'd remembered *something*, something her brother had let her forget for a little while there.

Jimmy followed the Skylark down off the Bayshore and into the city, the dropping left turn down into the Fillmore, heading west on Fell. For a quick flash, there was the skyline to his right, a clutter of blocks dropped in the foreground.

Lucy had the use of a third-floor flat in a Victorian in the regentrified Haight, on Central, a block up from Haight Street next to little

Buena Vista Park angling up the hill. Jimmy slowed at the corner where she'd turned, saw where she'd parked, halfway up the hill on the right.

He looped a block and came back on the intersecting side street. There was a lucky parking spot in the dim space between two streetlights. He parked, reached back, and hoisted up the top and snapped it down. It was cool. There was *moisture* in the air. Imagine that.

He watched. And waited. She just sat there, motor idling. Then she got something out of the glove compartment, maybe a white envelope, read something off the face of it, and looked over at the number on the corner building, the Victorian. She turned around in the intersection, put the car right in front, the nose pointed downhill now.

She sat there some more. The boy kept looking over at her.

A man with a white ponytail, a man in his sixties, came past on the sidewalk across the street, came down the hill from Buena Vista Park walking a dog, a chow with a loose black tongue and a tail curling up and over. The man seemed to Jimmy to make a point of *not* staring at the newcomers sitting in the Skylark under the circle of streetlight, kept on going down the hill. He lived over the wine shop at the lower corner, at Central and Haight. The chow waited, looking down at the ground like an old man, while his owner unlocked a black lacquered door. The man looked once back up the hill before he went in and the dog followed.

Across from the corner Victorian was a four-story building, a little too neat, too perfectly painted, with Catholic trappings, a cross on the crown of the roof and a flash of gold here and there. A nun in a blue habit was framed in a tall second-floor window with the white globe of a ceiling light over her head. Two girls played a board game framed in another window a floor above her, teenage girls in light blue smocks . . . What were they called? *Shifts.* On one girl, the cloth was stretched tight across her belly. Then Jimmy realized the other girl was pregnant, too, from the fullness in her face as much as anything. But not so far along. It was a home for unwed mothers.

It was a nice neighborhood. The Haight had been a lot wilder and woollier when he'd lived in San Francisco.

Lucy got out from behind the wheel. She went to the apartment building two doors down the hill on the same side, rang, waited there at the door. The boy got out a beat after she did and stood beside the car, looking up at the navy-gray sky. He looked like he was thinking that it was going to rain, but it was just the way the nights were in San Francisco in September, something else Jimmy remembered afresh. The boy looked over at his sister waiting there at the door, the way she was acting, but he didn't dwell on it. It was just one more thing he didn't get.

A woman answered Lucy's bell, came out onto the sidewalk, out under the streetlight, and the two of them talked for a second, the slanted sidewalk forcing them to stand oddly, a little uncertainly. In time the other woman, who was enough older than Lucy to have a little mother in her manner, a little sympathy (or at least *judgment*, which is a kind of concern), reached into the pocket of the long sweater coat she wore and came out with a key, a loose key, and an index card. She put the key and the card in Lucy's open palm and looked at her with that look again, the neighbor lady's own version of the tough-love look the waitress had given Lucy back at the café in Saugus.

Lucy nodded and thanked her and said something that looked like, "I will." The boy got his guitar and pack out of the backseat.

Five halting, unrhythmic tones sounded. Each of the three apartments in the Victorian had its own door at street level, on a marble stoop. Lucy had opened the center door, stepped just inside, the index card in hand, to punch a code into the alarm. There was another, longer tone, the all clear, and Les followed her in, climbed the stairs behind her carrying his gear, as the door closed itself. After a minute, a light came on in the front room on the third floor.

Jimmy started the Porsche. He pulled forward and turned right, drove up the hill on Central, alongside the Catholic home. He went to the top of the hill, to the park, and turned around and came back down and snugged the car in against the curb. From here he could see straight across into the apartment, from Lucy's top-floor flat on down. There were closed drapes in the living room, but in the bedroom the blinds were raised. The boy Les was in the kitchen, looking up at the light fixture.

It was wide-screen, like a drive-in.

The air had weathered up, gotten heavy with water. Jimmy suddenly felt a little hollow inside but shook it off. So he waited, behind the wheel. He smoked another cigarette, though he was already getting bored with it. Smoking. He spun the dial, found a good station on the radio. They were playing Zeppelin, *Houses of the Holy*, broadcasting from somewhere down on the waterfront.

Act two, Lucy came in and sat on the edge of a stripped bed in the front bedroom, alone, her hands on her knees. Her worries, her sadness, the *heaviness* had sure enough come round again. Big surprise, it was lying in wait for her four hundred miles north. Jimmy wondered if she had any idea that half the neighborhood could see in, could see her sitting there, if they looked.

The boy came into the bedroom. He looked at her but just stood there in the doorway.

"Say something to her," Jimmy said. "She's your sister."

But the boy just stared at her. Jimmy had decided a ways back down the road that they hadn't seen each other much lately, were unused to each other. Lucy lifted her head and said something. The boy nodded and left the room.

After a moment, the downstairs front door opened, and he came out onto the sidewalk. By now the night had that horror film look to it, fog hanging around the streetlights, making each of them look like something *alive* wrapped in a gauzy cocoon. She had given him the keys, to lock up the car. Les got behind the wheel and put the key in. He looked for a second like he was going to take it out for a spin. He canted the wheels to the curb. Maybe he knew more about San Francisco than his sister did. He sat there a minute with his hands on the wheel. Jimmy could see through the back window over the seat backs that the radio had come on when he'd unlocked the steering wheel. Maybe the kid liked Zep.

The kid leaned forward over the steering wheel and looked up at the apartment, at the light in the bedroom. He turned the key, and the radio light went out.

After he'd locked up the car again, he stood for a moment on the sidewalk looking down at the sideways traffic on Haight Street, an electric bus clicking by, rolling toward Ashbury, too fast, rocking, just this side of out of control. Les didn't see it, but the man with the white ponytail was watching him around the edge of the blinds in his second-floor bay window.

The kid went back up.

The overhead light was still on, but she wasn't in the front bedroom anymore.

"She sent you away," Jimmy said.

He watched as the boy went looking for her, worry in his manner, too.

Jimmy found her first. There she was, up on the roof, at the edge. Flat, no railing. She was looking out levelly, not up, not down, a look that said she just might take the next step in front of her, whether there was anything there or not.

So it's going to be *tonight* . . .

Jimmy got out fast, left the car door open.

But then Les came out onto the roof behind his sister.

Jimmy stopped.

When the boy said something, the first thing Lucy did was to take a step back from the edge.

CHAPTER TWO

Jimmy couldn't sleep, *didn't sleep*, so after he'd checked into a high suite at the Mark Hopkins on Nob Hill, he went back out into the night. He left the Porsche in the hotel garage and took a cab. He went by the house on Central. The lights were still on in the front bedroom, but now the shades were down. There was the blue flare of a television behind the drapes in the living room, and the kitchen was dark.

The cab driver didn't seem to make anything out of Jimmy telling him to just park at the top of the hill, looking down at the house. Ten minutes passed that way. Ten minutes of nothing. There was jazz on the radio, very low. The fog had settled in even thicker. July and August, Jimmy remembered, were the months when the fog really came in. Nobody told September the season was over. An electric bus blew past down on Haight Street. Jimmy motioned for the cabby, the same black man in his forties who always seemed to be driving the cab in San Francisco, schoolteacher's black-rim glasses and a Kangol cap, to roll on down the hill. The cabby rolled on down the hill. To the corner.

Jimmy got out, paid him off through the open window, with an extra twenty to really make him wonder what *that* had been about, and set out walking in the direction of Haight and Ashbury. He turned to watch the cab pull away, waiting to see the cabby's eyes in the rearview mirror, but the cabby never looked back.

It was San Francisco. Maybe he wasn't that weird here.

There was a Gap on the corner of Haight and Ashbury. No Starbucks. Yet. But a wannabe Starbucks a few doors down. There was a good crowd. By now it was almost midnight. It took Jimmy a second to remember what day of the week it was. Thursday. The coffee drinkers were mostly professionals, young, not so young. Dressed nice. Good haircuts. In pairs, most of them.

Jimmy got a tea and a madeleine and brought them outside and sat at one of the little white corporate tables. There was only one other smoker, a self-consciously scruffy man in his late twenties, in a rough-weave unbleached wool sweater, off-white, over dark green cords and what they used to call desert boots. Suede. Probably Tommy Hilfiger. He had one leg angled up into the chair. He was smoking a good cigar. With the gold band still on it. Jimmy wanted to put a fist in his face, but only because of how young he was, how apparently happy he was, and because the woman leaning into him looked a little, in the eyes, in the cheekbones, like Mary.

Mary.

A bus came. Jimmy jumped on it. It was the 43. He rode it out Fell along the Panhandle, halfway to the zoo and the ocean and then back again, back along Oak Street, along Market to the Embarcadero and then Fisherman's Wharf.

The night was still very alive down along the waterfront, post-midnight, out-of-towners most of them, honeymooners, lovers on lovers' long weekends, groups of three or four or five or six, more than a few in them in red sweatshirts with somebody's logo, a convention of somebodys.

And *Sailors.*

That didn't surprise Jimmy. This is where they'd be. And when. Was that why he'd come down here, looking for his kind? That felt a little pathetic to him. The bus he'd ridden in was one of the last of the night, five or six other passengers and Jimmy. Maybe there'd be another run, one last loop when the bars closed, whenever that was.

Most of the people were at Pier 41, where the red-and-white boats over to Alcatraz docked. The last Alcatraz boat came back at six or seven, but the ticket windows were still open for tomorrow's runs. It sat out there, Alcatraz, across the night, swathed in the clouds of fog that sat on the Bay. Other nights you'd be able to make it out from here, the lights, even the shape, the edges, but not tonight. Tonight there was only a sweeping light on the highest building, behind the cotton of the fog, and a moon up there somewhere, too, or a piece of one, a dull glow at two o'clock.

There were street entertainers, each with his own little knot of audience. There was a juggler. There was a close-up magician, making things disappear.

There was a man painted silver. Head to toe. In a silver tux and tails, silver spats and silver shoes and a silver top hat that stayed somehow on his silver head. With a boom box. Dancing like a robot.

The Sailors moved among the tourists, bumping into them like pickpockets, knocking into strangers just for the joy of it, for the harshness of it, with a rough laugh whenever a man from Kansas or a woman from Germany would excuse themselves, though it was the Sailor who had run into the innocent. Same as it ever was. Some of the tourists would check their pockets, to make sure.

But it wasn't their wallets that had been taken.

A couple of the crab stands were still open. Five bucks got you a red-and-white square paper tray of shredded Dungeness crab with a quarter lemon and a tear of sourdough baguette. Jimmy sat on the stool, close enough to be getting a facial from the stinking steam that came out of the stainless steel box. He'd already shoveled a forkful into his mouth. It was good.

"What do you want?" the teenager working the stand said. It was a Leone Brothers stand. This kid was likely a Leone grandson, maybe great-grandson.

His tone was a little quick. Jimmy waited.

"You look like you want something else."

"More cocktail sauce, I guess," Jimmy said.

The kid put an open paper cup of red sauce in front of Jimmy, the kind of little cup they put pills in, in a hospital. "You want horseradish, say it."

"I do."

The server spooned an amount of white horseradish that would have been too much for the average person into another paper cup and set it beside the first one.

"That's the way I eat it," the boy said.

"You still eat it?"

"Every day."

"I thought maybe you'd get sick of it."

"Every day. Ask him."

"Who?"

The boy looked over Jimmy's shoulder at a busboy pulling up black rubber mats, hosing off the underneath. The stand was in front of the mother restaurant, closed up at midnight.

"Do I eat crab?" the kid asked.

"Every day," the busboy said.

From twenty feet away, a Sailor was watching them, watching the dumb little play, the tourist getting stroked by the Welcome to San Francisco Committee. This one, this Sailor, sat on the closed lid of a Dumpster, a blond man who'd been a bit overinfluenced by Billy Idol, a little too pretty, lips too full in that pouty Billy Idol way. He wore what a lot of them wore, the ones with that certain attitude, the navy peacoat and watch cap. This one also wore black straight-leg 505s, pegged skintight, and pointy-toed fairy boots like The Beatles used to wear.

Only *red*.

"I know you, Brother," he mouthed to Jimmy. There was just a hint of blue around him, as if he were wrapped in another kind of fog. And he had that look, that Sailor sneer.

Why were they always so sour?

"Nice night for a white wedding," Jimmy said back at him, across the twenty feet between them.

The crab kid gave Jimmy a funny look.

Then everything started to speed up. Another Sailor came over to Red Boots with an *it's-happening-now* look on his face, and Red Boots jumped off the Dumpster. He didn't even look over at Jimmy as he went past. On a mission. None of it surprised Jimmy or made him wonder where they were headed. They were always scurrying around with sudden purpose, this kind, this time of night, like junkies energized by the rumored arrival of dope.

What did surprise Jimmy was that the crab kid was a Sailor, too. When the first two passed, the second Sailor caught the kid's eye, motioned with his head. The crab boy fell in step with them, abandoned his post at the stand. The trio headed off across the last hundred yards between restaurant row and the waterfront, leaving Jimmy to wonder if he was losing his sense of things, getting slow. He'd missed it. There was nothing about the kid that made him think this one was a Sailor. No lost look in the eye, no flare of blue. No fatalism. No bitterness.

He wondered something else, if the kid had read *him*.

Jimmy went after them, took his little twist-off split of Napa Chardonnay and what was left of the crab with him.

The drama was at Pier 35, one of the old World War II–era buildings, with its big, flat, blank face.

A matched pair of perfectly naked girls was on the lip of the two-story facade of the building. Black-haired, with cute helmet haircuts, turned under just below the ears, bangs straight across just above the eyes. They looked a little French, a little Godard. They were holding hands.

Girls Gone Wild.

They had a good-sized crowd of their own, five or six banks of peo-ple standing before them in concentric half circles, heads back, smiling, entertained.

But then there was a man, whom Jimmy hadn't even seen until just now, who *wasn't* naked, right behind the girls, all in black, hidden by the shadows on the ledge until now, who now leaned into the frame and said something into the space between their two heads, something that only took a second.

Or took half the night, depending on how tuned in you were.

And, next beat, the girls jumped, hand in hand. *Dove . . .*

They were so pretty, so *French*-seeming, had such beautiful bodies; it was clear the rapt crowd half expected them to arc back up into the air and land on their feet, like Cirque du Soleil. Instead, everybody got to watch as the two crashed into the cement in front of the dock build-ing face-first, shoulders and chests first, one girl somehow slightly ahead of the other and with a sound like hundred-pound sacks of pota-toes thrown off a loading dock.

Nobody stepped closer for a closer look. Nobody had to check to see if they were still alive.

Jimmy was in the second row, and he didn't step closer for a closer look, either, but he could *smell* it over the wet-dog musk of the Bay. It was a smell he knew.

When he looked up at the top of the facade again, the man in black was gone.

Crab Boy was behind Jimmy, over a row or two.

He looked at Jimmy. And *smiled*. How inappropriate.

The two Sailors in peacoats and watch caps, Red Boots and the other, didn't waste any time. They jumped on it, were already on the move, working together, doing this thing, Red Boots shoving people back and the other Sailor getting right in their faces for up-close scru-tiny, one person at a time, looking each person in the face.

It had a name. It was called, prosaically, *Looking*.

Then Crab Boy split. Something else had caught his eye, movement out at the edge of the crowd. Somebody chasing somebody.

Jimmy went after him. After them.

Three other peacoats chased a man down the alleyway between Pier 45 and the back of Alioto's. Crab Boy jogged after the three new Sailors and the one they chased, but at a pace that said he didn't mean to catch them, just wanted to be there when they all got to the end, when they caught the man.

The *silver* man. It was the silver-painted dancer.

The three overtook him and knocked him down and began a beating that scattered a clot of seabirds hunkered down in the shadow of what looked like a warehouse. Crab Boy came up and stood over the beaters, like a supervisor, like the boss's son who'd been made night shift manager. Not getting his hands dirty. There was an ugly rhythm to it, the way they beat him, taking turns on him, each of them hitting him in the face twice and, at the same time, saying something.

Two words.

Jimmy caught up, jumped right into the middle of it. He seized one Sailor by the back of his blue-black wool coat. (It felt damp, perpetually damp, out in the weather like this.) Jimmy pulled the Sailor away, off the silver man, cast the bigger man aside with a strength that surprised both of them, that even made Jimmy wonder why he was suddenly filled with rage, why he'd gotten into it without a hesitation, without thinking. The other two Sailors didn't miss a beat, kept pummeling the silver man, saying the same two words that Jimmy still couldn't make out.

"All right. Cool," the kid said after a minute. Instead of "Enough" or "Stop."

The other Sailors stepped off.

"*Damn!*" the silver man said, still on the ground. Turned out he was black under the paint.

They all caught their breath. Jimmy turned to stare at the Crab kid. The other Sailors were walking away.

"You look like you want something," the kid said to Jimmy's glare.

Now the kid flashed blue, but not in a way Jimmy had ever seen. A crackling, electric, staticky way, gone as soon as you noticed it.

Jimmy didn't crack wise back at the boy. He'd only been in town a few hours. It wouldn't get him anything. The kid turned in his very white Nikes and went back up the alley.

They were back behind the restaurants. The smell suddenly hit Jimmy, with his sinuses opened by the adrenaline coursing through his system. It was like ammonia.

"*Damn,*" the silver man said again.

Jimmy held out a hand to him, to pull him up.

The silver paint seemed to filter the man's blue edge, like a gel on a spotlight.

Another Sailor.

His silver top hat had gotten knocked off. He retrieved it, tried to straighten out a crease it had picked up. He stopped to look at it in his hand, as if he'd suddenly realized what an improbable thing he'd become.

"What were they saying, when they were pounding you?" Jimmy asked.

" 'Who's next?' " the silver man said in a way that meant that he didn't understand it, either.

CHAPTER THREE

"Machine Shop."

"What do your friends call you?" Jimmy asked.

"Jus' Shop. Or 'Shine."

"Really?"

"I'm not sensitive."

The lights atop the EMT ambulance were still on, a red pulsing sweep projected ten feet tall against the face of the building at Pier 35, where the girls had jumped, making the scene look like a rave. But with nobody there. Raved out. Most of the crowd had dispersed even before the coroner's van and a couple of news trucks had arrived.

The fog had descended thicker. Jimmy looked away from the death scene, up toward Coit Tower. It wasn't foggy there. Clear. Something else he remembered from his days in San Francisco, how the fog moved around, how you'd be talking about it on the phone to someone across town, making jokes about the doom and gloom (if they were new to what everyone here called The City), and the person on the other end would be just as likely to say, "It's clear here."

He and the silver man were on a bench in front of Pier 39, drinking coffee. Jimmy had said he'd buy the street performer a drink, a last drink before the waterfront bars closed, but they were outside drinking coffee instead. Good coffee. Black. Jimmy got the idea that Mr. Machine Shop here was a program drunk. A Twelve-Stepper.

"Why did they come after you?"

"I said something," Machine Shop said.

"Said what?"

"I yelled up at them. The girls. 'Don't do it! Don't listen to him!' "

Jimmy noticed his silver hand shaking a little as he brought the cup to his silver lips. The paint was wearing thin. He wondered if it was toxic, what the effects were of putting it on night after night.

"I shouldn't say it, but those girls were very sexual."

Jimmy nodded.

"I mean . . ."

"Yeah, they were beautiful," Jimmy said. "Very young."

"I know I shouldn't even be thinking that, but—"

"Did you know them?"

Machine Shop shook his head.

"Know anything about them?"

"I saw them earlier. In the ring."

"The ring."

"The audience."

"Did you know *him*, the guy who gave them the go?"

"Never saw him before tonight," said Shop a little too quickly. "You mean the skinny guy, in the black turtleneck? Maybe wearing a cape?"

Jimmy waited.

"OK, yes, I know him," Shop corrected.

"Who is he?"

"I know him. I don't know his name." There was another momentary delay. "OK, his name is Jeremy. Jeremy."

"He's a Sailor," Jimmy said. Not really a question.

"He's down in here all the time," Machine Shop said. He turned and looked for the big clock on the face of the mall of T-shirt shops. It was two forty. "He's all right."

Jimmy waited.

"I stay out of his way," Shop finished.

"Is he a Sailor?"

"Oh yeah," Machine Shop said. Then he said the same thing again, another way, a way that meant that the caped man was *really* a Sailor.

"Was he with them earlier in the night?"

"Not when I saw them."

"How did the girls look then?"

"All right. Kind of sad in the eyes maybe. They were holding hands then, too. Wore little white silky dresses."

"They were twins," Jimmy said.

Machine Shop nodded. "Don't get that every day. Barefoot, too." You could see him get lost in a thought about them. Then you could see him shake himself out of it. Here was a man trying to do right, be good. To walk the line. *What Would Johnny Cash Do?* He uncrossed his long legs and stood. "I guess that'd be a real bonus for them," he said. "Getting *two*. Twins."

Jimmy put that in his pocket, to think on later.

Machine Shop had retrieved his gear from where he'd stowed it behind a parked car before the trio had chased him down the alleyway. He reached down and snapped out the handle on his roll-away, the wheelie that carried his stuff, a silver-painted boom box and a plastic, silver-painted top hat, for "contributions."

"You make any money at this?" Jimmy said, looking up at him, still on the bench.

"It's a life," Machine Shop said.

Jimmy got the joke. A Sailor joke.

The trolley was coming up around the curve, up the Embarcadero from Pier 29. The night's last train.

"Where you *from*, man?" Machine Shop said. "I know you ain't from here. You ain't even from Oakland."

Jimmy told him.

"You just about the *bluest* man I ever saw," the other said. "You so blue sitting there, even a Norm could pick you out . . ."

JIMMY walked "home." Through North Beach, up Columbus. It was just a bit after three, and San Francisco was a late town, so he wasn't alone. Drunks and lovers. And drunk lovers. A cab would come by every thirty seconds. Every other one, the empty ones, would slow to look over at him. He'd just shake his head, headed up that straight, gentle slope. He was wearing a black suit, the black suit he'd had on all day, since six that morning. It was linen, over a white shirt. He turned up the collar. Maybe that would show the cabbies that he *meant* to be here.

Did he? Mean to be here? He remembered why he was here. He thought about his friend Angel, thought about Lucy, hoped she was asleep in her borrowed bed over in the Haight.

Then he went back to thinking about himself.

He realized he was looking for the U.S. Restaurant. It was gone. The U.S. had been there for fifty years, in a wedge-shaped building, a 24/7 place where bartenders came after their shifts, cooks and waiters, musicians after gigs, pimps and drug dealers, and *Rolling Stone* writers who counted themselves part of that crowd, somewhere in there. The stromboli-and-cannelloni-for-breakfast crowd.

But it was gone. Well, not gone, exactly: replaced by a new and improved version of itself four or five doors down. And closed at ten.

In the next block he found another open-late place. It was almost full. He ordered a glass of red. It came in a water tumbler, just like at the U.S. (So he wasn't the only sentimental one.) He sat at the bar. Alone.

Not exactly. Halfway up Columbus, he'd noticed the Sailors on the other side of the street climbing the opposite sidewalk, trying not to look over at him, Red Boots and his sidekick. Now they were here, in the corner in the restaurant, drinking espresso. The bad ones always came in pairs, and the good ones were always alone.

It was dogging him, had followed him the four hundred miles north from L.A. the same way Lucy's blues had followed her. It wasn't just the tails he'd picked up, the foreshadowing of trouble, the suggestion of the last act. What was on his shoulders, weighing him down was the reality of his state, of *their* state, even the ones he hated, like the murderer in the black cape. It had followed him. It was there every time he looked for it, every time whatever had distracted him away from it stopped distracting him from it. It was as present as the two tails across the room. It was his heartache. Everybody gets a heartache; this was his. It made every day a hole he had to claw his way out of, just to begin again. It was enough to make you dive off a roof, as if that'd fix anything, end anything.

Had he really thought that phrase, the *reality* of his state? Funny word for it. More like . . . unreality. More like . . . "*death's other Kingdom.*" A little T. S. Eliot for the fans.

Jimmy drank the last of the red. And only then noticed there was another full glass waiting beside it. Another Chianti.

He stared at it. The bartender came past.

"What's this?" Jimmy said.

"Somebody bought you a drink," she said. She was in her forties, with longer hair than most women her age. It was something else San Francisco had, bartenders and waiters who weren't just doing this while they were waiting to get famous. Or waiting to find someone to pair off with who was. She smiled the nicest, simplest smile. Jimmy had the instantaneous thought that he'd like to curl up in her arms on whatever quilt-covered Victorian bed she had in whatever vanilla candle–scented apartment in whatever working-class neighborhood she and her cat lived in. Or even just lie there and watch her as she pulled down the lacy shades to keep out the morning, while Mr. Kitty walked the infinity sign in and around her ankles.

"I bet you aren't working on a screenplay," he said.

"Oh no, you're from L.A.," she said with mock sadness.

"What did he look like, my secret admirer?" Jimmy asked, to set her up to correct him, to say *She.*

"Can't tell you," the bartender said instead. "That would violate the Bartenders' Code."

"A regular?"

"Never saw him before," she said. "But then again, I don't usually work Thursdays."

Jimmy turned on his bar stool to follow the bartender's eyes to an empty table, a table near the Sailors. Just looking in the tails' direction was enough to spook them. They left their coffees and headed for the door.

"What's your name?" Jimmy said, looking back.

It was Angelina.

He looked across the bar at her and recited . . .

Those who have crossed
With direct eyes, to death's other Kingdom
Remember us—if at all—not as lost
Violent souls, but only
As the hollow men
The stuffed men.

"What do you think of that, Angelina?" he said after he'd uttered the lines.

"I think it's the Chianti talking," she said.

He said, "No, if it was the Chianti talking, it would be . . .

Nel mezzo del cammin di nostra vita
mi ritrovai per una selva oscura
ché la diritta via era smarrita . . .

"OK, I admit it," she said "*I* bought you the drink."

Jimmy knew it wasn't true but appreciated the flirtation. "Dante's *Inferno*," he said. "Chicks always dig it."

He stood. The second glass of wine was untouched, catching the light.

The bartender looked sorry to see him go. "Aren't you going to drink it? Maybe she's coming back."

"Chianti makes me sentimental," Jimmy said. "I've had enough. Next thing you know, I'll be quoting poetry . . ."

On his way out, Jimmy went by the empty table. Where his admirer had been? A table in the corner. There was only an empty glass.

And, improbably, a scent still hanging in the air, the scent of a woman.

HE stood outside, looked up Columbus, the rise up the hill, a bigger hill to the right and the Financial District to the left, the point of the TransAmerica Pyramid piercing the lifting fog.

A bit more of the Dante he'd rattled off inside found its way into his mouth. Standing there looking up Columbus, he translated it . . .

So did my soul, that still was fleeting onward,
Turn itself back to re-behold the pass
Which never yet a living person left . . .

His new best friends were waiting in the shadows across the street. Jimmy set out to walk the rest of the way back to the Mark Hopkins, up and over another hill, Nob Hill, which took up most of two hours and what remained of the night, and left Red Boots and the other Sailor thoroughly winded.

He decided not to think about the dead girls. And he didn't.

CHAPTER FOUR

The morning broke eternal, bright, and fair.

Or so it looked to Jimmy. He was on the open top deck of the red-and-white ferry that crossed the Bay from Pier 41 to Sausalito. He'd gone back to the hotel to change, to shower, to go from the black linen suit he'd worn yesterday to another linen suit, this one the color of the little spoon of cream on the Irish coffee at the Buena Vista. A cream-colored suit over a black shirt, like today was going to be the opposite of last night. *As if*, as the kids say.

But it *was* a beautiful day; a few clouds pushed all the way back over to Oakland. Tiburon was in front of them, Alcatraz sliding by to the left. On the Rock, another red-and-white boat off-loaded the 10:10 crowd as the first-run-of-the-day people queued up for the trip back across to San Francisco. (Did they still call it that, "the Rock," after the movie, after the wrestler who'd named himself after the movie and then become a movie star?) Jimmy could hear the voices of the kids on the Alcatraz dock, loud, vacation loud.

Down below him a deck, Lucy *almost* looked caught up in the new morning thing herself. She sat out in the open in the middle of the first row of fiberglass benches, ten feet back from the splash zone, the V of the bow. She'd made a friend, a white-haired lady in a spiffy blue and white Nautica windbreaker, a happy lady, a talker. Lucy said a few words in reply now and then and nodded every few seconds. Women liked her, Lucy. Jimmy wondered why, what it was that was in her eyes or the shape of her mouth or the way she held herself that made women like her. And want to help her. He hadn't really looked her in the eye. Up close. Maybe it'd move him, too.

The boy Jimmy was calling Les Paul for the shape of his guitar case came out onto the deck with two hot chocolates in his hands and a frosted, sprinkled donut stuck in his mouth. It was a little cool out here on the water, but he was wearing just a T-shirt. He handed off one of the cocoas to his sister and sat a few places away on the end of the bench, so as not to intrude in the back-and-forth between the women. He sat there and went to work on his donut, eating the way kids do, taking a bite and then looking at the thing, studying it while he chewed. He looked over at Lucy and the Nautica lady. Jimmy got the sense that the boy knew his sister was hurting, off balance, and that he didn't much relish the role of helpmate, was glad for some help.

Training for the women ahead for you, Jimmy thought.

Les only stayed on the bench a minute. Too much energy. Too much juice running through the lines. He took his breakfast snack up to the bow, lay forward into the angle of the hull on the port side. A gull found him immediately, with that bright donut, took up a position in the air two feet above the boy's head, locked on, even when the boat rose or splashed to one side, powering through a swell. *This is his job,* Jimmy thought about the bird, *as much as popping and locking for the tourists is Machine Shop's job nights down on the waterfront.*

Les broke off a piece of the donut and ate it very deliberately and then another and then another until it was gone, and then the bird moved on to the next mark.

Jimmy lifted his gaze to Tiburon, getting bigger in the frame. It was like another Alcatraz in size and the lift of its hump, but an island of a whole other order in its hospitality, its richness. And its freedom? It was green, for one thing, and dotted with houses. Old Money. San Francisco doctors and lawyers. Second and third generation. Maybe fourth.

He saw that Lucy was looking at it, too, even as the white-haired lady prattled on.

"Is that Tiburon?" Lucy interrupted her to ask.

"Yes, it is," Jimmy saw the white-haired lady reply.

There was a change in pitch, and the boat slowed. It was a commuter ferry, with a stop in Tiburon before the turnaround in Sausalito. They were a good half mile out from Tiburon but, even over the sounds of the water, the engines, the wind across the decks, they could hear hammering. And old-school hammering, too, with a hammer, not an air gun. Jimmy scanned the houses up and down the hill and down to the rocks, the water's edge, until he found it, the grand old moss-green Craftsman "cottage" with a scar of new wood on one side of its face and a carpenter, now a third of a mile away, in khakis and a white sleeveless tee, raising and dropping that hammer, a half beat off from the sound that crossed the water.

SAUSALITO was Sausalito. You had to look hard to see how it could be a real place to real people, a place to live and not a happy hologram that zapped back into the projector once the last tourist turned his back to go up the ramp to the boat.

Lucy and Les had fish and chips at an H Salt Esquire that faced the waterfront and the marina. It was early yet, right at twelve, and there wasn't much of a line. They brought the food outside, very accommodating for the investigator tailing them. Lucy seemed to fall back into herself over lunch. She stopped eating and pushed away her little newspaper-lined basket of greasy fish.

Jimmy hated to say it, but he was already tired of her here-we-go-again soul-sink act. Les reacted to it immediately. Maybe that was what irritated Jimmy, how the boy scrambled each time to find in himself some sense of what to do to help.

"It's just a piece of fish," Jimmy said aloud.

The panhandler on a break on the bench beside him stirred. "You sure you can't help me out with gas money, man?" he said. "I'm stranded."

Jimmy got up, never even really looked at him.

"God bless you," the panhandler said.

Next, there was some jewelry for Lucy to look through, a rack out under the perfect sun alongside the very clean sidewalk in the bank of stores and bars along Bridgeway, the main drag. Jimmy strolled along across the street, stopping when she stopped, catching the mundane details to pass on to Angel. Lucy fingered a necklace while the bosomy young hippie woman who'd made it told her how good it looked on her. Les stood by, patient, putting on a good show of having no place he'd rather be than with his depressed sister in Disneyland. The boy pointed to another necklace, and the hippie girl took it down and handed it to Lucy. Lucy undid the clasp and held it up around her neck, but it was clear her heart wasn't in it anymore.

A passerby offered an opinion. "It looks good on you," Jimmy saw her say.

She was a real beauty, the passerby. Alone, too. With an expensive, trendy, flat leather bag over her shoulder, matching her expensive, trendy, pointy shoes, Jimmy guessed. The bag and shoes were bold yellow, goldenrod. She took off her sunglasses, shook out her hair. It was women like this with hair like this who made them come up with a new name for *brown*. She wore a white dress, full in the skirt, belted, V-necked, summery, so white it splashed light onto the storefront. She was Lucy's age, maybe a little older. The dress was long and had something of a *Town & Country* classy modesty about it. But it didn't stop Jimmy from imagining her legs pretty much all the way up to the top.

Lucy smiled and thanked the passerby but didn't want to talk. The woman smiled in return and walked on.

Lucy and Les took the bus.

Jimmy took a cab.

Right across the Golden Gate.

There was the city, off to the left. The day was still wonderfully, deceptively beautiful, clear and blue. And that moon. A daylight moon, almost full, sitting atop the point of the TransAmerica Pyramid like a balloon. The window was down, and the air smelled good. Jimmy realized he was happy. Go figure.

It was even a nice taxicab, patchouli and all. The driver was a Mr. Natural with dishwater blond dreads. The picture on his license had him with the same look, five or six years earlier. In the movie playing in Jimmy's head, here was the long-term live-in "husband" of the busty jewelry maker on the street back in Sausalito. He had the Pacifica station on the radio. They were against the war.

Lucy and Les's bus was four car lengths ahead. It was a commuter. With a rainbow running down the side. It changed lanes. The cab driver changed lanes with it.

"You're from L.A.," Mr. Natural said. He had his window down, too, enjoying the sea stink, too, the cool air. The cab was an excellent old Checker, with wing vents, as God intended, so there wasn't a roar that had to be shouted over.

"Yeah," Jimmy admitted.

"I can read people."

"So what was it? What said L.A.?"

"The suit, I guess. The extra button undone on your shirt. Your shoes. A little showbizzy but not executive suite. But not actor either."

"You've been reading my mail," Jimmy said.

"I used to be a haberdasher. Eleven years."

"Do they really call them haberdashers?"

"They did when I was doing it."

"Here? San Francisco?"

"Right on Union Square," the cabby said.

Jimmy tried to do the math. The driver looked late thirties at the most.

"You ever see that movie *The Conversation?*" the cabby-haberdasher said, taking one hand off the wheel, turning, looking back, getting eye to eye.

"Yeah," Jimmy said. "Gene Hackman." He waited.

"I love that movie," the other said.

The Sausalito bus blew by the toll booths in the far right lane and pulled over. There was a plaza at the head of the bridge and a small commuter parking lot.

There wasn't any chance of the bus pulling out anytime soon, so the cabby just slowed and picked a lane and waited through the minute that it took to come up to the toll booth.

"Be here now!" he said to the toll taker, a gruff-looking 1950s-looking man, probably Italian, as he handed over five bucks.

"Baba Ram Dass," the toll man said. "He's sick, you know. And broke."

Mr. Natural just shook his head sadly.

He held up his right hand so you could see it in the rear window and started across three lanes to the outside. Remarkably, people yielded. He left a car's length between him and the bus, so they had a clear view.

When the bus's door opened, the first one off was a leathery little man in his sixties in a serious bike rider's frog suit. He went around to the front of the bus and started unhitching his lean red and green Euro bike off the rack.

"Some don't like to ride across the bridge," the cabby said, narrating. "Guy that size, he might be right."

"When I was here before, they didn't used to let you ride across," Jimmy said.

Mr. Natural shook his head. "You got it wrong," he said. He turned around to look at Jimmy. "Unless you haven't been here in twenty years and you're a whole lot older than you look. They put the bike lane in, in 1992."

Lean Man mounted up, headed on south into the city.

"They used to be worried about jumpers," the cabby said. "Stupid. No bike rider is going to jump. Think about it."

"I was always surprised they let you *walk* across," Jimmy said.

"They couldn't stop people from walking," the cabby said. "It would be admitting something they're unable to admit."

Lucy and Les Paul got off the bus. Jimmy dug into his pocket for his sheaf of bills.

"I heard something on the radio this morning," the cabby said. "They said new figures show that the cost of living now outweighs the benefits."

Lucy and Les just stood in the sunlight a moment next to the bus. They looked like they were coming this way, coming back across the bridge. They'd walk right by him if Jimmy stayed in the cab. He got out.

He leaned in through the open passenger window, handed Mr. Natural two twenties. "Thanks," he said.

"It's a joke. Think about it."

"I'm laughing on the inside," Jimmy said.

BUT Lucy and Les didn't come back across the bridge. Not yet anyway. Instead, they found the stairs that led down to the Golden Gate Bridge observation area and gift shop, a round building with glass sides and an iron skeleton, probably the same iron from the bridge. Below the shop, down through the tops of the dark green trees, was brick Fort Point, built around the massive foot of the southern base of the bridge.

The shop was crowded. The "gifts" were grouped by languages. You couldn't call them trinkets. The "lap throws," whatever they were, were 129 U.S. dollars, which apparently was a sensational bargain if you were Japanese. Lucy and Les Paul stayed by themselves, as much as it was possible in the packed room.

She dug in her purse and came out with coins for Les for one odd hand-cranked vending machine. A penny and three quarters. The low-tech machine smashed an elongated image of the Golden Gate onto the raw stock of the penny—and kept the six bits for the trouble. Les turned the big handle and made one and got so happy he looked about ten. Lucy laughed off a handful of years, too, and then went back to her purse for more quarters and another penny for another go-around. A matching pair. Maybe they'd get the hippie girl back in Sausalito to turn the pennies into earrings.

And then Lucy was sad again.

What happens to happiness? Where does it go when it goes? And how? Out of the throat where the throaty laughter was born, across the tongue, across the teeth? Are there people who can *see* it leaving, drifting out? Is happiness exhaled like breath? Does it float into the clouds? Does it hover over our heads like a departing soul, hanging around to haunt us once we're low again, dead to joy again? *That's my happiness up there . . . It used to be mine.* Because Lucy *was* happy, Jimmy had seen it with his own eyes, as clearly as he could see anything else in the gift shop. And now it was gone, as gone as anything could be gone, sucked out of her, breathed out of her. She'd stepped out into the sunlight in her new jeans and white top. (Out of the wind, off the boat, and away from the water, she'd pulled off the jacket and tied it around her waist by the sleeves.) She'd stepped, still laughing, out of the gift shop, holding the bright flattened pennies up to her ears until Les snatched his away from her. The sun should have lifted her spirits, made her even happier, but the opposite happened.

Or *something* happened. As they came out onto the observation area, she just stopped (it was next to one of the coin-operated telescopes) and went from happy to sad. Jimmy had come out ahead of them, was across the way against the low wall that hemmed in the observation area. It was almost as if she'd seem him standing there and thrown on her depression again, like a wool overcoat, just for him.

But she had a savior. Or at least a friend. The woman in the white dress with the yellow purse and yellow shoes and the highlights in her chestnut hair. She was back, apparently hitting the same tourist spots as Lucy and Les, though she didn't exactly look the tourist. She stood, alone again, just this side of the snack bar on the observation deck. Was she in line? She never turned away once she'd seen Lucy, sad ol' Lucy, once she'd seen what was on her face, coming out of the gift shop.

She started toward her.

"Are you all right?" Jimmy watched the woman in white say, right into Lucy's ear. She touched her arm, just above the wrist, with just her fingertips.

Lucy nodded, but in a way that made it obvious she wasn't. Maybe too obvious.

Les was still standing there beside his sister. The woman in white said something to the boy that Jimmy couldn't read. Maybe it was, *Leave us alone a minute.* Les started away for the concession stand. He only made it a few feet before Lucy called him back and handed him a bill.

Les went to wait in line at the snack bar. For what? A water? Coffee?

Jimmy's impatience with Lucy was back again, too.

Get her a hankie. Get her a beer to cry in.

Get her a blue key light to stand in, to add to the effect. Get her the world's smallest violin.

The woman with the white dress and yellow purse led Lucy to a bench across the grassy observation area, held her by the arm as if she was eighty and in her vapors. A Japanese woman on the bench rose when she saw the distressed women approaching. She bowed and backed away.

The women sat. The woman in white had those long legs of hers crossed, showing through the inverted V in the skirt, unbuttoned two buttons.

"Sexy Sadie," Jimmy said.

Were they holding hands now? They were hip to hip. They were fifty feet away, as far away as you could get without going over the berm. Had they moved there because of him, out of earshot of any men, even the anonymous L.A. man in the off-white linen suit? Sexy Sadie would ask a quiet question, and Lucy would nod. And then, after the warm bond between them had bonded still warmer, Lucy would offer a question, and the woman would nod.

Where were the steaming cups of chamomile?

But then, when Lucy put her eyes on the ground and said nothing for a long time, the woman leaned close and whispered in her ear.

It made Jimmy remember something. From last night. Another whisper.

Les Paul was still waiting. He wasn't monitoring his sister, didn't even look over that way, seemingly glad to have been assigned a task that involved action and not emotion. At the head of the snack line was a barrel-shaped man, European, with a dictionary in his hand, squinting at the white plastic movable type on the black menu board. This could take awhile.

When Jimmy looked away from Les and back at the pity party on the bench, the two women had been joined by a third. Another woman.

When it came to this supporting cast, each woman was better-looking than the one before, though it was wrong to try to rank them. Each one was better-looking than she had a right to be. Professional-strength beauty. Sexy Sadie was on the tall side, model tall, brunette. This new one was almost short, black-haired, blue-black hair cut close to the head, with ragged bangs, that shake-it-out shaggy boy look. And vibrant blue-green eyes, bright enough to be read a mile away. (Or across the observation area, at any rate.) Maybe they were contacts. She had a killer body, stretch-wrapped in what was probably pleather, a sixties minidress and matching high sixties boots, so far on the other side of self-conscious she couldn't even see us from there, back here in Dullsville.

Polythene Pam. So good-looking she looked like a man.

The woman in the white dress had been alone walking down the street in Sausalito when she'd stopped to offer Lucy advice about the sidewalk jewelry. And she was still alone, or alone again, when she'd spotted Lucy this second time, in front of the gift shop. And now Sexy Sadie had just happened to run into her very best friend in the whole world, and just when another poor sister needed bucking up, too, because these two, Sadie and Pam, were definitely close. Hooked up. Not sisters certainly. Lovers? Welcome to San Francisco. Maybe they were just two very *on* women. Or maybe Jimmy was just lonely. They flanked Lucy, sitting so close the three of them still left room on either end of the bench.

They worked her, poor Lucy. There was no other way to look at it. They were going to console her or die trying. Sadie would say something in one ear, and Lucy would nod or just keep staring at the grass in front of her and then, before Lucy could nod again, Pam would lean in to say something in the other ear, both of them close enough to kiss the downhearted girl.

It was something to behold, and Jimmy beheld it.

He looked over at the snack bar. Les was coming back with a Coke and a bottle of water. He was accompanied now by the stout European man. Jimmy decided on second look he was probably Italian. Homme Italia carried a hot dog and another Coke. He said a few last words to the boy and then waved with the hot dog. He looked a little lonely, too.

Les headed toward the spot where his sister and the stranger had been when he'd left them, out in front of the gift shop, before they moved to the bench across the grass. Les didn't seem to realize they weren't there until he was right on top of the same spot. He looked confused.

"They're on the bench," Jimmy said to himself.

But they weren't.

When Jimmy panned right again, the bench was empty.

He had a hunch, a bad feeling. He tried to talk himself out of it, even as he ran up the metal stairs, back up to the level of the bridge.

Three steps at a time, and there she was.

Lucy was on the bridge, walking away, walking toward the center. She was already a hundred yards gone. Alone. Walking away. She wasn't in any hurry, but there was a kind of scary purposefulness to her gait, almost as if she was counting the steps.

Ninety-seven, ninety-eight, ninety-nine . . .

She was still fifty yards ahead of Jimmy when Les blew past him with a concussive blast that almost pushed Jimmy into the rail. The boy still had the two drinks in his hands, but he dropped them now, first the Coke and then the bottle of water. The water bottle skittered across the walk and bounced into the air and then under the railing that separated the walk and bike run from the fast traffic.

The water bottle bounced into the air and was struck by a north-bound Saab, dead in the windshield, bursting. The driver spooked at the splash, the flood, locked the brakes, and crunched the nose of the car into the rail and took the hit from a tailgating Ford Festiva, all in the time it took Jimmy to realize who'd blown past him.

Les never looked back, even as the line of cars in both hot lanes skidded and smoked and banged into each other.

Lucy kept walking. The inverted arc of the main immense suspension cable was beside her to her right, descending as she crossed the lateral plane toward some inevitable point of intersection, the descending curve and the baseline, as if the whole of the Golden Gate were a graph to illustrate the diminution of something. Hope? Promise? A fall from a great height.

But Les caught up to her.

When Jimmy saw that the boy was going to overtake her, or rather when he saw her reaction, when he saw Lucy let go of the dark thing she was holding on to, he stopped, let them have their moment. He had to remind himself that they didn't know who he was.

Lucy tried to cover with a line or two, and her brother offered her the grace of something close to a laugh, though he certainly didn't mean it. His face was flushed from the run. Now he bent over to catch his breath. It occasioned another line from her. The sidewalk was empty around them, had been empty for almost all of the boy's run after her. It was odd.

The two consoling beauties were nowhere to be seen. They'd just disappeared, like a magic trick, like a magician's two lovely assistants.

Now the traffic recovered, rolled past Lucy and Les, except for the cars that had crashed. The drivers were out of them now. From the passing cars, no one looked over.

CHAPTER FIVE

Jimmy sat with his eyes closed in a club chair by the window in his tenth-floor suite at the Mark.

For three hours.

There was a bedroom and a sitting room. He was in the bedroom, with the drapes open. When he'd first come back from the Golden Gate, from following Lucy and Les, from looking her right in the eye as she'd walked right back past him on the bridge, he had sat there for a long time and watched the light change, the clouds moving in across the Bay, their quick shadows crossing Alcatraz. Then he'd closed his eyes. Now it was five thirty. The day, which had begun so beautifully, was ending that way. At least for those looking at the sky.

Jimmy opened his eyes. He stood and took off the coat of his suit and laid it across the bed. He looked at the clock. He put on some music, the jazz the black cabby had been listening to, old jazz from a station that broadcast from down on the wharf and used Billie Holiday's "I Cover the Waterfront" under its station IDs. He walked back to the window. The low air conditioner under the tall picture window blew right at his groin. It would have been funny, worth a joke, a line, if he'd had anybody in the room with him. He found the little door to look in on the AC controls, fiddled with the knobs and buttons, but couldn't shut it off. You didn't need AC in San Francisco, and the hotel *didn't* have it for years, didn't have it the last time he was here. The windows used to open, even the tall ones. He felt his anger rise, felt it burn out to the surface from whatever tight, dark spot he usually kept it stuffed into.

"Goddamn it!" he said, slamming the little lid closed.

The machine wasn't a bit offended, responded only by blowing more cold air at his genitals.

Jimmy snatched up the phone and rang the front desk.

"Yes, Mr. Miles," a man with a young voice said, a beat sooner than you'd get for a regular room in a regular hotel.

"I can't turn off the air-conditioning," Jimmy said, *barked*, like some I'm-paying-a-thousand-dollars-a-day L.A. type. He heard the way he sounded but blew out the rest of it anyway. "I don't want it; I don't need it. I want to open the window. I'm not going to jump. I just want some pure air. I want my goddamn window to open the way it used to open."

"Yessir. Sorry."

The wall behind the bed was mirrored. Jimmy got a look at himself on the phone, the clench of his jaw.

He took what they call in childbirth pain-management classes "a cleansing breath."

"Mr. Miles?"

"Yeah, look, I'm sorry," he said with his normal voice. "Just tell me how to turn this thing off or send someone up."

"They're already on the way, Mr. Miles."

He hung up. There was a trio of water bottles on a smoked green glass tray on the table beside the bed, the Mark Hopkins label. He opened one and drank it down, standing there. He took a second one to the window, cracked the seal on the bottle.

Any time Jimmy cursed in front of his friend Angel, "took the Lord's name in vain," Angel rebuked him. Or thought of it. He should call him. He should have called him already. He hadn't reported in since he'd stood on the brown hillside west of Cholame. Yesterday morning.

What would he report? Lucy had looked all right when he left her a few hours ago. The brother and sister took a cab from the bridge back to the Haight. Jimmy was in a cab right behind them. He blew past them on Masonic, then had the cabby loop around up by the top notch on the park and came back down. He'd waited up the hill that way, like a jealous lover, like a nervous dad, for twenty or thirty minutes before the cabby shifted in his seat one more time, and Jimmy let him roll on. They were home. They were OK. But something *had* changed that morning. Jimmy had looked into her eyes, really looked. On the bridge, the boy had reached her in time, and she had put a look on her face that tried to laugh it off, to say that this couldn't possibly be what it appeared to be, a woman purposefully pacing off the last of her life. Jimmy had the details, if Angel wanted them. Les had made his awkward joke about dropping her Diet Coke and water. "I didn't know what you'd want," Jimmy saw him say. And then, as the traffic came back to speed, blasting past them headed north, as *life* had resumed, Lucy had put her arm in her brother's, very grown-up, and they had turned and started walking back. Jimmy was against the rail. He set out walking, *toward* them. So they wouldn't be suspicious of him. (He couldn't believe they hadn't yet made him, with all the close surveillance. But they weren't criminals. Why would they think anyone would be watching them?) And so, walking toward Marin, with the two of them walking back toward the visitor center, he came face-to-face with Lucille. Up close. Close enough to see into her eyes.

Here's what changed in that moment: Jimmy wasn't impatient with her anymore. He no longer doubted the genuineness of her melancholy.

He drained the second bottle of water. Now night was falling. He'd have to go back out there to her, back to the Haight, wait there at the apartment building until she came out. Or went to the roof again. He had to do what he could do. He had to go to work. It was what he did.

So why did he have this knot in his gut?

Why was he so full of anger?

There was a knock at the door, a little less subservient sounding than he would have expected. Maybe he hadn't intimidated the house staff after all.

It was a black man. Tall. Bony. He looked a little like Al Green, standing there, especially when he smiled, with big, perfect teeth.

He was wearing black-and-white suede shoes. With dice on the toes.

"I maybe got something for you," he said, stepping right on into the room after a quick look down the hallway in one direction. He closed the door behind him. "Little sumpin' sumpin'."

Jimmy looked from the shoes back up at his face.

"Machine Shop," he said.

"How are you, man?"

He looked naked, diminished, out of his silver paint. The face and neck were swollen in places from the beating he'd taken behind Alioto's, but Shop was dark-skinned, and the bruises would be hard to see. One eye had probably been swollen shut when he awoke that morning. It was still puffy, teary. There was a hematoma in one corner of the white of the eye, like a drop of red ink in a teaspoon of milk.

"I called, but . . ." He stopped. With Machine Shop, it was like there were two people in there, engaged in steady, often heated conversation. The other must have said something. "All right," Shop said, "I never called. I just came over."

"How'd you know where to find me?"

"You had matches from the Mark, when you were smoking. You smoke too much, man. The body is a temple."

"I just quit."

"Good. You had two packs of matches. You got to the end of one, and you had another pack. So you had to be staying here, not just using a pack of matches somebody gave you. And then I made some calls."

"Calls."

"I keep my ear to the anvil," Shop said.

"Called who?"

"All right," Machine Shop said, "I didn't call exactly. I just asked around about you. I have my network. Down on the water. Who you were. I knew where you were from, you told me that. I asked people who knew people. I found out, you know, what you do."

Jimmy waited.

"You know, that you're a detective and all. From Down Below."

"You mean hell?"

"L.A., that's what I call L.A. It's one of my trademarks." He heard another inner rebuke. "All right, that's what a friend of mine calls it. Los Angeles, Down Below. Or jus' D.L., short for Down 'Low."

"D.L. instead of L.A.," Jimmy said.

"That's jus' him," Machine Shop said. "Look, like I said, I maybe got something for you . . ."

"Tell me what you think you know about me," Jimmy said, an edge to his voice now.

"That you're a detective. You look into things for people. But not for the money. You work out of your house. That it has to be something that, you know, touches you in your soul."

"That it? Is that who I am?"

"That, you know, you're a Brother. Well, not a *brother*, but, you know, a . . ."

There was a knock at the door.

"That's probably him now," Machine Shop said.

Jimmy reached for the knob, not really hearing the last thing he'd said. "That eye looks bad," he said. "You know any Sailor doctors?"

"Look, before you—"

Jimmy opened the door.

Two people stood there. One was a very short man, built like a bomb. Brown cuffed trousers, a white short-sleeved shirt, tight over the biceps. Brown wing tips. A full head of straight black hair, oiled, combed back, a once-a-week barbershop haircut.

And a sad, Greek face.

The other guy standing there was a thirty-year-old boy in a Kelly green Mark Hopkins blazer who wondered who the man beside him was.

"Is this him?" the Greek man said to Machine Shop, pointing a finger at Jimmy.

"I said wait," Machine Shop said. "Downstairs."

"Mr. Miles?" the hotel boy started.

Jimmy dismissed the boy. "It's all right," he said, "I'll do it myself."

The green-blazered boy looked at the tiny, strong man and then at the tall black man with the beat-up face.

"You sure?" he said.

"Yeah, thanks," Jimmy said.

The hotel runner gave Machine Shop and the short Greek man another comprehensive look, as if he might be called upon to testify later, and nodded to Jimmy again and padded away.

So then it was just the three of them.

Jimmy let the Greek man come in, even let him close the door behind him. He didn't break five feet, but no doubt he could kick both of their asses.

"Have a seat," Jimmy said to the little guy. The Greek man took a seat.

Jimmy snagged Machine Shop's eye and tipped his head for him to follow him into the bedroom.

Shop came into the bedroom. Jimmy closed the door. He just looked at Shop, asking the obvious.

"It was his daughters who stepped off last night," Shop said.

Jimmy didn't exactly see *that* coming. People were always showing up with "a friend," some old grievance they thought Jimmy could fix, something "that should just take a couple hours." If you were a plumber, after you'd had a burger or hot dog out in the backyard, before the game started, they'd probably ask you if you'd mind taking a quick look under the toilet.

But this came at him from an unexpected angle. Had he forgotten about the beautiful naked girls, the dive off of Pier 35 last night, his first night in town? *It's not the going fast that kills you; it's the sudden stop.* He went over to the window. The city was purple all of a sudden, from one edge to the other. It was like a postcard with the color out of whack.

"The twins," Machine Shop said.

"Yeah, I know. What's he doing here?"

"He doesn't know how to deal with it," Shop said.

"I'm not a counselor," Jimmy said.

"He has all these questions. I thought of you."

"Yeah, I'm the answer man," Jimmy said, with his back still turned.

"He lives across the Bay, El Cerrito," Machine said. "They were just out of high school. They were younger than they looked. I thought they were from some other country, but they were just girls just out of school, come into the city for, I don't know, the nightlife. You see a lot of them down there, more than you'd think."

When Jimmy didn't say anything, didn't even seem to hear him, Machine Shop kept on, "He got the call at one-something in the morning. He came over there to the wharf. He was still there when I came back at dawn, like I always do, after I went home and got out of the paint. He was just walking around, standing there at the place where it happened. I hesitated to talk to him, but it was easy to see who he was."

"What did you tell him?"

"I tried to comfort him. Just that—"

"What did you tell him about me?"

"Just that you were a friend of mine and that you were a detective, that you looked into things."

"That's it?" Jimmy said, turning to look at him, a hard question.

"That's all I said," Shop said. This time there didn't seem to be a second voice in his head calling for a correction. After a second, he said, "They still lived at home."

"You're *playing* me," Jimmy said, looking back down on the bruised city. "Stop it."

Shop held up his hands. "He just needs—"

"He needs somebody else," Jimmy turned and said. "I'm not a shrink. I'm not a minister. How am I going to help him? I don't know shit. I'm not smart. My instincts are lousy. I hear something wise, and I make a joke about it."

"I understand," Shop said. "I fully understand."

"I have something I'm doing already. For a friend of mine. Tell him—"

But then the door opened, and the father stood there. He looked at Jimmy and then at Machine Shop and then back at Jimmy. Maybe he'd heard them through the door.

"He said you were there, too, that you saw it, too," the short man said. Only now did he let them hear the hint of an accent, a little Greek in the voice to match the shape of his face and the color of his eyes.

"Yes, I did," Jimmy said. "I'm sorry."

The man reached into the pocket of his shirt.

"Don't show me pictures," Jimmy said, raising a hand against him.

The man pushed the picture back down into his pocket.

That sad Greek face. It could have been half of the comedy/tragedy emblem. There's no tragedy like Greek tragedy.

"What's your name?" Jimmy said.

"George Leonidas."

Jimmy offered his hand. "Jimmy Miles."

"It means *lion*. My family's name."

"I know," Jimmy said.

"Why do you know?"

"I've been around." Jimmy was still standing at the window. He turned, took a step closer to the man, a sympathetic step. But what he said was, "I can't help you."

Machine Shop lowered his head and closed his eyes, his hands folded in front of him, like an elder standing before the first pew.

"I have to say," Jimmy said, with that same impossible mix of hard and tender, "there probably isn't anyone who *can* help you. What's happened is awful and wrong and impossible, but you have to take it. And probably alone. This time, it's your turn."

"God*damn*," George Leonidas said. It meant three or four things. *Goddamn you* was one of them.

Jimmy just stood there in front of him for a long time. Neither man moved, almost as if Jimmy was ready to take a shot to the mouth if that's what George the Lion needed to do next. But the small man just stood there, eyes on the floor. Jimmy could hear each breath he exhaled over the feathery whisper of the air conditioner.

It could have ended there, but then Leonidas said something, still staring at the muted green carpet in front of him, said it to himself more than to anybody else, or to God, something that flipped it all toward the other world.

"I saw Christina," George Leonidas said. "And she saw me."

"THERE is a place, a position, something, *a state*," Jimmy said, "between being alive and being dead. Not alive, not dead. In between."

There it was, for those who like their reveals cold and hard.

They were down in the Tenderloin. In the Porsche. Jimmy had the gray light of the dash on his face, the shining wood-rimmed wheel in his hands. He was riding in third gear with low revs, and the engine was purring. The Porsche was glad to be up out of the hotel garage, out breathing the night air. Jimmy was half lost but wouldn't admit it. It was a bit after nine, early yet, but the alleyways were already spotted with street people. Early yet, but there would still be a mad yell every once in a while, echoing off the emptied buildings. There wasn't much other traffic, a cab every once in a while or a lost, slightly spooked tourist or a box truck making a night delivery. Not even any cops. They'd roll in later, when the Tenderloin got its full freak on.

A place, a position, a state.

Something. He'd never found a noun for it. And as for the verbs . . . well, the verbs only added more confusion. To the uninitiated anyway.

"I know it makes no sense to you," Jimmy said. "How could it? You saw their bodies. But then you saw the one of them, up and walking, hours later. Who can understand that?"

George Leonidas was in the passenger seat, one hand on the grip bar on the dash, the way old people will do, or people unused to sports cars. Staring straight ahead, like he was scared. As if what he was wide-eyed about was the speed and the low-slung car. He didn't say anything.

Jimmy kept up the monologue. It was always a monologue. "They're called *Sailors*," he said, hearing himself pick the pronoun. *They.* "Not alive, not dead exactly. At least, not gone. Not a ghost, but flesh and blood." He thought of the mash of meat and blood where the two had impacted. He had seen the bodies, too, and before the sanitation death techs had cleaned things up.

He steered into the first of the real mysteries. "When this happens, when one of . . . them is born, they take on a new face, but, for the first hour or two, if the loved ones are around, the new might resemble the old, if they saw each other. But just for the first hours. Or, other times, it's not that way at all. It's not set. Each time is . . . each time."

His voice was low and steady, undramatic, like the engine of the car, just cruising through wild territory. He heard himself. It was like listening to his voice on a tape recorder. *Jimmy Miles Explaining It.* He remembered something he hadn't thought of in years, a ride with his father, when he was ten or eleven, when his father told him he and Jimmy's mother were divorcing. Middle of the afternoon, picked up from school. The tone was the same, Jimmy realized. The flat tone carrying the earth-rending news. Then it had been that speech that begins, "Sometimes a mother and a father grow apart . . ." *Grow apart.* Things don't grow apart. They either grow together, or they die.

The street was one-way. A half block ahead, the light went to yellow, but Jimmy kept on at the same speed. It was full red when he went under.

"Is it only when they kill themselves?"

George Leonidas had spoken.

"A lot of Sailors are suicides," Jimmy said, "but some were murdered. Some were accidents."

"I was electrocuted," Machine Shop said from the back, like another track on the stereo. He was wedged, long leg bones and bony arms and all, into the Porsche's jump seat, the little fold-down seats meant to hold bags of groceries or maybe a kid or two. His bent head was stuffed up against the leatherette headliner of the ragtop. It made him look like a giant in a very modern fairy tale.

Jimmy looked up at him in the center rearview mirror.

"A woman threw a plug-in radio into the bathtub with me," Machine Shop said. "I was just taking a bath." There was another millisecond for the corrective voice. "OK, I was with another lady friend . . ."

"All we know, or think we know," Jimmy said to Leonidas (and to himself, for the ten thousandth time), "is that it happens when there is some unfinished business. Maybe *because* there is unfinished business. Nobody knows. You're here as long as you're here. Then you move on."

"Where are you taking me?" George the Lion said.

"Nowhere," Jimmy said. "We're just talking."

He pulled it down into second and took the next right, onto Castro, took it a little faster than he had to.

IT was Friday night in the Castro. The after-work bar crowd had spilled out onto the street, drinks in hand, some of them. All men, in this block. They'd hang out there for an hour or two, and then the night crowd would start to show. Leonidas, even in his present stricken state, was put off by the scene, men with their arms around each other. He had his window up, but you could still hear the punch-bag sound of the bass speakers in the clubs. Techno and house.

Jimmy took a right, climbed a hill, just like he knew where he was going. There was a park to the right as the road curved around on top of the hill.

Buena Vista Park. So maybe he wasn't lost after all. He stopped. There, below, was Lucy's Victorian apartment building, lights in half the top-floor windows.

Les was in the dining room. He had the Les Paul guitar out of its case, had it on his knee where he sat at the head of the long dining

table. The table was mahogany, deep red, shiny, with the point of a
white lace cover hanging off each end.

So the borrowed apartment belonged to a lady. It would fit with
everything else, another woman putting her arms around the waif.
Jimmy wondered who she was.

There was a dim light in the front bedroom, Lucy's room. It said
she was there, that she was alive. Like Tinkerbell's little light.

Jimmy got out of the car. Machine Shop took the opportunity to
unpack himself from the jump seat. They stood beside the Porsche, left
Leonidas where he was, still gripping the bar, even with the car parked.

"I appreciate you doing this," Machine Shop said. "Saying the
words. I never been any good at that."

"I was mostly just talking to myself," Jimmy said.

"I hear you. If there's ever anything I can—"

Jimmy cut him off with, "There's a woman in that apartment.
That's her brother, in the dining room. Her name is Lucille. Lucy. I
don't know what his name is. I call him Les. I need you to watch them,
while I'm with him."

"I should be at work," Shop said.

"I have money."

"I don't do it just for the money," Shop said. "It's my witness, in its
own way."

"Her name is Lucy," Jimmy said and opened the car door. He went
to his pocket and took out a fold of bills. He gave a couple hundred to
Machine.

"What am I supposed to do?"

"Don't let her kill herself," Jimmy said.

THEN they were out of the car, walking, Jimmy and George Leonidas,
down on the waterfront. It was the happening part of the night, crowds
of tourists, even locals, enjoying the seafood joints and the street
dancers and the jugglers and each other. It was Friday night.

"Here," George said, pointing to a corner of one of the parking lots between the trolley tracks and the docks. "This is where I saw her, my Christina. There were no people then, or only three or four. Not all this."

"What time was it?"

"Four o'clock."

"Was she alone?"

"There were two others, a man and a woman. Away from her, but watching her."

"What do you mean, they were watching her?"

"Like I was watching her, like she was mine. Like she belonged with me. They were watching her like that, too."

"What did she look like?"

George Leonidas's hand went toward the pocket over his heart again.

"I meant the one you saw," Jimmy said.

The Greek father took the picture from his pocket anyway. He gave it to Jimmy. "Christina is on the right. She would always be on the right, Melina on the left. She looked like herself."

Jimmy looked at the picture: He expected a yearbook picture, maybe the officers of the high school Greek Club. Or an all-dressed-up-for-the-prom picture: full, frilly dresses, a pair of dorky boys in tuxes between the gorgeous twins. What he got instead was a shot of the teens in one-piece swimsuits, Speedos, one black, one silver, standing with water skis beside the stern of a low-slung powerboat on the shore of some big-acre reservoir somewhere inland, brown hills in the background. Maybe Bethany, looking down on Altamont. The name of the boat was *Zorba*. Their black hair wasn't wigs. It was real. They wore it longer and looser in the picture. And wet and ropey. The sun was dropping.

"I saw *Christina*," the father said. "I saw *her*."

His hands had tightened into fists. At his side. As if he was clutching an iron bar in each one.

Jimmy handed back the picture. It hurt to look at the girls.

"You said she saw you. What did she do?" he asked. "Did she say anything to you?"

The sad Greek face tightened up, especially around the eyes. It was as if someone had sprayed something corrosive at his face.

"What did she say?"

George Leonidas took one of those clenched fists and punched Jimmy right in the face. Just like that.

Jimmy took it. It snapped his head back and knocked him onto his heels, but he took it, and all the surprise that came with it. George the Lion stepped a step nearer, closed up the distance the head shot had knocked between them. Only a second had passed. As Jimmy was bringing a hand up to his jaw, where the first of the pain was pushing its way out past the stunned surface and into the bone at the same time, the little man hit him again. In the face again, in the same place.

This time, Jimmy fell away, as if he'd been "slain in the spirit" on some cable TV evangelist's stage. George came after him, punching him twice in the belly, dull thudding hits that, even as Jimmy fell onto his back, made him think, *Old World*. He was getting an old-world beating, an honorable, manly, *controlled* beating, though the man landing the blows had completely lost it.

They weren't in the most crowded area, but there were people nearby, and they turned to look with the sound of the first couple of hits and whatever sounds Jimmy had made. They stepped closer, the witnesses, but there wasn't any cheering or joviality, the way there is in bad movies. They were seeing it for what it was, a bloody shock.

Leonidas couldn't stop himself.

Jimmy just took it. He barely lifted his hands in defense. He tried to get to his feet, managed only to get to his knees.

Leonidas hesitated. Jimmy's let-me-have-it manner broke the heated spell the Greek was under. He dropped his fists back down to his sides, like he was letting go of something, almost like he was throwing away something with both hands.

Jimmy touched his cheek with the back of his hand. It came away with blood smeared across it. But his mouth wasn't cut, and his eyes still worked. And he knew he didn't hurt any more than the other did.

"I don't understand," George Leonidas said. And said it all.

But he had something else for Jimmy. "That's what she said to me. 'Daddy, I don't understand.'"

CHAPTER SIX

What Jimmy didn't tell George Leonidas was the most important thing, that last night someone else was on the roof with his girls, someone to whisper a word in their pretty ears, another sort of Sailor. What he didn't tell Leonidas was that there were two kinds of Sailors, two ways to respond to this impossible thing.

It wasn't exactly a fashionable idea these days, but some were Good and some were Bad.

What was that one's name? Jacob. Jason. Jamie. *Jeremy*. Machine Shop had offered up the name when his conscience had prompted him, when the other inside him had cleared its throat. *Jeremy*. There's a villain for you. A skinny kid in a black North Beach beatnik's turtleneck. And cape. A Jeremy.

But why would a Sailor, even a bad Sailor, want two innocents to die, to throw off their own lives? Why would a Sailor, even the darkest, the blackest-souled amongst their kind, climb up on a roof to encourage a suicide?

What would it profit?

Jimmy knew the Greek had already heard enough things he didn't understand, already had enough questions, standing there in the parking lot, on the waterfront. He didn't need to hear the rest of it, not yet. Maybe ever.

"Do you have a wife?" Jimmy said.

George Leonidas nodded. His hands were still throbbing with the flesh-memory of the beating. And hurting themselves, but he was in so much other pain that it didn't register.

"Go sit with her," Jimmy said. "Your wife."

Leonidas nodded.

"Don't tell her any of this, what I said to you," Jimmy said. "It won't help her. She'll believe it even less than you do."

"I tell her everything."

"Then tell her you met a crazy man, who talked crazy," Jimmy said.

"A man who just let me beat him . . ." Leonidas added.

Jimmy looked him right in the eye. "Don't tell her you saw your daughter. Christina. It will only make for more pain. Neither one of you will ever see either one of them again, do you understand that?"

"I understand the words," Leonidas said.

"Believe me," Jimmy said. "Neither one of you will ever see either one of them again. Not in this life."

Leonidas suddenly reached toward him. Jimmy flinched, thinking another blow was coming, but George the Lion just gripped him by the upper arm. "If they are where you say they are, then just tell me they are at peace. Go there and see them and come tell me that."

His grip hurt. "I will," Jimmy said.

If Jimmy had had his own nagging voice of conscience like Machine Shop did, now he would have taken it back. Because there was no way he could do what he said he would do, and Jimmy knew it. There wasn't even any reason to believe both girls were Sailors now, just the one. The other was probably just gone.

"Where can I reach you?" Jimmy said. He knew he'd probably never even try.

Leonidas had business cards in a leather fold-over holder. He

handed one over. He was in plumbing supplies. Across the Bay. He put
the card holder back in his front pants pocket and nodded at Jimmy
and turned and walked away.

Card. Nod. Turn. Walk.

Jimmy watched him go, watched to see if he would look over at the
pier where it had happened, Pier 35, where the girls had jumped, where
the seams of his world had been rent. But he didn't look over.

Jimmy let him get some distance ahead, then followed him. He
didn't exactly know why. He followed Leonidas through the crowds
of tourists, who only seemed to have grown in volume and *volume* in
the last hour, past the street performers, past everything his daughters
had passed the night before, past the last things they had seen in life,
across a packed open parking lot to a parking structure, open on the
sides, to a dark silver Cadillac DeVille, four or five years old, the last of
the "old man" Caddies. He unlocked it and got behind the wheel,
started the engine, pulled on the lights, never breaking down, never
looking back.

Leonidas had never looked back.

How do you do that? Jimmy thought.

HE thought it through three Chiantis, a few hours later, sitting in a
bar, looking back in spite of himself, remembering more than he wanted
to about a very specific time and place. And a person. And *Chianti*.
What he was drinking tonight was good wine, but then it was cheap,
youthful wine, Chianti out of basket-wrapped bottles, Italian-movie
Chianti. *La Dolce Vita. 8½*. Dan Tana's on Santa Monica in L.A. when
it was still just a good red-checkered-tablecloth Italian restaurant music
business and below-the-line movie people went to. Cheap, youthful.
She was the one Lucy had reminded him of, starting back in Saugus
Café. Mary.

Don't look back.

He was outside with the smokers. At one of those tall tables with
tall chairs designed to keep you from ever relaxing.

There Lucy was, right across the street. At a table in front of the Starbucks wannabe in the Haight.

With Machine Shop.

The coffee joint was packed, every table full, inside and out, busier than Jimmy's bar. Lucy and Machine Shop were about the only ones without big Friday night smiles on their faces.

Big surprise, she was a little down.

But Machine Shop was on the job, even if this wasn't exactly what Jimmy had in mind when he told him to look after her. They were like new best friends. They had coffees in front of them. Shop would stir his thoughtfully while she talked, stirring and nodding, just like a gal pal. Then Lucy would stop, get to the end of something, end it with a question. Jimmy could tell even from across the street that her voice raised at the end of the line. Machine Shop would stop stirring, nod a couple of times more, and then say a line or two. He was a good listener, leaning in, eye contact. Once he even reached a hand across the table to pat the back of hers, completely nonsexual. Two pats and out. His posture and performance made Jimmy think *Twelve Step* again. Shop had a sponsor somewhere, probably was a sponsor to somebody else, probably a good one, too.

Jimmy drained his glass. The first step is admitting you're powerless . . .

Across in the coffee bar, a fat guy moved, and Jimmy saw somebody else. Polythene Pam. Alone. She was inside, right on the other side of the window, watching Lucy and Machine Shop, watching them to the exclusion of everything else. She had a little demitasse in front of her, a shot.

A guy came up, stood over her. (There was an empty chair across from her.) He had an espresso of his own, had the cup and saucer on his flat palm, an odd way of presenting it. Maybe he was a waiter somewhere. In L.A., he would have been an actor. He was nice enough looking and expected more from her than he got. She didn't even shake her head no, just gave him a chilly "smile" that ended long before it got to her eyes. Dismissed.

She *did* look good tonight, very tempting, even hotter than out on that sunlit bench in front of the Golden Gate gift shop with Sexy Sadie. Even more mod. Tonight she wore a little plaid skirt, a Scottish schoolgirl's skirt. And a fuzzy sweater. And over-the-ankle Doc Martens.

"She's killer-diller when she's dressed to the hilt . . ." Jimmy sang. He tried to take another drink but found his glass empty.

He thought he had sung it to himself, but apparently it was loud enough for a young woman and her date two tables over to hear. The girl looked at him with some pity.

Time to go. He left a couple of bills on the table, weighted them down with the red glass bowl candle, and exited out the front, all but hopped over the low iron railing just to show anybody watching that he was in complete control of his faculties. He didn't look back to see if the girl had any parting pathos for him.

He found a wedge of shadow, even if it did smell pissy, in the entryway of a storefront next to the Chianti bar. From there he could watch the rest of the play over at the coffee joint. Everyone was still on their marks, Shop and Lucy talking, Pam looking a little put off, stirring her little coffee with a little spoon.

Then he figured it out. The empty chair across from Pam was meant for Lucy. It was a date. Spoiled by Machine Shop.

A band of hippies came past Jimmy, six or seven of them, girls and guys. Central casting. Freaky and fun. Hendrix headbands, striped bell-bottoms, fruit boots. One even clinked finger cymbals. If Disneyland had a Haight-Ashbury section, hippies like these would stroll past, saying things like, "What's *happening*, man?" and, "Be groovy."

The leader wore a fringey vest, a puffy-sleeved shirt, and a sho-nuff Vandyke. His right-hand girl, who wasn't much older than thirteen, blew Jimmy a kiss. Leader Hippie pulled her back in line. As the troupe moved on, there was a little edge of color to him, but not Sailor blue. Or maybe it was just the streetlight.

When the retro hippies had cleared the frame, over at the coffee bar the little scene was ending. Lucy was standing now. She said another line or two to Machine Shop, and he said something back to her. She smiled, and it looked like it was over, but then she tipped her head toward him and leaned into him for a hug, more her idea than his was the way Jimmy read it. Shop kept watching her as she walked up the sidewalk in the direction of the apartment. When she turned the corner at Central Avenue, a block and a half away, he left his place by the little round table and started after her. He was going to watch her all the way to her door. On the job.

Polythene Pam stood up to go.

PEOPLE make friends. People run into each other, find out they live a few blocks apart, make a date for coffee and commiseration. It happens all the time.

Or take a ride over into Marin on a beautiful, sunny day, like this morning . . .

Maybe he was seeing things that weren't there. Maybe it was innocent.

He didn't think that for a minute.

Jimmy kept ten cars back. Traffic was light. Last night, he had followed Polythene Pam away from the coffeehouse. She'd split a few minutes after Lucy. She was on foot, too. Pam stayed on one side of Haight Street, and Jimmy tailed her on the other, until she crossed the street in the middle of the block and came across to his side. She took the next right, walked across the wide greenbelt, the Panhandle, the eastern end of Golden Gate Park. There were a few street people out and people who lived in the park, but she never hurried her pace. Or looked back. (Here was another somebody who went through life looking straight ahead. With a purpose.) She turned left on Fell and walked two more short blocks.

To a black house.

The house had two-story columns out front and was painted black. There may have been some red trim here and there that didn't read in the darkness, but the house was *black*. And black lacquer at that.

It shined. Pam opened the iron gate and let herself in the outsized front door.

So she lived in the Haight. Innocent? Her house looked like a frat house in New Orleans, like a Goth sorority at Tulane.

Jimmy spent the rest of the night on the street. At dawn, he went home to the Mark for a change of clothes and to pick up the Porsche.

Maybe it was time to introduce himself to Lucy.

He made it back to the Haight just in time to watch the Catholic home for unwed mom-ettes come to life. (It didn't look as if anyone was awake up at Lucy's. He parked up the hill.) They had those girls up at the crack of dawn, scrubbing the sidewalks out front, watering the plants in the planters, scattering some bread crumbs for the birds who lived in the trees in the park behind them. They washed the windows. *All the better to see the bright future ahead.* The nun who acted as boss to the detention detail didn't seem too bad, called all the girls by name, even spoke Spanish to two of them, making them laugh. You never know. They say sometimes you're entertaining angels unaware.

There were some signs of life at Lucy's. Jimmy was *this close* to getting out of the car, to walking down the hill to the front door at 52 Central, when Pam pulled up.

Girls' day out. It was nine, a very civilized hour for an excursion. Pam drove a Land Rover County, dark green, deep dark forest green. She was alone. She parked at the curb, and Lucy came out the front door a second later, a sweatshirt tied around her waist, over sporty pants. Bright, springy, coordinated, Gappy colors. She got in the front seat, and Pam revved the engine and backed up a foot to straighten out the wheels, and away they went. The nun was back in her third-floor window, watching the whole thing with a neutral, preternaturally patient look.

Jimmy wished *he* knew how to do that.

Once across the GG, the Range Rover passed through the tunnel to Marin, under the rainbow painted on its concrete face. There was a second and a third exit for Sausalito, but Pam kept going.

The two women talked all the way. They had the windows down, the sunroof back. Pam had that short, chopped-off hairdo for her jet-black hair, so the wind made her look like she was in the stylist's chair the whole way, getting a new cut blown out. Lucy's hair was longer, was like a scarf out the window when the currents caught it right. Out in the bright, happy light of Marin County, her hair had all kinds of life to it, looked almost red.

They took an exit, east, and rolled along across the top limit of the Bay, through an industrial zone, marine industrial, shoulder-to-shoulder marinas and boat repair bays, all along the curve of the water's edge. Maybe they were taking a boat out. The roadway was elevated a bit. The city could be seen in the distance, white and silver, with the dark hump of Tiburon in the foreground.

Here it was. There was a park, a large greenbelt cleared of trees except at either end, an expanse of green that went all the way down to the water, to the big hauled-in rocks and the six-inch waves white-capped with foam and the detritus of the Bay. The Range Rover came around on the main highway and pulled into the lot.

From the water, from the south, Tiburon looked like an island at the top of the Bay, but close like this you could see that it was a knob at the end of a peninsula, a knobby knuckle on the end of one of the fingers reaching out into the Bay.

And on the end of the knuckle was another high-backed island. Belvedere. It was like the rich part of Tiburon, only almost all of it was rich.

Jimmy drove on past the park and the parking lot, went another half mile or so down to the ferry dock and the phony picturesque "seaport village" of shops and restaurants. There was a roundabout. Jimmy went around about it.

He came back up and pulled into the lot, parked where he could look out across the expanse of grass, all the way down to the water. He'd had the top down for the ride over. He got out and hoisted it up. He was in the first row of the lot, between two SUVs, hidden, dwarfed. A woman on one side of him was off-loading three boys in turquoise soccer gear, ten or eleven, a Jason and two Seans, and what looked like a hundred pounds of support equipment and a Hammacher

Schlemmer collapsible sideline parents' two-place couch with cup holders for the lattes from the back and side of a Ford Expedition long enough to be a gas line all by itself.

Jimmy took a book and a warm Red Bull from his cooler over to a picnic table ten feet from the cars.

Lucy and Pam had spread out a blanket. They sat. Pam had a picnic basket, opened the lid, unpacked something from it. Jimmy thought he saw her looking over at him. Maybe she was more aware than Lucy and Les, more suspicious of the same guy always somehow being around. Maybe she'd realized he'd followed her home last night, to the black house. But he was a hundred yards away from them. Not much for Pam to see. Still, he put his nose in his book. It was *Zen and the Art of Motorcycle Maintenance*.

Lucy was watching the little kids on the field. Beside "the big field" where the Seans and the Jasons would be playing there was a tiny-tots field lined out with little bitsy goals and four-year-olds. Girls. The Purple Unicorns versus Rainbow Ponies, though they didn't defend the goals, and only the dads kept score, so you couldn't really call it *versus*. Half of the girls ran around aimlessly while the other half stood and talked. Two held hands. One was lying on her back in the grass, looking at the fat white clouds, opening and closing her legs and clapping the heels of her rubber cleats, like she was making a snow angel.

Pam put her hand on Lucy's shoulder as Lucy watched the kids. Jimmy had wondered almost from the start if Lucy was pregnant, if that was what was at the bottom of her unhappiness. But wouldn't that be too much of a coincidence, with her landing in a borrowed apartment across the way from a home for unwed mothers? Still, he wondered it again, when he saw the way she watched the kids.

And then along came the other one. Sexy Sadie.

Probably just another coincidence . . .

The three of them seemed to have coordinated their outfits. Pam was wearing white ankle-length pants and a short pink top. Sexy Sadie wore a sea-green skirt, a full Katharine Hepburn skirt, and a cotton blouse with rolled-up sleeves. The three looked like catalog models, especially when Pam and Lucy stood to greet the third and they all touched each other's arms and Sadie kissed Pam.

Jimmy hadn't seen her arrive, Sadie. There was a white '57 T-Bird in the parking lot he hadn't noticed before, but that would be a little too perfect. He was guessing the classic Jag sedan, but it was black and seemed too gloomy for her.

Maybe she had parachuted in, rappelled from a rescue helicopter, because now the crack two-woman sympathy team really sprang into action. Again. The three settled back onto the blanket and began to talk. Serious as serious gets. The light changed. As if the god of weather were part of the plan, had just been waiting for his cue, the cottony clouds at the same time took on some color, dark enough and sudden enough to make the parents on the sidelines of the game look up at the sky.

Lucy, on the other hand, was looking down.

Now she was crying, pulling the sleeve of her sweatshirt over her hand to daub at her eyes.

Sexy Sadie patted her leg.

Polythene Pam stroked her hair.

They were whispering to her, every word hitting some soft, assailable spot.

Jimmy had a thought, that he was watching a murder in slow motion.

CHAPTER SEVEN

Machine Shop sat on the Market Street streetcar, in one of the side seats, one of the wooden slat benches. For some reason, San Francisco had bought up a half-dozen old New Orleans streetcars, refurbished them, kept the names.

Where was *Desire*?

Shop had all his gear with him, on the rollie. He was in his paint, fully, freshly silver.

"Look like you're moving out," a Chinese man seated across from him said.

"No, jus' headed toward my destination," Shop answered.

"You look like robot on vacation."

"Jus' making my witness," Shop said.

Jimmy was on the bench next to the Chinese man. It was an hour before sundown, not an easy time for him generally, the hour when the shadows tended to cross his soul.

But everybody else was happy. The Chinese man and almost everyone else on board were headed to a Giants game, a night game down at the new ballpark, the replacement for Candlestick, with some company's name crowbarred into its name. The streetcar riders were all decked out in Giants' shirts and jackets and hats, like the oddest, most overweight, most over-the-hill team imaginable.

It reminded Jimmy what a blue-collar town San Francisco was at its heart. There were plenty of the rich here, on Nob Hill, on Russian Hill, here in the City and over in Marin, on Tiburon, down in Hillsborough, but it was a city stocked with robust working men and women and their families. A union town. A proud town. A cohesive town. A public-transit town. A sweating town.

Going to work, just like Machine Shop.

They reached some stop, and the doors opened, front and back, and everybody else stood.

"Who're they playing?" Jimmy said to one kid on his way out, a boy eight or nine.

"Asshat *Dodgers*," the kid said, and got a laugh from the crowd.

Hey kid, at least in L.A. it's still just *Dodger* Stadium.

The streetcar rolled out again, empty except for Shop and Jimmy. Jimmy said, "I didn't mean you had to actually *sit* with Lucy last night."

"Yeah, that wasn't my plan," Machine Shop said. "It just happened."

Machine Shop didn't offer anything more, until he realized Jimmy was waiting for a report.

"She didn't come out of her place for a long time," Shop said. "The boy just played his guitar. I couldn't hear it, but I play a little myself. I believe he's good. I *used* to play, in my previous position." Shop went down a memory trail for a second. Jimmy waited.

"A light came on in the front bedroom about ten forty-five," Shop said. "I guess she was sleeping up until then. A few minutes before eleven, she came out. She was dressed up, kinda nice, but she had on a heavy coat, heavier than what she needed really. Had the collar up. Walked down the hill to Haight. She walked right straight to the corner, to the coffee place. She got a coffee, took it outside, sat down. I was watching from across the street, over there where you were later. She was pitiful. I couldn't stand it, came and sat with her, talked to the girl. She's just a child herself."

Shop exercised his lower face vigorously. "Am I cracking?" he asked.

"No, you look fine."

"I gotta get in character," Shop said.

"When you came up and sat down," Jimmy said, "did you get the idea she was meeting somebody?"

Machine Shop didn't answer for a long beat, staring straight ahead. Then he animated, straightened his spine, pivoted his shiny head robotically, and produced a mechanical sound without moving his lips.

"No," he said, unblinking.

The streetcar rolled on through the Financial District, empty, cold-looking, the wind stirring through it on a Saturday night, and made the big left turn onto the Embarcadero. *I Cover the Waterfront.* A Bay sunset cruise ship, out to the Golden Gate and back, was docked at Pier 39; a line of twenty ugly limos waited at the curb nose to tail, new-style prom haulers, stretched Escalades and Excursions. And a Hummer. The last time Jimmy was in San Francisco, the Embarcadero wasn't a tourist stop. The first time he came to San Francisco, there was still a freeway overhead, running along the curve of the docks and piers. It had been torn down a few years back. The docks had been just docks for all those years before that. Then somebody had gotten the idea tourists would come to the water's edge if they gussied it up a little. Come down to see where a hundred thousand wives and girlfriends said good-bye to a hundred thousand soldiers and sailors headed off to war. That was the scene in Jimmy's head as he looked out the streetcar window at the docks and the piers, *that* high drama, though it was before even his time. A lot of tears shed on these piers.

I cover the waterfront, watching the sea
Will the one I love be coming back to me?

Now it was home to another kind of sailor, off to another kind of war. One of their domains, one of their gathering places here. Every city had its Sailors, if some more than others. Even inland. Kansas City, Chicago. Even Orlando. (Though inland, they still tended to congregate near whatever big water was available.) But the big coastal cities collected the most Sailors, from inland, from all over. From small towns. You didn't like to be alone. You needed reinforcement, whether you were good or bad. (The new initiates straightway found out there were two ways to go.) Buses brought them every day, trains. They didn't much like to fly.

Jimmy saw a bright flash of blue around a young woman in a cluster of people at one of the stops. They were street kids, but not too ragged. One boy had a guitar. Even as the streetcar was pulling out again, with that surprising acceleration, Jimmy heard what he was playing, what they were singing, R.E.M., "Losing my religion . . ." Jimmy turned to look back at them, at the girl. Three of them were Sailors, though *her* blue, the edge of blue around her, was the strongest. So she was the newest, probably, or at least the newest to San Francisco. She had that New look in her eyes. She wore a T-shirt from some Oklahoma barbecue. He hoped that's where she was from. Oklahoma.

Machine Shop was looking back at her, too, at the cluster of Sailors. He mechanically rotated his head to the forward position again.

Jimmy rotated, too. He pulled the photo out of his pocket, the Leonidas girls beside the ski boat. With two days now past since she'd died, Christina would look different, but not completely different. He wouldn't have admitted it if someone had asked him, but he was down here to try to find her. There were things to look for. Sometimes the eyes would be the same, if you got up close enough. Jimmy hadn't known her, never spent any time with her before the dive off the roof. If he had, maybe he'd know her when he saw her. The surest link between the before and the after was gestures, the way you walked, nervous tics, the way you bit your lip, the way you brushed your hair out of your eyes. That was what was left. Maybe you could say that about anybody you remembered.

Jimmy watched Machine Shop do his act for twenty minutes. They'd gotten off two stops after they'd seen the Sailors losing their religion. Shop had been "on" since the Financial District, rolled his rollie down the streetcar steps as a robot, held the doors open for a middle-aged white lady as a robot, moved away as a robot, even sidestepped a cluster of pigeons feeding on a spilled bag of popcorn as a robot. He drew a crowd immediately.

Shop's act, at least what Jimmy saw, had two aspects: he interfaced with skeptics, and he danced. The interfacing was simple. They tried to make him laugh. Or get mad, in the case of a pair of blocky twenty-something boys, probably in town on liberty from their shitty East Bay jobs. Those two got right in Shop's face and sneered and said some things, worked in tandem, one on each side of him. In the end, Shop's answer was a perfectly executed 180-degree pivot.

The dancing was basically a robot on *Soul Train* or, when the demographic skewed older, *American Bandstand*. A lot of Ohio Players and Earth Wind & Fire. A little KC & the Sunshine Band, the early years. Jimmy pushed through from the second row and put a twenty in the overturned top hat, up until then empty except for Shop's own prime-the-pump fiver. A couple of others followed Jimmy's suggestion. Machine Shop bowed his appreciation in four mechanical stages.

The sun was gone. Here came the night. Jimmy ended up at the crab stand, where he'd gone that first night. Where he'd met the Sailor crab kid who had middle-managed Machine Shop's beating, apparently for the crime of trying to suggest maybe the twins didn't *have* to jump. In Jimmy's mind, this was Sailor Central. For now anyway.

Crab Boy. There he was in his perfectly white sneakers. The stand was busy, every stool taken, a cloud of steam engulfing the scene. A heat lamp kept the curly fries warm. The light turned the whole steam cloud red. Dante's Crab Stand. The kid recognized Jimmy, jerked his head up in a noncommittal greeting, but never slowed the pace of slinging that Dungeness into those red-and-white paper boats. A sheet of white wax paper, a handful of crab, a white plastic fork, a tear of sourdough bread, a look up at the customer for a nod or a no, and then a wedge of lemon. Or not.

"Gimme one," Jimmy said.

"Aye aye, Cap." There were four orders ahead of him.

"You seen Jeremy?" Jimmy said when a stool came free.

"Who?"

"Jeremy."

"I don't know any Jeremy," the kid said and made the name sound funny. "I just barely know *you*. Who's Jeremy?"

Since they were using lines out of movies, Jimmy had one of his own. "Somebody said look him up," he said.

Crab Boy didn't say anything for all of a minute while he filled orders, then got to Jimmy's.

"Where's your metal nigger friend?" he said.

Jimmy wondered if Crabby was related to the blockhead East Bay boys trying to make Shop crack.

"If he heard you say that, he'd . . . turn the other silver cheek."

The kid put the crab and a cup of horseradish in front of Jimmy. "You want that wine again?"

"A beer. An Anchor Steam."

"You're trying too hard, man," the kid said.

Jimmy waited him out.

"I'm just dicking around with you," Crab Boy said. Two more customers were coming up, a couple. "Jeremy's around somewhere. He usually comes later. What do you want with Jeremy?"

"I have ten grand to give him," Jimmy said. "Or is it twenty?"

"That's good," the kid said. He looked at the newcomer customers, raised his eyebrows, brightened his face a little, his version of, "What'll you have?" The man held up two fingers to order, but a forefinger and thumb. European.

"Where ya from?" the kid asked. "Deux. Due. Dos."

"France," the man said. "Montpellier?"

The kid rattled off three or four lines of French, but it was mostly wrong and more than a little confusing to the French couple. But Crab

Boy slung it with feeling. He was already prepping and filling the paper boats.

"Who's next?" Jimmy said, apropos of nothing.

It took the kid out of his crab-slinging rhythm, but he tried not to show it. "What did you say, sir?"

"Who's next?" Jimmy said. *"C'est qui, le prochain? Wer ist an der Reihe? Chi é prossimo?"* he added, for fun.

"Ask Jeremy when you see him," Crab Boy said after another delay that showed the kid was anxious about answering wrong.

Jimmy got up, surrendered his stool to the French lady. He overtipped the kid, which was a way of insulting him, because Jimmy knew he wasn't down here on the waterfront to make a living.

He went trolling for Jeremy.

It didn't make any sense, but he went first to the place where he'd last seen him, the only time he'd seen him, Pier 35. Where the girls had jumped. Tonight, nobody was naked, nobody was dying. But, hey, it was early yet. There was a crowd, gathered around a man with a trained cat act, cats walking a little tightrope, jumping from perch to perch. Then he'd have them walk back and forth across his shoulders to show that they enjoyed it as much as he did. For some reason, the ringmaster narrated the show with a thick French accent, at its thickest when one cat "pretended" not to want to do this tonight, and he had to go to his knees to scold her with a finger in her face. Jimmy turned away when the flaming hoop came out.

"Have you ever *smelled* burned cat hair?" he said to a girl as he was leaving.

She gave him a smile. He had seen her in the crowd. She was alone, maybe twenty, twenty-one. Or sixteen. A blonde. Pink Juicy knits, top and bottom. Cute sneakers. There was something about her eyes . . .

But she wasn't a Sailor. She certainly wasn't Christina Leonidas, unless she'd adjusted to her new state faster than anyone ever before. This girl looked more or less at peace, a place few Sailors ever found.

Jimmy bought a coffee and found a bench where he could sit alone to drink it.

He wasn't alone for long.

Meet Jeremy.

Suddenly, he was right in front of him, apparently dropped right out of the sky onto the bench across from him. Their knees were almost touching. Jimmy would have wondered if it was a gay attempt at a pickup if he hadn't recognized him right away, what with the length of long black coat (was it a cape?) thrown over the knee. Jeremy. And here was his "support staff," close by but not too close, three strong-looking ones ten feet away, sitting on other people's cars. Make that four. There was Red Boots. *Five*, Red Boots's sidekick. Good Lord, they *were* capes. Half of them wore long black capes. With silky rope ties to wrap them at the neck. New Romantics! One of them was one of the men who'd stood over Machine Shop on night one, punching him in the face.

"What's that smell?" Jimmy said.

"You're not in L.A. anymore, Brother," Jeremy said. Projected. Rumbled. He had an unnaturally deep voice, like a DJ, a DJ gone bad. Unless that's redundant. It was the kind of deep, dramatic voice that sounded worked on. Developed. Probably in front of a mirror. "*All* the senses can come into play here," he intoned.

"You know, I've noticed that," Jimmy said. "At home, I can't smell anything. Here, it's sea spray and patchouli and steamed crabs and . . . what's that purple flower, out under the Golden Gate?"

Jeremy's face was in the light. He wore a black turtleneck over black gabardine slacks. He liked jewelry. Silver. He was an *old* Sailor. Anyone passing by who didn't know him, or who didn't suspect anything about him, who didn't *know* who/what he really was, would peg him for early forties. That was another thing about them. It wasn't that Sailors didn't age, just that they aged on their own clock and calendar. There wasn't exactly an answer to how old he was, how old any of them were. You might as well just pick a number out of the air. Sometimes a Sailor looked ninety and had died at thirty and been in this state just ten years. Others times, more likely, a guy would look mid-thirties with fifty or sixty New Years on him. Doing the math didn't do you much good. This one had probably been a Sailor since the 1950s.

Maybe since the 1930s. At least the '40s. Maybe he'd been down here, this Jeremy, watching the wives and girlfriends saying good-bye in the war. Picture him sidling up to them, insinuating himself into their blues, offering his handkerchief for them to dry their tears. He was a predator. He'd probably be here another hundred years.

He looked like Charlie Watts. But without the happy-go-lucky disposition.

"So it's true?" Jeremy said.

"What's that?" Jimmy said.

"That the Sailors of the north have, what you call it, an identifying scent."

"I think I just meant your cologne," Jimmy said.

"I heard the scent is rather sweet," the other said. He was a familiar type among those on the bad side of the Sailor world, pretensions of sophistication, but a thug.

"I shouldn't have said anything," Jimmy said.

Over by the cars, Red Boots got a message from somewhere, just like the other night, another Sailor running up. There was action somewhere. It didn't seem important enough to involve Jeremy, but Red Boots went away with the runner.

A moment later, Jimmy saw Lucy. Lucy and company actually, Lucy and the two women moving through the crowd fifty yards away.

Jimmy looked away quickly. He didn't need for Jeremy to connect her to him.

"So who *is* next?" Jimmy said.

It was like Jeremy was ready and waiting for the line. No hesitation. "I was hoping *you* knew," he said. "They say you're a somebody down south."

"You ever been down south?"

"Man of the north, tried and true, Brother," he said. He uncrossed his legs and leaned back. He opened his thighs and hustled his balls, rearranging things in that way jocks do. And salesmen, trying to close the deal, man to man.

"What does killing a couple of girls get you?"

Jeremy just took the line like he'd probably take a two-by-four between the eyes. Rock steady. *What else you got?* That's what it meant to be an old Sailor. And this was sure enough a salty dog. Jimmy started wondering if maybe he'd been around for the '06 quake.

"One step forward, two steps back," Jeremy said. "They're in a better place, some would say."

Jimmy had had enough cryptic bullshit to last him awhile. "I believe I'm going to get me some more of that crab," he said.

But, before Jimmy could split, Jeremy suddenly sat up straight and lifted his nose in the air. One of his Watchers across the way perked up a second later, as if he'd gotten the silent signal, too. Suddenly they were all on their feet, Jeremy's crew, looking around in every direction. Like hunting dogs.

And then they were gone, all of them.

A second or two later, the background noise changed. A movie sound engineer could explain it, would know all the layers, would know what had built the previous sound, the ambient resonance of the water, the waves against the pilings of the docks, seabirds on top of that, the traffic near and far, and all the ways the crowds were noising, and would know what had changed.

It wasn't a silence exactly. It was nothing, turned up loud.

Jimmy looked over to the right. Whatever had happened, it was to the east, the Embarcadero.

He found it.

He walked into the back of the crowd. Here was another kind of audience. Jeremy and his men were already there, had already pushed through to the front.

It was a streetcar, stopped dead in its tracks.

It was a body, cleaved into halves.

It was a transit driver standing there with that nothing-I-could-do look.

And that smell in the air, spilled gore.

Jeremy dispatched his men. To Look. It was like the other night, the men circulating through the bands of spectators, staring individuals in the eyes. Looking.

Jimmy moved closer. He couldn't see if it was a man or a woman, old or young.

Of course he thought, *Lucy*. When he'd seen her, with Sadie and Pam, they were heading this way. If they were headed anywhere. They were just strolling. Pam had a drink with a straw, something bright red in clear plastic. Sadie had her arm in Lucy's.

It was a man. Two halves of a man.

Jimmy stepped closer.

The eyes were still open. The upper half was on its side. The lower was on its back. (Had this human being already lost the right to personal pronouns?)

The impact had torn open his pants. He had an erection. Jimmy had heard of it, a final jolt of nerve voltage through the cord, a last rude impulse. A last joke.

"Don't you have a tarp or something?" Jimmy said to the driver.

The driver shook his head. "You don't touch 'em. You just wait."

Then Jimmy saw Lucy in the crowd, across, on the far side of the halved man. She had seen it, and seeing it had changed her face.

But she was moving away, or being moved away, Sadie with her arm around her, Polythene Pam coming along behind them, finishing her drink, cute as a bug.

He went after them, pushed people out of the way to get to them, but they were too far ahead of him.

CHAPTER EIGHT

He heard the newspaper land on the carpet in the hallway, against the door.

Some call it morning.

He was in the club chair with the drapes open. There was a little blue on the right side of the sky, but it was still dark. He had a glass of vodka in his hand, the glass from the bathroom, but he wasn't drunk. It hadn't done anything for him. He never read the paper anymore. The news always seemed to be something he'd already gotten some other way. But he got up anyway and went to the door.

It was fat. A fat paper. He let the door close against his back standing there and then held the lever and let it close quietly, with just a click. No use waking anybody.

He went back to sit in the chair by the window. He put the paper on the ledge. He'd gone to get it not for the news but in the hope it could renew the sense that the world was still out there, remind him that maybe the world wasn't as small and as empty as it felt right now to him. The cold air from the AC ruffled the edges, made it flutter.

He turned the paper over to the front page.

It was below the fold, but there it was:

STREETCAR SUICIDE

With a picture. The body covered.

Things tend to be a little dead at a newspaper on a Saturday night. They'd given the assignment to a reporter, probably somebody young, maybe even an intern, and let him or her do a feature treatment rather than just the hard news. So the first graf wasn't the five W's, but more along the lines of . . .

The weekend revelers and visiting conventioneers in their matching T-shirts who congregated at the edge of the Bay on a Chamber of Commerce brochure–perfect Saturday night never expected . . .

The dead man was thirty-six years old. It said so, right there in the seventh paragraph. Jimmy made a point of not letting his eyes linger over the name.

He snatched up his cell phone and called the first number on the scroll. His "client."

"A voice from the past," Angel answered.

"And I haven't even said anything yet," Jimmy said.

"You caught me. I was just getting ready for services, just getting in the shower."

"I forgot it was Sunday."

"It's raining here. Maybe I'll just go stand outside."

"Rain . . ." Jimmy said, thinking about it.

"So what's up?"

"People killing themselves left and right," Jimmy said. "Three since I got here. And I was right there each time."

"But you didn't have anything to do with it."

"Not so far as I know. If *you* had been here, maybe you could have talked them out of it."

"It's never me," Angel said. "God through me. I'm just the . . . whatcha call it. Relay man."

"Lucy's all right," Jimmy said. "As far as I can tell."

"What is she doing up there?"

"I don't know. She's just been acting the tourist. With her brother."

"Her brother?"

"A kid maybe fourteen, fifteen. Plays guitar. Has a kind of retro look, a porkpie hat. I like him better than her."

"When did he come into the picture?"

"She stopped in Paso Robles for him."

"But she's all right. That's good," Angel said.

"She's dragging me around to see the sights. So far we've been to Sausalito and the Golden Gate, past Alcatraz, over to Tiburon, down to Fisherman's Wharf. All around the Haight."

"What's so funny 'bout peace, love, and understanding?"

"She's made a couple of friends. Girlfriends. They seem to . . . brighten her spirits."

There wasn't any use in talking about slow-motion murder. It would sound stupid if he said it out loud.

"People like her," Angel said.

"Who is she?" Jimmy asked. "Who is she to you?"

"I like her, too," was the answer, for all it didn't say.

"So what do you want me to do? Kidnap her, bring her home?"

"I don't know," Angel said. "Now I'm worried about *you*. Before, you sounded good, glad to be out of L.A. Now you sound like you're waiting for the other shoe to drop."

"Maybe," Jimmy said. "I'll watch her. I'll call you."

"God bless you," Angel said.

"That's what the panhandler said to me the other day up in Sausalito, when I blew him off," Jimmy said. "I'm not sure he really meant it."

He took a shower, a long shower with the water as hot as it would go. In L.A. you always heard the voices of the water conservation nags when you were in the shower, even when you were reaching for the handle on the toilet. Here, it rained, really rained, and San Francisco was that much closer to the mountains and the snowmelt to start with. They had water. So the shower flowed freely, almost washed away the heaviness in him.

The phone was ringing when he got out. The room phone.

It wasn't even eight o'clock yet.

He let it ring long enough for a wrong number to go away, give up. It kept ringing.

"Hello."

"This is Duncan Groner. The *Chronicle.*" It was a cracking voice, an old man's voice, a voice with some *coot* to it. Jimmy assumed the man meant the newspaper, not that he was an oracle. Even before he added, "I'm a reporter."

Something clicked about the odd name. Jimmy walked with the phone over to the window where the thick Sunday paper was. The by-line on the *Chron*'s suicide puff piece was Dana Gruber.

"You don't write under the name Dana Gruber, do you?" Jimmy said.

"Holy Mother of God, no," the voice on the phone said.

"The initials are the same."

"That's all. She's a *journalist* . . ." Then, without a breath between the words, he said, "So you were down there last night, too. I understand you were there for all three." It wasn't a question.

"Yeah, I was there."

"I'm doing a follow-up on the Leonidas girls, tying it in. I talked to George Leonidas. He said talk to you, that you had something to say about it. A different angel."

"Did you say *angel*?"

"I meant *angle*. Sometimes I'm a little dyslexic early in the morning."

"Mr. Leonidas got it wrong. I wouldn't be any help to you."

There was a little pause. "I know you, Brother," the man on the other end of the line said. He didn't say it like the secret Sailor code that it was, more like they were old friends. They weren't. They weren't even new friends. He waited. He expected the silence.

Jimmy said, "I guess I could use some fresh air. Where do you want to meet?"

"How do you feel about church?" the reporter said.

FRESH air? It was like being in an auditorium-sized pool hall. It was a ballroom in a hotel on Cathedral Hill. The cigarette smoke burned Jimmy's eyes and constricted his throat from the second he came in. It was like walking into a house afire.

But it *was* church. A pastor, a skinny man with a big, booming voice, was at a pulpit up front on the elevated platform with its white tacked-on pleated skirt. His voice was not just big but had a kind of authority, a kind of weight, a *been there/done that* intensity. He was talking about Peter, *Saint* Peter, and overcoming the past.

Jimmy squinted, looking for his date in the haze.

Duncan Groner was alone in the last row of hotel ballroom armless stackable chairs, against the wall, under an eight-foot-long mural of the completion of the transcontinental railroad, the driving of the golden spike. He had a fat, round, red eraserless pencil stuck over his ear and a long reporter's notebook on the empty seat beside him. And, Jimmy would learn in a second, a buzz on.

The banner strung up behind the preacher said: Western States Roundup Alcoholics Anonymous. Yee-haw.

Groner gave him a wave over, moved his reporter's notebook for him to sit.

"I thought San Francisco had a smoking ban."

"They do," Duncan Groner said. "They cut 'em a little slack. For the conventions. Especially this one." He had a cigarette of his own in his hand, a Player, a thick, unfiltered, English fag, smoked down to the nub. In his other hand, he had a tall coffee in a paper cup. He swirled it around a couple times and took a sip.

"Thanks for coming, Brother. God loves a cheerful giver." Groner's face matched the gravelly voice, ears a little gnome-ish, flappable, a bulbous nose, a weak chin, droopy dog eyes. Here was another old Sailor. He looked to be in his sixties, wiry, lanky. He wore loud checked wool pants and a yellow short-sleeved shirt with a press on it. And tan-and-white saddle shoes. He looked like he should be at the horse track with a stingy brim hat pushed back on his head. Or the dog track. "God says the past doesn't matter," he said. He snatched up his notebook and flipped back a page. "Or rather that 'the slate is wiped clean.' " He swirled his coffee again and took another hit. "God doesn't even care if you've inadvertently polluted your shorts at one time or another."

"Even advertently," Jimmy cracked.

"Oh, Mother of God, a free-willer!" Duncan Groner said, loud enough for a woman six rows forward to turn. "Sorry," he said. And lifted his coffee cup to her.

With a surreptitious slip of the fingers, he extracted a brass flask shaped like a kidney from his pants pocket. He kept it at his side, popped open the cap with his thumbnail, tipped it, and poured a dollop into the coffee cup kept down at his side and clipped the cap down again. And then he made the bottle disappear. For this, at least, he had the dexterity of a surgeon. He swirled the coffee again. Jimmy could smell the bourbon. A man twenty rows up turned and looked. Maybe he could he smell it, too.

Groner continued, "You have to accept that there is a Superior Being, a Higher Power, something greater than you." He flipped closed his notebook. "What they don't say is how can you *not* drink once you know *that* little piece of information."

"I believe the answer to that is, *God loves you*," Jimmy said.

"He doesn't know me," Groner said.

The reporter had what he needed for whatever he was writing, so they slipped out, retired to the hotel bar across the lobby. It wasn't even ten yet. The bartender and a busboy went to restocking the bar after the two lone customers had been served, an old-fashioned for Groner and a Virgin Mary for Jimmy.

There wasn't much restocking to do.

"I bet you love *this* convention crowd," Groner said.

The bartender smiled hatefully.

Groner stirred his drink with his finger. "By the way," he began, "George Leonidas isn't buying any of it. No sale." He lifted the drink to toast Jimmy and then all but drained the old-fashioned in the first "sip."

"He thinks you're insane," Groner finished.

"That's usually the intention," Jimmy said. "With third parties."

"Up here, we tend not to even try to explain things to third parties."

"That works, too."

"It never helps."

"No, it never does," Jimmy said.

Jimmy liked him. All Sailors were good liars, if they made it through the first weeks, months, without falling apart. You had to learn fast how to read each other and then trust what your instinct was telling you.

"So who's next?" Jimmy said and bit his stalk of celery in half.

Groner let a half minute go by. "Maybe it's you," he said.

"Or you," Jimmy said.

Groner laughed. "Is it that obvious?"

"What are you going to say about the Leonidas girls?"

"Mother of God, I saw their *room*," Groner said and shook his head. "It was like an explosion in a Dubble Bubble factory. They slept in matching canopy beds. One liked Justin, one liked Clay."

"That was probably last year," Jimmy said.

"They change so fast." The way Groner said the cliché, sour and sincere at the same time, made Jimmy wonder if the grizzled old cynic had been, of all things, a *daddy* once. "George had just bought them both a Kia. Two Kias. They came into the City in Melina's. It was in the covered parking lot across from Pier 41. It had a hundred and eleven miles on it."

"Did you find out why they wanted to die?" Jimmy said.

"You were there," Groner said. "I wasn't. What did you see?"

"In the moment, it was hard to get past the nakedness."

"The assumption was they were loaded, but they weren't. What they had in their stomachs was essentially a Jamba Juice mango smoothie. They'd each had one. One had some Midol in her blood. She was menstruating. Funny, you'd think the two girls would be in sync, but they weren't. There's always a detail like that. Maybe it's why I do this."

Jimmy said, "There hadn't been any signs of depression? High drama?"

"Happy and healthy."

"You said you were 'tying this in.' To what?"

The bartender came past. He pointed at Groner. Groner shook his head, though his glass was empty.

"In the last five days, there have been twenty-six suicides in the City. Usually, there are one or two a day. And more than half of them have been, as you say, the 'high drama' kind. Two off the Golden Gate last night, five minutes apart. Three last week. They usually get one jumper every two or three weeks. People are killing themselves spectacularly all over the city. Not the head-in-the-oven kind, alone in the garage with the Nova." He sucked the bitters-dashed sugar off the cubes at the bottom of his rocks glass.

"That's not what you meant when you said, 'Who's next?' is it?" he said, and looked at Jimmy.

Jimmy didn't answer.

"Why would a Sailor be up there with them, whispering in their ear just before they jumped?" he said instead.

"First I heard of it," the reporter said and almost made it sound like the truth.

Groner changed his mind about that second drink and, while he waited for it, asked Jimmy what had brought him to San Francisco.

Jimmy surprised himself with how much he said. About Lucy and Les. About Angel back home. About the boat ride over to Sausalito. About what he had thought had almost happened on the Golden Gate. About the park on Tiburon. About the two women who always seemed to be hovering.

It's getting to me, that's what he was thinking as he heard himself summarize the last days. There was too much death here, and it didn't have anything to do with him, however much they tried to make it be about him, however much he seemed to be right there when the bodies dropped. Sailors had their own kind of agoraphobia and for their own special reasons. They never liked to be too far from the home port. They started getting antsy. Maybe it was time to go home.

"Go to her, this Lucy, talk to her, tell her people are worried about her, take her home," he heard Groner say.

THE Haight. Lucy wasn't there. And the Skylark was gone. Maybe she'd figured it out on her own. Maybe she'd packed up and was headed south.

But he knew that wasn't true.

He drove across the Golden Gate, blew past the spot where the dropped Cokes had splashed into the oncoming traffic, where Lucy had stopped almost in the middle of the bridge, where Les had caught up to her. A couple was handing off their camera to another tourist for a shot of the two of them with the backdrop of the city, their backs against the low rail.

He took the first exit, dropped down into Sausalito. The baby-blue Skylark would be easy to spot, wherever they were, if he got lucky.

He didn't get lucky.

He kept on, stayed on the road that swung around the pinched curve of top of the Bay. It gave him time to practice his speech.

Tiburon. He found them. The Skylark was right there in the parking lot of the picnic place next to the playing fields, in the row of spaces closest to the highway. He couldn't have missed it if he wanted. It was sitting there all alone, like a big sign that said: Here!

So he *had* gotten lucky.

He pulled in and parked, found a place.

He watched them through the windshield of the Porsche. This time Lucy had brought Les with her. There was no sign of the others, the women, the helpmates. It was a sweet little scene. The sky was blue. The water was beautiful.

A little soccer player came running his way, right toward Jimmy. A boy six or seven with his shin guards over his socks, out of uniform, silky baggy pants and mismatched top. He had a set of keys jangling in his hand. Jimmy looked across the field. There weren't any games on. (It was Sunday. They probably didn't have games on Sunday.) But there were two or three boys at some distance and a few parents. (Lucy and Les were close by, but not right next to the parents and kids.) There was a chirp as the Tahoe two spaces away from the Porsche unlocked its doors.

The boy was impatient to get back to the field, to his friends. He yanked opened the passenger-side door and climbed in. Jimmy looked over, saw him rummaging between the Tahoe's front seats.

He came out with a white squeeze bottle of sunblock, slammed the door, was already running back across the field when he aimed the remote behind him and locked the Tahoe. California kids. Or maybe they were like this everywhere now.

As the boy closed in, a woman, who'd had her back turned away, standing, turned. Maybe she'd heard his voice. Maybe the boy had said something, maybe protested about the errand she'd sent him on, interrupting his play. "Here . . ." maybe he'd said, with an impatient edge to his voice. The boy was holding up the sunblock.

She took a few steps toward him, to meet him. She kneeled down.

It was all it took. She was far away, a hundred yards at least. She was across any number of gulfs, of chasms, of distances. Of time and space and reason. On the other side of possibility, across a wide field of coincidence and improbability. But it was all it took, the shape of her. The outline of her.

Her hair in the light.

The flash of white in the luster of her face, the teeth in her smile, the smile in her eyes . . .

As she knelt and finger-painted sunblock under the boy's eyes, across his forehead, and down the line of his nose.

Mary.

CHAPTER NINE

The same song was playing on a dozen radios, all tuned to KHJ. It was an AM kind of night. The sidewalks were more crowded than the four lanes of the street, and the street was plenty crowded, weekenders in from the suburbs to see how the other half lived, to pretend to be something wilder than what they were. It was the middle of summer. It was an even warmer night than usual, riot weather, but there wasn't any chance of a flare-up among this throng. The word was *mellow*. Moving along on the sidewalk, cruising out of the sound of one radio and then into the zone of the next, was like moving along *inside* the song, like walking with the singer, best friends.

It could have been Polk Street or MacDougal Street or South Beach, or even Fisherman's Wharf, but it was Sunset Boulevard, the Sunset Strip. It was L.A.

It could have been now, but it was 1995.

It could have been a lot of songs, probably should have been "London Calling" or "My Sharona" or even the Carpenters and "We've

Only Just Begun," but it was Tom Jones and "It's Not Unusual (To Be Loved by Anyone)." Another big pop lie.

She was with another guy the first time he saw her. *She* was Mary, her name was Mary, though it would take most of the night for him to find that out, to work his way through the jungle of playful protective coloration she threw up, *to break her down* was the way she always put it later when they were telling others about how they met, about that first night.

Jimmy and Mary.

He was with someone else, too. Most nights he was alone, particularly on the Strip. He lived nearby, a little house down below Sunset, below a restaurant everybody was going to at the time, Roy's. (Now it's the site of the House of Blues.) It was dead center in the Strip. It was close enough to the Chateau Marmont to walk over, which Jimmy did all the time.

The girl he was with that night worked as a secretary at a record label. She liked him more than he liked her. She brought him records, what they called "product." The LPs (they were still making them, along with cassettes and CDs) always had a hole drilled through some corner of the cover, a sign that they were meant for promotion. She'd bring him boxes of them. When she realized she liked him more than he liked her, trying to change that, she started bringing him boxes of "cleans," albums that weren't punched, that could be sold or traded for whatever you wanted. She hadn't figured out that Jimmy was different, different from everyone, and that he didn't care about money. (And, because he didn't care, he had a lot of it or could always get it.) She didn't know he was a Sailor. It was the secret he kept from almost everyone.

The guy Mary was with was a director.

It's not unusual to be loved by anyone
It's not unusual to have fun with anyone

She was twenty-two; the director was thirty-eight. She was five ten;

he was five eight. She was blond. He was blonder. Jimmy and the secretary, who had her arm threaded through his as they walked, were on the north side of Sunset, next to Tower Records. Mary and the director were across the street, going into a sushi place with a bamboo facade and glossy bright red paint around the door, making the entryway look like a garish mouth.

"Do you know her?" the secretary had said to Jimmy, when she saw him looking across the street.

The joke they said later, Jimmy and Mary, each taking a line in the telling of it, was that the director had looked back through the red mouth of that door and said to her, "Do you know him?"

Mary and the director had fought over dinner, and she had ended up walking away from him. From his white Jaguar sedan specifically, with the director standing next to it, sake-drunk, the valet standing there, too. She'd walked away on up Sunset, headed west, pretending to be drunk, too, which she wasn't at all. Jimmy had found her in Gil Turner's, a bright, glass-fronted, classic corner liquor store near the end of the Strip. She was inside, at the counter.

He was alone by then, too, behind the wheel of the only car he had, an oxidized white '68 Cadillac convertible, the punch line to some joke he'd forgotten. The top had long ago been knifed by vandals, so he left it down, at least once summer came. At the time, he thought he was just cruising, but he could admit later he was looking for her.

He parked. She came out. He set off after her. He caught up to her, walked alongside her. She was headed back toward the center of things. He didn't say anything for a half a block. That section of the strip was dead, the block before the Rainbow and The Roxy.

"Let's hear it," she said, when she realized that he was just weird enough to walk along beside her silently, maybe forever. "Your clever first line."

"I don't have one," Jimmy said. "I don't have a clever *last* line, either."

"Thinking ahead, are we?"

She was as tall as he was. And she had on flat shoes, dancer's shoes. Capezios. She was skinny but not a model. She probably wasn't a dancer, either. He thought of asking, but it sounded too much like a pickup line.

"You want these?" she said and offered him an unopened pack of cigarettes, after they'd walked another half block. She was setting the pace, not fast, not slow. Not an escape, not a stroll.

"Luckies," he said.

"I don't smoke," she said. "I felt sorry for the man in the store."

"That's Gil. Himself."

"I felt sorry for Gil."

"He's probably a millionaire," Jimmy said.

"So millionaires aren't worthy of our concern?" she said. Jimmy wondered if she *was* drunk, the way she chose her words. He'd learn soon enough that it was just *her*. Then, at least. The way she was then. She said, "I felt sorry for him because of the look in his eye, because he looked forsaken."

"What's your name?" he said.

"Lucky," she said.

Jimmy pulled the ribbon on the white-and-red pack of smokes and tapped it against the palm of his hand.

"Why do people do that?" she said.

"I don't know, I think it packs the tobacco tighter or something," Jimmy said.

"Or everyone saw someone do it in a movie."

"Are you an actress?" Jimmy said.

"No, you are," she said. "*You* are."

They walked almost as far as Tower Records and the sushi place. Jimmy was prepared to run into the boyfriend again, the director, but that would be overestimating him.

"Let's go somewhere. Where do you want to go?" Jimmy said, standing there on the sidewalk. In 1995.

"San Francisco," she said. "L.A. is bothering me. You're not the

Cut Killer, are you?" Lately, since the beginning of summer, there'd been a series of killings, girls' bodies left spread-eagle on road cuts, the sloping gouges into the rock where the highway sliced through. Nine of them.

"Where do you want to go?" Jimmy asked her again, as serious about anything as he'd been in a long, long time.

MARY wasn't a single mom. She wasn't alone.

He came late to the soccer practice or play date or picnic or whatever it was. Sunday afternoon in the park on Tiburon. Her husband. Jimmy saw him drive up in a black BMW X-5. On the phone. He parked and sat there another two minutes, finishing his call. There were two other mothers and a father next to Mary on the sidelines of the playing field. She had her back to the parking lot and didn't see him. She had her eyes on the boy, who was dribbling a ball down the field, or at least making an earnest six-year-old's attempt at dribbling.

Her son. It was hard for Jimmy to even think it. He didn't know much about kids but got close guessing the boy's age. He did the math. Everything in him wanted to get closer, to see more, but he knew that Mary would spot him, his shape, his coloration, as easily as he had hers. Or at least that was what he told himself, to keep himself inside the car. To stop himself. He turned the key and started the engine. The sound of the rev made Mary turn to look. It was then that she saw her husband walking toward her across the apron of the field. He wore a dark gray suit, but as he came closer he pulled off the necktie and unbuttoned the collar of the blue shirt. He folded the tie in half and slipped it into his coat pocket. (Who goes into the office on a Sunday? Even for a half day?) He was dark-haired. With a hundred-dollar haircut. He smiled at his wife from ten yards out and then looked away quickly to find the boy on the field, to wave, though the kid wasn't looking.

He came up and kissed Mary, put his hand on her back. Her hair was longer. And darker.

Jimmy drove away out the exit of the lot but turned left on the main road in and stopped on the shoulder. There was a little elevation, to look down on the field, the water behind it, Sausalito behind that. The boy had come over. The father had kneeled down to ruffle his hair. The mother was saying something. A family was laughing.

Jimmy let out the clutch and drove on. Fast and loud.

Very high school.

And what do you call sitting in the dark in a car on a hilly lane on Tiburon, on Belvedere, across from a black Craftsman house with a light in the second-floor window and a woman framed there, lifting a boy's T-shirt over his head, his arms raised as if surrendering?

MARY kept living in the director's house, though she said it wasn't "living *with* him . . ." In his rented long and low ranch house up at the top of a cul-de-sac in Benedict Canyon. ("Leased," she said. "He always makes me say *leased.*") Whatever it was now, it had been a family's house once, stuck up off in a rustic canyon, three bedrooms, two baths, a kidney-shaped pool, an enormous bank of rock behind it like a wave threatening to break. Now it was all white, inside and out, refrigerator white, and had bizarre white rocks the size of apples and grapefruits scattered across the white gravel of the roof.

"It's like the surface of the moon," Jimmy said the first time he saw it in the daytime.

"I like it," Mary said.

There were four girls living there. They didn't mind being called girls, except for the thirteen-year-old, who was the director's daughter, there for the summer. The others were Mary's friends. The girls. One was a friend from before Mary had moved in with the director; the other had become a friend. April and Michelle and Mary. They'd all three slept with the director at one time or another.

"You have to move," Jimmy said.

"You're always trying to relocate me," Mary said.

The director was Canadian, pretended to be French. He'd done one movie, limited release. It starred a rock star, and the movie was notably unprofitable, so a few people at the studios and the agencies got the idea the director was hip. So he had that to ride for a few years. But he didn't even have a deal anywhere now and was much angrier inside than anyone knew, even his agent. He'd shot another film with a little money from a horndog Pasadena dentist who liked the idea of the girls in the house up there in Benedict, liked the vodka-in-the-freezer thing, liked the old-school drugs they sometimes brought out for his sake. Everyone else thought *that* part of it was just too eighties. There were a pair of old-fashioned Moviolas in the bedroom where the director had stashed his daughter. Every once in awhile he'd go in to work on it, at least run some film through his hands, but most of the time he went to restaurants and out to parties and meetings when he could get them and looked for the next thing.

"Come live with me," Jimmy said.

It was the morning after they'd made love for the first time, four days after that first night on Sunset. They were at Hugo's, down on Santa Monica, a breakfast, brunch, and lunch place. Everybody else there was doing business.

"I don't even know what you do," she said.

"I don't do anything," he said. "I think about you."

"What did you do before I came along?"

"Think about you."

If anyone was close enough to hear him, hear them, Mary would have made fun of the line. But he meant it.

"Me, too," she said.

He could never tell anyone the things they said to each other.

They spent most of that day together, the day after they'd made love for the first time, rode out to the beach with the Cadillac's ragged ragtop down, out to Paradise Cove to watch the surfers trying to make something happen on a collapsed, glassy day, then ate drippy cheeseburgers at a joint while the red sun flattened out at the horizon. The burger place was on a rise above a south-facing beach, on one of the twists and turns along the line of the coast, and the effect of the right-hand, apparently northern sunset was unsettling, though neither of them noticed it then.

"Everything can change in just a day," she said.

They were riding back into the City, the back way, up and over Mulholland in from the coast, alone on the two-lane blacktop scrolling through the hills. He was watching the way the Caddy's high beams swept the manzanita, let himself think that the light going across the brush was what had released the scent that filled their nostrils. It hadn't rained in two or three months. There was a not-unpleasant dustiness to everything. What did the Eagles sing about in "Hotel California"? The "warm smell of colitas, rising up through the air." He wondered what it was, colitas. It sounded like a plant, like manzanitas.

"Everything can change in an *hour*," Jimmy said. "If it's the wrong hour."

"Or the *right* hour," Mary said. "You're so gloomy."

He left her at the gate of the white house. It wasn't that big a house, but the owners had put in a rolling iron gate and painted it white, too, so the renters, the *leasees*, could say they lived in a gated place in Benedict Canyon. Jimmy cranked the wheel, the power steering pump complaining, and turned around in the cul-de-sac. He wouldn't go in, didn't want to drop in on that scene again after so good a day, didn't want to have to try to make it all lie down in his head one more time. The director always had a crowd over, standing around the black-bottomed pool, looking down at the lights, drinks in their hands, or joints between their fingers like they were cigarettes. Strangers. New people every time.

In the rearview mirror, Jimmy saw her push the button on the squawk box and wait. She pushed it again.

He wasn't in any hurry to get home. In just a part of a week, she'd gotten him into some new music, new to him. Gloomy Canadian singer-songwriters, as it turned out. She'd made him a tape, two-sided, 120 minutes. So, driving around, killing time, he had Leonard Cohen and the last cigarette from the pack of Lucky Strikes she'd given him that first night. He almost hated to smoke it, but he smoked it, cruising

east on Sunset into East L.A. Lately he'd been spending more and more
time with his friend Angel, had come back around again, reconnected.
Everything seemed to go in circles. Angel was a Sailor who worked on
vintage cars, who had a shop downtown, who was also a preacher
in a way, a street preacher to gangbangers and their knocked-up girlfriends, to the people almost everybody else wrote off. He went by his
apartment, went by the storefront church where Angel spent a lot of
time, but never found him. He wanted to talk cars, nothing else. He
headed for home.

The phone was ringing when he came in. When he answered it, it
was just screaming.

CHAPTER TEN

He slept. The phone had detonated a couple of times, but he'd slept through it. He sat up. There was a knife-edge of light under the drapes. He'd drawn them when he came back from Tiburon. He'd *slept*. He'd even dreamed. It wasn't that Sailors never slept, but it was rare. They'd sleep an hour or two once a month. But they almost never dreamed. What had he dreamed? Like the rest of us, he couldn't exactly remember. Angel was in it. There was a gathering of some kind, characters moving in from all quarters, in some kind of empty room. It felt ordinary, obvious, pedestrian. The surprise was that Mary wasn't in it.

He ordered breakfast, a big breakfast. He was acting like a Norm all of a sudden. It came, and he ate it. He took a shower and put on a clean shirt. Like it was the first day of the rest of his life.

When he stepped out into the hallway in the hotel, he had to step over the *Chronicle*. If it had been facedown, he wouldn't have stopped, and his day might have gone a different way, but it was faceup, looking right at him, with a headline across half the page:

THREE GOLDEN GATE SUICIDES
WITHIN SPAN OF ONE HOUR

"Span." At least someone on the headline desk had a sense of humor about it. Jimmy picked up the paper and tucked it under his arm. He took the elevator straight down to the garage. While he waited for the car, he read the details. The three suicides off the bridge were unrelated. One was a German tourist, a woman. One was a woman in her nineties. (You had to wonder how she got up and over the rail.) The third was an anomaly, a man in his twenties who'd gone off the *west* side of the bridge, the side facing out to sea, something that almost never happened. Maybe he was a sailor. Small *s*.

It made Jimmy go back to the bridge. Maybe he was looking for something to bring him back to the present.

He drove along the Marina, the broad sweep of created land, a former marsh filled in a hundred years ago with '06 earthquake rubble. Now it was as if it had been there all along, another pricey district with its rows of two- and three-story houses, shoulder to shoulder on the left, red tile roofs and pale ice cream colors, and the expanse of Marina Green and St. Francis Yacht Club to the right. And the Presidio ahead.

And Fort Point, under the southern anchorage of the bridge. Jimmy parked in the lot next to the rocks, the water so close that the cars' windshields would all be grayed out, misted, when the drivers returned. The massive red/orange ironwork of the bridge, this end of it, was overhead. Sometimes you could hear the traffic noise above all the sounds of the Bay. To stand underneath it felt a little like being inside a hollow skyscraper. It also made you see how high it was off the water.

Jimmy walked along the shore on the paved path toward the angular brick fort. It had been built at the beginning of the Civil War, to guard the mouth of the Bay, set there long before the bridge. It was a Monday and still early, and tourist traffic was light. As vacationers' destinations go, Fort Point seemed not to mean much to non-

Americans. The crowd, what there was of it, seemed like Kansas people, men in short cargo pants with skinny white legs who looked like they'd been up since four thirty, their portly wives, and kids in Disneyland tees and knit Target shorts the colors of the houses back in the Marina District.

Jimmy knew Fort Point was a gathering place for Sailors. By night anyway. They weren't out now, or at least they wouldn't be expected to be, only the ones looking for trouble.

But George Leonidas was there.

"Hello, sir," Jimmy said, surprising himself with the deference, the formality.

The grieving father, if that's what he was here for, grieving, was sitting on a bench next to the freshly painted guest services restroom. He was wearing the same clothes, but a fresh version of the brown cuffed trousers and the white short-sleeved shirt. And the brown wing tips. He sat with his legs open, his forearms on his knees, one hand wrapped around the fist of the other, as if holding it back from doing what it wanted to do. His eyes were on the water but unfocused. He hadn't seen Jimmy until he spoke. But he didn't seemed surprised to come upon him here. Maybe nothing surprised him anymore. He nodded a greeting, tipped his head up.

When Jimmy got a good look at his eyes, it was hard to think of what to say to him.

"How's your wife doing?"

Leonidas nodded.

"Better than you, I bet," Jimmy said. He didn't mean it harshly, but Leonidas bowed up a little, seemed about ready to come at him, to say something, but didn't. He knew it was true.

Jimmy looked down at him. *I shouldn't have told you,* he thought. He almost said it out loud. *This is what you get, when you tell them. It doesn't make it easier; it makes it harder.* The truth doesn't always set you free. Sometimes it wraps you in a whole new set of chains.

"Why'd you come down here?" Jimmy asked him.

"A kid on the waterfront told me to. Works at one of the crab joints."

"Told you what?"

"That he thought he saw my Selene here."

"Selene."

"Christina," George Leonidas said. "I called her Selene."

He suddenly looked at Jimmy, very directly. "I never saw Melina," he said. "My other girl. Is she the same as . . . as what you said? Like Christina?"

"I don't know. Probably not. Stop thinking about what I told you. Forget me."

Jimmy watched as the Greek's eyes left him, went to the underside of the bridge, out across the bowed line of it toward the center.

"There were three more. Went off the Gate," he said.

"I know," Jimmy said.

"It's not anything I ever thought of. Before," Leonidas said, still looking where he was looking. "I was in the army. In Vietnam. You see people die, and it changes the way you think. You think different. You just want to come home, work hard, have your house."

Jimmy thought of the pink rooms Duncan Groner had described, the girls' rooms.

"One of them was an old lady," Leonidas said. "Ninety."

"Go home," Jimmy said. "Go back over to El Cerrito. Stay away from the City, from places like this."

Leonidas nodded. He got up, still nodding. Jimmy got the sense that something had scared him, something he'd felt in himself, an idea, an impulse. He was grateful to be yanked back to himself. He offered his hand, and Jimmy shook it.

Jimmy watched him walk away, watched him until the Greek was behind the wheel of the Cadillac, in the first slot in the lot. He'd been up all night, the first one there. Jimmy watched until he saw the Caddy's wide hood dip at one corner, when the engine started.

He stayed on the bench for a minute, then made a pass through the fort, walked across the open courtyard, but it was all just sea breezes and sunbeams.

He didn't know what he was looking for anyway.

CORONERS' offices have less security than you'd think. Jimmy walked in a back door, off the loading dock. He came down one corridor and then another, threaded his way into the interior, following his nose.

He was alone in a roomful of the dead for a good two minutes before anyone came in.

And *she* didn't work there.

"I'm sorry," she said. She was in her late fifties. She was dressed like a businesswoman but in particularly muted colors. Rich, but muted. *Dignified.*

Jimmy just smiled, the it's-all-right smile.

The coroner came in, a deputy coroner. He'd probably heard voices in the room. He was in his thirties and fleshy with heavy glasses that could have been military-issue. He looked like he should be working in a comic book store somewhere.

He looked at Jimmy first. He seemed to know the woman.

"Can I . . . ?" he asked.

"She was first," Jimmy said. Maybe it would give him time to figure out what he'd come here for.

The man let his eyes linger on Jimmy for another beat, then crossed the room to a steel desk, curved corners, a gray "marble" linoleum top, like an old schoolteacher's desk, or a cop's desk. There were clear plastic bags on top. He found the one he was looking for. It had a number on a tag. He lifted his glasses to read it—so he was nearsighted!—and then went to the wall of body drawers. He pulled one out, pulled away the polythene over the face, put it back, and checked the number on the end of the drawer.

He left it open and looked at the woman. She came over. He nodded at her. The woman pulled down the plastic and looked at the body.

Jimmy slipped out, left them alone. There was something that convinced him she wasn't a family member, but Jimmy couldn't decide who she was. Clergy? She looked too uncertain, too off balance for that. But she also didn't look like she was any stranger to morgues. He was at the water fountain, taking a good long drink, when she came out of the body room. She didn't stop to lean against the wall or anything, didn't twist a hankie in her hand. She wasn't distraught, but she had a tear in her eye. And, with this one, you got the idea those eyes hadn't cried in awhile, that her eyes were just a bit too old to tear up easily. Or had seen too much.

Jimmy came out into the parking lot in time to see what she drove, a pearlescent white Infiniti FX45 SUV that was probably almost pink in the right light. She pointed the remote at the door. There was a double click, and she went first to the hatchback and opened it and put the plastic bag there, on the carpet.

He didn't know why exactly, but Jimmy tailed her across town to Russian Hill.

The Infiniti was parked in the stubby driveway of a six-story apartment building, a vintage place, *some* vintage. It had character. He found a place down in the next block and hiked back up the incline. No wonder San Francisco women had such good-looking legs. He was about to go into the first floor—the door was propped open—when he saw something on the door of the Infiniti, letters impossible to read from any real distance. He came closer. They were silver on white. Dignified. Rich. Muted.

What they said was:

GRACEFUL EXITS
SENIOR MOVING — ESTATE CLOSURE

In the lobby was an old-fashioned elevator, with a brass arrow to point to the number of the floor. It was pointing at six. The top. As good a bet as any for where the woman had gone. Jimmy pushed the button to bring it down and stepped back. It was slow. It took twenty seconds just to creak down to five.

He leaned against the opposite wall. He'd been smoking all day, since he'd gotten in the Porsche in the basement garage of the Mark, since he'd dropped the metal door of the glove box, looking for his sunglasses, and had seen the pack of cigarettes he'd bought at the little store back down in Paso Robles.

Luckies.

He was snubbing out the cigarette in the sand in the canister ashtray across from the elevator when the Infiniti woman stepped out of a door at the end of the lobby, a door that had been left standing open but that he hadn't noticed.

"Hello," she said. "Again."

"Hi."

"Do you need a minute?"

Jimmy took one, to think what to say. He had been intending to work on his opening lines on the ride up in the elevator, have something worked out before he got to the top floor.

"I know it's difficult," the woman said.

"Unprecedented," Jimmy said.

She smiled and nodded. She'd been misting up again, just like she had in the coroner's office. He could see the teary sparkle in her eye. She turned around and left him there, went back through the door at the end of the lobby, left it open.

When he looked in, it was a small apartment. The door opened into a four-foot-square foyer and then a twelve-foot living room. It was tiny, but it was a deluxe apartment. The building was on the top of the hill, so even on the first floor there was a view, a blue and white pane of color, clear and bright, like a stained glass rendering of a slice of the skyline and the Bay beyond. The woman saw him looking out the window and for some reason got a bit flustered, apologetic.

"I opened the drapes," she said. "She kept it so dark in here."

"It's all right," Jimmy said. "It's a beautiful day."

She crossed to him, a card already in her hand. "Someone said you weren't coming in until this afternoon," she said. "Patricia Hatch."

Jimmy took the card. He convinced himself that he was working, working for some greater good, and just let the lie tell itself.

"Were you her only child?" she said. "No," she immediately corrected, "I'm sorry. A neighbor said she had a daughter here in the City who came to see her often. Who had just moved here?"

Jimmy kept quiet, took in the place. Every inch of wall, every flat surface, was covered with photographs, framed. On the coffee table was an ashtray from The Coconut Grove.

"Oh, I'm so sorry," she corrected again. "You would be *grand*children. I forgot how old she—she was *ninety*."

There was picture after picture of a beautiful, sassy girl, maybe twenty-two. In gowns. In a bathing suit, what they used to call a bather.

"Why were you crying?" Jimmy said, still scanning the pictures. "At the coroner's. And here, before I came in. I mean, in your business you must see the same thing, over and over. Was something different with her?"

The woman stepped closer, with a kind of familiarity, the same familiarity she'd been apologizing for ever since he came in.

"Can I show you my favorite picture?" she said.

"Please," Jimmy said.

"It's this one." It was a publicity shot, the young woman as a chorus girl. She handed it to him. "You see, I was a dancer, too," she said. "A million years ago."

"But not seventy," Jimmy said.

"No."

Jimmy put the picture back on the table.

"The world has changed so much," the woman said.

Jimmy couldn't argue with her there. "I don't have a sister," he said. "You said a woman had been coming by?" He tried to amend his tone, to keep from sounding like he was pushing. "Someone young?"

"That's what they said. A new friend. Maybe she's just someone in the neighborhood," the other said. "Someone like me. Who cared very much for your grandmother. It was good that she had a friend."

She went to her purse and started unpacking. A pad. A gold pen. A phone with a keyboard. A handheld tape recorder. A digital camera. "Timothy from our office will be here in a few minutes. If course, you can have your own Trusted Witness for the inventory." He heard her capitalize the *T* and the *W*. He thought, *That's what I'd like to be: a Trusted Witness.* Angel was a Trusted Witness. Jimmy knew a few others. "Of course, you can take anything today, before the walk-through," she said.

"I think I'll walk around the block," Jimmy said.

"Of course."

He made another scan of the room. There weren't any pictures anywhere of anyone who looked like a son or a daughter or a grandson or a granddaughter. Or a man friend. Or even the "new friend" she'd made. No friends, neighbors. Nobody. But don't you get used to being alone, being lonely, in ninety years? Don't you get used to outliving everyone, even get used to outliving yourself, at least what you used to be? Your perk? Your spark? The tone of young skin? The beauty, the sex that drew people to you? If she had been sixty, it would have made sense. Or seventy.

At least now he knew how she got her leg up and over the rail on the bridge. She had been a dancer.

"I wonder why I thought I should do this today," Jimmy looked at Patricia Hatch and said.

"Everyone is different," she said.

And he made his exit, graceful or otherwise.

THE world wasn't neat. The world didn't make sense, at least not moment by moment. Nobody knew that like Jimmy knew it, but still, he tried to neaten it up where he could, even if only in his own head. He made lists. He checked things off.

So, after Russian Hill, he looked into the other two suicides off the Golden Gate, the latest ones.

The German woman apparently was traveling alone, had checked in, alone, to a fairly expensive room at a blue-and-white nautical-themed hotel down on Fisherman's Wharf, a new hotel in an old, old brick building, a former cannery. You could look out every window and see the Buena Vista bar and the cable car turnaround and the water beyond. It didn't look like the kind of place a last-stage depressive would pick for herself. She'd been there three days, had made the rounds of all the sights, had asked the concierge for maps and restaurant picks. She was signed up for a wine country bus tour tomorrow, prepaid. (A *pair* of tickets. Why?) From here, it was on to L.A. for the woman. Alone.

Jimmy talked to a half-dozen guests and hotel staff. It didn't make sense to anybody, but everybody admitted they didn't know much about her, about how she was spending her days and nights. The concierge seemed particularly to feel the loss. The woman was German. Europeans understand that you tip the help at the end of your stay.

So that was two out of the three.

What about Mr. Wrong Side?

He had AIDS. That was the first thing Jimmy learned about him: he was dying of AIDS. It was right there in the paper, a sidebar bylined by Duncan Groner, who apparently owned the suicide beat. Jimmy had stopped for an Irish coffee at a place in North Beach. By night North Beach would be packed with tourists and locals, one of the neighborhoods that satisfied both of them, with good-as-Rome Italian restaurants and bars and hipster bookstores and strip joints. It was three in the afternoon, and the coffee and Irish whisky was good. Up and down in the same cup.

The young man was living in a hospice. Too weak to move out of his bed, they had thought. So he'd had some help. Jimmy didn't really want to follow up on it. He had the address for the hospice. It wasn't far away, four or five streets over. He didn't want to follow it up because the answer to the question of why the young man was dead was too clear. In spite of what he told himself all the time, he didn't like simple, obvious answers. A young man killed himself because he was dying in a slow, bad way. Jimmy wanted it to be something else. He wanted a little mystery. Not a lot, a small mystery, easily blown out, like a candle, by a professional with a modicum of sense, even if he was from out of town and wrapped in the cloak of his own mysteries, dragging around his own chains.

Then again, there was that detail . . .

The man dying of AIDS had to have had some help.

And something else . . .

Most of the day, Red Boots and another had been tailing Jimmy, neither one of them looking all that happy to be up in daylight.

CHAPTER ELEVEN

He stayed away for as long as he could, which turned out to be a day and a half. It was five thirty. Mary waited behind the wheel of her husband's black BMW X-5, in front of a dance studio on a side street in San Raphael. The light was what they call in the movie world the Golden Hour. Everything looked good at five thirty. She wasn't on the phone. Maybe she was listening to the radio. She had the window down. Jimmy was across the street, in the Porsche. He hadn't been this close to her before. Her hair was a little darker, at least in this light, than it had been back then when it was so blond it was almost white, when sometimes it looked like there were lights inside it, or at least electricity. He remembered the first time he saw her in daylight, walking toward him, away from the director's house up in the canyon, early enough in the morning that no one else was awake.

She put her head back against the headrest. She had one knee up against the door of the car, sitting like a man. She seemed happy, glad to be exactly where she was.

There was a reason Jimmy didn't like the simple, obvious answers. They hurt more.

She just doesn't love you.

You'll never see him again.

There is no God.

Everyone's afraid at the end.

The past is passed.

She is happily married now and has a little boy and never thinks of you and is out of your reach forever . . .

She's alive; you're dead.

Suddenly there were little dancers everywhere. The doors must have opened somewhere, sending them out to their parents and nannies.

But they weren't dancers. Mary was parked directly in front of a dance academy, but it was next door to a martial arts dojo, blocked by her car. Another kind of dance. The boys and girls, six and seven and eight and nine, spilled out in their gis, still all jacked up from the class, half of them kicking the air as they crab-walked across the asphalt, white belts or no belts, calling out things to each other, a happy little assault force.

The boy who was Mary's boy was one of the last to leave. He came out and stood in the angled sunlight just outside the glass door. The dojo had been a retail store of some kind in its previous life. The instructor came out behind the boy, a serious hand resting on his low shoulder. He was a black man with a Navy SEAL's body. Whatever he was saying to the boy, the boy kept nodding. By this age, living where he lived, living like he lived, the kid probably had five coaches in his life. He knew the coach drill.

The teacher dismissed the little warrior with a gentle hand on the back of his head. The black man's palms were so white they almost flashed in the bright, angled light. The boy ran the rest of the way to the SUV, opened the back door, and climbed up and in, buckling himself in and pulling the door closed. The front passenger-side window came down. The sensei leaned in with some words for the mom.

She is a mother, here, in this life. A wife, a mother.

There's your answer, simple as that. No mystery.

It made Jimmy's chest ache.

He followed them halfway home, halfway back to the hump of Tiburon, but he kept going straight when Mary turned left into the parking lot of a market. He'd had enough *obvious*.

He looked up in the rearview mirror. Had he caught her looking over at the departing Porsche? Following it with her eyes? Maybe he'd been tailgating or maybe she thought he had. He was wearing the blocky Ray-Ban Wayfarers from the glove compartment. That's what he had always worn then. *Then*. Maybe she'd seen him in her rearview mirror.

Maybe she . . .

No, it was something simpler than that. It had to be.

He watched the day die in a place that was almost painfully beautiful, Mount Tam, Tamalpais, one of the world's most scenic overlooks. At least if you loved California, if it spoke to you, the general drama of the coastline, the specific drama of San Francisco. The knob of the mountain was bare but for grass and outcroppings of smooth rock, hundreds of feet above the water, right at the Gate. The bridge was to the right. Though the sky was still full of light, the cars' headlights were all on, on the bridge, three lanes north and three lanes south, as if the curbs were channeling opposing flows of bright lava. Or surging white blood cells.

Two ways to go, he thought.

Southbound. He should be southbound. He should get the hell out of there. He turned and looked at the Porsche. With the riotous colors in the sky melting on the classic curves of the fenders, it looked like a model sitting there. The whole picture, and him in it, looked managed, staged, touched up. *A pensive, handsome young man and his automobile, the symbol of his success.* He should finish this cigarette and grind it dead on the ground and get behind the wood-rimmed wheel and turn the key and see the white light leap into the corners of the gauges, see the red-edged needle jump to three-quarters—plenty of gas to get well on down the road—turn the key further, hear the engine go, see the tach leap with the first punch of the gas. Hear and see everything that said *Go!* Everything that said leave the land of the dead before they all started coming to life.

Go.

He let the Lucky Strike burn all the way down, pinching it like a jay, staring at the car sitting there. He thought about the day he bought it. The car. He thought about who was with him. He thought about the ninety-year-old lady. He thought about the German tourist, about the wine-country wine she didn't drink that day. He thought about the young man dying of AIDS, until he died stepping off the wrong side of the Golden Gate. Everything he thought was complicated. None of it was self-evident. The voice in his head—the voice of himself, *Jimmy Miles*—was a dozen voices. He was like Machine Shop. But with Shop, at least what was in his head was a debate. With Jimmy, it was ten points of view. Twenty. It was like being in a bus station at midnight listening to crazy people, all of whom think they know you. It was like being in a room with every version of yourself you've ever been, hearing every lying man and boy you've ever been turning on you.

Maybe *that* was the gathering he'd dreamed of that morning.

Two ways to go.

He came down off the mountain and went north. To Tiburon.

A few minutes before seven, the babysitter drove up to the big Craftsman house in a yellow Volkswagen convertible. She looked college age. She parked on a curve just below the house. She got out, locked the car, started toward the gate in the hedge, then remembered something and went back to the bug. A book. In case her boyfriend wasn't home when she called. Mary's husband answered the door, stood there in the frame. White shirt, dark pants, tie around his neck waiting to be tied. He was a good-looking man. Jimmy still didn't know what his name was. He hadn't seen him again since the first time out in the park until now. He had a glass of red wine in his hand. Even from across the street, Jimmy could guess the lines in the joke he made with the young girl about it.

Mary was upstairs in the boy's room. Jimmy didn't know his name yet, either. She was getting him into PJs. Or trying to. He was jumping on the bed, taking advantage of the special circumstances, a weeknight left with a sitter. She caught him in midair on one jump and hugged him with such devotion it might have scared him a little. There must have been a voice they both heard from downstairs, mother and son, because they suddenly looked at each other and made the same funny face and turned for the door. A second later, the light went out.

There were two ways off the tip of Tiburon, two ends of the same road, but one way was more direct than the other. Jimmy couldn't keep himself from making assumptions about Mary's husband, filling the blanks. He didn't seem like the take-the-long-way kind of guy.

Jimmy guessed right; here came the X-5. Somebody had gotten it washed since the late afternoon. With the dark trees of Tiburon behind it on the dark street with its tasteful lighting, it was all black on black, glistening. Everything today looked like an upscale car ad.

Jimmy waited, let them get a ways up the road. He was parked in the lot of a closed gas station. The lights were out except for three moons of backlit white plastic, the signs over the pumps on the three bays.

Self Self Full, they said. Take your pick.

Jimmy was a little underdressed, a suit, no tie, but didn't have any trouble crashing the do in the St. Francis ballroom. It was a fund-raiser for some charity, something with *Heart* in the name. He wasn't on the list. He wrote a thousand-dollar check. Suddenly they knew him. A smiling woman who reminded him of Patricia Hatch from Graceful Exits pinned a red ceramic heart on his lapel.

"Good luck," she said.

"Thank you," Jimmy said. He was looking down at his new lapel jewelry.

"I mean in the auction," she said.

It wasn't hard to blend in, stay concealed. He had put on a black suit that morning and looked like every other man in the room, even the ones who'd thrown on a tux. You had to get close to see that Jimmy's shirt was taupe and that he wasn't wearing socks with the loafers. He hit the hosted bar for a champagne and crème de cassis, which is what everyone else seemed to be drinking, and found a shaggy arica palm to screen him.

Mary and her husband were at one of the front tables. With two other couples. Jimmy was across the broad room, with twenty tables between them, but he thought she looked his way once, fixed her eyes in his direction. But then someone in the foreground waved, and Mary waved back. So much for *I somehow sensed you were there.* She went back to her conversation with the man next to her. They were seated boy/girl.

Jimmy looked at her husband again. He was caught up in a conversation with the woman seated to his right. Or was pretending to be. Who was he? So far, Jimmy had held himself back from thinking too much on it. That was too high school, too. What difference did it make? He hadn't seen Mary in almost ten years. So what if she still looked the same to him? Ten years had passed. She had found someone. What did he think, that she had joined some I-can-never-love-another order? What was that phrase that everyone used now? She had *moved on.*

She flashed a smile to the others at the table and pushed back and stood. She took her clutch bag off the table. She moved toward opened double doors, the exit.

It was risky business, but Jimmy moved out from his blind and started on a line that, if he kept on it, would intersect her path. She stopped to talk to someone. She was only thirty feet away from him. He stopped. If she looked any direction except straight ahead when she finished talking, they'd be face-to-face. It would make for a dramatic scene, if drama was what he wanted.

So. It's you.

But she didn't look his way, walked straight out the exit.

He went through another open door into the hallway. He looked for the doorway where she would have come out. There were restrooms there.

Jimmy ducked back into the ballroom, found another potted plant to meld with. And snagged another kir royale from the tray of a passing waiter.

Mary's husband was impatient, maybe even suspicious of where his wife had gone. He kept up his end of the conversation with the woman next to him but still managed to look over at the exit every ten seconds. He did everything but check his watch.

Then he checked his watch. He got up, tossed the napkin in his lap onto the table. Jimmy realized he was older than he'd thought. Older than Mary. She'd be in her early thirties. Her husband was in his mid-forties.

He touched the shoulder of the woman he'd been talking with and said something and started off where he'd been looking all along, toward the exit.

And then she appeared in the doorway. She looked altogether innocent, refreshed, touched-up, relaxed. Until she saw the look on her husband's face, coming toward her.

He smiled but meant something nasty by it.

When he got close enough, she said something to him.

It didn't change the look on his face.

They were stopped beside one of the buffet tables, the dessert table. She said something else to him. Her tone had changed. She walked past him, or tried to. He took her by the wrist to stop her.

She said one word, glaring at him. Jimmy guessed it was probably his name.

He let go of her wrist.

Now it was his turn to say *her* name, as she walked away from him. She kept going.

Maybe it was the light, or that there was a tall ice sculpture behind him, but there was *blue* behind his head and shoulders, a blue edge. *Blue.*

But when Jimmy looked away, at Mary, and then looked back at her husband, the blue was gone.

Was it too late to get *simple* back?

On his way, he looked them up on the seating chart out in the foyer, where he'd laid down his check.

Dr. Marc Hesse and Mary Hesse.

WHEN he drove onto the plaza in front of the Mark Hopkins, to leave the Porsche with the valet instead of driving down into the garage himself, Machine Shop was there. Pacing. Scrubbed out of his silver paint.

He had a wild look in his eyes.

It was late. Jimmy was tired. When he got out, left the motor running, Shop was right there.

"Your girl killed herself," he said. "Your Lucy."

CHAPTER TWELVE

It was too nice a night for it, hot as hell, but clear. Jimmy roared up Benedict Canyon in Beverly Hills in the huffing old Cadillac, fouling the air behind him. It was a cruising car, not a ride-to-the-rescue car. Or whatever it was that he was riding to. In his head he could still hear Mary screaming on the phone. It was uphill all the way, twisting and turning. He stuffed the gas to the floor, and the land yacht shuddered, downshifted itself into first. It was like an old surfer digging hard to get a fat classic long board up and over a wave. Strange, the things you think of when you're thinking everything at once. Jimmy remembered a toast Ronald Reagan used to give, "May the road rise up to meet you . . ." He must not have meant this.

There were headlights way behind him. He was afraid he'd blown past a cop hiding on a side street, but he didn't slow down. He wasn't going to stop.

It *was* a cop. A black-and-white. It overtook him. The cops never even looked over at him.

We're headed the same place, Jimmy thought.

The cops' Gran Fury bottomed out on a dip in the road with an ugly sound and a splash of sparks, but the driver never let up.

There were *eight* cop cars under the streetlights at the end of the cul-de-sac, at the end of the road, counting the plain-wraps and the higher-up suits' cars with all the antennae. No press. Yet. Jimmy had gotten the screaming phone call at one ten. It was one twenty-five.

The gate was open for all the coming and going. A uniformed officer stood there, dead center.

"You can't park there."

Jimmy had just stopped the Cadillac in the middle of the street and gotten out. He took a step closer, saw the look on the cop's face. It seemed like a good time to lie.

"My sister lives here," he said.

The cop gave in quickly, too quickly, so quickly it scared Jimmy about what was inside.

"Go on," the cop said. "Just give me the key."

Jimmy didn't know he had it in his hand until he looked down.

The white house was doused in blank light from double floodlight fixtures on the corners of the garage and the far end, by the pool. There was another cop at the front door, after you crossed the driveway. A cop in a suit. The door stood open behind this one. It was a Dutch door, cut sideways across the middle so the top half could open on its own. They made doors like that for families with kids, to keep them in but to let air and light in, too. The two halves weren't lined up, locked together. There was blood around the knob outside but so dark it looked like chocolate. All the shine had gone out of it. What it looked like was shit. The cop in the suit wasn't standing guard; he was working, taking notes. He had twenty years on the officer out in the street, at the gate. He was a detective, a lieutenant.

"You can't go in there," he said, not looking away from whatever he was seeing on the face of the lower half of the door.

"My sister lives here."

Now the cop in the suit looked up at him but still used the same voice. "What's her name?"

It was only then that Jimmy realized how quiet it was, how nothing was coming out from the house. You'd think there'd be voices. Somebody. Something. There was a smell coming from the house he'd never smelled before.

He told him Mary's name.

A bit of the cop's steel shield came down, the slightest softening of his reserve, his self-protective distance. He was relieved.

"She's alive. She's all right. She's in the den." He even put his sentences in the right order, to save Jimmy the pain of even a half second of suspense.

Jimmy shifted, as if to go past him, through the door.

"Don't go in here," the cop said. "Go around."

"Thanks," Jimmy said.

"Better yet . . ." He called over another of the uniformed cops, who stood in front of the closed garage, his hand resting on his holstered revolver, as if something else was going to come out of the night.

"Yessir."

"Go in; if they're done with her, tell her that her brother is here."

The uniformed cop slipped in through the open door without touching it.

"He should have gone around, too," the veteran cop said, going back to the work. "Nobody needs to see that."

Jimmy knew what he meant by it, knew it was a tough guy's way of saying, *You're going to have to take care of your sister.*

Mary came around the corner of the house, but it took a few minutes. She stopped, just stood there in the middle of the driveway, her arms limp.

They let Jimmy take her through the gate, out to the end of the cul-de-sac, to the empty street across from the white house.

It wasn't something she could *tell*. Not yet. He saw that. She was trembling, but then it would stop, and she would be so still he would have shaken her if her eyes were closed. To see if she was alive. She just stood there, her back to the house, her eyes on the opposite ridgetop. It was only now that Jimmy realized where the city was, by the blue-gray edge to the scrub at the top of the hill. As if L.A. itself was a Sailor. It was what she was looking at.

"Which room were you in?" Jimmy said. He put his arm around her. She was as tall as he was, but that night, now, she seemed diminished.

"The study, the office," she said.

Maybe this was the way to let her unburden herself, a piece at a time. He didn't ask another question for a long time, long enough for a helicopter to fly over, coming in from the south, headed for Mulholland or the valley beyond. Jimmy wondered how long it would take for the first news cameras to arrive. He didn't want to be out in the open like this then.

"You were asleep?"

She nodded. She'd gone slack again, still. He dropped his hand from around her waist. She didn't seem to notice.

"David and Michelle were in my room," she said. "Off the hallway. So I went to the other end, to the office to sleep. The couch. I *told* them all this." She said the last imploringly, exasperated.

Then she seemed to remember who he was, who he wasn't.

"I'm sorry."

There were voices from somewhere. They both turned. Shafts of light were projected on the slab of hillside behind the house, sweeping flashlights. The cops were in the slice of concreted "backyard" between the house and the rock. The pool was on the other end of the house. Their voices, indistinct, guttural, masculine, rude, were rebounding off the rock, amplified somehow by the arrangement of things.

"I have to find someplace to go," Mary said, a crack of panic in her voice.

"You're going to stay with me," Jimmy said.

He took her home.

People always think someone should *sleep* when a thing like this happens, that the person *can* sleep. But Jimmy had been through his own version of a world-wrenching blowup. The ground had opened up in front of him once, too. He knew what it meant, knew what you saw when you closed your eyes in those first hours. *Everything can change in an hour, if it's the wrong hour.* So when he got Mary home, he asked her what she wanted to do. The bedroom door was open behind them.

"I guess lie down," she said.

He left her sitting on the bed, sitting in the center of it, with her legs crossed under her. He left the door open halfway. Something else he knew to do.

As he walked away, she came out of the bedroom, went into the bathroom. He listened at the door. He wasn't sure what he was listening for, but thought he should listen. She washed her hands for a long time, with the water on full.

"At first, they put my hands in plastic bags," she had told him before, as they were backing away down the cul-de-sac in the Cadillac. "Then they took them off. They never said why."

In the kitchen, Jimmy took a bottle of water from the icebox, left the door open for the cool and the light. He didn't turn on the overhead, sat at the turquoise Formica table, cracked the seal, and drank it down. He looked out at the lights of the city below his house. The kitchen window was closed. The little house didn't have air-conditioning, or even a wheezing window unit in the bedroom. He didn't know if opening the window would make it cooler or hotter. He reached back into the refrigerator, opened the freezer door, and pulled out an ice tray. He held it upside down over the table and twisted it. The cubes clattered out like dice in a complicated game. He picked up one and sucked it like a Popsicle.

He knew the layout of the house up in Benedict. Two nights ago there'd been a party he didn't want to go to, but went to anyway. It was Thursday night now, so that would have made it a Tuesday. Nobody in that crowd seemed to notice it wasn't the weekend. There were thirty people there, inside/outside, around the pool, a few of them famous, or at least famous somewhere. Recognizable. Actors, musicians. A high-hair metal band, whose look said they hadn't checked in at the record label lately, hadn't gotten the memo, came late and stayed late. Throughout the night they went everywhere together, side by side, in a cluster. Maybe they'd just shot a video that day and were still unnaturally synced. They stayed until the end. Or at least they were still there when Jimmy left.

That night Mary had met him at the door, at that Dutch door, and had kissed him. Other people were in the room, the living room. The girls. Michelle, April. In front of them, Mary had kissed him on both cheeks, Euro style. It had ticked him off. Somehow two kisses were less than one. He didn't see much of her for the next hours. He spent the first half of the night alone out by the black-bottomed pool, posing for a Hockney, a drink in hand, staring down at the reflective surface, maybe waiting for a coyote to come down out of the brush to drink. The rest of that night he spent in the office, the "study," though the director wasn't the type to study much of anything. He ended up being alone there, too. It was tucked away, off the master.

So he knew the rooms. He knew the layout. Stage right, stage left. The long hallway with its blank walls, where the director would have hung his awards if he had any. (That Tuesday night, he was off with some woman agent in his bedroom. Having sex would have been the least vulgar thing they could have been doing.) At one end of the hall was the living room, opening to a dining room and the kitchen, all opening onto the pool. At the other end of the hall were the bedrooms, two next to each other on the right, the "kids' rooms," the master at the end on the left, across the back of the house, with French doors to the concrete area behind the house, where the cops toward the middle of the night had focused their attention.

So he knew the layout.

Jimmy tried to put it together. Maybe *make it up* would be more accurate. He tried different scenarios, different entry points for the killer, different paths through the house. Different orders to the deaths. Who was first?

Then he realized something. The coroner's vans had never come the whole time he was there.

He was moving the melting ice around on the Formica tabletop. There was a siren somewhere down the hill or ripping across on Sunset, above the house. Maybe that was what had triggered the realization about the body wagons.

He had been on the scene for two or three hours, and no coroner's van had arrived.

What did that mean?

Jimmy and Mary stayed inside for the next three days. The scene had very little drama, only quiet talking, talk about nothing at all, about music, about the neighbor's cat who, even though Jimmy's kitchen window was twenty feet off the ground, came twice a day to tightrope-walk across the sill. Three days. Three days that way. Just the two of them. Angel brought in food sometimes. They drank a little. Mary started reading a book, something on the bookshelf left over from high school for Jimmy. The first day, in the first hours of pink light coming over the city, he had unhooked the television so neither one of them had to see the pictures from the news helicopters of the desecrated bodies spread-eagled on three road cuts in three disparate parts of the county. The director, Michelle, April.

CHAPTER THIRTEEN

There are rules; we just don't know what they are.

That was Angel's line. Over the years, he'd said it ten different ways to Jimmy. He'd said it the first night, when he'd found Jimmy on the street in Hollywood, standing across from the Chateau Marmont, in the crowd watching the ambulance, when he'd seen in his eyes whatever it is they see. Angel had spent the first three days with him. *First Days.* Angel had been the one who walked him through the first blue moon, though they didn't have a name for that person, that role. Handholder? You were lucky if you had one, if you weren't going through it all completely on your own, that first blue moon (and the ones after it), when some of the Sailors were called home, when some of them left whatever *this* was for whatever was next.

Everyone should have someone saying, "There are rules; we just don't know what they are." Whether it's true or not.

They were riding north on the 5, Jimmy and Angel, just now climbing up out of the San Fernando Valley.

It was night, when you think of the past.

"You should have took the cutoff, the Fourteen," Angel said. They were in Jimmy's Cadillac.

Jimmy didn't say anything.

"We should have took my car or something," Angel said.

"I wanted to go this way. Same difference. I was thinking of Saugus, the speedway," Jimmy said. "I'll cut across there." The top was down, but it wasn't too loud to talk. Mary's tape of Leonard Cohen and Joni Mitchell and Neil Young and Buffy Sainte-Marie was in the deck, down low, barely audible. Jimmy had been listening to it so much lately, it was full volume in his head, in his soul. Mary was back at his place. "Maybe I'll come up here this weekend, get her out of the city."

"She like cars?" Angel said.

"I doubt it. She doesn't have one."

"I didn't think *you* liked it, when you and me come up here."

"I liked it. What's not to like? It's loud and cheap and smoky and they run into each other."

"She's going to be all right," Angel said, because Mary was what they were really talking about, thinking about.

They'd already driven past five or six road cuts. Out here, where the highway opened up a little and the subdivisions of blunt, ugly houses only came along every two or three miles, the cuts were immense, great sloped gashes. Geology classes from UCLA took field trips up here. Field geology. Jimmy had seen something on TV about it once. It was a way to see what was under the surface, what primal sedimentary or metamorphic or igneous superstructure was there all along under ten feet of topsoil. Faults and folds. Layers of history. Shifting tectonic plates, north and south coming into collision. Jimmy remembered the professor's line. A road cut is like an *autopsy* on the earth.

"I mean, there was no connection to *her*, on her own," Angel said, when Jimmy didn't say anything. "She was just there. Wrong place, wrong time."

These days Mary was in that state of mind that said, *Why me? Why did I survive?* Jimmy, selfishly, without any evidence to point to, in his own mind had come up with the idea that she was spared because he loved her, because they loved each other. Jimmy and Mary. There was your reason.

They rolled on north, cut back east at Saugus, by Bouquet Junction into Placerita Canyon to the 14 and north again, past the great shoved-up plates of Vasquez Rocks off to the left, where so many sci-fi movies and Westerns had been filmed. For its otherworldliness, its sense of the edge, the frontier. A moon a bit past half side-lit the scene. Every time you saw Vasquez Rocks, especially by night, it looked weirder than your memory of it.

There was the long, easy climb up the grade. The Caddy was purring, running steady. At eighty-five. The forced march up Benedict Canyon the other night must have done it some good, blown out the pipes. Or put the fear of God into it.

"You should let me fix this up for you," Angel said.

"I like it the way it is," Jimmy said.

"It runs all right, but it looks sad. Does it even have a top?"

"It has one. It's ripped up."

Angel put his hand up to surf the wind. With the elevation, the air had gotten a little cooler, but not much.

"Here we go," Angel said, as they blew under the green rectangle of a sign. "Nine more miles."

"Nothing happens *fast* out here, does it?" Jimmy said.

"They get rattlesnakes in their garages," Angel said. "That can get fast on you."

Then they were cruising down one of the wide streets in a subdivision this side of Palmdale. It was three a.m. by then and real dead. The highway was a mile behind them, but if they'd pulled over and killed the engine they could have heard it, even over the sound of all the air conditioners, the steady river-sound of the cars, the interspersed basso profundo of the semis headed the back way toward the Central Valley, Bakersfield, and points beyond.

It was house after house, shoulder to shoulder, all the same color, at least under the moonlight, big stucco boxes, blank yards. L.A. was forty miles south. Some commute.

The motion-detector lights over each garage clicked on as they passed.

"You better have the number right," Jimmy said. "I mean, it's not like he can say, 'I'm in the white house with the little lawn boy out front.'"

"Watch it, Brother."

"This is a long way from L.A.," Jimmy said.

"Lot of cops live up here."

It was something he'd said, the cop at the door at the murder house, a beat after he'd let Jimmy know Mary was alive, that she was all right, that she was in the den. "It passed over her," he'd said. Angel had made a few calls, confirmed it. The detective was a Sailor. *Passed over* was their way of saying *spared*, though it meant something completely different. A good number of Sailors were cops, just like others were EMTs and emergency room doctors, people up all night anyway. They all took care of each other, like they took care of the new ones, stunned on sidewalks or beaches or beside overturned cars, in the first minutes of their new "lives." A Sailor tended not to say no to another Sailor, unless one or the other was one of the bad ones. (Who took care of each other in their own ways.)

And this was where he lived, the vet cop who wasn't as tough as he meant to be, in one of these big, ugly houses, a house he had probably tried to talk his ex-wife into taking.

"What is it? What's the number?"

"One one eight five two. Should be on the left side."

Jimmy looked up in the rearview mirror. The cop was standing in his unadorned front yard.

"Should be three houses back," Jimmy said.

The cop's name was Dill.

This was Dill's "day" off. He put a paper plate of Oreos and a gallon jug of whole milk and two glasses on the dining room table. He already had a glass of his own going. Cookies and milk. Sailors tended to eat exactly what they wanted, when they wanted. It could just as easily have been a bowl of raw Vidalia onions. Or ice cubes.

"They have their rules," Dill was saying. "They scrub the bodies. They shave the pubic hair. They always position the bodies faceup, head up. They close the eyes."

He'd put the Oreos right on top of *The Case*. He lifted the paper plate to pass it to Angel, and the face of a dead girl looked up at them, a close-up, outdoors. Full sunlight. Very white, white bordering blue. Jimmy and Angel recognized her from the news. She was the first of the dead. The first victim in what came to be called the Road Cut Killings, from two months ago, early in the summer.

"It's always high on the cut. Maximum light. Facing east usually."

"*They,*" Jimmy said. "You said *they.*"

The cop nodded.

"So the paper, the TV has it wrong," Angel said. "Road Cut *Killer.*"

"The papers and the TV have their own version of it," Dill said. "It's always that way. Personally, I treat reporters like they could just as well be the ones who did it. But that's just me. Long and short, they know about one-tenth what we know."

"How many have there been?" Jimmy said. "How many dead?"

"These three made thirteen."

Angel started to say something.

"Eleven that were in the papers," Dill finished.

"Who were the others?" Jimmy asked.

"A couple in Encino. They never made it out onto a cut. They were left in their house, in their bed."

The dining room table was covered with pictures, official pictures, and official documents and newspaper clippings, but only a few of those. The pics were hard to take. They were full color. It was the nineties. They were in color. With the old black-and-white, you could trick yourself into thinking it was a still from a bad movie. What this looked like was meat on rock. Angel shuddered involuntarily. He grabbed the handle of the jug of milk, poured himself half a glass, like it was whisky in a cowboy bar.

When Angel lifted the jug, there was Mary's picture.

Jimmy saw it.

Dill saw him looking at it. "No reason for her to be there," the cop said.

As it is with cops, the way they talk, there were a couple of ways you could take it.

"Your girlfriend," he added.

Jimmy nodded. He wondered just how early the cop had figured out that Mary wasn't his sister.

He picked up the picture of her. It was one the cops had taken that night, before he got there, inside, Mary standing in front of a white paneled wall in the study with her hands down at her side. It made her look so helpless. Small.

"How many of them are there?" Jimmy said, looking at her.

"I say two. Some think three. One detective thinks it's two men and a woman they share. But she's a woman. The detective."

What the cop did next was hard to take, even with the skewed view of the world Jimmy and Angel had, worse in a way than looking at the photographs, because what he did was walk them through every case. Starting at the beginning.

And it really meant *walking*, walking in behind the killers, a step behind them, seeing what they saw. It was almost like your feet stuck to the floor, made that bloody kissing noise. He started with victim one, at the beginning of the summer. He would pick up each photo and hold it through the telling. The setup for each story was the entry. The approach to the victim was Act Two. The killing was the climax, the body on the road cut the denouement. He would hold the picture and begin, each time, with a line like, "They parked on a street just below . . ." He might as well have started each line with a personal pronoun. And present tense.

We come in from the garage . . .

We walk down the hallway . . .

Jimmy looked up at the ceiling. There was a galvanized metal plate over an electrical box dead center above their heads. Chandeliers get repossessed? Or divvied up in divorce proceedings? Or maybe the couple had never gotten around to buying one. Angel said Detective Dill had been divorced a year. He'd married a woman with a kid, a boy, a teenager, but it had only lasted two years. There weren't any other details. There's hardly ever any story to it when a cop gets divorced, if what a story is, is something with at least a little surprise in it. Dill hadn't been a Sailor for a long time, four or five years, a lot less than Jimmy, an eternity less than Angel. Maybe what broke up the family was the truth, when he finally got around to telling it. Maybe at this selfsame table. Probably at this hour.

When Jimmy looked at Dill again, he could see the very faintest edge of blue around his head and shoulders. Very weak. Maybe he was a good man, but he was a weak Sailor, putting in his hours but mostly just waiting for release. Some blue moon to sail away.

"The French doors across the back of the house were never locked. They were probably open, with the heat. There was a shorted-out circuit breaker in the AC unit on the ground, mid-house. Either it had been out previously or they shorted it. There's a possibility one or both of them came earlier in the day to prepare the way. No one was home for two hours midafternoon. There were exterior lights, blue, but they weren't on. The lead put a hand, his right hand, high on the right-hand door of the double doors, and opened it, or opened it further. It opened out . . ."

Suddenly Jimmy was back in the scene. The episodic tale of the summer of murders had come round to the leased white house at the end of the cul-de-sac. To *him.* Not that he hadn't heard every word of the telling of the other killings, every detail, every footstep, every clicking drop of the blood onto every floor.

"They wore gloves," Dill said. "There were no prints left anywhere. And rubber-soled shoes. Converse."

Jimmy started filling in the details. He thought, *Mary stirred on the couch in the study . . .*

"Like the other times, they killed together, two together," Dill was saying. "The lead put his hand over the girl's mouth, the girl in bed in the master bedroom, and the second then choked her with both hands. Smoothly, with a strong, steady grip, tighter and tighter, but not enough to break any bones. This was Michelle Gandy. She struggled, broke two toes on her right foot, either on the footboard of the bed or striking one of the two on either side of her."

Did Mary hear something? Did her eyes open?

"They left her, for now," Dill continued. "The master bedroom opened onto the long hallway. One started through the doorway first. They apparently hadn't made any noise that had alerted the others in the house. They looked back." Dill looked over his shoulder. "The French doors were wide open, letting in whatever sounds out in the night there were, possibly masking any of the sounds of violence."

Jimmy thought, *Mary closed her eyes. It was nothing.*

"The man, David Fifthian, never woke up," Dill said next. "He was alone in the first small bedroom off the hallway. On his stomach. He was killed the same way, though facedown. Feathers were found all the way into his lungs, from the comforter, from trying to pull in what air he could. Both of them handled his neck." Dill made his two hands into an open circle. "One pair of hands on top of the other. He wore just a V-neck sweater. He had had sexual relations in the bed in the master bedroom and then left his partner there to come to this room. They wrapped his ankles with a leather belt from a pair of trousers on the floor near the door and used it as a strap to pull him off the bed and out into the hallway, once he was dead."

Stay asleep, Jimmy thought, as if he was standing over Mary.

"The third, April . . ."

Jimmy wanted to make him stop. What he wanted was to take Mary out of there, lift her off the couch, out of Dill's narration, before one more thing happened. He wanted to cut her out of the story, let all this happen to strangers, with no connection to him.

". . . April Joules. She was awake. Reading. In the second small bedroom. She couldn't have heard them. She was in a chair, beside a table with a gooseneck lamp, beside an open window."

Jimmy remembered something he should have remembered before. He interrupted, "Was his daughter there?"

It was the only interruption. Dill shook his head. "Vancouver."

It made Jimmy realize how little he and Mary had said about the whole thing over the three days, how little he had asked or she had offered.

"Because April Joules was awake, they stabbed her in the chest," Dill finished. "There was a different blood pattern."

Jimmy looked across at Angel. He had his head bowed. His lips were moving, mumbling a prayer. Or a curse.

"All of the bodies then were dragged into the living room for the desecration, and the body of at least one, probably the man, was dragged out the front door. The bodies of the women were likely packaged and carried out."

Did the wind blow the door shut? Once they'd left? Is that what woke her? Is that what brought Mary out into it, too late, or exactly late enough?

When it was finished, they talked a little more, about each other. "How are you doing?" was a question Sailors asked each other frequently, and it meant more than to the rest of us. And then, in the empty foyer, behind the closed front door, they formed a circle and held hands, like a prayer circle, only they didn't bow their heads but rather looked straight at each other, a scene someone from the outside world would never have understood.

Jimmy dropped Angel off at home in Silver Lake. It was six in the morning by then. Some of Angel's neighbors were breaking the day, loading tools into their trucks. (They couldn't leave the trucks loaded on the streets all night.) They'd gotten used to seeing Jimmy in the old Cadillac, Angel's friend. A couple of them waved. They were even used to them being out all night together. They probably thought they were just partying.

Mary wasn't in the house when Jimmy got back.

The light was full then, bright and hot, coming in through the east-facing windows. He looked for her in every room. He looked in the closets. He looked under the bed, feeling foolish on top of his sense of panic. He tried to tell himself maybe she'd gone for a walk, gone to a friend's.

He circled the base of the house, calling her name.

She was in the storage room beneath the kitchen. She was covered with dirt. There was no floor. She cowered in the corner, in a jail of rakes and hoes and shovels. In as much dark as she could find.

"They came back after me," she said before he could say anything.

He got her out of the corner and held her. He said the words to calm her, to dismiss it, the way men do to women.

She pulled away from him.

"They were here," she said. "They came an hour after you left. There were two of them. They wore black. Black pants and coats and black sneakers . . ."

CHAPTER FOURTEEN

It became Jimmy's first case.

He got up that morning and moved Mary to another house, a friend of Angel's down so deep into Latino territory that it'd be next to impossible for anybody who wasn't Latino to get to her.

Now it was noon, and he was headed west on Sunset, west all the way out to Temescal Canyon.

He had "looked into things" for people before, tracked down a lost soul here or there for Angel or for some other Sailor or friend. Or friend of a friend. He had tailed people, to make sure they were all right. To make sure they had made it home, made it back to a safe place. He had tucked in his share of desperate, hurting people, sat up all night with people who needed someone there to keep them from falling apart. Others, he had "looked into" to see just how bad they were. To confirm that here was someone for an innocent, a friend, a Sailor to steer clear of.

But this was something new. Something closer, with higher stakes.

The first of the Road Cut Killings had come in a cabin out at the end of a tight, twisting road, a road that all but turned into a footpath as it climbed higher into the hills. The farther you went, the narrower it got, like a capillary. Temescal, Benedict. Maybe there was a canyon connection. It was a one-bedroom cabin. She was young. An actress. Or would-be. Like everybody else, she'd been in a few commercials, was up for a pilot or a continuing role on an episodic. Or at least that's what she'd probably told the folks back home. Maybe there was a Hollywood connection, but that was too easy. Everyone was connected to Hollywood. Jimmy had spent nearly the entirety of his existence here. From time to time he had to remind himself that dry cleaners and hot dog stands and churches in other parts of the country didn't brag on the famous people they served. Some places weren't about the show. Some people just *watched* movies and television shows.

There was a bleached-out plastic For Rent sign out front stapled to an oak, as if anyone could just happen by the place. Word must have gotten out. There had been no takers in three months. Jimmy parked the Cadillac, turned off the engine and the music with it.

There was a cicada somewhere, with that high-tension sound, like a rattler on crank. He left the driver's door open, stood in place, turned a full circle. You could see the rooftop of another cabin halfway up the side of another canyon across the way, but that was it. Nothing else that had anything of a human stamp on it. Hard to believe the towers of Century City were three or four miles from here, in the air anyway. It was a good place to kill somebody.

"Hello?" he said, louder than he'd intended.

There was a little yodel slapback from the other hillside, but nothing else, not even a dog barking back at him. As he started toward the cabin, he stopped to pick up a straight length of branch dropped out of one of the oaks. What was he going to do with a stick? Use it the way a kid uses a stick to poke a dead thing? To make sure? He was more spooked than he'd thought he'd be. Detective Dill had done too good a job at painting a picture of what had gone down inside.

He tried the knob on the front door. It was locked. The door was baby blue with hand-painted flowers, years old. Temescal had been a favorite hippie canyon in the '70s. Hippies and bikers. After that, it was rich Hollywood types, weekenders, weed smokers. Who told themselves their new jobs hadn't changed them. *It* hadn't changed them. Then they got bored, and the drive was too much trouble. (*It* won.) And the next wave moved in, whatever it was. That the actress lived up here told Jimmy she'd probably come from someplace real and missed it, *real* like trees and birds that go to sleep and shut up when the sun goes down. Real like mice. And mud daubers.

Real like dying of old age. With your clothes on. With your heart still on the inside of your body.

There was a back door to the cabin, but it was locked, a dead bolt and a clasp and padlock to boot. New locks, a little late. Jimmy found a loose window, old rippled glass, and was just about to get it forced open when it decided to shatter instead. He reached in, unlatched it, pushed it up, and crawled through. And it wasn't until he was inside, standing in the cabin's one bedroom, that he saw that he'd cut himself, cut his hand, badly enough to bleed all over his T-shirt, where he'd scratched himself on his shoulder. He looked down at the floor. There was a puddle like a rose petal under where his hand hung down.

He didn't learn anything in Temescal Canyon. Or at least nothing that clicked into place at the time, anything that meant anything to him then.

So he went to the movies.

The Vista. They showed foreign films and American classics, double bills that didn't seem at first to belong together. This week it was *The Searchers* and *The Road Warrior*. It was a Monday night. He was all but alone in the place, just three or four film buffs sitting in their favorite seats, and the kid from behind the popcorn counter who was a film buff, too, who knew so much about movies that it crowded out the unimportant stuff like human relations and the future. Jimmy sat dead center, two-thirds of the way back. The four hours of screen murder and mayhem for some reason felt like a nice, long, warm, cleansing shower.

Not that he didn't keep thinking about the Temescal Canyon girl. He hoped she wasn't the kind of aspiring actress who just wanted to be famous. He had stood in her living room. The cabin really only had one main room, with the kitchen against one wall, and the bedroom and bathroom. (It was like the low-ceilinged cabin in *The Searchers* John Wayne kept coming back to, without an answer.) Jimmy had stood there, in the middle of that front room. It was sad. It was easier to get inside the actress's head than the killers'. She was only twenty-four, but Jimmy's mother was twenty-one when she became a star. A star. Miss Temescal, or Miss Wherever She'd Come From, was only twenty-four but must have wondered if she was already too late.

And, as it turned out, she was.

The bathroom had a big old porcelain tub with claw-and-ball feet. Jimmy had crawled into it. From it, you could see up the hillside out a high, sideways window. Up there was a firebreak cut into the scrub brush, a gap to stop the flames from eating up and over the crest line. In fire season, the manzanita and scrub ground cover got a new name: *fuel*. Detective Dill had told Jimmy and Angel where the young woman was killed, the bedroom, but he had said they didn't know the particulars, or not all of them. And not the beginning of the slaughter, the horror. Maybe she had been here, taking a bath. Candles? Maybe she'd pushed open the window to let in the smell of the trumpet vine that curled up over the back of the cabin. Had she heard something? The hills would be filled with coyotes. She would have gotten used to them right away, heard their yipping and seen them for the dogs they were. Had she heard something else? A car coming up the hill? There were no tracks, just the tracks of her Jeep CJ-7. Had they come down on foot on the firebreak? They pulled casts of the Converse shoe prints from behind the cabin, from under the window where Jimmy had come in. The cops knew from the beginning this was going to be bad. And showy. Her brown heart had been left on the counter beside an antique tortoiseshell comb and a burned-down candle.

He left twenty minutes into *The Road Warrior*. The rescue motif had got to him. And the burnout in the two heroes' eyes.

Jimmy drove by the house in East L.A. that held Mary. He didn't stop. He'd had the feeling someone was following him earlier in the day, and it still hung over him. Two of Angel's men were out front, leaning against the fender of a glossy lowrider. They knew him, raised their beers in salute. Or to tell him she was OK. There was a light in the third-floor window. It was an apartment building. He wasn't sure, but he told himself that the light was her. That she was reading.

The next to die, after the actress, was inland, Ontario, out half-way to Palm Springs. It was a good thing he liked to drive, had nowhere else to be. And the third was south, halfway to Orange County, a teenager on the streets, a girl in the hard-core surf scene, down in Redondo.

An actress.

A middle-aged man, a fifth-grade teacher.

A street girl.

White.

Black.

Filipino.

It was a triangle, if that mattered. On a map. West, east, south. The cop Dill had said that the beginning and the end, the old alpha and omega, was always *motive*. The job was to find the logic. What you were looking for was the obvious.

Four, five, six. Seven, eight, nine.

No more triangle. The murder scenes were all over the place.

The surfer girl was the youngest, seventeen. The oldest was ninety, snatched from his bed in a convalescent hospital in Long Beach.

Eight women, five men.

Then there was the couple in Encino, the ones who didn't make it onto the official list, into the papers, onto the TV. (The cops liked to keep a card or two facedown.) The scene was out in the Valley, a house south of Ventura Boulevard, a quarter-way up into the hills, in a neigh-borhood of big houses but close together, which is maybe why the couple never ended up on a road cut, were left there in the house where they were eviscerated.

Jimmy came in from the back, came in across the golf course. He stopped fifty feet out. The house was Moderne. Most of the rear of it was glass, floor-to-ceiling, tinted black squares tucked under the flat roof. It was three in the morning. The man had been a television writer, hour cop shows when what they wanted was hour cop shows, true-crime woman-in-jeopardy movies of the week when *their* time came around, shifting as easily as he'd gone from Mercedes to Lexuses. Or would it be *Lexi*? When the long-form writing work ended, nothing much else came his way, but he had money in the bank and this house, for which he'd paid seventy-six thousand dollars. His wife sold real estate. Jimmy wondered if her agency was handling the house. There was a For Sale sign in the backyard, aimed toward the water hazard. Apparently no buyers for this one yet either.

He was about to move closer to the house when a light snapped on. Jimmy jumped, though he was still fifty feet out. The windows weren't covered, no drapes or shades, or they were pulled open. The light had come on in what was the den. It was a table lamp. No one was visible. Jimmy waited. Maybe the light was on a timer. But set to snap on at three a.m.?

Then an overweight kid stepped into the frame of the interior door-way. He just stood there, looking into the big, wide room, as if he was uncertain about stepping in. He wasn't a kid exactly, except in L.A. showbiz terms. He was probably in his late thirties. He wasn't over-weight exactly either, just fleshy. In L.A. showbiz terms. He was bare-foot and wore silky running pants, a white T-shirt.

The light went out. Jimmy waited.

The light came on in the kitchen. There was the fridge, a stainless steel side-by-side Sub-Zero. Jimmy expected the kid to come in, go over, open it, look in, the way people do in the middle of the night. But he stayed standing in the doorway again, this time with his hand still hovering over the wall switch. The rooms were all bare, stripped down, hyper clean. Open House clean. *Show* ready. The light went out.

Now the kid picked up the pace. He went from room to room, light on, a beat, light off. He was like a scared little boy or girl looking for the source of the out-of-place noise he'd heard, home alone, hoping there'd be reassurance at the end of the search, when he'd checked everywhere.

Jimmy knew what it was. He had run through this routine himself. It wasn't about what was *there*, under the bed or in the shadows in the closet. It was about what was missing. Jimmy called it the I-can't-believe-it dance, though he threw an obscenity in the middle.

They're gone.

The light came on upstairs, in the upper right-hand corner of the house, where there was a balcony. It went out. Ten seconds later it came on again. This time the kid stepped in, left the doorway, crossed the room, and stood at the foot of a king-sized bed. The bed where they'd been found, in that horrible configuration. (Jimmy had seen the picture, could see it too clearly still.) He just stood there.

This was the second part of the story.

The first part was the actual loss of the thirteen human lives. The reality of what they did in life, their jobs, their work, what they filled their days with. And the potential. What the writers at the papers and the TV stations like to call "the hopes and dreams." Maybe she would have been a star. He might have been Teacher of the Year. She didn't get to see her daughter graduate from preschool. Maybe they would have made a movie remake of one of his TV shows.

But the second part of the story was the subplot, the story of those who'd been left. Left in pieces. Left not understanding much of anything anymore. Left with your heart ripped out, too, or at least a deadweight in your chest. Left in a foreign country where somehow you don't speak the language and the people don't like you. Left with pictures you can't look at. Left with songs you can't stand to hear anymore.

Left to stand in his parents' bedroom, "house-sitting" in his own life.

Jimmy ended the night, or at least the night ended around him, standing outside another house, standing at the foot of the Chateau Marmont on Sunset, his eyes on the penthouse and the railing.

CHAPTER FIFTEEN

"Where's your little doggy?"

It took Jimmy a second to hear the spite in her voice. She was in her sixties, maybe seventies, and stood an arm's length away from him with her feet apart and her hands on her hips, as if braced against a wind or on the pitching deck of a ship. She wore all black, a dress, a sweater, a shawl over that. Old Country. He was on the sidewalk across the street from a pricey condo building in Brentwood, a four-story taupe job with black trim, black wrought iron around the windows.

The seventh of the dead. A twenty-year-old woman.

"I don't have a dog."

"Today you don't," the woman said. "The other nights you did."

"Must have been somebody else," Jimmy said. What he didn't say was that, generally speaking, dogs don't like Sailors.

"I *saw* you," the woman said. She pointed her finger at him.

Jimmy just let her go on to her next line.

"I think it's revolting, you coming around here, over and over," she said. "Let the dead bury the dead."

Jimmy decided to take a shot with her. Maybe there was something here. "I don't even like dogs," he said.

She tilted her head.

Jimmy pressed on. "I think they're a menace, fouling people's yards with their feces. Snarling, snapping. Urinating willy-nilly."

She liked the sound of this. "It wasn't you?" she said.

"Not if the person had a dog," Jimmy said.

"I don't like dogs," she said.

"I'm like you, then," he said. "You live in the neighborhood?" Jimmy asked.

"Right behind you," she said. Right behind him was a cute little Spanish-style bungalow. Covered with tile. From top to bottom, side to side. Ceramic tile, blue and white and green and yellow, every inch of the face of the house, every surface, and out into the yard, up and over fountains and benches and from the front steps to the street on a curving sidewalk. Tile. If it had had a pattern, it would have been a mosaic, but there was no pattern to it. It was a crazy-quilt house.

Jimmy hadn't really looked at it when he'd parked the car and gotten out, his eyes on the condo, checking the number.

"Damn," he said now, scanning the tile house. He tried to add a flip to it, to make it sound like he meant it admiringly.

"You're as bad as him," she said.

"How so?"

"Coming out here, drooling over this. The death of that poor girl."

"I was just going for a walk . . ."

"No, you weren't. You were rubbernecking. Or worse. Let the dead bury—"

"I *am* the dead," Jimmy said.

She took a step back.

He let her wonder for a minute.

"I write television scripts," he said. He named a show with a creepy attitude, then tried to look as much like Rod Serling as possible. He tossed his head in the direction of the condo. "I thought this might make a good episode."

"But you'd change the names," she said. There was something plaintive about the way she said it.

"So you knew her?"

The woman shook her head. She pointed toward an arched-top picture window on the front of her house, a table, a chair, a Tiffany lamp there. "I sit there. I would see her come and go, out of the underground parking. She never walked anywhere."

"What did he look like?"

"Who?"

"The one you thought was me."

"Like you. But with motorcycle boots."

He knew he wasn't going to get much else out of her. The "colorful" have their limits as information sources.

"How many times did you see him?"

"Three nights. Just standing there, where you are."

"When?"

"The night after it happened. And then the next night. And then a week later."

"Did you ever talk to him?"

"Are you going to use him in your story, too?"

"I don't know."

"Not with that dog, I wouldn't talk to him. That was the idea. The idea of the dog. To keep you back. To scare you."

"What kind of dog was it?"

"Some black kind, the kind you don't even see until it shows its teeth."

There was steady west-side traffic up and down Barrington the whole time they stood there talking. Brentwood had its gentle hills, curving streets, all very easy. If you had the money. The tile house was one of the last of the single homes left on this stretch of Barrington. The rest were condominiums. She probably didn't even know that the developers called her a holdout.

A car stopped in the middle of the street right in front of them. A Bentley, a ten-year-old Bentley. Black. Waiting for oncoming traffic to clear before it turned left. It made the turn. The window came down as the driver stopped in the driveway beside a keypad switch on a post. A hand came out and tapped a code onto the keys. A hand with a Rolex. The iron gate of the car park rose in recognition.

"That's him," the neighbor lady said. "Her father."

The Bentley went down the sloping drive. The gate closed.

The woman turned to go. "You can stand out here and embarrass yourself all you want," she said, hard-ass again. "Don't think I don't know who you are. Boots or no boots, dog or no dog." She walked away up her tiled walk, which looked from this distance like walking on broken glass.

Twenty minutes later, the Bentley came back up out of the building. The window was coming up.

You didn't have to see any more of the man at the wheel behind the black-tinted glass to know who he was. He was everywhere, or his face was. Looking down from billboards, on the sides and backs of buses. And always with a single word across his chest, over his heart: *trust.* The dead girl's father was Mike Roberts. Of Channel 8. Now he'd gone white-haired and slipped from the network wholly owned and operated down to an independent station, but he'd brought half of his viewers with him, and whatever the ratings were or weren't, he was still *The Anchorman* in Los Angeles for anyone who'd been here longer than five years. For the new arrivals, he must have seemed like *El Presidente* or *El Jefe* or *The Pakhan*, staring down at his people from every rentable, printable surface.

He was no pretty boy. He had a face like a marine, or a movie star playing a marine. And they *did* trust him. He was the one who went out and stood in the rain for the rest of them, hillsides sliding in the b.g., the one who raced in a panel van on the crest line in Angeles Forest with the flames "leaping across the highway, Trish!" for the sake of the safe at home in their living rooms. Even if all that was years ago.

When his little girl was still a little girl.

But her name wasn't Roberts. It was Weinstein. Rachel. And as far as Jimmy knew nobody had ever connected the daughter to the father.

At least there wasn't anything in any of the newspaper clips Dill had given him. It wasn't public knowledge. Another card facedown. She'd been seventh in line.

Jimmy thought back. The coverage had ramped up about then. Maybe that was why: one of their own had been taken. *If it can happen to us . . .*

Along about then was when the people of the city really started feeling threatened. He/they were out there.

Who was next?

Jimmy was following him, following the Bentley. Roberts took Sunset all the way in from Brentwood into Hollywood. The Action Eight studios were in a block-long, solid white Greek Revival curiosity on Sunset, the old Warner studio, where Warner Brothers had started, where *The Jazz Singer* had been shot a thousand years ago. *Mammy!* The Bentley slowed at the gate, and the window came down so the anchorman could chat up the guard, who obviously knew the car, who already had the crossing arm up. The biggest billboard of all was over the studios.

Trust.

Rachel Weinstein had been dead two months. Jimmy wondered who or what Mike Roberts trusted now.

He had pulled to the curb across the street. Jimmy didn't know why he'd followed him. He stayed there an hour, waiting for an answer. All he got for his trouble was a glimpse of the Bentley behind the gates in the parking lot. A young man came out, opened the unlocked trunk, removed a white cardboard box, something not too heavy. The kid, the intern, was trying to balance it on one leg so he could reach up and close the trunk when the guard from the gatehouse came running over to assist.

Maybe the anchorman had given his girl his Emmys and now was getting them back. Prick a famous man, and does he not bleed?

Jimmy ended the day back in Encino, Encino by daylight this time. He parked the Cadillac across from the television writer's long, low house. He didn't know what he was looking for here, either. He was still new to this.

On the For Sale sign out front there was a radio frequency, a lightning bolt logo that explained it. The Realtors had a new trick. Jimmy tuned it in on the car radio. It was a two-minute commercial for "the property." Which, it turned out, was spectacularly more valuable even than it appeared. Or at least priced that way. It was a woman's voice, warm as the smell of fresh-baked cookies, probably another actor doing this to pay the bills, waiting for that big break. Music played in the background, George Winston, if Jimmy knew his New Age tone poems. He shut it off just as she was getting to the square footage of the "bonus room" and got out.

He stood there on the sidewalk across the street for five minutes, just stood there. He could almost hear the screams from out here, through the tinted, double-glazed glass. Is that what he wanted? Is that what he was looking for? Is that why he'd come back? Is that what he was waiting for? For it to get *real*?

He heard a sharp sound behind him, metal scraping on something, and turned. It was a gardener with a grass rake raking the lawn next to a concrete driveway, hitting it every third or fourth stroke, his eyes down. He was a South American, hard to say what country. A few years back, they were all "Mexicans"; people thought that, but they weren't, many of them. There were Salvadorans, Guatemalans, Costa Ricans. It also was hard to say how old the man was. He wore clean khakis and had a red kerchief knotted around his neck. Put him in a suit on a telenovela, and you'd realize how handsome he was.

"Amigo," Jimmy said.

The tile house lady in Brentwood may have stepped back from Jimmy when he spoke, but this man *jumped* back. Five feet. With a scared-to-death look, an I-know-you look. He backed over a rosebush, lifted his rake, and turned the handle sideways, as if he was going to make the sign of the cross with it. From the reaction, Jimmy might as well been a monster, out in broad daylight.

A monster the gardener had seen standing there before.

The man kept looking around, as if looking for the black dog . . .

• • •

ANGEL picked up Jimmy in front of his house. In a primer-red Porsche Cabriolet with no top, just the metal birdcage frame folded back without any cloth over it. It was a '64. A 356C. It had already been lowered a bit, lost all the chrome, the radio antenna frenched in, but in a way that didn't look wrong. The seats were bare-bones, but they'd already been rebuilt, too, had a Tijuana border-crossing five-dollar blanket thrown over them.

The engine had a perfect sound to it. It had gotten the first dollars.

"Whose car is this?"

"Nobody's," Angel said. "Mine. Yours. I'm just doing it for myself, for the glory of God."

"Jesus is gonna love it," Jimmy said.

For now, they were headed nowhere. On Western Avenue, south. It was what they did instead of talking on the phone. It was ten thirty or so. A weeknight. There wasn't much traffic.

Angel took Jimmy's Jesus line with a smile. He always did. He was content in his belief and easygoing about others' disbelief. It worried him, made some part of him sad, but he repeated the same line ten times a day, usually out loud: "It's in God's hands." There was so much doom around him, he had to pick his battles. *Let go, let God* was another one, another line he repeated.

"Let me ask you something," Jimmy said. " 'Let the dead bury the dead.' What's that about?"

"It's in Matthew."

"Yeah, I know. I looked it up. I thought it was Shakespeare."

"What do you think it's about?"

"I think it's *harsh*, is what I think. You read the story. Jesus is heading out, some guy wants to follow him but says first he has to go take care of his father's funeral. And Jesus says, 'Let the dead bury the dead.' "

"I used to think it was about *us*," Angel said. "Back about a hundred New Years ago . . ." That was what they called the increments of time since they'd become Sailors, since it'd happened to them, since they'd crossed over to death's other kingdom: New Days, New Weeks, New Years . . . Angel Figueroa had been a Sailor almost seventy years. But looked mid-thirties, in his white T-shirt and baggy starched jeans, and long, hipster-straight-back black hair.

"I mean, I thought, here we are, we were the dead, walking around, here was a job for us."

"What does it mean?" Jimmy pressed.

"Jesus was a rebel leader." Angel always said Jesus like the gringos, not *Hay-soos*, at least when talking to white men. "It was the beginning of things. He was starting the revolution. Jesus *was* the revolution. 'Follow me and become fishers of men,' he said when he was talking to fishermen. He meets you where you are."

"So what did he mean by it?"

"You sound like you're mad at him."

"What did he mean?" Jimmy said, harder. He was looking away, looking at the whores on opposite corners of an intersection they blew past. If you didn't slow down, they didn't even look like *people*. They just looked like sex. Sex and money.

Bad sex and dirty money.

Angel was nothing if not patient. "'Let the dead bury the dead.' All that matters is what happens now. Next. There's no purpose in the past."

Jimmy let a block go by. "But *you're* the guy who restores old cars," he said.

"I don't restore anything," the other said quickly. "I make something new out of the old. *Too* new for some."

Angel shifted gears, literally and figuratively. "Are we looking for something? Somebody?"

"Yeah, somebody who looks like me," Jimmy said. He told Angel the story of the tile house woman in Brentwood and then the yard man in Encino.

"He got a name?"

"Three or four or five. I just call him Handsome."

They drove around the rest of the night, looking where they knew to look, looking for trouble, but they didn't find him, the man who maybe looked like Jimmy, the man in black with the black dog.

They didn't find him the next night, either.

Or the next day. Or the day after that.

But they found him.

Or at least they found his den.

It was six o'clock. They came walking down the alleyway between two brick buildings in a "neighborhood" of shit-hole apartments and rooms by the week in the shadow of downtown. And not one of those *romantic* shadows of downtown where painters rent lofts and documentarians make movies of each other and the beautiful poor. Angel's body shop was five blocks away, so he'd met Jimmy here. Six o'clock. Anywhere else in L.A. that would have meant the light was pretty, but down here the shadows had won the battle between light and dark a half hour ago. Here the Golden Hour only meant you couldn't quite see.

What Jimmy had was an address, a location, a home base for the man with the black dog, the man who'd shown up at eight of the murder sites, from what Jimmy had learned. Who'd just stood there across the street, whichever street it was, the day after. And sometimes the next. Reliving it? Funny word for it. In the end, after a few days, Jimmy found somebody who knew somebody who knew something. So a few words, an idea, maybe even a lie, had led Jimmy to this alleyway. Maybe to the man.

But what did he know about detective work? He'd heard a line once, about art, about sculpture. About a sculptor known for his enormous, very realistic sculptures of horses. He had been asked how he could do it, his technique. "It's simple," the sculptor had said, "I just chip away everything that doesn't look like a horse." What did Jimmy know about detective work? Nothing, except to go everywhere he could go, cut away everything it wasn't, until a shape emerged. What did he know, except that almost everything was a mystery and that what was most true about a thing you usually didn't see until it was too late.

"Which floor?" Angel said. He was stopped, looking up at the side of the brick building at the end of the alley. It was six floors, old arched windows bricked in years ago, covered by a picture of something, signage. If it was one of those romantic alleyways in a documentary about the poor, the old sign would have been a fading picture of an orange tree with a lush, fading, green Promised Land behind it. What it was instead was a man in a bowler hat wearing a truss.

"My guy didn't say," Jimmy said. "Just that this was his squat, that he slept in the daytime. Or at least people only seemed to see him at night."

So they went inside. The first floor of the brick building was open from side to side, with posts, with high windows with arched tops, with unfinished, worn wood on the deck. It had been a factory. Jimmy and Angel crossed to a pile of rubble in the middle of things. Angel picked through it and found a length of hardwood, like a table leg. Maybe it had been a furniture factory. Or a coffin factory. He gripped it by the skinny end.

"You look like a caveman," Jimmy said.

To tell the truth, both of them were spooked. They'd bought into the hysteria. They'd been carrying it around, a gnawing unease, both of them, for six days. Since the killings up in Benedict. There hadn't been any more murders since the director and the two women, but that had only increased the apprehension somehow. The whole town's apprehension.

They went upstairs. The staircase was wooden but strong.

There wasn't any dust in the center of the treads. Somebody had been coming and going.

"You should have called that cop Dill," Angel said.

"He was gone," Jimmy said. "Out."

"I got his cell somewhere."

"We're here, we might as well go on up."

"I wasn't saying don't go up," Angel said defensively.

The second floor and the third floor were open side to side like the ground floor. Open and empty. The light was all but gone. Now they had to put their hands on the railing to feel their way up.

But there was light above. Golden light.

They came out of the stairwell onto the fourth floor. It was wide and empty, too, but across it there was a single tall window bringing in a sharp-edged quadrilateral of gold light.

They moved toward it. There was a heap of clothes, a bedroll.

And a body.

He was on his side, the upper quarter of his head smashed in from a blow that could have been inflicted by a club like the one still in Angel's hand. Angel looked down at it, as if he was thinking the same thing.

Angel said, "He doesn't look anything like you."

"It's not him," Jimmy said. A moment passed that wasn't as long as it seemed. "It's the guy who sent me down here, from out in Van Nuys."

There was dog shit everywhere.

ON the drive home, Jimmy and Angel saw people standing outside an electronics store, looking in at the bank of TVs. Same thing at another store down the street.

The radios in all the cars around them weren't playing music. It was just talking. All talk.

It was like the end of the world. Or the beginning. The people they passed on the sidewalks and the people in the cars around them seemed to be, if not happy, lightened. The Porsche had a hole in the dash where the radio used to be or Jimmy and Angel would have tuned in the news themselves.

Jimmy went straight to the television when he walked in the door of his house.

Mary was there, startling him, coming out of the bedroom.

She let the TV tell him. They'd caught the killers, black Converse high-tops, bone saws, leather gloves, in an apartment in North Hollywood.

Two Russian brothers.

Neither one of whom looked anything at all like Jimmy.

CHAPTER SIXTEEN

"Your girl killed herself."

In Jimmy's state of mind, with where he'd just been, what he'd just seen, *who* he'd seen, Mary and her husband, it took him a second to think which girl.

But he figured it out. And the guilt started.

"Get in," Jimmy said.

From the circle out in front of the Mark Hopkins the two of them went across the city to the scene of the thing, the place where she'd done it. And then to the morgue. In that order, Jimmy delaying the latter as long as possible. It was Machine Shop who'd said, when Jimmy showed some hesitation, that they *had* to go see the body, to be sure it was really her, be sure that Shop had gotten it right, though it had happened almost right in front of him down at the waterfront. Plus, Shop had a friend who worked nights in the coroner's office, a Sailor.

They'd already hauled the crumpled car away, the little baby-blue Skylark. Bad for business. They'd already hosed off the blood. The car hadn't caught fire—when Lucy had driven it at fifty or sixty into the concrete face of Pier 35, the same blank building where the Leonidas girls had jumped.

"There was nobody with her, right?" Jimmy said to Shop, standing there next to the circles of oil and transmission fluid and the white blanket of the powdery flame-killer SFFD had sprayed down just in case. Atop the engine gunk was pebbly absorbent, what at the old Saugus Speedway they used to call "kitty litter." They'd be back later that night to sweep that up.

"No, nobody," Shop said.

"Where were you?"

"Over there," Shop said and pointed to the corner of a parking lot. "Working. It was all just getting going. Where were you?"

Jimmy didn't answer that question. He looked from the end of the story in front of him back over his shoulder to the beginning, at least this last chapter of Lucy's story. She had come on a straight shot down the Embarcadero. There was a curve in the wide boulevard but not enough to make her slow. It wouldn't be hard to get up to speed. Pedal down, go. It's the long skinny one on the right. You don't want to be going too slow, embarrass yourself.

"Was she thrown out?"

Machine Shop just nodded. Jimmy remembered the scene in front of the store down in Paso Robles, how she hadn't put on her seat belt.

It was rocking Jimmy, standing there. Everybody knows how they'd kill themselves, if it came to that. What sad, sorry method they'd pick from the list. This right here was the way Jimmy had thought of, from the time he was a kid. And just about every time he came up on a freeway overpass abutment. Speed meets an unmovable object.

"It was a sweet little car," he said. "Too bad."

Shop didn't have anything to say to that. He wasn't into cars, not the way Jimmy was, not the way Los Angelenos were. (Who was?) Now wasn't the time to bring that up, that old north/south row.

"She didn't suffer," Shop said. One of those things you say.

Jimmy scanned the flat face of the pier building. Pour-and-fill concrete. Probably three feet thick, given its age. Barely a scratch.

You could throw any number of little sad girls at it and not make a dent.

"Let's get to that morgue," Jimmy said.

Turned out she hit face-first. But there was that baby-blue dress, the one she'd been wearing the first time he saw her, in the café in Saugus, the dress that made him think of Mary. There wasn't much blue left, stained as it was. He wondered what her purpose was, putting it on again, for her last scene, for the end. Or maybe she hadn't had a purpose. Maybe he was the only one who saw purpose everywhere. Seeing the dress again made his skin crawl.

"Maybe you can start looking for her brother," Jimmy said to Machine Shop as the coroner's assistant drew the sheet back over Lucy, like a magician trying again when the trick didn't work. "Go by the apartment first, but he hasn't been there for a couple of days, as far as I could see. Maybe he doesn't even know what happened to her. I don't know if he was close by or what. I hope not. I don't know *who* was there."

"What are you going to do?" Machine Shop said.

Jimmy turned away. "Try to get this smell out of my clothes," he said.

The coroner's assistant said, "There's no paperwork yet. You want a prep?" His name was Hugh. A Sailor.

"What do you mean?"

"Any family?"

"I don't know," Jimmy said.

"Normally, when we get the word from the family, if they're out of town, we just bag 'em for chilled shipping."

"I don't know," Jimmy said again. It was getting to be the thing he thought and said more than anything else.

"Because I could do a prep," Hugh said. "On my own. In case there's any viewing or anything. Here. I mean, this isn't a funeral home, but—"

"Sure," Jimmy said. "Why not? Make her look good. Do what you can."

He was thinking of Angel.

. . .

THEY call it *nightside*. The second shift at the newspaper. The business offices are closed, but the guts of the paper are churning. It's the time of day when it all looks most like you'd expect a newspaper shop to look. Maybe no chain-smoking, green-shade-wearing editors anymore, shouting "Get me rewrite!" to the copy boy, not even any clattering typewriters these days, but busy, purposeful, noisy, even dramatic. That was nightside at the *Chronicle*. There was work to do. In the morning there would be San Franciscans waiting to be pulled back into their communal lives by the slap of the paper on the driveway, on the doorstep, on the plush green cut pile carpet of the Mark Hopkins.

Like the coroner's office, the *Chron* by night was surprisingly wide open as far as security went. It wasn't midnight yet. Maybe the bomb-throwers came around later. Jimmy parked the Porsche on the street, on Mission Street, and came in one of the workers' entrances. The first floor was where the presses were, where the pressmen wore square hats folded out of newsprint, at least the old-timers, what was left of them. Jimmy came in as if he belonged there, and nobody stopped him.

Duncan Groner wasn't in the city room. They said he was in the library, what they used to call the morgue. (Back at the coroner's, did they call it the library now?) Once Jimmy had gotten up to editorial, he had run into a few questions. He talked his line, spoke Groner's name. He got an escort, a kid. Good thing, because the library was in the windowless bowels of the place. He never would have found it on his own. There were big leather couches. Groner was asleep on one, flat on his back, his hands over his sternum, fingers laced. He looked like he was positioned to go down the chute at a water park. Only he was snoring. The kind of snoring that comes with exclamation marks at the end of each declining sentence. One terminating snort was loud enough to wake him. His eyes popped full open.

"How long have you been there?"

"Just walked in," Jimmy said.

"I've been *sleeping* lately," Groner said, sitting up. "Odd."

Jimmy didn't say anything.

"Have *you*?" Groner said.

"As a matter of fact, yes."

"And *wanting to* other times when I'm unable."

"It must be spring," Jimmy said.

"That's it," Groner said. "Spring." He extracted his flask from his trouser pocket and popped the cap and took a boy-oh-howdy. "Spring in September."

"I don't get any blue from you," Jimmy said, looking down on him on the couch. "Same with a lot of the Sailors here. Some do, some don't."

"I probably extinguished it," Groner said and raised his bottle to finish the thought.

"A clean-cut kid down on the waterfront working at a crab stand . . . A pair of thug boys I saw beating another Sailor, my first night in town . . ."

"I've always heard the azure edge was stronger down your way," Groner said. "More visible. Readable."

"I never heard that," Jimmy said.

"Funny, you don't look bluish," Groner said. Before his nap he had taken off his shoes, placed them side by side on the carpet next to the couch. He retrieved them, slipped them on. When he went to tie the laces, his fingers were uncooperative, a little shaky. You couldn't tell if it was age or alcohol.

He must have noticed being noticed. "'Sure, I'm a old gnawed bone now,'" he said in a rangy voice, "'but don't you boys think the spirit is gone. I'm all set to shoulder a pickax and shovel anytime somebody's willing to share expenses.' Now there's a movie. *The Treasure of the Sierra Madre.* Why don't you make them like that anymore down there in Lost Angeles?"

"I don't make movies."

"I meant the collective, editorial *you*."

"So why are all these people killing themselves?" Jimmy said. He was still standing over the other.

Groner leaned back on the couch. "If you ask me, a better question is why not?"

Jimmy waited him out.

"I guess the ten of them this morning prompted this," Groner said.

Ten?

"And then there was another one tonight," Groner finished. "But the overnight ones were the headline. It's a helluva story, I have to admit. Dayside got it, unfortunately."

"The one tonight was the girl I told you about," Jimmy said.

Groner heard that and knocked off some of the "colorful character" show.

"The girl I was supposed to be watching out for."

"We didn't have a name for her."

"Lucy," Jimmy said. "Her name was Lucille. I didn't know her last name."

"Hers was one of the better ones, actually," Groner said. "Very public." In the next breath, he said, "I was considerably less . . . *entertaining* myself."

You never asked a Sailor how they'd died. You waited for them to say it, if you cared to know one way or another. Jimmy didn't usually care. He had found out early that it never really added much to his understanding of another Sailor man or woman, so he never asked. Some people needed to tell you. If they decided to tell you, you listened. Or at least stood there and let them empty the bucket.

"A bullet to the brain, which I thought at the time was the source of my gloom," Groner said. "Small caliber. A little chrome-plated Colt .25 automatic. I thought I was minimizing the mess. I had no surviving family, so I guess my concern was for the sensibilities of what we now call 'the first responders.' I didn't know then how quickly they become dulled to the offal."

"What year?" Jimmy said, surprising himself.

"Nineteen twenty-two," Groner said. "So I didn't even have the excuse of the crash, Black Friday. It was a Black *Tuesday*, actually. I was fifty-one."

"What are the overall suicide numbers now? How many total?"

"Aha, you're looking for a reason! For your Lucy's act of negation."

"Is there anything that ties them together?"

"United only in death . . . Twenty-eight Romeos and nineteen Juliets. Which is unusual, the ratio, the high number of women. Usually the men far outpace the women. As whites do blacks. Hispanics are moving up on the outside rail. Asian women, almost never. Asian men, after the age of sixty. Before sixty, they lag behind almost everyone, hari-kari, seppuku in popular entertainment aside. They're spread all over the city, which is something of a surprise."

"What about suicide contagion?" Jimmy asked.

Duncan Groner wasn't the sort to raise an eyebrow in surprise, but *something* registered on his face. And it took him a beat before he spoke, as if things had to be aligned in his head. Or realigned.

"You *are* engaged in the subject," he said.

"Well?"

"Even as we speak, I'm sure great committees are meeting, with the wringing of Great Hands," Groner said. And here he paused with intent. "A number of the suicides now appear to be in response to the earlier ones, to the publicity. In response to, as you say, 'the contagion,' a wonderfully melodramatic phrase."

Suicide contagion wasn't the result of some recent research on Jimmy's part. He'd run into it before.

"Copycats."

"Not exactly," Groner said. "More like, *Now I see that life is maybe not so sacrosanct after all.* With people hurling it at the fronts of buildings and such." He stood and put a hand on Jimmy's shoulder and said, "Something we in the brotherhood have known for some time."

Jimmy looked at the bony, skeletal hand on his shoulder.

"I'm off work," Groner said. "Rested and refreshed. Let's go pretend it's happy hour. I know a place where Sailors drink free. And freely."

CHAPTER SEVENTEEN

The people of San Francisco didn't *look* like they all wanted to die. Of course it was morning and, if the sun wasn't exactly shining, it was up there somewhere on the far side of the "marine layer." Jimmy was walking. Marina Green. They didn't *look* suicidal. They didn't look like the creeping cloud of death had o'ertaken them. The people of San Francisco looked like they wanted to play tennis, at least the ones standing at the back of the open hatch of the Porsche Cayenne all in white, in the parking lot of the private waterfront tennis club. They looked like they were thinking ahead to dinner, the ones coming out of the Safeway with a bag of groceries in each arm, a stick of French bread sticking out of one, just like in the movies. They looked like they wanted to go to work, the ones going past him in their cars all fresh and clean in their laundered starched shirts, in their ties, with their suit jackets folded lengthwise at the collar, like a butterfly, and laid over the back of the empty passenger seats beside them.

Die? They looked like they wanted to jog in matching outfits, earbuds in their ears. Then meet for brunch. They looked like they'd just had their teeth bleached and wanted everybody to see 'em. They looked like they wanted to sail the bay in forty-footers, loop around Alcatraz, out and back under the Golden Gate, the kids up front with their legs over the side. They looked like death was the furthest thing from their minds.

An old familiar feeling came over Jimmy, that *I'm here all alone* feeling. He had his own kind of hope, but he didn't have it this morning.

When he made it back to where he'd parked the car there was a white flyer tucked under the wiper, white with a rainbow. A free concert on the Panhandle in Golden Gate Park. Three or four bands, food, holistic healers . . . Just like the last thirty-some years hadn't happened. Over the rainbow, it said: Celebrate Life!

OK!

Midmorning. The Haight was just coming alive. The sun had broken through. Down at the corner on Central, down the hill from Lucy's, the white-haired, ponytailed man who lived over the wine store with his black-tongued dog was out on the side of his place with a hose, watering a color-coordinated square of flowers around the base of a sapling staked out in the tilted sidewalk. The chow sat on the stoop in another of his old-man poses.

The ponytailed man made a point of not looking up when Jimmy parked the Porsche against the curb halfway up the hill, halfway between the corner and the Victorian apartment.

The nonlook made Jimmy go up to him. Or, rather, down.

"How's it going?"

"Good morning," the man said. He kept watering, kept his eyes on the stream as if he had to watch it or it would all go wrong.

"The woman who was staying on the top floor, up at the corner . . ." Jimmy began. The man nodded, nodded in a way that said he knew what Jimmy was going to say next.

"So you know she's dead?"

The man nodded again. Jimmy got the idea somehow that this one had known more death than most, maybe even more suicides. But he still watered flowers.

"I was looking for the boy," Jimmy said.

The man shook his head.

"Her brother."

Nothing.

"You haven't seen him?"

The man shook his head again.

Jimmy decided to see if he could blow things wide open. "I'm an investigator. From L.A. I followed her here."

At least now the man looked at him.

"I was supposed to keep her safe, keep an eye on her, anyway."

"Nothing you could do," the other said.

Jimmy saw him look up the street. Machine Shop was standing on the corner next to the apartment, on the corner across from the Catholic Home.

Jimmy thanked the man with a wave. The man said *No problem* with a lift of his head. The rain from the garden hose kept falling on the petunias, which by now must have been screaming for help.

Jimmy climbed back up to the corner. "You got leaves in your hair," Jimmy said to Machine Shop.

"I slept up there, in the park," Shop said. Then he heard what he'd said. *Slept.* "I've been sleeping lately. Funny."

"Why up there? You got a place, right?"

"I thought the kid might have gone up into the park," Shop said. "You know, when you can't stand to be around the other person's stuff . . ."

Jimmy knew.

"Actually, I used to live up in here."

"In Buena Vista Park?"

"Sometimes," Shop said. "First Days. First Month."

Maybe Machine Shop was about to tell the rest of his story, after the part about the plug-in radio landing in his bathtub.

But Shop stopped short. "So what are we going to do?"

Jimmy looked up at the apartment. "You sure he's not up there?"

"I pushed the button. I heard it ringing. I tried last night, this morning. There was one light burning all night, in the hallway. He's not up there."

"Well then, let's break in," Jimmy said.

There was a way around the back of the apartment building, up a little alleyway where they stored the garbage cans, behind a white latticework shield. They really *were* fixing up the Haight. Even the alleys looked healthy.

"How many times you done this?" Jimmy said, when they were standing in the middle of the living room.

"I've done it. Seeing what's in the icebox, that's what creeps me out," Shop said. "Or a half an apple, on the table."

"Like the people at Pompeii," Jimmy said.

"Pompeii. I used to put that shit on my hair," Shop said, which was another way of saying, *Can we talk about something else?* He walked off toward the bedroom.

There were two toothbrushes in a Coke glass on the back of the white old-style pedestal porcelain sink. Hygiene, right up to the end. For Lucy, anyway. The boy had left his behind, wherever he'd gone. Jimmy had to find him. He had a special worry for the people left behind. The faucet was dripping, slow, three seconds apart. With the kind of sound that yanks you out of bed at midnight, that a Sailor can hear when nobody else does, day or night, anywhere. Anything like a clock.

Jimmy tightened it down. And then stood there until the last drop formed and fell.

"The Wind Cries Mary," Shop said behind him.

Jimmy felt like he'd been stuck in the chest.

"What? What did you say?"

Machine Shop held up a square bar coaster. And then, in the other hand, five more, all the same. "Your boy's been hanging at The Wind Cries Mary, a guitar joint over in the Fillmore. He had these all laid out on a little table beside his bed."

The Wind Cries Mary. Doesn't it though.

IT said "Open @ Eight" on the door of the club, but ten was probably more likely. It was painted purple, a box that had expanded into the windowless box beside it. An expressionistic suggestion of a Fender Stratocaster stretched in broken neon across the face of it, like a poor man's Hard Rock Café. A marquee spelled out the name of the guitar slinger of the moment, if the moment was ten years ago. Or twenty. One-night stands. A different player for the next three nights. Maybe the place looked better at night.

Jimmy parked at the curb out front, and he and Shop got out. They split up to circle the club and check out the alleyways. They met up again in back. Nothing, though there were a couple of street people living around the trash bins.

"I don't like to think about him, just being out there somewhere," Shop said. "It's not good."

They were about to get back into the Porsche.

"Wait a minute," Jimmy said.

He had seen a face, a part of a face. A young face, in the window of a liquor store across the street and down a couple of numbers.

A kid in a hat.

Jimmy crossed between a speeding bus and lagging truck and made it into the liquor store in time to see the form of the kid duck into a hallway in back, between the coolers. (He was wearing a *knit* hat.) The boy went through a door and slammed it behind him but it banged back open, and Jimmy went after him.

"Hey!" a hard voice said behind him. "What the—"

The kid had run into a storage room. There was another door out, on the back. The room was stacked to the ceiling with cases of booze. The gaps between the towers were more the kid's size than Jimmy's size, and the boy threaded the needle, ten feet ahead of his pursuer, and got his hand on the knob of what looked like an exit.

"It's all right," Jimmy said. "Wait."

The exit door opened. Light blew in. Jimmy found his own way through the boxes and ran outside.

He caught the kid in the paved space behind the store.

It was somebody else's little brother.

"*What?*" the boy said, that way only fifteen-year-olds can. "What?"

"Sorry," Jimmy said to the kid.

He didn't know what to say to the clerk with the shotgun standing in the doorway, the gun held down low and braced against his hip like he knew what it was.

When they all settled down, Jimmy apologized, said he was looking for his brother.

"You forgot what your brother looks like?" the clerk said.

CHAPTER EIGHTEEN

Sailors never flew, unless drugged and bound and gagged, so Angel came north on the train. The Coast Starlight. Two of his guys had dropped him off at Union Station in downtown L.A. Then it was across through the San Fernando Valley, coming out at Oxnard, then up the coastline on into the Central Valley, sunset about Salinas, in the dining car if you were in the mood, then rolling miles of dark fields, just enough time to think of all the things you should have done differently since ninth grade. The Starlight left SoCal midmorning and made it into Oakland after nine.

When Jimmy drove up out in front of the station, Angel was standing there. The train had gotten in early.

Then they were crossing the Bay Bridge back toward the City.

"How did she get in touch with you?" Jimmy said. It was almost the first thing he said to Angel.

"What do you mean?"

"How did you know she was in trouble?"

"Lucy never got in touch with me," Angel said. "A friend of hers come to me."

"And said what?" Jimmy said.

Jimmy's tone had some accusation in it, but Angel didn't let himself react to it. He knew what it was, what was behind it. Guilt. Jimmy's anger at himself. Angel cut people a lot of slack.

"It was one of Lucille's girlfriends, a girl I didn't really know but who knew about me," Angel said.

"Knew what about you?"

Jimmy had two hands gripping the wheel. He noticed them, his hands, as the Porsche rolled under another pole light on the bridge, as the orange light flared in the cockpit and he got a shot of the taut skin across his knuckles.

"I just meant—" Jimmy started.

"I *loved* her," Angel said, cool and calm. "But where's that gonna go? She was young. I'm old and a Sailor on top of that. Or, I'm a Sailor and old on top of *that*. You know how that works." The last was as much a rebuke of Jimmy (and his own past, his own history with women) as Angel would offer in this story. "So I never told her right to her face. I was 'her friend,' helping her out when I could, talking to her when some guy did her wrong one way or another. This girl, Mariel, she knew that, the last part, that I cared about Lucy."

Jimmy stared at the backs of his hands, willing some of the tenseness out of them. He stared until one relented and let itself drop off the wheel onto the leather-wrapped shifter knob.

"I even introduced her to the last guy," Angel said. "Guy I stripped and cleaned the Skylark for."

"So what happened, after the other girl came to you?" Jimmy asked. "I'm just trying to start at the beginning."

"I know what you're trying to do," Angel said. He reached to the floor between his knees for his leather gym bag. He unzipped it and took out a pint of Courvoisier. Jimmy had smelled the sweet stink on Angel when he'd embraced him on the concrete in the front of the station in Oakland. Angel never drank at home. Too many of the people around him, the boys and men he was trying to help, had drink and drug problems. Things were confused enough for them. He never offered the bottle to Jimmy. Angel unscrewed the cap and took a sip. "You're trying to start at the beginning. You're trying to *find* the beginning." He had a little edge to his voice. He took a second hit.

"I'm sorry," Jimmy said. It had a kind of all-purpose quality to it.

They rode in silence for half a minute, crossed Yerba Buena Island in the middle of the two halves of the bridge. It was like a fist of rock in the middle of the Bay.

When they went through the tunnel, there were no cars close around them in the lanes going into San Francisco. The Porsche engine sounded a good rumble.

"Love that tuned exhaust," Angel said. "L.A. Symphonic." He screwed the metal cap back on the cognac and dropped it into his bag.

"*Lil' Bitch,*" Jimmy said. It was what Angel had named the car when it had been reborn in his shop back in L.A. years ago. James Dean's Porsche 550 Spyder was named *Lil' Bastard*. Jimmy and Angel never said the name to anybody else.

Out the tunnel, off to the right across the slate water, was Alcatraz. And, dark at its side, Angel Island.

"There's your island," Jimmy said.

"Yeah, I wonder if they'd let me camp out," Angel said.

"I got a room for you," Jimmy said.

"So after I got the call from Mariel," Angel said, "I went all crazy-like and drove over there, right then, that night. I took this old piece of shit car of my neighbor's so Lucy wouldn't look out the window and know it was me. I parked up the hill a little bit, but I could see everything. She was in her front room. She has this house." He paused. Jimmy knew Angel was adjusting the tenses in his head. *Has* to *had*. Or trying to.

"It's all right," Jimmy said. "I don't need to know any more."

"She was sitting right in the front window, where I could see her, like a picture in a frame," Angel said. "Like she was waiting for me.

But, of course, she was waiting for this guy. To come back. Or just, I don't know, waiting for things to get better again for her."

"Yeah, I saw that look," Jimmy said.

"She just sat there."

"So when was that?"

"The night before she left. To come up here. Last week. The Sky-lark was parked out front of her house, and I was on the other side of the street. She shouldn't have left it out like that, where people could see it."

"You talk to the boyfriend?" Jimmy said.

"The dead don't talk," Angel said. Then he said, the way he always did, one of his jokes, "Oh, yeah, I forgot, sometimes they do."

"He was a gangbanger?"

"Yeah. But he was just out with his sister, down in San Diego, leaving SeaWorld, in the parking lot, when they hit him. Friend of mine down in Diego said it was another gang."

"When was that?"

"I don't know, sometime. A week before she left to come up here."

"She was waiting for him to come back to her. But he was already dead, and she knew it."

"Well, you know how that is, don't you? Holding out hope."

"You didn't go to him before? To find out what the problem was between them, what broke them up?"

"Never thought of it. I guess, inside, I was glad about it. That they broke up." Angel looked at Jimmy. "So I feel it, too," he said. "Responsible. Guilty. Like I could have done something. Should have." He looked out at the lights of the City to the right flashing through the bars of the railing, the curve of the waterfront, the Embarcadero. "And that don't make any more sense than *you* feeling the same thing."

Jimmy wondered if Angel knew he was looking at where it had happened.

"What about her brother?" Angel said.

"He's out there somewhere. I don't know where."

"I didn't know she had a brother, until you told me," Angel said. "She never talked about him."

Jimmy told him about The Wind Cries Mary.

"So we find him," Angel said. "Bring him in, get him home."

Jimmy had gotten Angel a room next door to his at the Mark.

"I'd rather sleep in a ten-dollar-a-night place, down around Market," Angel said, standing in the middle of the room with Jimmy and a bellhop.

"You gotta get out more, bud," Jimmy said. "The ten-dollar-a-night places are forty now."

"Sixty, I believe, sir," the bellman said.

"I was going to say *five*," Angel said and tossed his leather bag on the turned-down bed. And Jimmy tipped the boy.

By then it was eleven thirty. They came downstairs again. They'd left the Porsche in front of the hotel.

"I guess you can't do *that* down in the Tenderloin," Angel said.

They went across town to The Wind Cries Mary. It was about all they had to run with when it came to finding Les Paul. (Finding him and then getting out of San Francisco, while they still could?) He wasn't there. They sat through the second half of a set by a doodling jazz player who played too many notes. For Jimmy's ear, anyway. There were three or four *other* Les Pauls there. They were hanging around the front when Jimmy and Angel pulled up, kids fifteen or sixteen, a couple of them with guitars in cases. And it was a school night, too. The doorman seemed to have been hired for the flat look on his face and the size of his biceps, especially when his arms were folded across his chest. But at least one kid had made it in. He stood in the back next to the door in and out of the kitchen. The mesmerized look on the boy's face made Jimmy think maybe he was missing something when it came to the jazzbo on-stage with the fat hollow body. But none of the boys was *their* Les Paul.

The star of the night came on, a black player with a scarred Strat that looked like it had already been on the road ten years by the time Hendrix was joining the army. And the player was older than his guitar. Jimmy wondered what the man looked like in daylight, out front under the stage light. Maybe he never saw daylight. He was out there with just a bass player and a drummer, both white. The bass player was in his twenties, the drummer a chewed-up-and-spat-out rocker with dyed black hair, maybe a wig. The band played almost nothing, just stood back, literally, figuratively, while the man went where he went. For most of an hour, an idiot in the crowd called out the name of a song, *the* song, the one the Rolling Stones had "discovered" and covered and hit with. And everybody else before the Stones and after. When the player finally got to it, the idiot shouted, *"Hoo!"* for a half minute until Jimmy threw a wadded napkin at the back of his head and told him to shut up.

The guitar player managed an impossible thing: he somehow went back to the original ache, the initiating heartbreak behind the song, however many years ago it was. His guitar had a baby picture laminated onto the front of it. The mother of his new baby couldn't even have been born when the *other* she broke his heart, but the way he played and sang, the wound sounded fresh, still sore to the touch.

"Let's go," Jimmy said when the song was done.

He had told Angel about Les Paul and about The Wind Cries Mary, but she was the only Mary Jimmy told Angel about that night.

CHAPTER NINETEEN

The night Lucy had died and Jimmy had ended up in the library at the *Chron* with Duncan Groner, they'd talked Sailors, suicides, and San Francisco.

But Jimmy hadn't left it at that. At the end, as they were walking out to go get that drink, Jimmy spoke her name, almost as if it was just an afterthought.

Mary Hesse.

Or rather, he spoke *his* name, Dr. Marc Hesse.

There was a beat. "Don't personally know him," Groner said.

He plopped down into an armless roll-around chair and rolled over to one of the terminals. His two index fingers went to work, typing hunt-and-peck at a furious speed, more peck than hunt. He hit *Enter* with his elbow, to be funny.

"There used to be black steel file cabinets in here, wall to wall, floor to ceiling," he said. "Mother of God, I miss them. Now you put in a name and you end up with pictures of some gentleman servicing his wife in Quito, Ecuador."

The screen filled up in front of him. Text and pictures. But fully clothed.

"Cardiologist," Groner said first. "Who is he to you?"

Now it was Jimmy's turn to hesitate, to shove aside all the words that were gathering around the truth. To come up with the right lie.

"Something I'm working on," was the one he settled on. It was true in its own way. He'd been working on the idea of Mary over all the years since they'd been together, trying to tame it in his head. Trying to get over it.

"I thought what you were working on was a sad little Mexican girl who came up here and killed herself," Groner said.

"It goes where it goes," Jimmy said. He was looking past Groner to the image of Hesse on the screen, a color shot of the doctor in another tuxedo at another charity event. Or maybe the same tuxedo. Jimmy couldn't help but see a cold, unpleasant look in the other's eye, in the shape of his face, in the reluctance of the muscles around his mouth to gentle into anything remotely like a real smile. That face said, *I can do anything I want to you.* To Jimmy, anyway.

"Cardiologists are cold bastards," Groner said, like he was inside Jimmy's head. Maybe the San Francisco Sailors had come up with some powers their brothers to the south had missed out on, like mind reading.

Another screen full of information replaced the first.

"Not much about his years back East," Groner said, reading. "Sketchy. A liberal arts college in central Florida, then Duke for med school. He's thirty-eight, one kid."

Jimmy held himself back from asking what he really wanted to know. About Mary. *Her* past. What she had been doing since their time together in L.A.

"He's on boards, professional and philanthropic, *loves* stray animals apparently, believes in neutering, plays tennis." The bony index fingers went to work again. "Oh, this is rich. He's a Mormon. So that means he has a year's worth of food and water in the basement of the nine-bedroom house in Hillsborough."

Jimmy waited.

"He has a house on Tiburon, too," Groner said, reading. "And probably a cabin up in Sebastopol, where he dances naked in a fern-ringed redwood glen with a secret assemblage of men at solstice."

Groner spun in the chair to look at Jimmy. "His wife is beautiful," he said after a long beat. Then he looked back at the screen.

"Mary," Groner said. "He doesn't deserve her. Maybe none of us do."

Jimmy took the reporter's obvious, immediate dislike of Marc Hesse as an act of friendship, though Groner couldn't know why Jimmy hated him.

"Any chance he's a Sailor?"

Groner shook his head and said, "I'd know."

And then they'd gone off into the night for that drink.

Hesse had offices downtown, in a building across from the TransAmerica Pyramid.

Midmorning, Jimmy was standing out front. Groner had called him at the Mark with the address. Hesse had just moved from previous digs. This new place wasn't even listed yet.

Jimmy knew enough about movies to know it was the building with the "florist's shop" on the ground floor where Dirty Harry had faced down somebody, said something sharp while the punk was left to stare into the holey end of the .44 magnum. It wasn't *Dirty Harry* itself or even *Magnum Force*. It wasn't "You have to ask yourself, do I feel lucky?" or "Go ahead, make my day." The movie was probably *Sudden Impact*, and the line wasn't good enough to get remembered, the way it was with sequels.

He should have been off with Angel, looking for Les Paul. He hadn't even knocked on Angel's door when he left the Mark.

Jimmy rode up in the elevator. He felt lucky.

He didn't know what his intentions were, what the plan was. What was he going to do, slap Hesse in the face with a glove? Challenge him to a duel? *Go ahead, make my midmorning.*

It never came to that. The doctor was in surgery.

The waiting room was empty. Everything was perfect. The magazines were unmussed, in neat stacks. Unread. Even the sports magazines. Even the swimsuit issue. Everything had a new smell to it. The receptionist was cute, didn't have a drop of blood on her. She was a little flirty, maybe bored with a long, slow morning. Or it could have been that everybody who came in was old and pale and short of breath. Jimmy's breath was just fine.

The art on the walls was original. Oils. One canvas pulled Jimmy closer. It was of a boat entering a harbor, a black-and-white sloop, a storm behind it like a giant with a puffed-out chest. The painting even had a name: *In Time*. It wasn't pretty, as pictures went. It went right up to the edge of pretty, stopped just short; *art* that way, not decoration or entertainment. Jimmy wondered why a doctor, a cardiologist, would choose it for the eyes of those waiting. *We found the blockage just in time? You're safe here?*

It made Jimmy want to eat a steak, drink a martini, *Celebrate Life!* with the new hippies in the Haight. What he remembered of it.

It made him want to hold Mary.

"Bye," the flirty receptionist said to his back.

A call to Groner on the run got him the name of the hospital where Hesse was. Under the hood of some poor bastard. Valve job.

Groner kept the info coming, a second call. He told Jimmy to look for a deep dark red, big-dog Mercedes, a CLS500.

"A color called Bordeaux Metallic."

"Sounds delicious," Jimmy said. "Fruity, but not casky, I hope. But how am I going to find out what row he's parked in?"

Jimmy was already at the hospital, in the corner of the lot. He was making a joke.

"Where are you?" Groner said.

Jimmy told him.

"Look straight ahead, on the right," Groner said. "Under the carport."

"Now you're starting to creep me out," Jimmy said.

"I can see through walls, across town, but only if the conditions are exactly right," Groner said. "A friend works there, in the ER. I just called her. Hesse's name is on a parking place."

"Your friend a Sailor?"

"Yes."

"So you're sure Hesse isn't a Sailor."

"I would say no," Groner said.

"Would you say any more?"

"I've never heard of him, never heard anybody speak of him," Groner said. "Remember, I've been here a very long time. And then there's the boy."

"Yeah," Jimmy said.

Sailors were sterile. Some cosmic safeguard. Or joke.

"Of course, the boy is six. Hesse could have fathered him Before."

"Yeah."

"But then why would they so resemble each other? You haven't seen the boy. I'm sitting here looking at a picture of him."

Of course Jimmy had seen him. The boy didn't look anything like Mary, but Jimmy wondered if he'd just thought that because he liked that idea, because it made the reality of the situation a little less painful for him. So the boy looked like his father.

"I have work to do," Groner said. "People to bury, mysteries to de-mystify. Good luck. With whatever it is you're doing." And he was gone.

Hesse didn't appear for two hours, two hours before he got into the bulbous new Mercedes and backed out of a reserved parking place. (His name wasn't on it.) The hospital was the medical center at UCSF. On Divisadero.

He came back toward downtown. He disappeared into the Sequoia Club on Hyde, the private club, pulled up in front, left the Mercedes with a valet. He stayed inside for a half hour and came out into the afternoon looking fresh, clean shirt, pressed suit. Came out under the SC's arched doorway, under the letters cut into the stone . . .

GREAT GEARS TURN

Hesse then drove west on Geary, through the Richmond District, out to Fourteenth Avenue, where he turned right, headed north. He stayed with it as Fourteenth turned into California 1 in a tunnel of tall old trees, a corridor of mystic greens and almost black browns that kept closing in tighter until it burst open into the Presidio, then onto the Golden Gate. Dr. Hesse was headed home.

Jimmy stayed right behind the Mercedes on the bridge until he realized how close he was following. It was borderline road rage. He eased off, let a BMW motorcycle and an Accord pulling a U-Haul trailer pass him and then tuck back in, so he had a wall between him and the Mercedes. A cool-down zone was another way to look at it.

Jimmy had a *What am I doing?* moment. He hadn't learned anything so far, nothing except that Marc Hesse was fairly young, fairly good-looking. Rich, clean. A member of society in good standing. Belonging to all the right clubs. Paying rent, fixing heart valves. Buying good art. Friendly when it came to the little people. He'd waved to a pair of nurses coming in as he was leaving the hospital. So what if they only tentatively lifted their hands, as if they didn't exactly recognize him? It was the thought that counted.

A wearer of Italian suits.

A brand-name shopper when it came to cars.

A neuterer of strays.

A *giver*. What else?

Oh yeah, not sterile.

Alive, not dead. Living a life with the one woman who had shown Jimmy what love could look like, when it finally came round to you.

Jimmy yanked the wheel right, took the exit for Sausalito. It was just about the last self-protective instinct he'd have for a good, long time.

CHAPTER TWENTY

You know you've got it bad when you start lying to your friends. About her. About you. About *it*. Or just leaving it unsaid, which is another way to lie. Jimmy was on the same bench as before in the little pocket park on the north end of Sausalito, when he had been tailing Lucy and Les Paul four or five days ago. But he wasn't thinking about them. He was looking, through the trees, past the red-and-white ferry boats, one coming in/one going out, past the sailboats in the marina, across the water to the knob of Tiburon. The tip of it was shaped like a turtle. Maybe that's what *tiburon* meant. There was a light chop on the water, a little wind. Sitting there, he was wondering why he hadn't told Angel straight out about seeing Mary. About the hole seeing her again had pulled him into. Angel knew more of the story of Jimmy and Mary than anybody, knew it from all angles. Start to finish, beginning to end.

Maybe he'd tell him now. Because Angel was walking across the grass toward him.

"He's here somewhere," Angel said from ten feet out. "We lost him. He came in on the boat."

Les Paul.

"What are *you* doing here?" Angel said.

"Just out riding around," Jimmy said.

"Come on, let's go find him."

Jimmy didn't move off the bench. Angel looked at him.

"*Maria, mi Maria, esta aqui,*" Jimmy said. *Mary, my Mary, is here.* He'd gone to Spanish without thinking about it, but it made sense. The Spanish Jimmy knew he learned from Angel, back in those L.A. days.

"Where?" Angel said.

"There. Tiburon." He lifted a finger to point at the arched back of land across the way.

"That's bad," Angel said.

"She's married. Has a little boy."

"You talked to her?"

Jimmy shook his head.

Now Machine Shop was walking toward them across the grass.

"That's bad," Angel said again. "Bad for you, bad for us."

"He's down here," Shop said. "I found him."

Jimmy got up.

Les was in a bar. And he had a beer in front of him.

"Doesn't anybody check IDs in this town?" Jimmy said. They were in the doorway. The bar was open in the front with French doors that slid aside, and open on the back to the water. Heavy, dark, carved curving wood, a stained glass skylight. It was about as Sausalito a bar as there could be. The boy was alone at a round table with his back to them, across the half-filled room. With his beer.

"Let's get him," Angel said.

"Wait," Jimmy said.

There was a drink next to Les's beer glass. A pretty pink cosmo in a martini glass. Down a sip.

"Did he have somebody with him before?" Jimmy said.

"Not when I saw him," Shop said. "He was just sitting there by himself, looking out at the water."

Jimmy saw her, saw *somebody*. Moving away. The restrooms were in the corner. *A flash of white.*

They waited a moment, to let her come back, but she never did.

"Come on," Jimmy said, and they started in.

The boy probably heard Jimmy's voice. He got some signal, maybe just instinct, and turned.

He didn't stop to think. He ran like hell, bolted away from the table so fast and rough it knocked over the beer glass. Ran like an underage teen in a bar.

They'd say later they'd forgotten how fast a teenage kid can be, how much go a boy has. He went out the back. For a second, Jimmy thought Les had jumped in the water, right into the Bay, but there were sailboats and houseboats moored all along the back sides of the bars and restaurants, and Les Paul leapt from one rocking deck to the next, broad-jumping, scissoring over rails and deck chairs like a middle school record holder. *Running for his life* is what you'd call it if you saw it.

He got away from the men. It was never even close.

Jimmy went back into the bar, straight into the ladies' room. It was empty.

Or at least there was nobody in a white dress.

OTHER people seemed to take comfort in the circularity of things, how things doubled back, repeated, came round again, but Jimmy hated it, had always hated it, that fact of physics or metaphysics or the cosmos or whatever it was. He wanted something new to happen, something unprecedented, instead of the same old thing recycling itself. And the same people.

At least that's what he told himself, sitting there behind the wheel of the Porsche in the parking lot of the waterfront park out on Tiburon. *Again.*

What he told himself was that he was there because it was where he'd seen the woman in the white dress. But he knew why he was really there.

He had his own kind of hope. That afternoon, scanning the park, he had too much of it.

The cosmos made him wait two hours.

Mary walked across the grass from the parking lot. Today she and the boy had ridden their bikes over, had come in from the south on a bike path, the boy on a terminally cute scaled-down ten-speed, probably titanium, probably a thousand bucks' worth. The bikes were just left in a rack. Not even locked. Mary walked with a tall coffee in her hand, a stainless steel Thermos cup. The boy had a net sack with his soccer gear thrown over his shoulder. It was a good life. This is what stay-at-home mom meant for the wife and son of a San Francisco cardiologist.

Mary spread out a blanket, while the boy kicked a ball around. She looked over at the car, the Porsche. The top was up. With the sun sliding down in back of the water behind her, there had to be glare on the windshield. Jimmy knew she couldn't see in, couldn't see him. So why did she keep looking over? Did she remember the car? Why did she just stare, stare off at nothing, as if someone was reading an old, familiar story to her?

The soccer ball rolled over to the blanket, to pull her back from wherever she'd gone, from whatever had taken her away. She threw it back to the kid.

Jimmy realized he'd made a point of *not* learning the boy's name. That night in the newspaper library Groner could have dug it up, on the registry of whatever pricey preschool the boy had gone to, the team list of his little soccer crew, his bike registration. Groner knew it now, had to.

"What's his name?" Easy question.

The boy was kicking the ball and going after it, getting in front of it, playing all of the game in his head. Jimmy remembered the way he used to do the same thing with baseball when he was seven or eight, remembered how he'd throw the ball up and hit it and run the bases, even if they were just his mother's magazines laid out in the backyard, run until he'd switch sides and go after the ball in the outfield, throw it into the air again and catch it and throw it home.

He let his mind slip out of gear, let himself pretend that he'd just pulled up, that she was expecting him, that this was one of those moments where you stop yourself. *Stop and smell the roses.* Where you hold back a second and look at the other out there on the grass, unguarded, waiting for you, and you think, *She loves me.* Before she sees you and puts on whatever face that calls for.

Mary was staring at the car again.

He waited until she looked away again and then started the engine and backed up and drove away.

But not far enough.

Today was the day when he was going to meet Mary face-to-face, and he knew it. He just didn't know where.

He drove into the village of Tiburon, the little loop of shops and restaurants at the end of the road that went out to the top of the peninsula, by Belvedere, out at the water. He parked in plain sight, lending a hand to Fate. He didn't put any money in the parking meter, whatever that meant.

He drank a beer, out on the deck behind a place. There were hardly any men anywhere, just pretty women, most of them young. Married. In tennis clothes, in white jeans. Drinking white wine. There was an imposing view, the ferry docks, the expanse of water, Alcatraz and Angel Island, the cityscape behind, all with an impossible depth of field.

He'd ditched Angel and Machine Shop back in Sausalito. He thought of all the things he *should* be doing. He thought of the weight of what he knew was coming next.

But not enough.

"Are you ready for another?" a voice said.

The waitress looked like one of the Tiburon wives, minus the BMW X-5 and the tennis togs and the portfolio. And the cardiologist.

"I don't know," Jimmy answered honestly. His glass was still half full. Or was it half empty?

He drained it before the next wave of sarcasm rolled in.

. . .

"LET go, let God," Angel was always saying.

Surrender to the Force, Luke.

"Any port in a storm," Jimmy said aloud as he walked up the street in the village toward the Porsche, with the second beer in him, with the edge off. Everything was a little soft-focus.

Give up, that'll make it happen. Things happen when you stop trying to make them happen.

Just do it.

"So that's what I want," Jimmy said to himself, stepped from word to word with a rhythm that matched his footfalls on the sidewalk. *"Another man's wife. A little boy's mother. Amen."*

"Jimmy," Mary said.

She was sitting on the steps in front of a shop right beside the nose of the Porsche, the Porsche with the parking ticket flapping in the breeze. The shop was closed. It was a place that sold pillows, all of them shades of yellow, from what you could see in the window. It had a cute name.

She stood.

He meant to be prepared with an opening line. He knew he'd remember it, whatever he said, whether she did or not. He knew he'd probably regret it, whatever it was.

She was more self-assured. Or maybe it was that it was her town.

"You always wanted us to come to San Francisco," she said. "I never knew why."

"And we never did," he said.

Are you ready for another?

"It's a kinder place than L.A.," Jimmy said. "Maybe that was it. I knew you'd like it. But, you know, back then I thought and did a lot of things for no reason at all."

She sat back down on the steps, straightening the skirt of her dress, pulling it tight across her backside just as she sat. All the women were wearing skirts and dresses. Maybe it was just San Francisco. Or they were dressed the way he liked because it was his fantasy. In her skirt, on the blanket in the park, Mary had looked like Lucy. Or like the girl in foreground in the Wyeth painting, *Christina's World*, with her legs stretched out to the side. Mary used to like that painting, had a print of it on her wall, the one everyone liked, but that didn't diminish it for her. Jimmy wondered if she remembered how they used to talk about whether she was crippled or not.

He sat beside her. She'd left him space. They were tucked away, with a low hedge on either side of them. *Out of view,* he thought.

"You still have your car," she said.

"You saw me, in the park," Jimmy said.

"Yeah. I mean, I didn't know it was you."

"You always did like the car more than me."

"That's not true," she said. It made him remember something about her, something she did, turning back a smart-ass answer with directness. By being straight.

She was still looking at the car in front of them and not at him. There wasn't much traffic, but she turned her face aside or looked down whenever a car did pass. She didn't want to be seen. She couldn't. She wasn't going to sit there forever, he knew that. He knew she was thinking of something besides him.

"You saw my little boy," she said.

Don't say his name, Jimmy thought.

She didn't.

He realized that she'd taken the boy home before she came looking for him. She'd changed her shoes, left her bicycle somewhere. Was her car close by? Had she walked back into the village? Did she have a nanny? Had she taken the boy somewhere else?

He was looking at the side of her face. This close, he could see how changed she was. She had aged a little but not much, a little around the eyes. But she had changed in other ways. He wondered if he would have recognized her right away if he'd seen her up close first, instead of across the park. Maybe she'd had some plastic surgery done. She was married to a doctor, after all.

"You look good," he said.

She let her hand touch his, the edge of it. It was as much as he'd get, but it was *her* touch, unchanged. It was just enough to mess him up good.

A clot of clouds went over the sun. She stood, brushed off the back of her skirt, as if she'd been sitting in a pile of leaves.

She was about to say something when Jimmy said, "It's still so strong."

It was the only line he spoke all afternoon that he didn't rethink later, that was naked and true.

Even if it didn't stop her from walking away.

CHAPTER TWENTY-ONE

Turn the page, things change.

Since the day of the ten suicides, spread all over the city, a dark meanness had rolled into town, a jittery *Now what?* that everyone felt. Ten plus Lucy. They were back down on the waterfront, Jimmy and Angel, coming around the Embarcadero in the Porsche. If he was home in L.A., Jimmy would know how to describe it, that dark sense hanging over everything. And how to duck it. In Los Angeles it would manifest itself in freeway gunplay, "cutoff shootings," boys on overpasses blowing out windshields with fist-size nuts stolen from job sites. It'd be the dry winds they called Santa Anas, ushering in "homicide summer," "earthquake weather," baseball bat attacks at kids' games in the parks. It'd be fistfights at gas stations, gang dustups at Magic Mountain.

Here it had its own style. You felt it in the waves of nervous energy that came off the knots of men standing around the piers. Each cluster of Sailors, out here almost all of them men, would turn and look at the

Porsche as it rolled past. Put a fire in a barrel in the middle of them and it'd look like the old newsreels of the Depression. Waiting for something to happen, for whatever was next, *wanting* it, even if everybody knew it would probably be worse.

"Man, look at this," Jimmy said.

"It's been getting strange back home, too," Angel said. "Everybody's got the jitterbugs."

Jimmy hadn't thought about L.A. in awhile, not the L.A. of the present. And he'd stopped wanting to run there. He wanted to be here now.

"Who was the last one Lucy talked to?" Angel said. They were driving through a corridor of waterfront Sailors now, waiting for them to part like herd animals on a Land Rover safari. The men opened a path. They seemed to be a polite lot, for beasts. Almost intentional. It was after two in the morning. Another hour or two, they'd have the world to themselves.

"Did you try to find out?" Angel pressed when Jimmy didn't say anything.

"No."

"When was the last time you saw her?"

Jimmy felt like he was in the dean of boys' office. Or a cop station.

Then he remembered. "Down here," he said. "The night of one of the suicides. A guy stepped in front of a streetcar."

"Did you ever talk to her, face-to-face?"

"No."

"Machine Shop said he talked to her, had a cup with her one night."

"I was across the street," Jimmy said defensively.

"He said she was a real talker," Angel said. "Baring her soul." He was quiet for a minute. "She was never that way with me, just said something when it needed to be said, not even then most of the time. She was real sweet."

What do you want me to say? Jimmy was thinking.

The Sailors were packed in tight around the car now. And not so fast to move out of the way. Angel saw where they were. Pier 35, where Lucy had died.

"I don't need to *see* it," Angel said.

"Shop called, thought he saw Les Paul down here. With the woman in the white dress."

"She was with Lucy, the last time you saw her?"

"Yeah. And another woman. Short black hair."

Les Paul. Sexy Sadie. Polythene Pam. The Leonidas girls. Truth was, Jimmy was looking for everybody.

Anybody except Mary.

TURN the page, you got another day. Whether you wanted one or not. Duncan Groner had had his own way of bringing Jimmy back to the case, of pressing his fingers down on the fiery Braille again, of dragging him back across the bridge from Marin to San Francisco.

"Page A-6," Groner had said, a wake-up call at the hotel, though Jimmy had never turned toward the bed that night. "The *Chronicle*, All the News That's Fit for Fools."

It was a full page of faces. The dead. The suicides.

"Some friends of yours . . ." Groner said.

Jimmy opened the newspaper standing in the doorway to the suite, and there they were, all the suicides, in clean rows with their names underneath, way too much like a high school yearbook. He'd expected something else, the latest edition of *the present* maybe, not the past.

What he'd expected was something about Mary. Or her husband.

The accompanying copy was bylined. Duncan Groner apparently had become the go-to guy for self-murder. There wasn't much "story" to the layout, one long graf in which the reporter laid out the terms: San Francisco proper usually had eight to ten suicide deaths a month. (The Golden Gate had its own segregated stats, *two a month* since the plainclothes patrollers had been instated, "blending in" with the despairing.) Since the first of September, all told there'd been forty-eight suicides, *successful suicides* was the term, bringing to mind dozens more with *half*-slashed wrists, with only a *half* bottle of pills to be suctioned out in the ER, jumpers off one-story roofs, shooters firing starter's pistols at their temples. Groner ended the lead-in with a few sentences of behind-the-scenes stuff, the disclosure that the editors "vociferously debated" the "dangers" of "publicizing" the suicides (of telling the truth, in other words), for fear that the "suggestible" in San Francisco might think the unthinkable, and act on it, join the club. Even if the initiation ceremony was a tad severe.

Faces. Hairstyles, forced smiles. The retoucher's craft. Lives smoothed out, flattened onto cheap pulp paper, tamed in black and white, gussied up. There was the old lady, the ninety-year-old chorus girl. The young man with AIDS. The German tourist. All the pictures shaved off years, decades in some cases. Now the AIDS man from the hospice was outdoors, resurrected into a brighter yesterday, coastal cliffs behind him, his perfect thick hair wild in the wind up off the water, a white smile on his face that made you wish you could see the cutoff person at his shoulder, the man, Jimmy guessed, who'd gone through the drawer of pictures to pick this one. There were the Greek twins. There they *all* were.

"What exactly are we looking for?" Angel said.

"*New,*" Jimmy said. It was a vulgar term.

Some of the Sailors, the more dramatic ones, used the word *aboard* when they were talking about new Sailors: a new Sailor was "aboard." New meant "new meat."

"You don't think Lucy's down here, do you?" Angel said. For Angel, the whole thing had more than enough drama on its own, he didn't go seeking more in language.

Lucy *could* be down here, Lucy as a Sailor. A lot of them were suicides, *successful* suicides. The murdered were another contingent, especially among the darkest of the Sailors, the ones who liked the shadows. The rest had died in accidents. But a loose definition of the term. More than a few had been the ill "misdiagnosed" into this state. Before their time.

Everybody had their own unfinished business, even if none of them knew exactly what it was.

Jimmy had only glanced at her picture in the *Chron*, Lucy's picture. A portrait from a few years after high school. From Sears? Kmart? Old enough and fuzzy enough almost to be someone else. (He wondered where they'd gotten it. From family in Paso Robles?) He didn't look at it long because in the picture Lucy looked a little like Mary. Not the hair, but . . . Why hadn't he seen it before? (Or had he? He'd flashed on *something* in the café down in Saugus.) More likely, it was some trippy side effect brought on by the acid of his guilt. He was supposed to save Lucy, and Lucy *wasn't* saved.

"Did you see the pictures of all of them? In the paper?" Jimmy said. "They had a picture of Lucy."

Angel shook his head. "I got my own pictures of her."

The Sailors were blocking the way now. Jimmy thought about a tap on the horn. Maybe in San Francisco they wouldn't kill you for it.

Then he saw the Sailor right in front of him, across the hood. This one was very tall. He was black, but light-skinned. He had spotted skin, looked particularly African.

And he carried a staff, a wooden rod taller than he was.

Jimmy and Angel looked at each other.

"Let my people go," Angel said.

But this Moses wasn't there to part anything, not yet anyway. He just stared at Jimmy and Angel. The other Sailors seemed to press in closer, surround the car. Moses stayed where he was, in front of the hood, one of the Porsche's chrome sissy bar bumpers against his leg. Against his calf. That was how tall he was.

"I guess this is the valet parking," Jimmy said, and turned off the engine.

They both opened their doors at the same time, pushing back the men on the side, and got out.

There didn't seem to be any women Sailors down here. It was a rough-looking crowd.

"They're going to mess with the car," Angel said.

"Maybe not," Jimmy said. "Maybe they'll cut a couple of out-of-towners some slack."

"It's not going to be here when we get back," Angel said.

The man with the staff had started away. Jimmy and Angel set out after him, figuring that was the plan. Somebody's plan.

There were hundreds of them down there. Something about the gathering, the whole scene, felt ceremonial. The general agitation in the air, in the San Francisco night, seemed to have found a focal point.

But they were all silent. Like obedient spectators for a play.

"Maybe we should do this tomorrow," Angel said.

"This isn't something *we're* doing," Jimmy said. Now the San Francisco Sailors were moving the two outsiders along. Jimmy and Angel were just going with the flow. There wasn't any resisting, no use. It felt inevitable, whatever it was.

Jimmy lost sight of the tall African.

One of the grimmest-looking Sailors got right in Jimmy's face. "We fell away," he hissed at Jimmy. Or at least that's what Jimmy thought he said.

Jimmy tried to get past him. The man said his line again.

This time Jimmy heard it right. "We follow Wayne," the man was saying.

The others around him joined in. "We follow Wayne . . ."

"Good for you," Angel said. "I follow Jesus."

A brutish Sailor shoved him. Angel shoved back. "Step off."

"We serve the Russian!" one of the few women said defiantly.

"Look," Jimmy said.

Just in time. The tall black man with the staff was waiting next to a door in the front of one of the waterfront warehouses. Jimmy and Angel and their escorts had crossed two hundred yards of pavement. The Sailors had closed in behind them. Wherever the Porsche was, it was swallowed up.

The door on the front of the warehouse was closed.

Jimmy walked to it. He expected it to open. It didn't.

"Knock," Moses said.

Jimmy went along with the gag.

Even before the door opened, Jimmy and Angel heard it. Wailing, spacey guitar. Live. They'd found Les Paul.

He played real good.

CHAPTER TWENTY-TWO

Through the doorway, there was a corridor. There was a nobody dressed all in black. They followed him. There was nothing on the walls, nothing on the floor. After a few yards, another door, with a raised threshold, like a hatch, like the mouth of a trap. From here on, the walls seemed cold, slippery. Not that Jimmy or Angel were reaching out to touch them. Everything from the door on in was painted black. Or, if not black, some deep red.

The crying guitar got louder.

They stepped over another threshold and found themselves in a space three levels high, a single room a hundred feet from end to end. They still couldn't spot Les, but the sound had a location now, the far end of the big, hollow room. The chamber was lit by gaslights positioned along the side, flamboyant brass curves, feminine shapes, clear glass globes. And real flame, not some electric update. Now they could see that the walls were metal. Iron or steel. There didn't seem to be any windows, but there were drapes, red velvet, to match what furniture there was, preposterous curvy Victorian divans and claw-foot mahogany tables atop thick rugs, like the great rooms halfway down the coast at San Simeon or, farther down, in Hollywood, in Charles Foster Kane's Xanadu. Somebody had a flair for the dramatic.

The room was a great jam room. Some combination of the slick walls and the baffles created by the yards of pleated velvet made the guitar notes swoop around the room like a special-effects ghost. Like the ghost of Jimi himself, because what the boy was playing was soaring and free-form. A sound to match, to fill the plush void of the space.

"There," Angel said.

Lucy's baby brother was on a second-level landing, behind an iron railing, beside a lowboy Fender amp with a red-glowing jewel light on its face. He had his eyes open as he played but wasn't looking at anything, certainly not at them. Jimmy realized he had never gotten the kid's real name. The kid had on his black porkpie hat from that first day up in Paso Robles. He still looked fourteen, even if he sounded ninety-nine.

Then they weren't alone anymore.

It was Jeremy. Cape-wearing Jeremy. All-in-black Jeremy, who whispered in your ear and told you to jump.

He came in from offstage, stage right, walked with an ivory-headed cane, looking, in that setting, like a turn-of-the-century opium dealer who pimped on the side. But without the happy-go-lucky disposition.

But it turned out this wasn't *his* play, Jeremy's. He was just a supporting character. He greeted Jimmy, "met" Angel, which meant he saw him and nodded in his direction. Les reached the end of his jam, let the last of it sustain for twenty or thirty seconds, then killed it off with a last strike at the strings.

"Cool," Jeremy said.

The kid started sketching out something else, heading off elsewhere, a new set of chords and changes.

Everyone seemed to know what they were doing there, everyone except Jimmy and Angel.

Someone else was coming, footsteps on the hard floor. Was the floor metal, too?

"Whitehead," MC Jeremy said to Jimmy and Angel a second before the man himself appeared.

Whitehead.

He looked to be in his sixties, thin but with weight to him. The skin on his face was tight and smooth, his hair silver, buzz-cut. His eyes were pure black at the center, at least looked so here, on this stage. He wore a suit that fell the way expensive suits fall, a politician's suit, the color of coal, black or blue, depending on where the light was. He seemed to hesitate under one of the flickering gas wall lamps, his hands folded in front of him, as if to let Jimmy and Angel get the full effect. Jimmy knew the type, the kind of man who liked to think a person would remember forever the first time he saw him. The tip of his third finger on his right hand was gone, from the knuckle out. He wore an onyx ring, to draw attention to it.

A shudder went through the room, strong enough to make the boy up top stop playing. It was as if someone had backed a truck into the side of the warehouse.

Jimmy wondered if it was a quake, though it was already over if it was. He looked at Angel. Angel had spread his feet apart, for balance.

Les Paul started playing again, rolling with the punches.

Whitehead turned to an intercom on the wall behind him, a Bakelite and brass device as out of the past as the rest of the furnishings. He depressed a switch and spoke into a conical mouthpiece.

Jimmy realized that what was coming up his legs was not the aftereffects of the shake but a low, regular vibration in the floor itself, as if there was a generator in the next room. Whoever's place this was, you got the idea they were off the Pacific Gas and Electric grid.

Angel leaned in a little closer to Jimmy. "Let's just see if we can get the kid and go. I don't get this."

There was another shudder, the floor shifting under them.

"Sit, please," Whitehead came closer and said. "You'll be more comfortable."

There was a smell, a new scent, heavier than the sickly sweet perfume of the two men, the marker of the Sailors of the north. This was a thicker smell, a pungency that rode a little lower in the air. *Diesel.*

In the same moment Jimmy put a name to it, there was a sense of movement. And the floor under their feet became *the deck*, the walls around them *the bulkheads*, the doors *hatches*.

They had cast off.

Les Paul played on.

"I exhausted part of my youth in Los Angeles," Whitehead began as he stepped toward a wing chair in the center of the room. He sat and crossed his legs at the knee. The nobody who'd ushered them in, *aboard*, crossed to his master's side with a silver tray, a snifter of something golden. Nothing was offered to Jimmy and Angel.

Jimmy dropped down onto one of the couches, stretched out his arms along the top of the back, right at home. He looked up at the dark recesses of the rumbling chamber.

"Great gears turn," Jimmy said.

It was sufficient to make Whitehead turn his black eyes toward his impudent guest.

"What does that *mean*, anyway?" Jimmy said, trying to sound like a teenager.

Whitehead ignored the distraction, the question. Angel was still standing.

"Sit, please," Whitehead said. And then, after the comma, "Mr. Figueroa."

Angel picked a chair.

The pitch of the vibration changed. Things stilled for a moment; then there was a stronger tremble, and the room's equilibrium shifted. The rocking was polite.

Whitehead began again, said his first line again, "I exhausted part of my youth in Los Angeles," with just the hint of irritation at having to repeat it. It made it seem as rehearsed as it was, as thought-out. It made what came next feel like a politician's stump speech. Too repeated, probably not true. "I had been in the Brotherhood—we still called it that then—two or three years. San Francisco was exhausted for me. Gratefully, I say only temporarily." He wasn't drinking his drink, hadn't even lifted it to his nose to admire, just palmed it like the prop it was.

Jimmy wished he had it. He thought of a line to interject into the proceedings, to throw the other off balance, but decided instead to rear back on the couch, be cool. Let the man empty his bucket.

"I was alone. On the train, of course." Whitehead looked at Angel. "The Coast *Day*light. Of course, this was before the Coast Starlight, years before." He waited. When Angel nodded, Whitehead's eyes released him.

"I remember coming into Union Station at sunset. I remember the sound of it, the echo. I came outside, into that very striking Los Angeles sunset panorama. Spectacular. I was met at the station by a man, an actor whose name you would recognize, who of course was a Sailor, too. I admit I was a little starstruck. I had seen so many of his movies. And not all of them on the late show, I have to admit. He was waiting, parked at the curb in—"

Jimmy held up a finger, pointed at the air. "Jefferson Airplane," he said. Les Paul was working allusions to a few classics into the set.

Whitehead put some steel in his voice. "I met Red Steadman that trip, that very night, as a matter of fact," he said.

The name wiped the joke off Jimmy's face. Walter E. C. "Red" Steadman was the leader of the Sailors to the south. He and Jimmy had had their clashes over the years. The young man and the old man. If they had made any kind of peace, it was an uneasy one.

Whitehead enjoyed the moment. And the next even more. "Of course, I was something of an emissary. Steadman wasn't receiving *me*, Wayne Whitehead, but rather the one I represented, whose card I carried in my vest pocket."

He tapped his heart.

And then he spoke the name.

The night, the drama, the episode dutifully had followed the principle of rising action, starting with Black Moses out on the pier parking lot with his rod and his staff, who led them to Jeremy. Then Jeremy led them to Whitehead—and Whitehead, in speech at any rate, to the unnamed famous actor and then, "that very night," to Steadman, untitled leader of the Southern California Sailors.

And then, by nothing more than the utterance of his name, to the man himself. It was designed to take Jimmy and Angel to the top of the mountain, let them see the view.

And how far there was to fall.

"The Brotherhood—we still called it that then—was a different animal in those days," Wayne Whitehead continued, his voice now confident, steady, impressive, as if he knew he'd already met the most important of his objectives. "Everyone knew everyone, or at least acted in that spirit. We looked each other in the eye. We *measured* each other. I wouldn't say we trusted each other, but there was understanding. Cooperation, after a fashion."

"We just want to get our people out of here," Jimmy said. "The ones who are still alive. Actually, all we want is the kid up there, Johnny Guitar. We get him and we go home. It's actually simple."

"Just the boy?" Whitehead said. "Really?"

He knew about Mary. Jimmy could feel it.

"I've been back to Los Angeles many times . . ." Whitehead said, starting down a new line.

Jimmy stood. "How about we all go up top?"

He looked at Jeremy to see if he got the joke: the warehouse building they'd first entered was the selfsame one the Leonidas girls had dived off, Pier 35. Where Lucy had met her end, too.

"Get a little fresh air, see the city lights? Maybe we're cruising past Alcatraz. Angel gets seasick, I'm just telling you."

"I was there in Los Angeles for the murders, in the nineties," the host said, bringing it all back home.

It wiped another smile off Jimmy's face.

"And, of course, the aftermath," Whitehead said. "That was the last time, actually. And the first time I heard *your* name."

Jimmy was still standing.

"I'm nobody," he said.

"Those who know you best say otherwise," Whitehead said.

There was a bump. They'd arrived back at the mooring, back at the wharf. The little play was over. At least the first act.

The nobody Sailor made ready, stepping over to open the hatch.

Whitehead stayed in his chair. He made a little church out of his hands, looked at them over his nine fingertips.

THEY weren't back at the waterfront, or at least not Fisherman's Wharf. When they went through the last door, they were somewhere else, stepping out of another warehouse building with its back against another pier. There were ships all around, but it was dark, *past* dark. The ships looked to be old navy ships being stripped for salvage and old freighters, some of them navy gray, too, some black, some rust red, all dead-seeming, under a blurred navy gray half moon.

"Where are we?" Angel said.

"Go ask Alice," Jimmy said.

Then *they* started to emerge. Forms, shadows coalescing into human forms. People. There were scores of them, coming in from all quarters. A show of strength. Or *need*, because they all had looks of expectation on their faces. Anticipation, hope, fear. Waiting.

Who's next?

Jimmy and Angel had left Whitehead and Jeremy behind them in the hold of the ship, had just followed the nobody out.

But now Whitehead was standing right behind Jimmy, seeing what he saw.

"They know who you are," he said, just loudly enough for Jimmy to hear. "You have a reputation."

There began a reverberation coming up from the gathered, a vibration like the engine on the boat, low and indistinct. They were saying something over and again. It was like the noise they call for from a crowd of extras in a movie, vague mumbling that sounds like a hundred conversations but is really only a few words repeated. The same words. With the crowd of them, it was oddly melodious.

It got clearer as they synced up. "We follow Wayne . . ."

Whitehead stepped around Jimmy and waded into their midst.

Jeremy had come out from the ship, too, with his long cape draped over his arm. Now he came forward and, hoping at least some in the crowd were watching *him*, unfurled it and let it fall over his shoulders. These San Franciscans liked their Romanticism, if that's what it was. Jeremy stood with his hands on his hips but still looked like what he was, a sidekick, a right-hand man.

Jimmy was watching Whitehead and his congregation. "Funny, I wouldn't take him for a people person," he said to Jeremy, who seemed to like the line.

"Thought maybe you'd want to know: The Greek girls, what's left of them, are down here," Jeremy said.

"They're both Sailors?"

"Double down, I say," Jeremy said. "Whenever you can."

Now it was Jimmy who went into the crowd, into the wake closing behind Whitehead.

"Where are you going?" Angel called after him.

Jimmy kept going and didn't answer his friend.

Jeremy turned and grinned at Angel, a look Angel didn't get at all.

CHAPTER

TWENTY-THREE

Two girls were holding hands. It was a start.

Jimmy found them down by the piers, walking apart from the others. One of them kept looking over her shoulder at him. She smiled, in fact. The girls wore matching clothes, long blue dresses out of some cheap goods. It looked rough to the skin and the color uneven, as if hand-dyed. It made Jimmy think of cult clothes, pretty hippie girls on a commune, flowers in their hair but a dreary, frightened servitude in their hearts, following the master. (The trick was to not want to be the master.)

"Wait," Jimmy said when the one turned to look at him again.

She waited, held back her sister.

When he got closer, he saw how young they were. With Sailors the new form matched the old, at least in age and usually in size. From a distance, or in a photograph, one might pass for his or her former self, except to the eyes of a close loved one, to whom the new person always looked like a stranger.

It wasn't a logical thing. The Sailor way was a ball of mystery, surrounded by a hundred miles of fog. There was a famous fog in the

Central Valley, starting south of Bakersfield on Old 99 when you came up from L.A., Thule fog, so thick it looked like dishwater. Whenever Jimmy drove through it, or up to it (you couldn't drive through it at its worst), he thought, *This is what it's like to be a Sailor.* A sailor at the wheel of his boat.

"Hi," the girls said together. They weren't twins in this domain, but they looked alike.

"Hi," Jimmy said.

They seemed so trusting, so open. Unafraid, now that they had each other. They also seemed to know who he was. He wondered why, what they'd been told about him.

They were *New.* It was all over them. Jimmy had already decided they probably weren't the Greek girls, the reborn Leonidas twins. He just had a feeling about them. The fog. He was about to ask them, gently, about themselves, when they just smiled again, or at least the one of them did, and they walked away.

Down the rabbit hole again . . .

Jimmy followed them into a room in an old military building, World War II–era, wooden, with brown linoleum floors. One of those buildings built fast, when the world was coming apart on two fronts. It had a ten-foot ceiling, exposed rafters, all very intentional. There were windows along both sides, but they were covered with blackout cloths, just like in the war. It was an officers' mess, with a long table.

An odd one, because the table was set with candelabra and a tablecloth. And a meal on silver serving plates.

The chairs were filled with women. The two sisters were seated on either side of a woman who looked a little French, with short-cropped hair. They stopped talking and eating when he stepped in, then went back to it. They were different ages, but there was something in their faces, all of the women, something about their pale skin, that made Jimmy think of the Procol Harum line about the sixteen vestal virgins leaving for the coast. (And, although his eyes were open, they might just as well have been closed.) It was a little like a scene from a dream, like a memory of an event that never took place.

A couple of the women looked familiar. It took him a second to realize that some voice in his head was telling him that two or three of them resembled women out of his past. *That* dream. At his right, closest to him, was a dark-haired beauty who reminded him of a woman from a year or so ago in his life, a "client" who'd become much more before it was over. And next to her was a girl who instantly made him think of a girl he'd fallen hard for when he was just a kid, maybe the last real love before he'd become a Sailor. (Maybe they'd slipped him something on the boat.) Right in front of him was a punky-looking girl with silver hair. *Eighties Girl.* She stuck out her tongue at him. Jimmy almost laughed. He'd accepted the trippiness of the scene, was going with it.

Then he realized the short-haired woman at the other end of the table looked a little like his mother. He didn't exactly want to dwell on that.

There was an open place at the table. Was it meant for him? There was a glass of wine there. He decided now would be a good time to drink half of it.

It wasn't all women. Machine Shop was there. Shop had dressed for the occasion, whatever the occasion was, a maroon suit that could have been sewn from the remnants of the velvet hanging on Whitehead's vessel. Put him in a plush red Al Green suit and the seventies really came out. Shop hadn't even noticed Jimmy. He was totally into the women around him, full shuck and jive, a bit of the old "And how are you fine ladies this evening?" When his eyes met Jimmy's, he looked embarrassed, guilty, caught. He was supposed to meet Jimmy at the Wharf.

"Sorry, man," Shop said.

"Yeah, I was looking for you up there."

"And now you're here."

"How'd *you* get here?" Jimmy said.

"They brought me in a limousine," Shop said.

Jimmy guessed that all this was part of Whitehead's master plan, whatever it was.

Then he saw Mary. Or rather "Mary."

At the far end of the table. If the lights were up, she probably wouldn't have looked a thing like Mary. Not the twenty-two-year-old Mary Jimmy had met on Sunset Strip in 1995, not the woman now, out in Tiburon. But the hair was close, the face the same shape. She was wearing a dress that made Jimmy remember the one Lucy had been wearing there at the start. But that was all right, too; all of them were getting tangled up in each other's stories in his head.

He took his wine over to her. Nobody paid him much mind. He stood over her.

She looked up at him, stopped whatever conversation she was having. This close, she didn't look like Mary at all.

"Come sit by me," Jimmy said to her. "There's a seat down there by me." He sounded drunker than he was.

"You're always trying to relocate me," the Mary *almost* lookalike said. Or Jimmy thought she did.

CHAPTER TWENTY-FOUR

"I still see them," Mary said.

She had just said it, blank-faced, sitting there in her white slip-covered armless chair, the light of a cream candle dancing on her face. They were in a restaurant on the Sunset Strip. Le Dome.

Back then it was the kind of place Jimmy wouldn't have sought out on his own. A little rich, a little too hushed. He'd go if someone else suggested it, but it was too snow-white and *round* for him.

Mary had picked the place. "I want to talk to you about something," she had said.

He had assumed it was one of those girl talks about commitment, about "moving to the next level." In a way it was. But he was way ahead of her, ready to relocate to any level she named. He loved her, simple and sure.

But what she had said in Le Dome was, "I still see them."

"It's over," he said. He knew what she meant.

"I know," she said. "I know it's *supposed* to be over. I know everything you know, everything everybody else knows. They arrested two brothers. Russian brothers. There is all the evidence against them. I don't care. I *still* see them."

"Where?"

Jimmy leaned closer. Everybody knew about Le Dome. The arch of the smooth, plastered ceiling meant the sound bounced around in funny ways. Conversations ended up where they weren't meant to go. Jimmy had been there one night, late, alone, stood up by someone, and heard more than he wanted to about the problems in the marriage of a fading television star and his young wife all the way across the room. He was worried about who else was hearing Mary. The place was almost full.

"I was on Melrose," Mary said. "Two of them were following me. In the middle of the afternoon."

He didn't say anything.

"I told you when I met you I was crazy," she said.

"What did they look like?" Jimmy said.

"Just like before," she said. "Black on black. Sneakers. Black jeans. Black T-shirts. One of them was maybe one of the ones who came to your house after me."

"What did they do?"

"They just followed me. I'd go in one store and when I came out, they were waiting, hanging back two stores up the street."

"Why did you want to come *here* to talk about this?"

"I didn't want to fall apart. I feel like I've been doing that lately anyway. I wanted to be out. Among the living."

Jimmy asked her if she'd been thinking much about the others in the house up in Benedict. Whom she'd survived.

"Yes."

He reached across the white linen to her. "It's over," he said. "They caught the two men. They were the ones. The killings stopped."

"No, they didn't," she said. "They *didn't*."

There'd been a copycat murder two weeks after the Russian brothers had been arrested.

"I have friends who are cops, Mary."

"Yeah," she said. "Why is that?"

He didn't have a quick answer for her.

Wait a second or two and that *is* your answer.

"Why is that?" she said. "You're a record producer."

Remember, they were both young. It was a time, and they were an age, when *what you do* could be a very roomy jacket. And you could have three or four of them on the rack by the door. Pick one. Nobody checked the label, as long as it looked good on you. He was a "record producer" working on a demo for a band in the Valley anytime they got some money together, and sometimes when they didn't. She was an "actress." Or was it "singer"?

"I know people from lots of different . . . areas," Jimmy said. "It's an L.A. thing. I'm just saying: The cops are convinced they got the people who did the murders. All of the murders."

"Why did you go downtown that day?"

"What day?"

He knew exactly the day she meant. In the scene they were playing out in the restaurant that night, Jimmy had been behind Mary from the start. Running to catch up.

She just waited him out.

"Angel had heard about somebody else who could have been responsible, involved in the killings. We were downtown checking it out."

He should have stopped there.

Instead, he made a joke. "Going to see a man about a dog."

Mary said, right back at him, "There was a man with a dog, all in black and a black dog. *I* saw a man with a dog."

It was like laying down the first card in her hand.

"Twice," she said. "I saw him twice."

There was the second card.

"Where?" Jimmy said.

"The first time in daylight, when I went back up to the house in Benedict."

"When? You went back up to the house? Why?"

"Last week. Sunday."

The third and fourth cards.

"Why did you go up there?"

"I don't know," she said. "I was just thinking about it. Too much. I just wanted to see it again."

He was shaking his head. "You shouldn't go up there. Or you should have told me. I would have taken you."

"Always riding to the rescue," she said. "That's my Jim."

"When was the second time you saw him?" Jimmy said.

"A couple of nights ago," Mary said. "In the yard." She meant *his* yard, *their* yard. "You were gone somewhere."

The fifth card.

She had ordered a glass of red wine after they'd cleared away their dinner plates, but she hadn't touched it until now. "I was feeling . . . desperate," she said, drawing the wine to her. "I was feeling . . . pushed into a corner. He was just standing there, down the slope from the house, with that black dog, looking up at me in the kitchen window, as if waiting for me to *do* something."

She tasted the wine. "I don't like it that you have a gun," she said. "And I especially don't like it that you left it where I could find it."

He held his question. About her, about the gun, about what she had been considering that day. He held his question. And, he realized later, held his breath, too, the same as if he had walked in on her in that moment, holding the gun, precisely at the time in her life when she didn't need to find a gun.

"I put it away," Mary said. "In the hall closet, under all those books, in the back. Tell me you'll get rid of it. I don't want to see it again. Not when I'm going through this kind of shit, feeling this."

Jimmy didn't have a gun.

TWO days later there was another copycat killing, another heart ripped out, another body spread-eagle on another road cut, and a secondary wave of panic in the L.A. basin. There wouldn't be any more, but it was enough.

This time, the killing seemed to trigger suicides, a half-dozen of them. "Panic suicides," the article in the *Times* called them. Maybe they'd happened before, in the first wave of killings, the *real* killings, but it hadn't been reported.

There was another term they used, official psychologists, to describe what they were afraid of, if reason didn't prevail.

Suicide contagion.

If reason didn't prevail. As if reason ever prevails.

JIMMY moved the two of them up to a house at the edge of Angeles Forest, high in the rocks and woods above Altadena. A house with a pool. The owner was a Sailor friend of Angel's; Jimmy didn't know him. The owner called it a "cabin," but it had three bedrooms and was behind gates, though the back of the property was open, open to the woods and the rocks behind it. It was all the way at the end of its own road. The view from the window over the kitchen sink was of Mount Baldy.

It helped. Mary felt better. Safer.

She assumed Jimmy didn't believe her, didn't believe that the Cut Killers could still be out there, looking in people's windows. Or tying up loose ends, whatever it was that they were doing. Killing again. Maybe he *did* believe her. She didn't know what he was thinking. She got up each morning and made a big breakfast, the kind of breakfast her mother used to make for her father, eggs and bacon and fresh orange juice and pancakes or waffles. She'd found a waffle iron in the cabinets. (There wasn't a phone, but there was a waffle iron.) She'd eat everything she'd made. Jimmy had trouble keeping up with her. He'd make the runs down to the store. She would make the lists, apparently having decided to cook her way through every one of her mother's recipes, as best she could remember them.

He came "home" one day, and she'd painted "Good Day Sunshine . . ." with clear red fingernail polish on the kitchen window.

Without ever deciding to, without ever talking about what should happen next, they stayed in "the cabin" like that for two weeks straight, Mary never leaving the house and grounds, and Jimmy only leaving to make the supply runs. And to make a few calls. There was no TV. What they had for entertainment was each other and a few board games, cards, and a beautiful old tube Zenith stereo with three-foot-high stained cherry speakers and a cabinet full of old LPs.

All day Mary played *The White Album* over and over.

SHE came out from the kitchen, the dinner dishes done.

"Honey, I'm home," she said.

"That's supposed be my line, Lucy," Jimmy said.

"I'm more *June*, June Cleaver." She crossed to him. He was in a chair, an old man's recliner, reading. There was a cabinet of *Popular Science* magazines. From thirty years back.

"I was just reading about the future," Jimmy said. "We're all going to have personal helicopters by nineteen eighty."

"Nineteen eighty! It sounds so futuristic . . . I was *seven* in 1980. I was born in 1973. When were *you* born?"

He had made a pitcher of martinis. He had found the glasses and everything behind a little bar, the kind covered in black pleat-and-tuck leatherette. He'd delivered one to her in the kitchen while she was cleaning up. Now she took a sip of his. First, she kissed him. He could smell the gin on her breath.

When were you born?

"I don't think June and Ward Cleaver were drinkers," he said, letting her question evaporate.

She plopped down into his lap. "Sure they were. The Beav drove them to it."

He kissed her.

After a second, she said, "I love you," and said it in a way that made him think she wasn't used to saying it. He thought that, even after the voice in his head ridiculed him for it.

"I love you, too," he said.

"I feel safe," she said. "I feel safe."

"Nobody knows we're here. In the middle of nowhere."

"It's like we're lost," she said, against his neck. "Or is it *saved*? Can you be lost and saved at the same time?"

"I'll ask Angel."

She jumped up. "Check this out!"

She was like a girl again, more girlish than before. Than when they met. She went over to the stereo on the bookcase. She turned on the amp. The speakers thumped, then buzzed up to attention.

"I figured this out, how to do it, all by myself this afternoon," she said.

She took hold of the mechanical control on the side of the turntable and shifted it out of gear. "You put it between forty-five and thirty-three and a third . . ."

She took *The White Album* off the shelf. She unsheathed one of the disks, checked the label.

"Wait," she said, to herself.

She reengaged the speed control lever. When it got up to speed, she put the needle down. After a second of click and sputter, it began.

"Revolution No. 9."

She waited until it came to the refrain, "Number nine . . . number nine . . . number nine . . ."

"OK," she said. "Got it? Now . . ."

She disengaged the speed lever again, slipped it into neutral. Then she put her finger in the center, on one side of the label, right on the bright green apple, and turned it backwards, counterclockwise.

"I didn't know you could actually do this," she said over the wobbly, warpy backwards noises, music for aliens.

"All right, I hear it, stop," Jimmy said, with an edge to his voice she didn't understand. And a *sadness* she couldn't understand.

"Not yet," she said. She was still spinning the record backwards with her finger, coaxing the guttural discord out of the vinyl, trying to keep the rhythm, what there was of it.

Jimmy sank into himself.

She reached the place in the "song" where the announcer spoke, said his syllables over and over atop the orchestral noises, atop Beethoven's Ninth or strings tuning or whatever it was.

"Turn me on, dead man . . . Turn me on, dead man . . . Turn me on, dead man . . ."

She turned her face to him. She looked like a teenager, so happy in the moment. "It's one of the clues! 'Paul is dead.' Remember?"

Turn me on, Deadman.

He went outside, out onto the deck, beside the pool. The bleached-out water was just a step down from a huge rock that jutted out of the side of the hill, looked like a natural pool that way, in that "California perfect" way. A dragonfly skimmed the surface, like something out of a future war.

The windows were open. The music came out after him. Mary had flipped the record, and now she played the side over and over, Disk 2, Side 1, lifting the needle over "Helter Skelter" each time "Sexy Sadie" ended.

CHAPTER
TWENTY-FIVE

This time on the night run over the desert mountains north on the 5 to his new cop friend, Jimmy was alone. Angel was elsewhere. L.A. was panicky again. The suicide toll was climbing. And there were frayed nerves in the Sailor world, too, a generalized high anxiety that meant Angel had home calls to make, hands to hold, people to talk down off the ledge. It was what Angel did.

Nobody seemed to know what it was. Sailors were just wound up tight, waiting for something. Looking for somebody who could change things or even bring back the old status quo, when things were straight. Maybe they'd caught the same bug that was testing the nerves of the rest of L.A., driving even the Norms to start thinking the unthinkable.

Angel had handed him the key to the "new" Porsche, the '64 Cabriolet with no top, primer red, halfway to restoration. No top, no leather on the seats, a metal floor, but with the motor *there*, twenty foot-pounds past tight.

"I got a ticket on the way up," Jimmy said, when he dropped into a lawn chair in Detective Dill's backyard.

"The down side of Boiling Point Ridge?"

"Bingo."

"Rookie," the cop said. "Fish in a barrel, man."

They had walked straight through the house from the front door. The divorced cop hadn't done a bunch of decorating since the last time. Dill lagged behind a beat, then came out after Jimmy onto the patio with two bottles of beer and a brown leather briefcase. He handed one Negra Modelo to Jimmy and held out the neck of his for a clank.

"You know, Boiling Point's actually a town a mile or two from here," Dill said. "What's left of it. They could have named the subdivision Boiling Point Estates or some such, but they didn't. I don't know why."

"Well, I'm not a marketing person," Jimmy said.

"So what do you want to know?" the cop said in one of his other voices, a cop voice. "What else?"

Jimmy told him everything Mary had told him.

The question was: Had they really caught the killers? Or could they still be out there? Could they be somebody else?

Dill opened the briefcase. He flipped through some papers, but when he spoke it wasn't as if he was having to look at anything to refresh his memory. "They had knives and saws, including a Czech-made, Russian Army–issue bayonet, with blood and tissue, matches to victims one, seven, and eleven. Cleaned with paint thinner, but not enough. The girl up in Temescal Canyon. The schoolteacher out in Riverside, the woman but not the man. The old lady Jehovah's Witness in Santa Monica."

He handed Jimmy a police photo, color. A power tool.

"Milwaukee Sawzall. Cordless, so they could take it with them. A number fourteen drywall blade. Blood and organ tissue from the last victim on the blade."

Dill dealt out another photo. It was of a section of floor, kitchen floor from the looks of the linoleum, ripped up, a hidey-hole space between the floor joists exposed. And a tin box with the lid ajar.

"New blades, used blades," Dill went on. "Victims four, five, nine, and ten."

"How noisy is a Sawzall?"

"They never had to worry about noise."

"The news just said *saw*. Nobody said anything about power tools."

"There's always what's real and what's *news*. It's the way we play it. One advantage we keep."

Dill handed Jimmy some photocopies. "Receipt from the Sherman Way Home Depot for the Sawzall with the signature of one of the Russian brothers. Receipt from Home Depot for blades, the other brother. A second battery pack, the first brother again. The tin box is what a kind of Russian cookie comes in. They call them biscuits. The receipt is from a Russian specialty store in Glendale. They taste like they were baked under Khrushchev, but what do I know?"

"Why didn't they confess?" Jimmy said, handing the pictures back. "With all this against them."

"They usually do," Dill said. "I don't know. They got a famous lawyer. Early. They went quiet . . ."

"What do you have on the copycats?"

"Not as much, but enough. Whoever it is—and it's the same person both times—he's missing some of the details."

"Which means he isn't inside," Jimmy said, forgetting in the moment whose backyard he was in.

"Cops wouldn't kill like this," the vet detective said. "Cops like to *save* people. Even bad cops. Bad cops do things like kill the wives of dirty bookstore owners for five hundred bucks and all the videos they can carry. But even then, they think they're performing a service for society. Say what you want about those of us who are Jehovah's Witnesses, nobody thinks we should have our hearts cut out and left on the side of the road." The last was the cop's idea of a joke. He wasn't a Witness.

Dill sat back. "What's it say on the car door?"

"To protect and serve."

"That's right," the other said. "There's no *inside* in this one. These two are all the way *outside*. You can see it in their eyes. I don't know who the copycats might be, but the Russians are locked-down bad guys."

The cop saw what was on Jimmy's face, saw the way he was sitting, the way he had lined up the photos and photocopies on the low white plastic Costco table. Jimmy looked like a lawyer who wished he'd drawn a different case.

"But . . . but . . . but . . . But what?" Detective Dill said.

"What if the people killing now are the real ones? What if these Russian brothers were made up, set up?"

"Come here," Dill said, halfway out of the chair already.

Jimmy followed Dill into his bedroom. High angled ceiling, a ceiling fan on high, sounding frantic. Not much else. There was a king-sized bed with a pressed wood headboard and just a white sheet stretched tight across the mattress. And a single pillow.

Across from the bed was a tall dresser with a Costco TV/VCR combination on it, nineteen-inch. It opened its mouth and took the unlabeled VHS tape from Dill's hand.

Jimmy stood there. They both stood there, holding their beers, glad to have them once it started.

The Russian brothers had seen a few too many movies. Or too much "reality TV." Somehow they'd gotten the idea that what they were doing would make a good show, even if no one could ever see it. Or maybe some part of them wanted to make sure they'd be convicted, when the time came. Wanted it *certain*, that would be another theory.

Their shooting style favored the extreme close-up.

THE cop and Jimmy Miles stood out in the front yard beside the Porsche at the curb. It was almost three in the morning.

"Sprinklers are going to come on in a minute here," Dill said.

"When do you work next?"

"Six. Third shift."

"So what should I do?" Jimmy said. "About this girl."

"Your sister."

"Got any ideas?" Jimmy said.

"You moved?"

Jimmy told him a limited version of where he'd gone.

"Stay there," Dill said. "There is more shit hidden in Angeles Forest than even God knows. Stay up there. Let her forget about it, or at least file it away. Kill your TV. Let the panic blow over. It'll come to trial."

Jimmy nodded. The scene felt so empty, so *desert*, it was hard to remember there were a couple of thousand others sleeping all around them. Norms.

"In my experience, people—and by 'people' I mean 'women'—are always afraid of the wrong things. Afraid when they shouldn't be, not afraid when they should be. Of course, when I said that to my wife one time, when we were out with some friends, she said, 'What I'm afraid of is twenty-odd more years of that rich of bullshit.' So there's that."

"What about the men?"

"They're afraid of everything," Dill said. "At least the ones I have any respect for."

It was still hot. The streetlights staggered down the streets in the subdivision were the yellow/orange kind, the kind that gave everything that sickly look city planners seem to prefer. Even the Porsche looked tired, out-of-date, sad, there in the driveway.

Jimmy was staring at something out in the road, something four or five feet long, stretched out, like a strip of shredded tire or something. There was another a few feet away.

"Those are rattlers," Dill said. "They like the heat soaked up in the asphalt all day. I used to run over them but then I . . ." He trailed off. "Live and let live. Some time of year, I forget when, they shed their skins. You find them under the bushes and hedges and shit. They look like the rubbers in the parking lots out at the beach."

Jimmy said, "Got any idea what's up with Sailors these days?" Dill hadn't been a Sailor all that long as these things went, four or five years, but he'd been on the streets as a cop a lot of years before that. One thing Sailors all did, the good and the bad ones, was respect experience.

"I was hoping you'd tell me," the cop said. "*I've* never seen it like this. People I trust say they haven't seen anything like this for a lot of years."

"Since when? When was the last time?"

"When the man stepped up, the Passing. Fifty years ago."

Jimmy dug in his pocket for the loose key to the Porsche.

"I know your man in black with the dog," Dill said.

It stopped Jimmy.

"They call him Kingman. For Kingman, Arizona. Bad town for a Sailor."

"He's a Sailor?"

"*Old* salt. Made his way out here twenty years ago."

"But he has a dog."

"I don't get it, either," Dill said. "Maybe it's the one dog in the world that likes us. Maybe it's a *Sailor* dog, something new. I hate new."

"WHAT time is it?" Mary said when she felt him move in against her in bed.

"After midnight," Jimmy said.

"It was after midnight when I went to bed."

"That was the last song on the radio, coming up the road. 'After Midnight.' "

She made a sound like a laugh. "Don't wake me up," she said, dreamy.

CHAPTER TWENTY-SIX

There was a place called the Pipe in Long Beach. Jimmy waited until late afternoon before he rode down out of Angeles Forest. There wasn't much use in going in earlier.

He figured he'd start at the sea, out on the edge, and work his way inland, looking for Kingman.

Just because. Because the son of a bitch had stood in his yard, looking up at his troubled girl in the kitchen window.

Because maybe he'd planted a gun in Jimmy's house, where Mary could find it.

Just because.

There was still a little light left in the sky. It was pretty, the last light of the day, the light of surrender, as night moved in. The light was pretty, but nothing else was. The Pipe was wetlands, soggy marsh littered with what floats, whatever is cast aside and floats. Sailors, a certain kind of them, lived down here in the hulls of beached boats, boats on their sides, demasted sailboats and the rusting iron skin of a trawler.

The "leaders" would be there, the dominant ones. There was a chance Kingman would be among them.

There were different kinds of Sailors, different levels. *Ranks* wouldn't be the right term, because it would imply they were linked in service to some mission. In the end, Sailors were all just dealing with themselves, in it for themselves, trying to make sense of it. Even Jimmy Miles. Even Angel Figueroa.

But there was a kind of Sailor easy to spot: Walkers. Everybody said there were more of them in Los Angeles than almost any other city. Go figure, the one place where *nobody* walked. They'd lost all hope, given up, gone slack, checked out of the whole world of Good or Bad, and were a real danger because of it. The Pipe was always thick with them. Down here they tended to stand around fires, hard as it was to keep them going with everything wet, staring into the flames as if waiting for the fiery face of a god to appear, to tell them at last what to do.

"I'm looking for Kingman," he said, to anybody who would let their eyes meet his.

Jimmy didn't like doing this alone, but he hadn't been able to find Angel. He called him. He kept calling him. Angel's phone rang and rang. And he wasn't in his usual haunts. His men didn't know where he was, just that someone had come for him at noon.

There were a lot of ragged-looking Sailors down at the Pipe, shaking their heads *no*. But no Kingman, no black dog.

Jimmy cruised through Hollywood, down a back alleyway in the shadow of the Hotel Roosevelt, another gathering place for Sailors. The alleyway, not the hotel, which had gotten almost toney again. He was driving the Porsche. Angel had thrown a race-tuned exhaust on it. In the canyon of buildings, it provided a rolling thunder effect that made the men and the few women who were down here turn and look. He parked and got out.

Up close, the men looked like they were all on speed. Full-on jittery. Dilated pupils. Moving hands. It was what Angel had been talking about, the *jitterbugs* in the Sailor world.

"Who are you, Brother? What do you hear?" one of the men said before Jimmy could even get out of the car.

Two other men gathered closer, in anticipation of an answer.

No Kingman.

Jimmy drove by his house, stopped out on the street but didn't turn off the motor. One of Angel's men was staying there, in case anybody showed up who wasn't on the guest list. After a moment, some fingers came around the corner of the heavy drapes in the window in the front room, moved them a half inch.

"Water the plants out front, bud," he said, letting out the clutch to pull away. "They're looking a little brown."

The Sailors downtown that night were the worst off.

Same as it ever was.

Jimmy didn't come down here unless he had to. The downtown Sailor scene had a certain drama to it that he tried to avoid. And so far he had avoided it, except for the couple of times they had dragged him into it, into the arch ceremonial bullshit they reveled in. Their head-quarters was an "abandoned" courtroom with its high soiled marble walls on the top floor of the old Hall of Justice building. On Spring Street.

Jimmy kept going right on past it. Even sped up a little.

He went in on foot. His hands were sweaty. It was a funky neigh-borhood. Sixth Street. He'd done what he could, put the Porsche right across from Cole's, a street-level, five-steps-down antique saloon with a bloodred mahogany bar and booths carved with the initials of traveling salesmen and USC frat boys from the thirties. But it was a Wednesday night and early yet, not even ten, and Cole's was still dead. The Porsche looked wide-eyed as he walked away from it.

He came east two blocks. He'd been down here enough to know it wasn't as dangerous as it looked. Most of the people whose eyes met yours weren't thinking what you thought they were, didn't want your watch, weren't trying to guess which pocket you kept your cash in, weren't drawing lots for your garments. The dangerous ones you probably never saw coming. Street people were mostly just people on a street.

He stopped in front of the hollow, dead building where he and Angel had climbed the stairs and found what they thought was the "home" of the man with the black dog, and the body of the North Hollywood street person who'd directed Jimmy there.

The House of Kingman.

The homemade video Dill had shown to Jimmy to close the deal with him had had the opposite effect. It had blown the deal apart, and just when Jimmy had the pen in hand, too, hovering over the long sideways line with his name under it. It didn't happen right away, not even on the ride home. It came later that night, or maybe came the same hour dawn came to the house in Angeles Forest, while Mary still slept beside him.

Jimmy knew something about movies. His mother was a star. His father was a director. There was a screening room in the house Jimmy was born into. A studio nanny pushed him around the Fox lot in a French perambulator. All of his parents' friends, and all of their enemies, were in the business: actors, directors, shooters, composers, editors.

Editors. What was missing were the two-shots. There were no shots of either one of the brothers and a victim in the same frame. The shot list: A brother alone. A victim alone, usually in close. A wide shot, pulling out, a brother looking down at the floor. An extreme close-up of an incision. Sometimes the brother would be looking at the camera, sometimes waving it off. Sometimes there'd be a smile, a kind of sour smile that gave off a sex vibe. Naughty. There was one shot of blood on hands, in close. Holding a gutting knife. *Someone's* hands.

There were no two-shots.

Jimmy was circling the base of the building, outside. The House of Kingman. You could walk all the way around it, alleys on the sides and on the back, Sixth Street out front. He and Angel had come in from the back. Jimmy headed that way. He didn't think Kingman would still be there, but maybe there'd be somebody else inside who knew something.

Or maybe there was some value to standing again over the spot where they'd found the body.

Where Jimmy had had to look at the face of someone who'd died because of him.

It was dark ahead. The light on the corner of the building was out. A black, dead bulb. (Shouldn't that be the ultimate version of a *stop*-light?) But Jimmy had a light in his hand, his own light, a foot-and-a-half-long Maglite he'd thrown onto the other seat of the Porsche when he left the cabin to drive down into whatever was supposed to happen next. Half light, half club, a cop flashlight.

He came around the corner with the light. Somebody scurried away at the other corner of the back of the building.

There was a flash of blue.

"Brother!" Jimmy called out.

The door was closed. A metal fire door. Jimmy watched his hand reach out toward it.

A shoe crunching glass. A sound effect.

Behind him. He spun around.

The shape had already stopped. It spoke.

"Knock knock," Dill said.

Jimmy felt the way a Rhodesian Ridgeback looks, bowed up.

"Come on," the cop said, stepping forward out into a little more light. "There's nobody in there. Certainly not Kingman."

He turned and walked back up the alley toward Sixth. "Come on, let's get in out of the rain," Dill said. It hadn't rained in three months. Jimmy fell in behind him.

A black-on-black LAPD detective's Crown Vic was on the street.

"Get in," Dill said and got behind the wheel. Jimmy got in up front. He left his door open out onto the sidewalk. Cop cars don't have automatic dome lights. Nothing dings or talks.

"You been busy tonight," Dill said. "Forget about Kingman. I shouldn't have said anything."

Jimmy thought a second before he did it, but he began to spit out his doubts about the videotape. He only got two sentences in when Dill leaned forward and started the engine.

Jimmy closed his door, and they pulled away.

"I have the Porsche up here on the street," he said.

"It'll be taken care of," Dill said.

It was about the last thing Dill said as they drove across downtown to the 101 north. Traffic was light. Dill slid straight over to the inside lane and stayed there, rolled up to seventy, seventy-five.

All the way to Universal City. Maybe he was going to take Jimmy on the *Psycho* ride, take him in through the midnight VIP gate, buy him a churro.

They drove east on North Glenoaks Boulevard. And pulled into a motel, an old-style, single-story, U-shaped motor court.

A dark motel. With the sign off. Not even a No Vacancy.

A man dressed in LAPD blues but without a badge on his chest, stripped of anything that shined or named, stepped out of the office. On Dill's side of the car. Jimmy looked to his right and saw another cop next to the ice machine with a pistol in his hand, down at his side. They both wore body armor vests.

Jimmy liked drama as much as the next guy, but . . .

"What's this?"

"The Federovs."

"Here?"

"Live and in color."

"So who's in the special cells they built down at Terminal Island?"

"Russians all look alike," Dill said. "Actually, the Federov brothers aren't Russians. They're Ukrainians. That's one of the things that honks them off. So I make sure and call them Russians."

By then, they were out of the car and walking toward the back of the U. Another guard stood in front of the door to a unit.

They'd ripped out the partitions between three or four units across the back of the motel, taken them down to the studs, and pulled out the ceiling up to the rafters. They'd sprayed what was left of the framing flat black. The cage that held the two brothers was dead center in the

space, built out of gate and handrail iron and metal mesh. And painted
black. They'd left the motel carpet on the floor, the bathroom in the
corner. The carpet was dirty green. Another guard was fussing over a
coffeemaker in the corner, in what remained of a kitchenette.

The brothers were playing chess at a Formica table. They didn't
look up until the door opened again, and the guard stepped outside for
a second, on some signal from Dill.

"I brought a friend of yours to visit," Dill said. "He thinks you're
being framed."

"Yah," one of the brothers said, the younger one, the bigger one.
Everybody knew all about them.

"He *loves* Russians," Dill said.

"He's right," the other brother said. "Innocent. Not guilty."

"Leave us alone!" the first bellowed.

"Go ahead," Dill said to Jimmy. "Look them in the eye. You tell me."

"Yah!" the first brother said. "Innocent!"

And then he laughed.

When Jimmy came out, there was the Porsche, waiting for him. It
was such a Sailor thing to do.

Jimmy opened the door.

"So. You all right, Brother?" Dill said, right behind him. "Did you
see what you needed to see?

"Yeah," Jimmy said. And he almost meant it.

What did he know about cracking a case?

Or even about guilt or innocence?

WHEN Jimmy made it to the gate at the end of the long private road
up in Angeles Forest, he yanked up the parking brake and killed the
headlights but left the motor running. He got out. The gate wasn't
automatic. There wasn't a remote control. In fact, he'd locked the gate
when he left, a length of chain and a padlock. He unlocked it, shoved
it open. He stood there a moment in the open gateway. After being in
the city and then in the traffic, it all looked really dark. He thought he

heard something out in the trees. The woods were thick all around him. He listened for the sound, but it didn't repeat.

He'd had enough of noises, enough of suspicions.

Mary was in a deep sleep, but a gentle one. In the bedroom. With just a low light on beside the chair. She'd felt safe enough to turn out all the lights in the rest of the house and go to sleep in the bedroom. He pulled the wool Pendleton Indian striped blanket up over her shoulder, to send her even deeper into that peace.

He was about to sit in the chair at the end of the bed, to read away what was left of the night, when he heard their footsteps on the deck.

Loud. There was no intention to be quiet. Loud enough to make Mary stir.

He leaned over her, awakened her the rest of the way.

"Get in the closet," he said when her eyes came open.

There was a sliding door from the living room out to the deck, to the pool. He could see them out there as he crossed the room.

Six of them.

He opened the door and stepped out.

He had already recognized one of the shapes: Angel. Detective Dill was next to Angel. Even in the dim light, Jimmy could see that Dill had an embarrassed look on his face. It was harder to say what the look on Angel's face meant.

The blue edge around them was vibrant, all of them. This was official business.

Angel waited for Jimmy to look at him directly. When Jimmy did, Angel's face said, *It's all right.*

Whether it was or not.

The other men were less . . . conflicted.

There was a round man, cartoonishly large, Orson Welles–size. And in a suit with a vest, like some Daddy Warbucks. They were in a semicircle, facing him, like a tribunal. Next to the fat man was a man who had *cop* written all over him, but *ranking officer*. Next to him was a man, not small, not big, who didn't give off much.

And then there was the biggest man.

Who wore a hat. Whose face, save the eyes, was covered by a wool scarf, like this was London. Who even wore gloves, gray doeskin, lest his hands somehow give him away.

It was Walter E. C. "Red" Steadman, who in a way was their king. It was the first time Jimmy had ever been face-to-face with him.

It turned out Steadman was just there for the visual effect. And the scent of almost ultimate power he gave off. Steadman nodded to the nondescript man, who delivered the word.

"You are not incorrect in your conclusions," the mouthpiece said, "but this matter suits our larger purposes at this particular point in time."

A hoot owl picked now to hoot. *"Who?"*

"And now it's over," the nondescript man finished. "Your part in it, at any rate. It is over. Do you understand?"

He said the last with a surprising kindness.

"What about the threats?" Jimmy said.

"There were no threats," the high-rank cop said.

Red Steadman looked at the ranking cop to silence him. Jimmy noticed that Steadman didn't move his neck, as if he'd been injured somewhere along the line. Or as if he was very old. The "chief" wouldn't speak again.

"Who?" the owl said again.

"It's over," the mouthpiece said. "Anything that happens now will not happen to you."

Jimmy looked like he was about to jump in with something.

"Or to yours," the man added.

"Why are the two Russians going along with it?" Jimmy said. "Just curious."

No one thought it was necessary to answer.

"You should, in the morning, go back to your house," the mouthpiece finished. "Stop trying to see the bigger picture. Just live for yourself, for as long as you are here."

It was a line Sailors told each other, the last phrase anyway.

The nondescript man turned to Angel. "And you, too. Bless you, Brother."

Jimmy wouldn't let it go. "Why do Sailors want people murdered, and other people, Norms, panicked, killing themselves? Why do you want all these people to die?"

Jimmy was looking Steadman in the eye when he said it.

This time, there wasn't any thought any of them would answer. Their eyes had moved to the house behind him.

Mary stood in the open doorway.

She ran out of the house and past them.

Jimmy came after her. "Mary!"

It was steep, it was downhill, it was dangerous. And the woods had gotten even darker.

CHAPTER

TWENTY-SEVEN

There is an angry, ugly rhythm to an argument. You don't have to hear the actual words; the sounds are enough. They're like blows in a fight. Three or four jabbing syllables and then the louder thud of the knock-out punch. But the other isn't knocked out. Not yet. It's never over that quickly, no early-round knockdowns. There's always more. You rephrase. You repeat. Redundancy is a given. You aren't judged on grammar, maybe on the number of fricatives and glottal stops. The percussion. Or the footwork, the angry, ugly dance of it. There's a reason arguments end in violence, in hurled glassware, in slammed doors, in slaps, in gunshots. Punctuation is everything.

Dr. Marc Hesse slammed the bedroom door on his way out, and Mrs. Mary Hesse came to the window and looked out at the night, tears running down her cheeks like commas.

Jimmy was across the street but fifty yards away, close enough to hear the angry, ugly sounds but not to see those tears. So maybe he just filled in the blanks, seeing what he wanted, what he needed to see. Just enough to hate Hesse.

The other night in front of the Victorian apartment house, with the Greek father and Machine Shop packed into the Porsche, Jimmy had remembered the ride with his own father when he was ten or eleven, when his father told him he and Jimmy's mother were divorcing, that speech that begins, "Sometimes a mother and a father grow apart . . ." Jimmy remembered something else. When he was sixteen, he told his mother what his father had said that night, and what she had said back to Jimmy was, *"Les chaînes de mariage sont si lourdes qu'il faut deux pour les porter. Et parfois trois."* They were in a car, too, the huge white Chrysler 400 that was her last car, top down, somewhere in Hollywood. "The chains of matrimony are so heavy it takes two to carry them. And sometimes three."

The garage door came up. The Mercedes's red taillights and white backup lights flared, and the SUV charged out, the automatic radio antenna extending so fast it dragged across the last of the garage door hurrying to get out of the way. Mary stood witness in the upstairs window, in the master suite, over the garage. It was a big window, with true divides, beveled leaded glass, black frames dividing her into eight-by-tens.

Jimmy hated him for making her cry, for bringing her to the window to watch him go. He hated him.

Given what he was about to do, it was a useful emotion.

A sound made Mary turn toward the door. A woman stepped into the bedroom, a young woman wearing a dark suit, a uniform of some kind. A nanny? They spoke. Something was determined. Mary came out of the house a few minutes later, a sweater over her shoulders. Jimmy stepped back into the deeper shadows. The street they lived on, Alcatraz Lane, went two ways down the hill. She started off to the right, toward San Francisco, toward the view rustling through the gaps in the evergreens. Jimmy went the other way. All the streets out on the point of Tiburon emptied down onto the drive that circled the tip of the peninsula and led to the village.

Mary walked along the fronts of the shops and restaurants. It was eight or nine. The shops were closed, the restaurants busy. With the indoor smoking ban, every place now had tall stools and tables out front, where the happiest people seemed to gather. Or at least the loudest. Jimmy was a hundred yards behind her, coming up the same side of the street. He saw her look over at them, the happy, loud people. She kept on walking.

There was a compact marina just past the traffic roundabout and the heart of the village. She walked out to the end of a dock. It should have gotten cooler out on the dock, with the wind off the water, but somehow it felt warmer. Maybe it was just Jimmy. The air smelled fresher here than on the other side of the Bay.

Mary stood there with her back to him. There was the sound of the wind, the sound of the boat tackle banging against itself, but still, she had to have heard his footsteps on the planks, coming toward her. Didn't she? But she didn't turn. She must have known it was him. At last. Again.

When he was five feet away, she turned.

He stopped.

There was a moment. The sliver of a moon over her shoulder clicked into a new phase.

"What are you doing here?" she said.

He didn't say anything, let her make up her own answer.

"This isn't a good night," she began, as vague as that.

He crossed the last few feet between them. Could be she moved at least a step closer to him. He put his arms around her and drew her in. There was some exotic perfume behind her ear, somewhere on her, that he almost knew, though not from their time together. Not from the past, at least not *their* past.

He waited. And then he kissed her.

He hadn't kissed anyone in months. When it's that way, you could forget how smooth lips were, how warm. How unlike any other skin.

"Besides that," she said. Her voice had changed into something more comfortable. "What are you doing here? San Francisco."

Jimmy wished she'd asked something else, almost anything else. He wished he had it in him to lie. "Angel had a friend," he said. He noticed the tense. "A girl, a girlfriend maybe. She had just broken up with somebody else, came up here. She was kind of messed up. I was keeping an eye on her."

Mary waited.

"She killed herself," Jimmy said. "Down on Fisherman's Wharf."

"That's sad," Mary said. "That's sad." It was something else he had remembered about her, the way she repeated lines sometimes. She pulled away from him, turned back toward the water, the lights across. It was as if the word about Lucy had broken her will about something. "There have been so many of them lately. It's all people are talking about."

After a moment, she said, "That's something I never thought of. As bad as it ever got."

Jimmy knew that wasn't true. "Let's get a drink," he said.

She turned to him. "We can't do that," she said.

"We'll go somewhere. I have the car."

She looked at him a long time, judging him, he thought, and wondered on what count. How. Was she judging him for *then*, or for now?

"Come on," she said, and started past him up the dock.

They walked over to the last pier. There were three fingers of docks and slips. Jimmy just followed her lead. Halfway there, he took her hand, but she let go after only a few seconds, a few steps. He sensed she was angry, but also sensed that it wasn't entirely focused. It was a rising anger looking for something to form around, something to be about. Something to beat her fist against.

She walked out to the end of the last dock. It was where the big sailboats were, thirty-footers and up.

One of them had her name on it.

Queen Mary.

The cockpit was open, uncovered. It was a Swan, a beautiful Swan, a forty-five footer. She climbed over the lifeline and into the cockpit. There didn't look to be any live-aboards in the boats in the neighborhood, but there were voices from somewhere close. Voices over the water, that sound. Jimmy looked until he found them, two or three guys in the cockpit of a Hunter 38 out near the head of the next pier, the glow of a cigar or two and the good smell of it winging over. Here behind the curve of the little bay there was barely any wind. Jimmy stepped over the lifeline onto the boat.

Mary was unlocking the cabin. She slid the panel door up and out of the way and stepped down. After a minute, she reappeared with a bottle of wine and two glasses. Plastic glasses, but stemware, a nice shape. Boat drinks.

"I drink a lot of wine now," she said and handed him the bottle and a corkscrew to open it with. She plopped down in the seat beside the wheel and pulled her legs up and wrapped her arms around them. All the years that had passed since they'd been together in L.A. blew away.

Jimmy opened the wine. When it popped, there was a response from the guys on the boat across the way. Maybe, "Cheers!"

"I don't know them," Mary said. "They came in a few days ago, sailing down the coast, I think."

Jimmy got that she was also saying, *I wouldn't be here if I knew them.*

But at least she seemed to have lost the anger. "You know what you said yesterday?" she said. "About how it was still so strong?"

He gave her a glass, found a place to stow the bottle, and sat beside her. He didn't know if it was a question she meant for him to answer or not.

She seemed to finish her own thought by drinking half of the glass of wine. Punctuation.

She took his hand now. He brought their hands up and kissed the back of hers, something he never would have done if anyone could have seen. He was different when they were together. Always.

He tasted the wine. It was a rich Chianti.

"Are you cold?" she said.

"No."

"People from L.A. are always cold up here, always talking about it."

"I hate L.A.," Jimmy said. He didn't mean it.

"That's not true."

"I'm never going back."

She surprised him by taking him seriously, like the girl she used to be. It was something else she used to do, something else that made her different from all the rest.

"You know, it never stopped for me," he said.

The sailing-down-the-coast guys laughed loud and rough at something.

Mary moved away from him just enough for him to notice. He followed her eyes. She was looking at the dots of house lights out on the point, above the village, or maybe she was reacting to the intrusion of the guys on the other dock.

"Is the boat yours or his?"

"Mine. He never comes down. He bought it, but he forgets it's even here."

There was another laugh from the men across the way, as if her last line was the punch line to the one about the cardiologist and his restless young wife.

Jimmy stood. He put his wineglass in the teak holder next to the wheel and went forward.

Mary thought he was going to say something to the other sailors. "Jimmy," she said.

But then she saw him kick off his slip-on shoes.

The *Queen Mary*, this *Queen Mary*, was stern-out, its back to the Bay. Jimmy stepped off the boat onto the dock with the balance of a dancer, already getting into the rhythm. He unhitched the bowline with a twirling figure eight, like a cowboy with a lariat. He stepped back onto the boat and curled the line in a circle on the deck, one-handed, another trick. He lifted the white fenders up and over the rail as he came aft and undid the second sheet and the stopper line. He put his foot against the dock and gave it a gentle push. The planks, the cap of the piling backed away.

Mary just watched him through all this. There seemed to be pleasure in it for her, whether it was because of a memory or just the pleasure for women that comes when men finally act. And become themselves, or at least what they think of as themselves. She took the key out of her sweater pocket, a single key on a chain with a fat marshmallow float. She held it out to him. He put it in the ignition and turned it over a click, but not enough to start the engine. He snapped on the nav lights.

He hoisted the main while the stern was still coming around, the boat sliding away from the dock, all from his one push. When she was around, with the sail still just coming up, it caught wind, and the boat started forward across the flat marina water splattered with reflected lights.

It was all pretty slick as moves go, slick and quiet, no engine, and when Jimmy sailed by the men aboard the Hunter on the other dock, they tapped their beer bottles against the rub rail in approval.

Mary went below. She was gone a minute. When she came back to the cockpit, she had on full weather gear, jacket and pants. Everything but a nor'wester hat.

Jimmy had gotten them out past the tip of Belevedere Island already, headed toward the Golden Gate, Sausalito off to the right.

"So, we're making a passage," he said, about her change of clothes. "Hawaii."

"Catalina," she said. That's where they used to sail.

She settled back in beside him. He was standing behind the wheel, one hand down to steer. The sail began to luff a little. Without thinking about it, Mary leaned forward and pulled in the sheet looped around the winch and cleated it.

"Who's sailing this boat?" Jimmy said.

"You are, sir," she said.

And then they didn't say anything for thirty minutes.

Not a word.

Not a memory, not a question.

Not a promise, not a hope, not a regret, though their heads must have been filled with all of those things.

Night sailing. Jimmy didn't know anything like it, anything that combined the serenity, the mysticism, the calm, with that underlying sense of danger, that sense of things that *could* go bump in the night. There was the bright fire of the City to his left, the rust red arc of the bridge ahead, and, beyond it, a kind of darkness not duplicated anywhere else, only over water. There it was, all of it, wide-screen. The wind was light, but there was enough of it to raise some chop, to occasionally throw up a burst of spray, like a handful of confetti. Everything was warmer than Jimmy would have expected it to be. Maybe it was the tide, the famous tide that caught the Alcatraz escapees all those years ago. So the cops said, anyway. The Bay seemed empty. Maybe it was just a trick of the mind. Jimmy wondered when it was most crowded.

He also wondered what would happen if he just kept going.

He stayed on the same track until just shy of the Golden Gate when he came about. It was then that Mary came up beside him at the wheel. She reached across him, put her hands over his. He thought first that it was a tender gesture, but then he realized she wanted the helm. He pulled his hands out from under hers.

She changed his course. She changed his trim on the sail. The boat immediately picked up speed, moved more cleanly through the water. He found his Chianti and sat with his back to the cabin, sailing backwards so he could look at her, with the lights behind her, almost like a corona. It was something else he remembered about her, the way she didn't just sit there, even when she was just sitting there. She was always moving. It was like each moment made him replace some soft-focus sense of her from memory with the reality of her. Of Mary. Now what was before him was vivid and strong and undeniable. Here.

He wanted to give her whatever she wanted.

He had *that* feeling.

Jimmy followed her eyes, looked over his shoulder. Ahead there was a large fishing trawler, halfway across the Bay, heading out from Oakland probably, ablaze with deck lights, covered with fast-moving shapes, crew, draped with nets on cranes. It was still a half mile away but bearing down, an intersecting course, insistent enough, big enough, to stir something in the blood.

Mary kept her hand on the wheel as she dug in the cabinet under the seat and came out with a yellow and black battery lantern. She pointed it up at the sail, not turning it on until it was aimed away from their eyes, to preserve their night vision.

The sail sprang into whiteness, tall as a billboard.

"Let them see us," she said.

Even from a third of a mile out, they heard the change in the pitch of the other's engines. A big thing had yielded.

On the lee of Alcatraz, the wind slacked. Mary eased the boat up into it, to catch what she could. Jimmy tried to suss which cluster of lights ahead was Tiburon, the marina, the restaurants. He thought she was turning for home.

But he was wrong.

She reached forward and started the engine, waited to see that it caught, then started forward to drop the main. Jimmy reached over to steady the wheel, though it was steady enough on its own. He could tell that she was used to sailing alone, even a boat this big. She stood by the boom on the foredeck, atop the cabin, pleating the sail, left right left, as it collapsed onto itself, then looping and tying the stays when it was down. She came back to the helm, pushed the throttle forward a little.

She powered out from under the sweep of the light on Alcatraz, out of its reach, then across a sudden section of chop.

To Angel Island.

It was black, had a mountain in the center of it, was fifty times the size of Alcatraz. Mary steered to the windward side but cruised on past the cove where the overnighters were moored and the campers gone ashore.

She found their own blank section of water. She steered into the wind and cut the engine back to idle. The last of the momentum spent itself. The boat drifted its last foot. They stopped. She listened. They were alone.

"You want to drop an anchor?" Jimmy asked.

"Yeah," she said.

He went forward and let down the anchor, hand over hand, because it was quieter than the electric winch.

She backed up the boat until the hook set. She shut off the engine.

When he came back to the cockpit, she was drinking the last of her glass of wine.

"You were smoking when I saw you in the park," she said, so quiet he could hardly hear her, right next to her.

He sat beside her. She put her head back.

"I bought a pack of Lucky Strikes, on the road, on the way up here," he said. "Something made me think of you. And Luckies. That first night on the Strip."

He didn't tell her about all the other times something made him think of her these last few days.

"I wondered what you would remember."

"The house up above Altadena, in Angeles Forest," he said.

"I would hope you'd remember better times," she said.

Not the end of it, Jimmy thought. *Everything before.*

"That isn't what I remembered about you and me on the way up here, but . . ." He stopped himself. "What do you remember?" he said.

"The way we were together," Mary said. "What we were like. The way people always said we were exactly the same, just alike, and we weren't at all, but there was something when we were together that made it seem that way. That made me better."

"Do you want the rest of the wine?" he said.

She shook her head. Chianti. It was what they always drank. Then. His first night in San Francisco, his unnamed, unseen admirer had bought him a glass in the bar on Columbus. Another thing that sent him down this road, aimed him toward this. Could it have been her? Could she have seen him then? Why wouldn't she say so now?

He leaned over her. He could feel the heat coming off of her. He remembered pulling the blanket up across her shoulders as she slept in the cabin above Altadena. The last seconds . . . The last seconds before it all changed, before she saw just enough of who he was, who he really was, to rend things. *Forever,* he thought, *until now.* He put his hand on the side of her neck. He could feel her carotid, her pulse. His wrist was against the cold knife of the tab of the zipper.

He pulled it down, the zipper. It made a sound like a murmur.

She lifted her back for him.

His hand moved across her breastbone, found another pulse. She wasn't wearing anything under the weather gear.

They moved from the cockpit to the forward cabin. Inside. The physical part was as good as it had always been. Unthinking, natural, confident, unequivocal. The expected and the surprising at the same time. It had always been that way with them, even when they were on the run in L.A. and scared, up in the Angeles Forest, maybe especially then.

The intervening years, gone. At least in this.

When it was over, they talked, or Mary talked and Jimmy listened. He listened to her and studied her face in the indefinite light, while the boat rocked, like a car alone on a good night road. (Was it only the light of the City, coming across the water?) Her face. She'd changed more than he'd thought. How could it be otherwise? Years had passed. And she wasn't like him. He had to keep reminding himself of that. Of course time would change her. The shape of her face was the same, but her eyes seemed stiffened, the line of her nose drawn straighter. He thought again she'd probably had some preemptive cutting and sewing, the kind doctors' wives get. He wanted to reach out to touch her cheek but held back.

She was talkative. She seemed caught up in purpose. That was something new. Before, after sex, in the L.A. days, she'd been soft, conforming, quiet but not sullen, a perfect definition of *easy*. Making love then seemed to take her out of the world. Tonight it seemed to have set her up to want something more from it.

That, he didn't understand.

"I want us to be together," she said to him.

Mary left the cabin, went aft, naked.

She looked back at him. And then just stepped off the stern. It made the smallest of sounds, the water receiving her.

He couldn't help but think about the suicides.

He stood looking down at her, standing on the aft deck.

"Come on," she said. He was naked, too.

He knew why she'd gone into the water, that she had to wash the sex off of her before she went home, exchange its scent for some other, for something innocent. Salt for salt.

He had understood that much.

MARY'S nanny, or whatever she was, stood at the head of the dock, waiting for them as they walked away from *Queen Mary*. Her suit, in this setting, seemed almost nautical, a first mate's uniform. She was almost at attention.

She pulled Mary close and said something. Mary turned and cast Jimmy a complicated look and then started away, with the young woman falling in behind her, leaving him there.

CHAPTER TWENTY-EIGHT

A white rose in a vase filled with milk.

It was waiting for Jimmy on the table in front of the bay window in the living room of the hotel suite when he came back from Tiburon. At midnight.

The thorns hadn't been trimmed.

It felt equal parts threat and seduction.

Jimmy called downstairs for the bellman.

"What is this?"

The bellman squirmed, once he was standing there before it. "I don't know, sir?" he said.

"You didn't bring it up?"

"No, sir?"

"The bellman before you?"

"No, sir?"

"Stop turning everything into a question," Jimmy said. "I'm confused enough."

"Yes, sir. No, sir, I didn't bring it up. And I've been here since . . . yesterday. Someone called in sick."

Its scent filled the room. You couldn't avoid it.

"Do you want me to take it away, sir?"

"No, I like it," Jimmy said.

"Yes, sir," the boy said. "It's very . . . white."

"You don't have to understand something to enjoy it."

"No, sir."

Jimmy gave him a twenty. The bellman started for the door.

"You were here all day, all night? Is that what you said?"

The bellman stopped. "Yes, sir."

"Anybody leave any messages for me?"

"No, sir. Not that I know of."

"My friend in the room next door, have you seen him?"

"No, sir."

"When you go back down, see if anybody called."

"There were no messages. I was at the desk."

"Thanks." Jimmy gave him another twenty. He turned for the bedroom, to change clothes.

"I believe they came up from the kitchen, sir," the bell said, when it looked like the scene was over.

"What came up from the kitchen?"

"The flowers. I didn't actually see them, but I understand they had their own delivery persons. For all of them."

"Other people got these?"

"Yes, sir. The men on the sixteenth floor. Above you. From L.A."

Jimmy had half talked himself into the idea that the flower had come from Mary.

He took a shower. A midnight shower. He was going to go look for Angel. He felt bad about the way he'd left him the last time he'd seen him, never even looked back as he walked away from him down on the docks on the second stretch of waterfront, the old navy base or whatever it was. When Jimmy had followed the two cute girls into the mess hall full of women.

Over the downpour of the shower, he heard a thud, the outside door slamming closed. It shook the wall. He listened, but there wasn't anything else. He turned off the water.

He'd left the bathroom door standing open, the door into the bedroom. He wrapped a robe around himself and came out.

The door to the living room was open. There was Angel.

Angel stood looking at the rose.

"What's this shit?" Angel said, feeling Jimmy's presence behind him.

"I thought maybe you'd know," Jimmy said.

"Did *she* send it?" Angel was changed. He turned with a look on his face Jimmy had never seen before. He looked like he'd been beat up. And left ready to dish some out.

Angel didn't look like Angel.

"I'm sorry I left you back down there, at the navy base, or whatever it was," Jimmy said. After the scene with the women in the dining hall, he'd looked for Angel but couldn't find him.

"Is that what you're sorry for?"

Jimmy didn't say anything.

Angel advanced on him, shoved him. "Is that what you're sorry for?" he said again.

"What happened? Where have you been?"

Angel pushed him again. Jimmy stayed on his feet.

"You go chasing after *her*, and Lucy dies!"

It hit Jimmy like an iron bar, hurt all the more because Angel had waited so long to throw it in Jimmy's face. Jimmy didn't say anything, didn't try to counterpunch. Because Angel was right. Once Jimmy had seen Mary, everything else had fallen away. He had wrapped himself in the past from then on, walked those streets again, not these. He had looked for her, not for Lucy. He worried about her, not Lucy. Before long Lucy had her new best friends whispering in her ear, and he was glad. Let *them* take care of her. He had stood by and watched a slow-motion murder. Was it only in that moment, standing there in his hotel room, that he was able to admit what was obvious, that the two women were agents of . . . Of *what?* Of something that wanted death.

And that he had stood by and watched it, like it was slow-motion crash test footage, projected drive-in style onto the end of a building. Onto Pier 35.

"Tell me what you know," Angel said. "About Lucy. What happened to her?" Angel was shorter than Jimmy, but somehow now he loomed over him. "All of it." His fists were still clenched at his sides.

So Jimmy told him.

He told him all of it. About the first day, about Sexy Sadie and then Polythene Pam outside the Golden Gate gift shop, felt foolish using the nicknames, but what else was he going to say? The woman in the yellow dress, matching purse? The cutie in the too-short skirt and Doc Martens? He could have taken the trouble that first day to find out their names, but he was content calling them Beatles names, from *The White Album*. Because that was the trip he was on. He told Angel the real deal on the two women, how they'd started out looking like helpmates for Lucy, sympathetic ears, but then transmuted into something else. Into the opposite. (He left out the part about not figuring it out in time.) He told Angel about the last night when he had seen Lucy with the two of them, down at Fisherman's Wharf, the night the man had been cleaved in two by the streetcar. On the suicide list, it would have been number . . . *What was it?* He even told Angel about the second time he'd tailed Lucy and the women to the grass out on Tiburon, how he never looked over at Lucy again once he'd seen Mary and her boy playing fifty yards away.

That day.

THEY were in the Porsche, Jimmy and Angel, just driving, a loop around the fingerprint of the City, the perimeter, then into the center, driving nowhere, until most of Lucy's story had been told. It was after two.

Angel had lost his anger, or buried it. "The radio is better here," he said. "Why is that?"

"Everything is better," Jimmy said. "I think that every time I come here."

"Then, after awhile, you start missing L.A."

"I start missing L.A."

"Everything is too *free* here, that's the problem," Angel said.

Jimmy looked over at him.

"Everything comes too easy," Angel said. "Back home, you have to *earn* everything. Work for it, fight for it. A lungful of good air, a piece of shade, something green. Somebody nice. Here it's like they just give it to you."

Jimmy had told Angel everything about Lucy, everything he had, even about the day in the waterfront park when it was Lucy and the women and Mary. But he hadn't said anything about *Queen Mary*, about the night sail, about where he'd been just a few hours ago.

He was still trying to figure out what it meant.

Jimmy stopped at the top of a hill. It was the rise above the Victorian on Central. He hadn't realized he was headed here until he turned the last corner, looping around little Buena Vista Park. He was on autopilot.

"This is the apartment," he said. "Lucy's."

Angel got out of the car, gently closed the door behind him. He looked across at the top-floor windows. There was a light on. In the living room.

"Who's in it now?"

"I don't know," Jimmy said. "It belongs to a lady two doors down the street. Or she manages it. Lucy got the key from her. And the combination to the alarm, which Lucy never set again. I never talked to the woman, the landlady, never found out what the connection to Lucy was. The light's probably just on a timer or something."

A single table lamp burned in the foyer of the Catholic Home, a light that seemed to say, *We're here, anytime.* Jimmy wondered if it was true, if the door was unlocked, if they'd come if you rang, even now, at two in the morning.

"Across the street that's some kind of home for pregnant girls."

Angel turned to look at the home, but not for long. A two-second look.

Angel had seen enough. He got back in.

Jimmy rolled on down the street, not even starting the engine. Quiet. He stopped at the corner. Haight and Central. He looked left.

"There's a guy, white hair, ponytail, lives above the store."

"Yeah?" Angel said, looking over.

"If I was back home, I'd think he was a Sailor. The kind that watches everything. Reports in."

"Yeah."

"Except he's got a dog, kind with the black tongue."

"You never know," Angel said, uninterested.

Jimmy turned left on Haight Street, drove by the coffee place where Lucy had had her "date" with Machine Shop. While Polythene Pam watched. Jimmy spotted the culty girls again, the "sisters" who held hands, the wispy-dress girls from the other night down at the shipyard. Tonight they were hanging with the central casting hippies, the Sailor hippies, at the mouth of an alley. The leader with the Vandyke, Shakespeare in his pointed shoes and his bells, gave them the old *I know you* smile as they passed.

"He may be a Brother," Angel said. "Hippie Boy. Something about him."

Jimmy looked up in the mirror. One of the sisters was watching him go with an imploring look. Jimmy wondered why.

"Sailors are all acting hinky up here, too," Angel said.

"Yeah."

They drove by the black house a few blocks over, down on the Panhandle. Jimmy pulled to the curb.

"What's this?" Angel said. "Besides about the weirdest house I ever saw."

"One of the girls I told you about who hung out with Lucy lives here. Pam. Or at least I tracked her back here."

"It's *black*, right?"

"Yeah, I came back in daytime, hoping it was purple."

So they made the loop, hit the highlights, did the tour. The Lucy tour. The apartment on Central, the coffee place, the black house. They'd already cruised by the place where she'd died, Fisherman's Wharf, Pier 35. It was what Jimmy should have done the first night when Angel came in on the Amtrak Coast Starlight, would have if it wasn't for his mind being elsewhere.

They had the top down on the Porsche. They kept hearing sirens. Echoing. In a city built on hills, sound moves curiously. They stopped at a blind intersection, hearing the wail. Both of them looked left, but then it came in from the right, two city ambulances, racing west, nose to tail.

Jimmy took Van Ness and then Mason and drove out along the water to Fort Point, not because Lucy had ever been there but because he'd run out of places to go.

Except for the morgue. Which was where Jimmy already knew he would end the chapter.

Fort Point. A cop stopped them in the parking lot before they even made it close to the redbrick fort, raising a hand. He was just standing there, no car, nothing. His uniform wasn't even all there. He looked as if he'd come over from home on his bicycle. Extra duty.

"What's up?" Jimmy said.

"Private party," the cop said.

It was a quarter mile away, whatever it was. At the far end of the parking lot under the rumbling undercarriage of the bridge there were a couple of buses, curved metallic shapes catching the light. You couldn't see much of anything else from here. A few knots of people.

The officer leaned over and looked into the interior of the car, just enough for Jimmy to catch the scent on him, the marker. A Sailor cop.

"What year is this?" the cop said. "Sixty-five, sixty-six?"

"Sixty-four," Jimmy said. "Three fifty-six C. The first 911s came along in sixty-six."

"Sweet."

"We'll just turn around," Jimmy said, and eased forward.

"Have a nice night," the cop said.

But instead of turning around, Jimmy went straight. Gunned it. Charged toward the far end of the lot like it was a gymkhana in a shopping center parking lot. The cop shook his head but didn't run after them, didn't unholster his service piece, didn't even radio ahead.

"Guy just flipped me off," Jimmy said, watching in the rearview.

Sitting there were two old-style streamline buses, one in front of the other. Polished aluminum. Without markings. People were disembarking, orderly, in line, joining those who'd already stepped off.

Blue people.

"Those are Chick Warren's buses," Angel said. "Tito Nava did the roll and pleat on the seats. They're tricked out. Blue lights in the headliners."

"They're all L.A. Sailors," Angel said. "What are *they* doing here?"

Another group watched the new arrivals, from a distance, standing together, silent. Not blue, most of them, but on fire in their own way. San Francisco Sailors.

"Field trip, I don't know," Jimmy said. "It doesn't involve us."

He popped the clutch and roared out of there. The SFPD cop stepped out of their way with a sweeping gesture, like a wiseass matador.

THERE was a helicopter overhead, a news helo.

There was a line of ambulances, like a parade, lights spinning, splashing light onto the buildings that surrounded it. There were already spectators on the sidewalks.

The morgue.

"What's this?" Angel said.

"I got a call," Jimmy said. "They're shipping Lucy's body out in the morning. To Paso Robles."

It was Angel's turn to look like he'd been struck between the eyes.

Jimmy said, "But I don't know what all this is."

He parked, got out. Angel took a minute in the front seat, alone, then got out, too.

"Maybe you don't want to do this," Jimmy said.

Angel just shook his head.

"She'll be dressed up and everything," Jimmy said. "A guy here took care of her. A friend of Shop's."

They had to walk past the line of ambulances. There were five or six of them, waiting, engines running, lights rotating like idling heli-copter blades. Every thirty seconds, the news copter came round again with that thudding Vietnam sound. It hurt the head. It felt like being in-side a lawn mower.

Duncan Groner was on the loading dock. When they got closer, up to the ambulance at the head of the line, they could see the first of the bodies.

Wrapped in white, like mummies. Head to toe.

Groner waved to Jimmy. The old reporter was trying for cool and collected, but the story had him excited. The lights from all the ambulances made him look like he'd been doused in blood, standing there.

"What happened?" Jimmy said.

"*Eighteen,*" Groner said. "Eighteen of them."

"What happened?"

"A cult," Groner said. "Over on Fulton Street. They have a house, a four-story Victorian, five bedrooms, four to a room. A flying saucer–tethering pylon on the roof, everything inside painted white, like John and Yoko."

A wrapped body was rolled past and through the double doors. A wheel on the gurney squeaked. The body was small.

"The youngest was sixteen, the oldest twenty-eight, except for their maximum leader. He'll be bringing up the rear. He and his lovely assis-tant, Rita."

"Suicides?" Jimmy said.

"Drink the Kool-Aid," Groner said. "The cosmos awaits."

Jimmy looked at the spectators across the street, saw a familiar face or two. When he turned back, Angel wasn't there.

"What are you doing here?" Groner said, but Jimmy was already headed inside.

The latest suicides had brought out the senior coroners. And deputy coroners and body probers and morticians and, already, politicians in suits. Angel stood in the middle of them, lost.

The late-shift Sailor mortician named Hugh was there, Machine Shop's buddy. He and Jimmy saw each other. Hugh raised his hand, high, like a kid in class. Jimmy led Angel over to him.

"It's kind of wack here, but I already had her out," Hugh said. "I put her in the D Room."

Angel had a freaked-out look in his eyes.

"Come on," Jimmy said. "Then we'll get out of here."

There was a commotion behind them, at the pneumatic doors, which kept trying to close but never got a break. Another body had come in on a gurney. This one wasn't skinny, but he, too, was wrapped like a mummy. And tight, as if this was some ultimate spa treatment. Some final reduction. The cult's leader. Groner walked alongside, enjoying all this more than was becoming. Rolling in immediately behind the fat man was, just a guess, Rita. Whose wrap could not fully blunt her curves.

As Jimmy and Angel walked down the hallway, away from the action, the volume came down.

From the many to the one.

The black linoleum was shined to an absurd pitch, the way it is in prisons, that shine that can only come from people with all the time in the world. It was like walking on obsidian in some Egyptian temple.

Here was the D Room.

The door was closed but unlocked. The lights were on. It was the barest room in the world. The room at the end of the world.

She was covered. On a wooden table.

Propped against her hip was a hand-lettered index card with her name and *vitals*, if that was the word.

Somebody had taken a calligraphy class.

Lucille Estella Maria Valdez

Her elbow stuck out from under the covering. Her sleeve. White satin. She was dressed in white satin now. At least Jimmy wouldn't have to look at that baby-blue dress again.

There was motion beside him, Angel crossing himself.

It was Angel who peeled down the covering sheet.

And it was Angel who said, after a second, there at the end of the world, "That's not her."

CHAPTER TWENTY-NINE

Think *dark*. *Darker*.

Who did this? What exactly happened?

When a big question was thrown in Jimmy's face, his usual first response was to look for the answer in Coincidence. *Shit happens*, wasn't that the bumper sticker? You find out something wasn't at all the way you thought it was, and you're scrambling to make sense of it. And you think, *Coincidence*. You think that if you pull back a little bit, go over all the pieces, see this leading to that leading to this and this, you'll see that it was coincidence, chance, the roll of the bones that made it happen. That made this particular shit happen.

So some other Lucy-looking girl with a 1978 baby-blue Buick Skylark convertible just happened to plow into the flat face of Pier 35 right around the time the real Lucy, Lucille Estella Maria Valdez of Paso Robles, was getting suicidal?

What's next?

Think dark. When *Coincidence* isn't the answer, look next for a human explanation. Skullduggery. Conspiracy. Men in shadows pulling strings for dark purposes. Jimmy Miles probably had a lower opinion of the human animal than most people, men in or out of shadows, pulling strings or dancing on the ends of them, but it didn't wash. Why? How? Who? For what purpose? If this wasn't Lucy, the Lucy he'd followed here all the way from her house in L.A., who was it? *Why* wasn't it Lucy? Who would it profit? How would they do it?

Coincidence. Conspiracy.

Too many questions, you went to *Cosmic*. Some cosmic Somebody is working out His (or Her) will, moving chess pieces on a whole other plane. You only thought that was Lucy you were seeing on the slab in the morgue in the baby-blue dress, her face smashed in. It was just a trick of the gods, a bit in a skit that amuses them ever so slightly. Part of the plan. What they wanted you to see and think about and act upon, for some reason. There was a time when Jimmy's mother went religious, Angelus Temple religious. Jimmy was ten or eleven. She dragged him down there with her to Echo Park for three-hour Sunday services for the half year it lasted. He remembered some of the songs, the old rawboned hillbilly hymns. One of them said,

Farther along we'll know all about it,
Farther along we'll understand why.

But Jimmy didn't have the luxury of waiting for it all to make sense later. This was way too here and now. And human. On *this* plane.

Think *darker*. Darker than dark.

Who set this up? Why? Who would it profit? What would he gain?

"Look, you're sure?" Jimmy said. "I mean—"

"She looks a little like her," Angel said. "But not enough." He pointed at her face, with two fingers together, almost touching her forehead and then her cheek. It was a gesture that looked like he was blessing the girl. "Her eyes, her nose. It's not her. This one's older, for one thing. Ten years, maybe. She's also more mestizo. She's also probably Salvadoran. Lucy was Mexican."

Jimmy hadn't really looked at the girl on the table until now. And now when he looked at her . . . But how could you know? What do you go by? She'd gone into the wall face-first. Her skull had been smashed. Who knew what mortician skills Hugh had. Maybe he just wasn't any good at this. It *didn't* look like Lucy. But what did Jimmy know? How close had he ever really been to her? Ten feet away in the café in Saugus?

"This is somebody else," Angel said. "Lucy is still alive out there somewhere. I know it . . ."

Jimmy covered the body. The face.

"So who's this Hugh?" Angel said. "The one who sent us down here."

Jimmy knew what Angel meant. Start at what's right in front of you and backtrack. Go from man to man to man until it started making sense. New sense.

"He's a Sailor," Jimmy said.

"Yeah, I know. I got that. That can mean a couple of things."

"Friend of Machine Shop's. He works nights here."

Angel said, "So lay it out for me."

"Machine Shop was right there, Pier 35," Jimmy said. "He didn't see it happen, but he was on the scene right after, saw them load the body. She was wearing the blue dress."

"Did *anybody* actually see it happen?"

"I don't know. I guess. It must have been crowded down there."

"Then what?"

"They brought her here. Shop and me came here, after we'd gone back down to the waterfront together."

"And this girl is the one you saw that night? That same night. Here."

"Her face was crushed in," Jimmy said. "I don't know."

Angel said, "I never *knew* Lucy was dead. You know what I mean? I never felt it."

The intensity was still there, but his anger was gone. And Jimmy knew why.

"She's alive out there somewhere," Angel said. "Her and her brother."

• • •

ANGEL wasn't even three feet from the car when he put a Sailor on his back in the parking lot with a single shot to the face. Angel wasn't that big, so a good part of what knocked the man down was just surprise.

"Sorry," Angel said. "Don't come at me like that."

They were on Fisherman's Wharf. It was three in the morning. The tourists were long gone, but there were two or three hundred Sailors between the Porsche and the warehouse building. And no Black Moses to part the Red Sea this time.

Whatever tension, noise that had been in the air before, it had been cranked up a few notches. The waterfront Sailors saw Jimmy and Angel for what they were, two guys looking for trouble, or for something on the other side of trouble, and most of them backed out of the way.

But not the guard at the door. It was Red Boots, the blond, pouty Billy Idol in the peacoat and navy watch cap who'd tailed Jimmy his first night in town.

"Hold up there, mate," he said, putting a hand on Jimmy's chest.

Jimmy slammed his face into the metal door, something of an over-reaction.

But effective. It knocked the door ajar.

Jimmy and Angel came down the same corridor as before, but this time it opened out onto a dock, inside the huge, unlit warehouse space.

They got their first look at the exterior of the ship.

It was painted black, or some dark color that looked black in this gloom. It was big, a refitted oceangoing trawler. With its three-deck-high square windowless cabin, it came off looking like a missile cruiser.

"What's the difference between a boat and a ship?" Angel said.

"This is a ship," Jimmy said.

There was a gangway that was level with the dock, a double-wide hatch at the end of it on the other side. It was probably where they'd been led in the other night for their audience with Wayne Whitehead.

Jimmy snatched up a three-foot wrench propped against a mooring winch and went aboard, Angel behind him.

Nobody home.

And no bent guitar notes sustaining in the air.

The oil lamps on the walls burned. Just enough light to illumine the oval, black marble-topped table in the center of the room and the white rose in the vase of milk.

Jimmy gripped the wrench a little tighter.

He yelled. "Hey!"

They waited.

"We should have took him that night, instead of playing whatever game that was," Angel said. He meant Les Paul.

When they came out through the hatch again, they weren't alone. Twenty or thirty of the Sailors from outside had come into the warehouse. They were still not saying a word, quiet enough to make it creepy.

Just staring at the two out-of-towners.

Jimmy shifted the wrench to the other hand, but they weren't any threat.

"We follow Wayne," one of them said without much behind it. A few of the others gave him a look.

They were staring at Jimmy as if he was somebody. As if his reputation had preceded him. As far as Jimmy knew, he didn't have a reputation. Not here.

"Go," he said.

Surprisingly, they went.

Maybe it was the wrench.

"Come on," he said to Angel. "We'll go south, to the shipyards where we were before. It was where all the women were."

"She's not dead," Angel said. He said it in an odd way, different from before.

"Maybe he's there," Jimmy answered. "Maybe he's looking for her there."

Angel was looking into the shadows.

"What?" Jimmy said.

Angel waited a second, still looking into the shadows, then said, "We know she's not dead, son. Where is she?"

There was a rope locker on the dock. "Come on out, it's all right," Angel said. "We're the good guys. We just want to find her, too, get you guys home."

There was a scurrying rat sound, and the kid exploded up out of the plywood bin. Angel charged in, crossed twenty feet in two seconds, but it was only fast enough to catch an ankle.

"I'm Angel, man, Lucy's friend!"

But the ankle was slick, wet from sweat. The boy escaped Angel's grip but fell hard, on his face, onto the dock. He didn't stop moving. He jumped to his feet and made it another ten yards before Angel was even sure he wasn't still holding him.

"Stop! Come on, man!" Angel said. "You gotta stay with us! We know she's still alive!"

The kid turned with a look of hurt and confusion and anger and suspicion all at once, but only slowed for a second.

And then he was out, through an open door at the far end of the long room, lost into the night again.

When Jimmy and Angel came out of the warehouse building, things had changed yet again. The numbers had swelled. It looked and felt and even smelled like the exercise yard at a prison.

Familiar faces. Some of the L.A. Sailors had come calling, had come over from Fort Point. Some of the roughest ones. Angel knew most of their names. Jimmy knew to stay away from them. The ranks of the San Francisco Sailors had grown. There was a face-off going on, maybe just starting. Some of them, on both sides, had weapons in hand, clubs, lengths of chain or heavy marine rope. There was an ugly sound in the air, ugly anticipation, like the sound in the auditorium before a heavyweight fight.

But then it stopped. When they saw Jimmy and Angel.

They followed them with their eyes.

Or was it just Jimmy?

They split open a path before him. *Yea, though I walk through the parking lot of the shadow of death . . .*

A woman they'd seen earlier stepped in front of Jimmy again and said her line again. *"We serve the Russian . . ."*

"I don't know what that means," Jimmy said.

To answer, she pointed. Across the skyline, the winking cityscape behind them, like a backdrop in a play.

"I don't understand," Jimmy said again. She was right in his face.

She kept pointing. Now he saw it. Maybe. Was that what she wanted him to see?

A violet light atop one of the hills, brighter than anything around it, brighter than there was an immediate explanation for. It burned with the intensity of an airport runway light.

Violet.

The Porsche had been left unmolested.

Jimmy got in the car, but Angel didn't.

"I'm going to stay down here," he said after a second. "In case Lucy's here. In case the kid pops out again. Maybe he'll lead me to her."

"We should stay together," Jimmy said. "Until we understand more of this, what this is about."

Angel shook his head. "I don't care what it's about," he said. He set out back toward the waterfront and all the Sailors.

JIMMY crossed the empty foyer of the Mark.

There it was again. *Hope.* It was all over Angel. He was walking with it like it was his new best friend. Jimmy hadn't run after Les Paul because he wouldn't have known what to say to him if he caught him. He saw the look on the boy's face when Angel had said his sister was alive.

The kid knew she was dead. He knew. He was her brother. He knew.

And now Jimmy was back to knowing it, too. Lucy was dead. Angel had talked himself into something.

Angel had hope. Sometimes it gives you perfect vision, sometimes it blinds you.

It all made Jimmy's head hurt. It made him want to lie down. *Sleep.* He looked over at the first-floor sitting room as he went past, the big pink divans. He had tried all night, through all the death and death talk, through the gathering storm, not to think about Mary, to keep it in some safe spot, the way when something is really good you don't want to connect it to the world, you don't want to dirty it, you want to leave it where it is, perfect. He wanted to let a day or two go by, to think on all of it. To think of her. Of them. He wanted it to be waiting for him, whenever he got through with this, whatever this was.

The last thing he wanted was to see her again now.

But there she was.

Mary stood in the corner of the sitting room. The far corner. She had changed her clothes from what she wore on the dock, the last time he saw her. She was wearing black pants and a long coat, a coat that seemed too heavy for the night, for the season. She looked severe.

"What's the matter?" he said.

She took his hand but then let it go a second later, self-conscious. Even if there was no one there to see anything.

"Can I stay with you?" she said. It was a line she'd never said to him.

But if she wanted rescue, she came to the right guy.

He didn't ask any questions. He took her hand and led her away, across the lobby, toward the elevator.

They got in. He didn't want her to say anything else. He didn't want to know what it was. At least not out here, not now.

But she said it anyway. "He knows about you," she said, as the elevator doors closed.

Jimmy just pushed the button for the fifteenth floor.

"When I came home—"

Before anything happened, the doors opened again, as if he'd pushed the wrong button.

Four men. In dark suits.

The biggest one was Red Steadman. Walter E. C. "Red" Steadman. He flashed blue, strong blue. It made Jimmy take a step back and take Mary with him, though he knew she wouldn't have seen what he saw. The blue.

Steadman. From the deck behind the house in Angeles Forest that night. From other nights.

At Steadman's side was a portly man with a briefcase in hand, a short man as far around as he was tall. (Who had also been on the deck that night.) On the other side was an average man of average size. He wore a hat, or carried it in his hand, a gentleman, if one out of another time. He nodded to Jimmy, all polite, familiar. As if they were all just fellow guests of the Mark. The fourth was a thug of some kind, but a well-dressed one.

They stepped forward into the elevator. The thug made it one too many. The average man flicked his hand, and the thug stepped out again. The doors closed.

It was Steadman who reached across and pushed the button for the sixteenth floor.

"We're just above you," he said.

Jimmy had let go of Mary's hand, but he could feel her trembling beside him. Staring straight ahead.

Steadman seemed to catch the scent of her perfume but never looked at her directly.

"Did you get your flowers?" Steadman said. He slowly turned to look at Jimmy. "Did we *all* get them?"

Jimmy shrugged.

"Interesting gesture," Steadman said, looking forward again. "What do we think of it?"

"I don't think anything."

"Must be . . . new management," Steadman said.

It was a long few silent seconds before the doors opened again. At fifteen. The men moved aside to let Jimmy and Mary out.

Steadman was standing next to the polished brass wall of the elevator, so Jimmy had two views of the last look he gave them before the doors closed.

Mary was still trembling, standing at the door to Jimmy's suite while he found the key. He wasn't sure she'd recognized Steadman. Them. She'd never actually seen Steadman's face on the deck that night. That night, he was wrapped in a scarf and wearing a hat, his face covered. Even his hands. Maybe she had gotten it just from his shape, from his vibe, from the dark richness of his suit. Maybe she remembered the fat man. And the other, the nondescript man with his hat in his hand, the mouthpiece. He'd been there that night, too.

All she really needed to get from seeing them was that Jimmy was the same thing now that he had been then, the same impossible thing. Whatever name they called themselves. She didn't have to see a flash of blue to know that.

He opened the door, and she went in ahead of him, not looking back.

She never said a word about the men. Or of the coded, elliptical talk of flowers, of "gestures" and "new management."

Or of her husband.

She went to bed. They went to bed together but didn't make love again. They didn't talk about the future or about the past. Jimmy just put his arm around her until she went to sleep. He stared at the ceiling, not ever realizing that she wasn't asleep at all.

CHAPTER THIRTY

They had words and she left.

What they said to each other didn't matter. What it was really about was the impossibility of the two of them. What they both knew. Morning reality.

Jimmy asked her where she was going. What he meant was, *Are you going back to him?* Mary didn't answer.

She wasn't even ten feet away, out of Jimmy's reach, before he knew that she wasn't angry—she was scared. And very alone.

ALMOST any time's a good time to meet when you hardly ever sleep. Jimmy had called Duncan Groner. Now they were in the all-night restaurant on Columbus. At five in the morning.

Jimmy asked for and got a glass of Chianti. And a couple of poached eggs.

Groner was sticking to black coffee.

"So is she dead or what?"

"I never met the lady," Groner said.

Jimmy had told him everything about Lucy. Everything.

"You were there, at the scene. You wrote the obit. Tell me what it was like. Take me through it."

Groner said, "Did *you* ever think of going out that way, behind the wheel? Or maybe you did go out that way . . ."

"When did you get there? To the waterfront."

"Twenty minutes after it happened. I was home. I live in Colma."

"Was the body still in the car?"

"She wasn't wearing a seat belt."

"Was the body *on* the car? In front of the car? Under the car?"

"Now *that* would violate a basic law of motion," Groner said. "And be a justifiable cause for suspicion."

"Help me," Jimmy said. He drank about a third of his breakfast wine. A businessman at the next table gave him a look.

"There wasn't anybody around in the immediate vicinity when the car hit the wall," Groner said. "Somebody could have rammed the car into the wall, run from the scene, while some other somebodies—it would take more than one—deposited the body there. Oh. And cast some blood around. A good deal, actually. I don't know where they would have had this body stowed beforehand. What are you thinking, in the ambulance?"

"I'm not thinking anything," Jimmy said.

"Here's another scenario," Groner said. "The car was operated by remote control. The girl, Miss Nobody, was already dead. A body. Yet full of blood, like a ripe pomegranate, ready to burst."

"I guess sarcasm is something you use every day in your line of work," Jimmy said.

"Yes, it is. And on the weekends. Even sitting alone in my little backyard."

"How about this?" Jimmy said. "Somebody talked another girl into killing herself, put the idea in her head and put her behind the wheel?"

There was a several-second delay before Groner laughed, a lag Jimmy would think about later, would try to calibrate.

"Yeah, crazy," Jimmy said. "What's next?"

"How about this?" Groner said. "Dr. Hesse is a Sailor."

Jimmy had to remember to breathe.

"You said he wasn't when I asked you."

"I believe I said I wouldn't think so," Groner said. "I'm afraid I made the mistake of assuming something didn't exist because I hadn't heard of it."

"Where is he on the local organizational chart?"

"Not on it, as far as I can tell. Though he may have pretensions. Just lives the good life. Wink wink."

"How long has he been a Sailor?"

"Years. Thirty?"

Groner studied Jimmy's face. Jimmy was chewing on the inside of his cheek.

"So I guess the boy, who looks just like Hesse, is adopted," Groner continued. "Or he was hers from some previous dead end. I don't know, maybe Hesse put the kid under a knife to make him look more like 'Daddy.' "

"How did you find out?"

"People were asking about you," Groner said. "I in turn asked about those people. You go back up the line."

"When? When did my name come up?"

"For me, the first question about you came a few days ago, just when the girl died. Your Lucy."

Jimmy waited for the rest.

"But the Jimmy Miles File had already been pulled. He'd made inquiries of others before it got around to me. Or I surely would have alerted you."

"He."

"Hesse."

"When? When did Hesse start asking about me?"

"That's what I don't understand," Groner said. "A month ago. Before you came north. Great gears turn."

He put a little drama in his voice. "So maybe *he's* the mind reader, the prognosticator."

A minute earlier, a pair of men had walked by the restaurant, and one of them had looked in, looked only at Groner. Jimmy wasn't sure Groner had noticed.

But Groner noticed now, when the two men came in the front door, shoulder to shoulder, wide enough to block the exit of the businessman.

"I believe *you'll* be getting the check," Groner said, with a little shake in his voice.

Jimmy got up defensively.

"It's all right," Groner said, getting to his feet, too. "It's nice to be noticed."

"Who do they work for?" Jimmy said.

"Oh, could be any number of people," Groner said. "These days."

The men took a step closer, like starting a sentence.

Groner raised his open hands in surrender. He had spotted two more of the same subspecies on the sidewalk out front. And a car.

Jimmy just watched it go down. They hustled Groner out and into the back of the car.

At least it wasn't Hesse's big wine-red Mercedes.

THEN *it became visible . . .*

Jimmy stopped the car, driving westbound on Haight. The nouveaux hippies were bopping down the street. He'd just passed them. It was minutes after sunset. Haight at Ashbury.

They were flashing red auras, faint to Jimmy's eye, but unmistakable.

"Are you seeing that?"

Machine Shop looked back over his shoulder at the hippies. "Uh-huh, *red*," he said.

"I never saw it before," Jimmy said.

"It's the moon. Or all this *meshugas*. All this *activity*."

"What about the moon?" Jimmy said.

"We're goin' into a new moon. Man, you don't know much, for being a emissary from the south and all. Everybody's different—San Francisco is different from L.A. You're blue, we're red. Blue sometimes but red sometimes, too, when the moon goes into a certain phase. You and me together will make purple. The world's a rainbow, man."

"Let's walk," Jimmy said.

"You're the one driving . . ." Shop said.

The two of them had been cruising for hours in fairly aimless loops. Not that Machine Shop was complaining. Jimmy had gone by Shop's Tenderloin hotel around noon, talked him out of going to work down on the waterfront. Jimmy needed the company, needed someone around him, beside him, someone from the time before everything started doubling back onto itself. A week ago seemed like a long time now.

Angel had never come back to the Mark.

"Maybe I need a night off. Sometimes I wonder if that silver paint is bad for you," Shop had said as they were getting into the Porsche.

They made the run up across the Golden Gate to Marin. Past the house on Alcatraz Lane out on Tiburon. It was buttoned up, the black shutters closed. Jimmy drove around the circle in the village, then past the marina. The Swan, *Queen Mary*, was at the dock, a cover over the cockpit now, the mainsail sheathed. The cruise-down-the-coast guys in the Hunter 38 were long gone. Jimmy was beginning to wish he had made friends with them and gone along. Nothing was much simpler than a boat on the ocean, out of sight of land.

He took the 280 south out of the city to Hillsborough, a community of gated homes big enough to look Euro rich. He'd tried to reach Groner all day on the phone, at work and on his cell, but he never answered. He needed another address for Hesse. He pulled into a little branch library and dug into a city directory. There was nothing listed. But there Hesse was, in an old number of the local weekly, a picture in a backyard in a black short-sleeved shirt and tan linen shorts, a fund-raiser for a preschool, though there wasn't any mention of Little Marc and no pictures of his smiling, supportive wife.

And no mention at all of the undead.

The article didn't let slip a street address but referred three times to "Butternut Drive" and even ". . . at the end of Butternut Drive . . ." As they cruised by the numbers, single- and double-digit and nothing more, Jimmy asked Machine Shop what he knew about Hesse.

Nothing, it turned out.

"I move around at the *bottom*," was the way Shop put it.

They found the house. The circular driveway was clean and clear, right up to the four-car garage. It didn't look lived in, but that seemed to be the idea with all the homes on Butternut Drive. Show houses.

Machine Shop didn't ask any questions, not a one all day, seemed content to just be along for the ride. They stopped for lunch at a sawdust-floor burger joint next to Stanford, a bit on down the peninsula, and then came back up on the 101 into the City. With the working stiffs.

They made one last stop, the building downtown where Hesse's office was. Jimmy stayed in the car at the curb in a loading zone, let Shop ride the elevator up.

"It's closed, locked," Shop said when he came back down.

Which didn't seem exactly right.

Night fell. Jimmy found a place to park on Haight, and he and Shop set out. They walked up one side of Haight Street eight or ten blocks and then crossed and came down the other. It was a midweek night but the tourists were out anyway. Jimmy and Shop came past the nouveaux hippies again, face-on this time. Nobody seemed to be in any hurry to get anywhere. More laid-back than the sixties, actually. The leader, with his Vandyke beard, who had seemed a little hostile to Jimmy before, this time put his hands together and bowed.

"I know you, Brother," he said self-consciously, stiffly, the way you greet a foreigner with a phrase not your own.

"Right," Jimmy said. "Hola."

There was a flash of red from Shakespeare.

The young sisters were in the back of the group.

"Can I talk to him?" the one with the imploring eyes pressed forward and said. Her sister tried to hold her back.

"Of course," the leader said. "If he is willing."

"Hi," Jimmy said to the girl. She looked about fourteen.

There was a stiff moment, and then the hippie leader said, "We'll dig you later, Babygirl. We'll be at The 'Choke."

And he led his merry band away up Haight. Babygirl's sister looked back at her, not happy.

"I'm going to get a tea," Machine Shop said, when he picked up that Babygirl was still hanging back, with him there.

"Got any idea what The 'Choke is?" Jimmy said.

"Yeah, down the street. That's where I'll be."

When Shop was gone, the girl leaned against the wall, took refuge beside a rainspout pipe. She said, "He calls me that, Babygirl, or Cry Baby Cry," she said.

Jimmy was about to say something.

"But my name is Christina," she said. "Christina Leonidas?"

Everything's a question. Maybe everybody's name is a question.

"Are you doing OK?" Jimmy said.

"My dad calls me Selene," she said.

"Yeah, I know. He told me."

He heard a breath, or an unformed word, catch in her throat. The perfect word, that explained everything.

"He'll be all right," Jimmy said. "I'm watching him."

"I thought I saw him the other night."

Jimmy nodded.

"No, I mean . . . again. Out at the Yards."

"You mean the Point, Fort Point," Jimmy corrected.

"No, the Yards. Where we saw you. Down south. I mean, I thought I saw him, but—"

"That's your sister, right?" Jimmy interrupted. "That's Melina?"

Christina nodded. Cry Baby Cry nodded.

"She's . . . different from me," she said. "She has all these 'friends.' I just feel like going home." She looked at him directly. "I know I can't, so don't even."

"I wasn't going to say it," Jimmy said.

"I mean, I know how it is. Sorta."

"Where are you staying?"

"We were in this apartment place, down in North Beach, with these really nice people, you know . . . Sailors. But then Melina said things were changing, that something big was going to happen now, that we had to move, to be with the right people."

"So where are you now?"

"With these people, the hippies. But we go back down to the Yards a lot, too. Where the women are, where The Lady is. Sometimes. That's how I knew about you."

"The Lady."

"That's what she told us to call her. She is so nice. She even let us go to her house."

Jimmy decided to break the rule.

"Why did you jump off the roof? What was going on that night?"

She flushed red, so bright and so sudden it was as if she'd expelled vaporized blood into the air around her head and shoulders.

"It's so stupid, I don't know," she said. "We were just hanging out with this guy Jeremy. We were just having fun. He knew all about everything. It was fun. I guess we were drinking, but it wasn't that. Suddenly, we were both so *sad*. We were like crying and everything. And Jeremy was crying with us."

"Stay away from him," Jimmy said.

"Well I know that now," she said, with a little fight in her voice that made Jimmy want to hold her.

"The Lady knows who I am?" he said.

"Of course," she said. "I told you . . ."

"You mean from the other night. At the Yards."

He was remembering that moment when he first saw her, the woman with the short-cropped hair, when he thought she looked like a version of his mother.

"From before that."

"What did she say about me?"

"Just that you were a good person. Someone who understood stuff. Someone to follow. And that was why you had been brought here."

"To the Yards?"

"I guess."

Click. A fragment of light appeared in the angled space between the tops of two buildings across the street, a lamp, a flame, a mirror behind the trees, that hadn't been there a second ago. And a rustling sound at the same time, though there couldn't be any real connection. Jimmy followed her eyes to it. It was the moon. What there was of it.

"Do you know what Selene means?" she said. "In Greek?" She didn't wait for him. "It means *moon*. When I tell people that now, they think it is so cool."

He walked her down the street to The 'Choke, a coffeehouse. A coffeehouse for real, not like the Starbucks wannabe. Yesterday's coffeehouse, not today's. Jimmy didn't tarry. Once he saw the hippies, saw Christina's hard-eyed sister, once he had delivered her back to them safe and sound, he bought a pack of American Spirit smokes and then came back out the front.

And into the shadows across the street.

Machine Shop was already there.

"What are you doing out here?" Jimmy said, lighting up.

"I can't take too many people inside a place," Shop said.

"Too bad, since you're an entertainer," Jimmy said, his eyes across the street at The 'Choke.

"It's limited me," Shop said.

After a few minutes, the group came out en masse. Shakespeare bade the Leonidas sisters adieu, standing there on the sidewalk, kissed his fingertips and then touched each of them on the forehead. The girls got on the first eastbound bus that galloped up. The lights on the bus were bright, and the sisters squinted as they made their way down the aisle to the wide seat across the back. Christina saw Jimmy through the window and waved. Jimmy waved back.

"Youngest Sailors I ever saw," Machine Shop said. "The two of them."

"I was seventeen," Jimmy said and started away.

The remaining hippies, two girls and two guys and their leader, had taken a left, heading away up Ashbury.

Jimmy and Machine Shop followed them, on foot, across Oak to Fell, across the Panhandle.

To the black house, where the band let themselves in.

CHAPTER THIRTY-ONE

"I have to be back before dark," Mary said.

She drove a car Jimmy hadn't seen before, a two-seater Mercedes convertible. Early seventies and perfect. Light silver, the color of a knife. The road was in the country, with a nice gentle back and forth to it, through a valley where they grew flowers, mile after mile, color by color, in strict, clean rows. It was like being led by the hand across a color chart. It was like driving through a rainbow, only the colors were harder. Even to the two of them, even in the moment, it felt like a dream. With that same sense that it had to end, and probably abruptly.

Mary had called the Mark and told him where to meet her, a corner away from Nob Hill. She told him to take the cable car and where to get off. She had called at eight that morning. Something made him think she'd just dropped her boy off at school. They took the 280 out of town, the same way Jimmy and Machine Shop had headed south the day before, and then along the reservoir lakes, lakes to the right, the moneyed communities to the left. He watched to see if she looked over at Hillsborough, in the direction of Butternut Drive. She didn't. Another

ten miles, and she veered off right onto San Mateo Road, the road up
and over the ridge of mountains between the Bay and the peninsula
towns and the coast.

"I have to be back before dark."

She didn't give a reason. He could come up with three or four on
his own, and he didn't want to think about any of them. He certainly
wasn't going to ask her why. He just looked at her, what the wind was
doing to her hair, the shifting light to her eyes.

"I never rode in a car with you, you driving," he said.

She didn't say anything.

The fields of flowers ended, and the road came out at Half Moon
Bay. It was a Thursday. There wasn't much traffic, local or otherwise,
through the main strip of town. Half Moon had been there awhile, had
some character, some Western to it. It also had that nobody-will-know-
us-here feel.

They went to the beach, parked, and walked down onto the sand.
The waves were gentle. And empty. Pillar Point was to the right, a confusion of sailboat masts and The Breakwater. Even that had an unpeopled
look to it.

The two of them had a way of not talking in settings like this, a history of *un*pregnant silence. Back when they were first together they
would go out to the beach at Malibu or Paradise Cove or up into the
mountains or out to some alluvial plain in Joshua Tree and just be
there, side by side, no pressure to talk, no impulse to frame things with
words. It was one of the first pop-up signs that told Jimmy he loved her,
when he realized that she didn't need to say anything, especially in
those situations when anything either one of them might have said
would probably be weak. Or just wrong.

But he spoke now.

"This is where Mavericks is, right? The big waves."

She pointed straight out. "In the winter months, December. A half
mile out past the point. It's tow-in surfing. I don't even know what you
can see from here. They go out in boats, on Jet Skis. The waves are
forty, fifty feet."

The calm in front of them suddenly seemed like something else that could end abruptly. She took his hand. She looked up the beach in one direction. Someone with a dog was coming, too far away to even tell if it was a man or woman, throwing something to send the dog out ahead.

"Are you afraid of him?" Jimmy said. He meant her husband, Hesse.

She didn't have a quick answer. Or a defiant one, which surprised him.

She pulled him to her. "I'm glad you're here," she said. Was that the answer?

"What did he say? When you were arguing?"

"This isn't about him," she said. "In the end."

"Of all the city parks in all the towns in the world, I walk onto yours," Jimmy said, holding her.

She wasn't going to let him throw movie lines at her. "L.A. is only a few hundred miles away," she said. "We would have run into each other again eventually."

"You knew where I was; I didn't know where you were."

"You're the one who used to talk about Fate all the time," she said. They still held each other. It didn't sound as harsh coming out of her mouth as the words would look on a page. Or would seem, remembered. "You were the one who always said that we were meant to be together."

"We were young."

"What are we now?" she said.

"Together," Jimmy said.

He wanted to say one more line. He wanted to ask her why she went into the arms of a Sailor, why she married a Sailor. Was it possible she didn't know about Hesse? Even he didn't believe in a Fate that blind. Or blinding.

She seemed to sense how close he was to asking the real question about her husband.

"Come on," she said. "There's a motel up the way. I called ahead."

The man with the dog had reached them. Mary didn't look his way, but Jimmy did. The man didn't want their eyes to meet, put all his attention on the dog.

"Rex!" the man yelled and threw the stick again.

Mary was looking up at the sun. Or maybe she was gauging the time left by the position of the faint curl of daylight moon.

THEY made it back before dark, time to spare. In time.

In time for Jimmy to be waiting at dusk for Hesse to exit the medical center. To tail him. Maybe in time for Mary to pick up the kid and make it home and shower and change into evening clothes for a reconciliatory dinner with her husband someplace nice in the City, because Hesse never went home. He drove from the UCSF med center to the Sequoia Club to get cleaned up, emerged a half hour later in a slick suit for a dinner date.

Only the doctor met someone else for dinner. A *woman not his wife* is the phrase.

Great gears turn. And not-so-great ones, too.

Jimmy had seen all the detective movies, so he knew, Jake Gittes and *Chinatown* aside, no self-respecting investigator did divorce work. The money wasn't any good, the hours blew, and the customers were never satisfied at the end of the thing, were more likely to hate *you* more for telling the truth than the guilty party for living the lie. When he started "looking into things" for people, formally and informally, for money or, more often, for his own private reasons, he knew what he *wasn't* going to do. He wasn't going to follow husbands to dinner dates. But here he was.

Why was it always husbands? Because husbands tried to pull it off in town. Women at least had the sense to go out of town. Out to some sleepy little beach town for instance. On a Thursday afternoon.

Jimmy didn't have any reason to think Hesse had identified the Porsche, so he'd only stayed two car lengths behind the corpuscular red Mercedes as it left the Sequoia Club. He had the top up, but that was because it felt like rain, the air thickening, clouds descending onto the hills of San Francisco like a stage curtain dropping. He was working. He had half a pack of the American Spirits left. Angel's pint of Cour-voisier was in the glove box if he needed it. There was good music on the radio. He'd made love hours ago in a motel at the beach with the only woman he cared about, still had her scent on him. Life was con-fusing, but it was good. A wave bigger than Mavericks might be build-ing a thousand miles offshore, but it wasn't here yet.

Hesse and the woman met at the restaurant. Separate cars, meet out front. They'd picked a restaurant on top of a high-rise with glass eleva-tors on the outside of the building, right downtown. Maybe they thought it would look like some kind of business meeting, on the up-and-up. Sophisticates in a sophisticated city. The woman wore a stylish hat, a two-hundred-dollar version of a skateboarder's sock hat. Nothing sexier than that.

They left their cars, rode up together.

Somebody else was there. The man who'd been on the Half Moon Bay beach with the dog was there, too. Minus Rex.

Jimmy waited a beat, dodged the dog man, rode on up after them.

Their first courses arrived.

She had her head bare now. It was the short-haired woman Jimmy had identified as The Lady, the Sailor the New Leonidas girl had talked about, the one from the mess hall with the candelabra who'd reminded him a little, but not all the way, of a young Teresa Miles.

There didn't seem to be much passion to the thing. But, just as Jimmy thought that, Hesse reached across the table to touch her hand, to make some point. They *almost* looked like lovers. She drank. He didn't. The view of the city was lovely behind them. It was a very busi-nesslike date. Jimmy remembered Groner's line about cardiologists and their cold, cold hearts. And Hesse a Mormon on top.

Jimmy was almost enjoying it, watching them, a great position at the bar, a gin to make it look right.

Then The Lady said something, and he said something back. And the lovebirds flashed red. Mauve, actually. And he remembered the twisted-together threads of story that had brought him here, that had twisted tighter with this.

A half hour later, Hesse and the woman were coming down in one elevator, and Jimmy was in the other. They were a bit ahead in the race for the street level.

While they waited for their cars, they stood close and talked. She even touched his hand.

Jimmy watched from the Porsche.

Hesse kissed her lightly. She pulled him back for another, this one with a little more intent behind it. She walked to her car, and he walked to his. He didn't look back at her. She didn't look back at him. The two cars pulled away, the red Mercedes and a silver Prius. The Mercedes with a refined roar, the Prius with an electric hum.

So what did it mean? Jimmy had seen the San Francisco movie called *The Conversation*, too, knew lovers' talk was code, that there was always something else being said, that it could look like one thing but be something else.

But it sure looked like unfaithfulness, betrayal. Or maybe Jimmy was just hoping to dirty up his rival.

He saw movement across the street. It was the man with the dog from the beach, coming out of the shadows, on the phone, with a little hurry in his step. Out at Half Moon Bay, Jimmy had decided that he worked for Hesse, was tailing Mary, Mary and the new man in her life. Now, he didn't know what to think.

He started the Porsche and pulled forward.

Dog Man walked four blocks, fast, with Jimmy lagging behind in the Porsche. The man stayed on the phone.

He went down a side street.

Jimmy drove by and looped back. Mary's black SUV was parked down the alley, and the man was at the driver's-side window.

He finished reporting in. He nodded. He walked away from her.

She sat there a minute, then left her car, walked away toward the waterfront.

CHAPTER THIRTY-TWO

He had left so many hanging out there.

Angel.

Machine Shop.

Les Paul.

George Leonidas. His daughters.

Duncan Groner.

Maybe even Lucy.

Now Mary.

And with the wave building, big enough to cover them all.

He parked the Porsche on Battery and walked down to the Wharf. He was looking for Mary. But he was looking for Angel, too. For any of the rest of them, *all* of them. Unfinished business. It was as if they were all Sailors now. Left hanging until it was finished. Or until *It* was finished with them.

On Fisherman's Wharf, things were Balkanized. Territorialized. Any Thursday night tourists left were clearing out, looking over their shoulders as they split for higher ground.

Because tonight the waterfront was all Sailors. Sailors from the south. San Francisco Sailors. Blue. Red.

The blues were around the restaurants and bars to the west. The reds were gathering to the east, closer to the piers. The docks for the Alcatraz boats were dead center between them. There were further divisions within the two nations, subsets, breakout groups of fifty or a hundred Sailors formed around some leader. Or wannabe leader. There were a thousand Sailors all counted. It felt like the floor of a political convention, minus the signs on staffs. They weren't needed. They knew who they were, and any who didn't, didn't care, didn't care where they stood as long as someone else objected, as long as someone else claimed it as theirs, wanted to push and shove for it.

Whitehead moved among the crowd.

Steadman and his crew.

Jimmy thought he saw Hesse.

He saw Sexy Sadie and Polythene Pam, but just a glimpse, not even enough to tell if they were with the Sailors or in among the last of the escaping Norms.

He'd see them again.

He jumped onto the top of a Dumpster to see over the heads of the others, looking for Angel. In seconds, dozens of Sailors gathered around him. He knew some of them. L.A. Sailors. Some good, some bad. A kid named Drew he'd taken off the streets himself two years back, a nurse, an L.A. cop in street clothes. S.F. Sailors. Two of the women from the Yards, who'd been at the long table. Eighties Girl. There was Angelina, the first-night Columbus Street bartender who he'd wanted to go home and curl up with after seeing the suicides on the docks, who gave him the glass of Chianti from his secret admirer. So she was a Sailor.

But the rest of them were strangers to him.

Jimmy heard his name. Then he heard his name repeated, passed from one Sailor to another, from one to the others around him, and others drawing in. A whisper at first, then openly. He'd never heard his name repeated by a crowd. Who had?

The kid Drew raised his hand to wave.

Jimmy jumped down and tried to get away from it. They only pressed in closer. It started to rain. Soft, steady. Nobody seemed to notice. Jimmy only managed to move another few feet.

Suddenly the kid Drew was pushed up against him.

"Hey, bud."

"Hey," Jimmy said.

"How ya been?"

"I'm looking for Angel."

"Haven't seen him," Drew said. "He's here?"

"Somewhere. Why are you even here?"

"I don't know," the kid said and smiled about it. "I just went with everybody else. The bus up was a trip."

"Be careful," Jimmy said.

"Dude, what's the light about? Up there."

Through the rain, the violet light on one of the city hills was still burning. Steady, iconic, cloud-piercing.

"I don't know," Jimmy said.

"It's *Russian* Hill," a man beside Drew said.

"What does that mean?" Drew said.

The man put a hand on the kid's shoulder and started talking to him, leading him away, putting the word on him. *Some* word. Jimmy tried to move, but a new set had discovered him, crowding in, crowding him, whoever they thought he was. With the soft rain, now it felt like a rock concert, without the music, without the mud. With what was already in the air, more Altamont than Woodstock.

A hand seized him by the wrist. Jimmy looked down. A silver hand.

He found the face. Under the silver top hat.

"She's over here," Machine Shop said.

Shop pushed and shoved, cleared a path, like a bodyguard. Now the crowd really had something to look at.

Jimmy and Shop made it to a place between two dockside buildings, a space that seemed to be guarded by two or three of Jeremy's crew. They stepped aside when they saw Machine Shop coming and Jimmy behind him.

"I saw him over in here about ten minutes ago," Machine Shop said.

"You said *she*."

"No, I said he."

"Who?"

"*Angel*," Shop said. "That's who you're looking for, right?" The rain was beading down his face and hands, off his painted skin, huge rolling drops of it. He looked like he was sweating like a runner, or crying great tears. "I maybe saw those girls, too," he said. "The ones from last night, who hold hands." It sounded suspicious. It sounded too much like, *Whatever you want, I got it.* Something, or someone, had gotten to Shop. Gone was the verbal tic that characterized him, the self-correction. Everything he said tonight he said once and stuck by it. He was on message. It felt wrong.

"What's the matter with you?" Jimmy said. "You're acting like you're high."

"I haven't been high since 1976. Gerald Ford."

"So where's Angel? Did you talk to him?"

"He said everything was cool. He was looking for you. To tell you. You stay here; I'll go get him and bring him here."

This was beginning to feel like a trap.

"Go back to work, man," Jimmy said, shaking his head.

He'd had enough. He started toward the wall of people on the other side of Jeremy's boys, disappeared into it.

Behind him, Machine Shop said, "Yeah, you're right, I got to get back over to Pier 41."

JIMMY was finished with the Wharf, but it wasn't finished with him. As he pushed his way through the edgy throng, he caught sight again of Sadie and Pam.

One and one, on a bench, on either side of a woman who looked like she needed a couple of friends.

On either side of Mary.

Jimmy tried to get through the sea of Sailors, but they seemed to have something else in mind for him, and he was taken away by it and lost sight of Mary and the women, forced to watch the three of them get smaller and smaller, like the victims of a shipwreck drifting away.

And, in the end, the ocean spat him out elsewhere.

He walked back up to Battery Street. He got in the Porsche and fired it up. He didn't know where he was going.

He didn't get *any*where.

A black Bentley Arnage rolled out of an alley to block his path.

Groner had only gotten a Lincoln Town Car when they came for him.

I T was another house that looked black, but it was probably just the rain. It was large, four stories, a blockish gingerbread Victorian but done in dark colors, greens and browns and black, with gold edging where it counted. A slate roof.

It was a man's house, you could see from the curb.

The Bentley waited in the stub of a driveway. Jimmy looked out the rain-streaked window at the Goth house. All that was missing were bolts of lightning. Maybe he was supposed to get out. Nobody had said the first word to him. Or to each other. There was a driver and the best-looking muscle Jimmy had ever seen.

A garage door opened on its own, and the house swallowed the Bentley.

The elevator was an ornate cage, black and gold wrought iron. And small. And slow. They'd deposited Jimmy in it and stepped back. It felt a little like carrying out a sentence.

Another man in another black suit was waiting at the other end, with his hands folded in front of him like a funeral director. He made Jimmy remember the woman from Graceful Exits in the ninety-year-old chorus girl's living room.

The room had the same air of the dead to it.

The attendant stepped away into nothing.

Jimmy was worried about Mary, adrift out there, but was afraid to give himself over to it.

"I know that light switch is around here someplace," he said.

There was a rough laugh from the deeper darkness across the room.

"You're young," a voice said.

"Only here," Jimmy said. "Everywhere else, I'm old. When I'm around kids, I correct their grammar."

Jimmy had come in out of a dark, rainy night, physically and emotionally, but it was darker still here. His eyes began to adjust from what, in retrospect, was the blinding brilliance of the elevator. There were a few candles. On tables. They had a scent he'd never caught before, the best candles in the world, from some country Jimmy guessed he'd never visit.

He began to make out the man's shape. The face came last. He was in a wheelchair, a wood and wicker chair. He was a bigger man than his voice suggested. And he'd been even bigger before. A diminished man. Chest sunken, arms gone thin. A man from *then*.

The room began to establish itself. It was large, what once was called a drawing room. There were boxed beams on the ceiling. The floors were dark wood and uncovered. There wasn't much furniture, so the chair could roll without obstructions. There was a large picture window, but the man wasn't beside it. The window was uncovered. There was the waterfront far below, a grid of lights looking like a bed of embers.

Mary was down there somewhere. The other night, down at the Yards, that roomful of women had reminded him of the women he'd known. There was something else about the women in his life: He'd thought he was rescuing each one, one way or another. It was what he did, or tried to do. Save them. More than a few of them threw it in his face on their way out the door.

Now Jimmy could see the man. His hair was white. And full. His head was tipped back against the headrest, until he realized Jimmy was looking at him. He was dressed in dark silk, a jacket or robe. His legs were uncrossed. His feet were bare. His leathery hands were out to the ends of the armrests, as if the chair was a throne. He wore a ring with a red stone. The ring seemed loose enough to fall off.

"Who's next?" Jimmy said. To break the ice.

"That's why we're all here, isn't it?" the man said. "Do you understand the particulars of the process?"

"I don't even understand what you just said."

"Step closer. I'm having some difficulty getting a sense of you," the man said. He took several breaths. Labored. But then seemed to find himself again. "I don't automatically assume that's a bad thing."

Jimmy stayed where he was. "I've got things I could be doing. Why am I here? Why did you have me brought here?"

"You don't know."

"I don't know."

"*Mene, mene, tekel, uparsin,*" the man said. Under the circumstances, with this stagecraft, with the rain running down the outside of the picture window like anointing oil, it was a bit chilling.

Jimmy said, "'You have been weighed in the balances and found wanting.' Daniel interpreting the words that appeared on King Belshazzar's palace walls."

The man seemed impressed. "Are you a Jew?"

"No. My parents were both in the movie business, if that counts."

"A Christian?"

"No. So somebody has found me wanting? Is that why I'm here? Who? Found wanting for what?"

"Actually I was talking to myself, about myself," the man said. He hesitated for another couple of rough breaths, to force a little more oxygen into the blood. "The three words were *three* messages. *Mene.* God has numbered the days of your reign and brought it to an end. *Tekel.* You have been weighed on the scales and been found wanting. *Uparsin.* Your kingdom is divided and given to your enemies."

Before the man spoke again, he waited almost a full minute, long enough for Jimmy to hear a clock ticking somewhere.

"So," the other said, "You see it *is* about me. Though I stopped believing in God a hundred years ago. Took from him his uppercase *G*. Corrected *his* grammar, you might say. Come closer, boy. Young Mr. Miles."

"Who are your enemies?" Jimmy said. "Wayne Whitehead? Red Steadman? Hesse? Marc Hesse?"

"Who?"

"Who else then? The Lady? Who's next?"

"Soon enough it will be beyond me. All that is certain is that this kingdom will outlive me. And *someone* will be king." He shifted in his chair, uneasy, restless. "Come closer, I still can't see you. My eyes . . . Everything is going away. What can I say about you if I can't even see you, son?"

"So is that what the business down at the Wharf was about, people looking at me as if I was somebody?"

The man took the question as rhetorical.

"I'm not up for your job," Jimmy said. "It's a joke somebody's playing. I'm not built for it. I don't lead, I don't follow."

The man reached down and unlatched the brake on the chair.

"Take me over to the window," he said.

Jimmy stepped behind him and wheeled him twenty feet across the room to the window. A reflection of the two of them rolled out of the night sky to meet them.

"Help me stand, James."

There was rustling in the wings. The attendant had never left.

"Go away!"

The rustling quieted.

"Help me."

Jimmy reached around him in the chair with both arms to the small of his back. His body was dry. He didn't hold much heat. Jimmy lifted him to his feet. His hip popped. He felt to Jimmy like he weighed less than a heavy winter coat on a hanger.

The man took a second to steady. He tightened his dressing gown around himself modestly, around his straight hips, over his bony white legs, over the knobs of his knees.

"They said you came north on a mission of mercy, a favor for a friend," he said, standing there at the glass, a shaky pile of sticks. "A favor for another Sailor." He drew in another labored breath. "There was a time when a sentimental gesture like that would have impressed me."

"Well, it all pretty much went bad," Jimmy said. "My 'mission of mercy.' So I'm with you."

There was another dry, rasping laugh. "You remind me of myself," the other said. "A hundred years ago, when I was foolish."

"Thanks," Jimmy said. "I guess."

"*Ah yes!*" the man said suddenly. His focus had shifted, his depth of field.

The rain had lifted. Some hand had moved aside the clouds. There was Alcatraz, alone amid a range of black like the electrified capitol of a dark, dead, desert country.

With that nothing moon overhead.

CHAPTER
THIRTY-THREE

The Bentley boys deposited Jimmy back where they'd found him and whispered away up the rain-slick street.

He drove over a couple of blocks. Mary's SUV was gone.

He took a minute. What he hoped was that the dog man from the beach had found Mary down on the waterfront, gotten her home, and calmed her down. And then he had come back for the car.

Hope. It came and went. And was always ridiculous, if you stared hard enough at it.

He put the Porsche in gear, but before he could pull out, there was thunder. Familiar thunder.

L.A. thunder.

Coming at Jimmy from the far end of Battery was a lowrider. But not just any lowrider: a lowered and sectioned '56 Mercury, white over midnight metalflake blue.

Angel's lowered and sectioned '56.

He parked nose to nose with the Porsche, but ten yards out, killed the headlights. There were two heads in the frame of the windshield.

There was some talk between the two, or Angel talked and the other nodded. And waited.

Angel got out. Jimmy got out.

"You all right?" Angel said.

"Yeah."

Jimmy waited for an explanation, but wasn't going to wait for long.

"I went back to L.A.," Angel said. "Twelve-hour turnaround. I've been driving around, looking for you. I just saw Machine Shop down on the waterfront. He said you were somewhere around here. Said to tell you he was sorry, for some reason. It's crazy down there."

Jimmy was looking at the Mercury. At the girl in the front seat. Angel looked back at her, too.

"Get ready for something heavy," Angel said.

He walked back to the car, to the passenger side, and opened the door. The woman got out. She was wearing a full skirt, like a fifties girl. She had dark hair. She straightened her skirt. She looked as if she'd like to be almost anywhere else.

Angel walked her forward. She was in her twenties.

"This is Lucy," he said. "Lucy Valdez."

She looked scared. She looked guilty. She looked away. She looked like nobody had had to make up the part about her being sad.

"Tell him," Angel said to her. "It's all right, he's cool."

"I couldn't see how anyone would get hurt," Lucy Valdez said. She had almost no accent. L.A. raised. L.A. Unified School District. "I tried to think it through. I couldn't see how anyone would get hurt by it."

Jimmy wanted to hit her. He knew he wouldn't, couldn't, knew his anger had other targets. One of them the man in the mirror.

"They come to her," Angel said. "A guy."

"Let her tell it," Jimmy said.

Lucy took a step back, a step that put her halfway behind Angel.

"A man called me, from up here," she said. *Lucy* said. "But he didn't say where he was. The phone said four-one-five. He said, 'A man will come see you.' He said that when the other man came, he would tell me what it was, the details. And how I would be paid."

Jimmy said, "Do you have a brother?"

The girl shook her head and started to cry.

Jimmy turned his back on them and walked away, halfway up the block.

Angel came after him.

Jimmy turned.

"They gave her five grand," Angel said. "The guy who came down to L.A. did. All she had to do was be there at her house that one night, the night I saw her in the window from the street, and be out of there at two that next morning. The guy would take things over from there. And she had to leave the keys to the Skylark."

"Who was the girl I was following?"

"A friend of Lucy's. From an acting class she took. They asked her if she had a friend."

"What did they tell her it was about?" Jimmy said.

Angel didn't want to say the next word. "Me."

"How?"

"They told her that some men wanted me in San Francisco."

"They thought *you'd* tail her? It doesn't make sense. Like you didn't know what she looked like?"

"They knew I'd send somebody, one of my guys or somebody, and then I'd come up here eventually."

"When the bait was *dead*," Jimmy said.

"She didn't think that far," Angel said. "She's just a kid. She's *con-victed*, man. She knows she did wrong. I found her still out at her cousin's in Duarte. She can't even go home. She can't stand to be there."

"You have enemies here?"

"I didn't think so until now."

Jimmy turned and started back toward the cars, with a sense of purpose that sent Angel after him. "What are you doing?"

Lucy backed up when she saw Jimmy coming, the look on his face.

He grabbed her by the wrist. "Come on," he said, already pulling her up the street, toward the waterfront. "We're going to find the man you met with. You're going to point the finger at him. Lucky for us, seems like everybody's here . . . "

"Maybe he isn't even a Sailor," Angel said.

"It's a start," Jimmy said.

"I never said anybody was in the navy," Lucy said.

"Shut up," Jimmy said.

THEY *were* all there. It was like a living mug book of Sailor suspects.

Jimmy still had Lucy by the arm. Angel was on the other side of her.

Things had gotten even rougher. It was all in boldface now. The segregation had only become more pronounced, the lines drawn clearer. Each knot of Sailors had a speaker at its center, only most of them weren't speaking, just on display, like a dictator on his palace balcony with his arms outstretched to receive the love of the people. But it wasn't love exactly. For some, it was fear. Or that crash at the intersection of admiration and fear that is respect.

Fights were breaking out everywhere. There was Steadman, with the L.A. Sailors around him, bad and good, and a few converts from the north. And a few undecideds, whatever that meant in this context. They'd brought one of the tricked-out buses over from Fort Point, positioned it in the middle of the parking lot. Steadman stood atop it. On the polished, curved aluminum of the bus like that, he looked like Howard Hughes on the wing of a plane. He looked like what he had been in life, an airplane man.

Jimmy didn't imagine that Steadman was behind bringing him or Angel north, but he still made Lucy look at his face and at the faces of his men. The fat man was beside the bus. The hat man was there. And Steadman's muscles, L.A. handlers, one named Boney M and a particularly singular-minded little man they called Perversito.

Lucy just kept shaking her head no at each face Jimmy made her judge. She was scared. She was still crying. She wasn't a Sailor. It was hard to take this in, in one big dose. And she was just a kid.

They came upon Hesse. With him it was hard to tell if he was a focal point, a point of attention, or just another lieutenant moving through the crowd. Maybe he was looking for a crowd, waiting for one to gather around him.

Jimmy dragged Lucy right up to him.

Hesse didn't know who Jimmy was. Or didn't betray it if he did.

"No," Lucy said. "That's not who came to see me. I don't know him. Please. It wasn't even—"

"Shut up."

They pressed on, eastward, leaving a perplexed Hesse behind.

There were groups Jimmy hadn't seen before, with men in the middle he'd never seen, either. There were News everywhere. They were the ones with the stunned looks, the ones with roaring red auras. The ones who shuffled from place to place, waiting for things to start making sense.

"The suicides," Angel said.

"What?" Jimmy said.

"A lot of them are probably these suicides. Somebody trying to run up the numbers."

"When did you start caring about the leadership?"

"I care about it when it touches innocence."

They'd made it to Pier 35, Whitehead's home base. Wayne Whitehead himself stood on top of the face of the building tonight, like the Leonidas girls a million years ago. Last weekend. Only he wasn't naked.

He wore a white suit with a white rose in the lapel.

Jimmy pushed through to the front. Whitehead looked down on him. He raised a hand in greeting.

"Does he think we're his guys now?" Angel said.

"I don't know; I don't care," Jimmy said.

He knew Whitehead wouldn't have made the trip to L.A. to meet with Lucy. He turned her so that she faced Jeremy, scarred Old Salt Jeremy, who stood in his cape at the door into the warehouse, where the ship was.

"*Him*," Jimmy said. "Do you recognize him?"

She shook her head. "I told you—"

"I know what you told me."

As Jimmy took her by the wrist again, to lead her away, Lucy said, "She looked a little like *her*. But not really."

She.

Lucy pointed to a girl beside Jeremy. It was the nobody who'd ushered Jimmy and Angel into Whitehead's hold, aboard the ship in the warehouse. That night, she wore a navy watch cap and peacoat. They hadn't even noticed she was a girl.

"Just the hair," Lucy finished.

"You said it was a man."

"It was. On the phone."

"You said another man came to see you in L.A."

"The first man said it would be a man, but a *woman* came to see me." Lucy touched her own hair. "She had short hair, like a man."

The Lady.

It took awhile, but Jimmy found her, near where Hesse had been. Hesse was gone, and the short-haired woman was in his place. (Or maybe *he* had been in *her* place.) She wore the same clothes from the date with the doctor. The Lady.

"That's her," Lucy said.

"Who is she?" Angel said to Jimmy, lost.

Jimmy didn't have a quick answer for him. "She was down at the shipyards that night. She's a leader. She wanted to meet me. Or at least she wanted something."

"So what does this mean?"

"I means it's about me, not you. They did this to bring *me* up here, not you."

"Why?"

"I don't know."

The short-haired woman was talking to a cluster of women Sailors, some familiar from the Yards. When one turned his way, she was Christina Leonidas. This was about as far away as you could get from where she and her sister had jumped that night.

Selene, her father called her.

Jimmy looked up at the sliver of moon. The clouds were gone.

The woman finished her pitch, or whatever it was. She put her hands on the shoulders of the women around her, smiled, then stepped away a few feet to another group.

But something caught her eye.

Just as it caught a hundred eyes.

People pointed. Across the way, up the hill.

The violet light. It grew brighter and brighter.

When everyone was looking at it, it began to pulse.

In, out . . . Here, away . . .

And then it stopped.

They waited. It never returned.

Some began to cry. Some dropped to their knees.

When Jimmy looked for the woman with the short-cropped, mannish hair, she was moving away through the frozen crowd, the only one in motion.

CHAPTER THIRTY-FOUR

The Lady led Jimmy to the Haight. In her silver Prius.

He didn't have any trouble keeping up. He'd left Angel and Lucy behind at the waterfront, left them and the others and almost everything else behind, left the gathered Sailors to cry and wonder what was next, for those so inclined. There wasn't any traffic. Anywhere. It was as if the city had gotten the word: Tonight belongs to Others.

She parked in front of The 'Choke.

And the stories started to knit themselves together. The way broken bones are said to. And scar tissue.

She got out of the Prius in a hurry and didn't lock it. She went into The 'Choke. Jimmy went past the coffeehouse and turned around and came back up on the other side of the street, stopping three storefronts away. He could use a cup of coffee. He already knew he was only hours away from the end, whatever it was.

The violet light of the story had begun to pulse.

He didn't know exactly what he expected to find in The 'Choke, but what he found was Mary.

They were all working on her. Or at least they were all around her. She was in the center of the group, with her hands around a cup of tea or something. The hippie with the Vandyke and his people, Sexy Sadie and Polythene Pam, they were all there, listening to what Mary was saying and nodding. She had that end-of-a-long-day look but smiled more than you would expect, but the kind of wistful smile that admits defeat. That wants the day to end, whether there's another one after it or not.

The Lady stood by, five feet away, almost at attention.

Mary finished what she was saying, and Sadie and Pam stood and leaned over her and hugged her, that way women do, draping themselves over the other. *I understand.*

Mary saw Jimmy.

He just stood there in the doorway. As if he was in charge, as if *he* was going to determine what happened next.

As if he could save her.

When the others saw him, they closed the circle around Mary, made her disappear. Like bodyguards. Like magic. They were already in motion, leading her away, out the other entrance, the one on Ashbury.

Jimmy went after them. "Don't go with them," he said.

He saw her eyes in the middle of them.

And then they were gone. All of them. They were already crossing the Panhandle at Ashbury, the whole merry band of them. And not waiting for the light. He went after them.

Beatles music was in the air.

With every mistake, we must surely be learning.

Maybe, maybe not.

So this was the black house. Inside.

They had left the door open. He had the idea they never locked it. There probably wasn't even a key.

The living room, the first room in the front of the house, had twenty-foot ceilings and red velvet drapes, Persian rugs on the floor. Mahogany furniture, a wall covered with prints of birds, in different-sized frames, gold frames. There were velvet pillows everywhere and a collection of hats on pegs on another wall.

It was a woman's house. Or *women's*.

He kept expecting to be jumped. Maybe hippies never attack. Next to the living room was a dining room, with a twelve-foot table. Fresh flowers. The kitchen was done in white octagonal tile with a strip of black around the backsplash, looked a little institutional, but on the glass of the window over the double sinks some hand had painted "Good Day Sunshine . . ." in clear acrylic, yellows and blues.

The Beatles' music was coming from the back of the house somewhere. It only made clearer to Jimmy that they were gone already, that they'd run in here and then out the back, to buy time. The sound somehow said empty house.

I don't know why nobody told you how to unfold your love.
I don't know how someone controlled you.

He found the CD player. There was a den in the back of the house. Painted purple, semigloss. The speakers were built into the ceiling, made it sound like God was listening to *The White Album*.

Jimmy eyed the stairs, thinking maybe they were still in the house, upstairs. But then there was a mechanical sound, from the anteroom outside the den.

An elevator stood open. It was integrated into the dark woodwork. He hadn't noticed it before when he came through. It wasn't standing open before. There didn't seem to be a call button for it. He stepped in. He could smell Mary's perfume, floating above the patchouli of the hippies.

There were three buttons. He went with Up.

But it had other ideas. As soon as he'd stepped into it, the elevator had started to make noises, motors and levers. Not-so-great gears turn, too. It went down. One floor. It stopped, but the doors didn't open. Jimmy pushed the bottom button, and it continued. A light over the door pulsed, a soft light behind a circle of ivory, that seemed to be measuring time and not distance. If it *was* distance, it felt like ten floors. It stopped, roughly.

It opened onto a ten-foot-square room, a room hewn out of rock. With an arched opening to the right, a tunnel leading away.

In the tunnel there were train tracks and a shiny electrical contact centered overhead. It was small.

OK, I'll bite, he thought, and started down the tunnel.

He could stand upright but thought to keep his head and hands away from the power line. There were lights on the wall every fifty feet, gaslights refitted with clear incandescent bulbs.

He walked a half mile. It stayed level. It was dry. He would have thought it would be damp, wondered how they did it. He came through a section with a great rumbling nearby, vibrating gear sounds from the other side of the rock. (A cable car barn?) Near the end, there was an intersection with a larger tunnel, this one tiled, a look from another age, a hint of Le Métro. It all seemed automatic, as transportation networks go. There was a light, red/green, at the intersection.

It shined green, so he kept going.

There was a sound behind him. He turned just as an open train car stopped inches away from running him down. It was simple, inelegant, an open box on wheels, eight feet long. A Sailor manned the helm, standing in the rear, like a gondolier. His face wore no expression. Back home, this kind of Sailor was called a Walker. It was a good job for a Walker.

He rode a good distance in the second tunnel, was brought into a room. The tunnel and cart and driver continued on beyond it. He stepped out. The conveyance stayed put.

It was a waiting room. There was a pair of empty wingback chairs. And three doors.

One opened, saving Jimmy from any test of character or intuition.

It was the dog man. "Here," he said, "this way," and held the door open.

Jimmy just put one foot in front of the other.

• • •

THEY came out into a room, a room where everybody had a purpose. People came and went, carrying things. Most of the people Jimmy didn't recognize, but the hippies were there and some of the women from the Yards. There was an air of imminent departure, the train leaving the station. Another train, another station. Jimmy looked for a clock, but there wasn't one.

Duncan Groner came through carrying a wooden box, what could have been a case of booze. He came out of one doorway and headed toward another.

"You still here?" Groner said, didn't wait for an answer.

The woman with the short-cropped hair and that French look was right at the center of things. The Lady. She'd changed her clothes. Now she wore a dark business suit, blue almost to black, with a waist-length jacket, a straight skirt, a white collar, heels. Like a stewardess on the *Titanic*, if they'd had them.

There was something familiar about the outfit. Then Jimmy remembered the nanny that night on the dock. This was the officers' version of the suit she wore.

The woman gave Jimmy a pleasant smile.

Christina Leonidas came through. She seemed happy, excited, energized, the way schoolgirls are when they're working on a project. Putting on a play, a fashion show, a fund-raiser.

"Did you see her yet?" she said. "The Lady?"

"The Lady" was still standing there, maintaining the same smile, standing by. So Jimmy didn't get it.

"The Queen?" Christina said. "She told us to call her The Lady, or even just Mary, but everyone calls her that, The Queen. *Queen Mary*," she said and giggled.

And there was a flash of red, like a wink.

Jimmy's heart fell through a hundred floors.

"She prefers just Mary," the woman in the suit said to Christina.

Then she turned to Jimmy. "She's in the drawing room."

THIRTY-FIVE

She stood facing him when he came in. The woman in the suit had deposited him on the other side of the door and then clicked away in her heels.

The room was lit up bright, the way a child puts on all the lights when a night turns scary, when questions threaten to overtake everything. There were deep green drapes, a heavy weave, closed across whatever windows there were. Two of the four walls were covered with dark books, floor to ceiling. There wasn't much furniture, and the wooden floors were bare, polished to a shine that made it look like the two of them, Jimmy and Mary, were standing on water, looking at each other across a gulf.

She stayed where she was.

Jimmy stepped in through the doorway but nothing more. For now.

"I don't know if you knew or not, but The Man is gone," Mary said.

"Yeah, I don't get that," Jimmy said. "Explain it to me."

She smoothed out the front of her dress, or dried the palms of her hands on it, if they were damp. She had changed clothes, too, from what she was wearing at The 'Choke, when she was being "consoled," or he thought she was. Now she was in a gray suit, with a long coat over a long skirt. It was a little odd, high-collared, a little Eva Perón–theatrical.

"There must be other things you want me to explain first," she said.

"You started with that." He heard the edge in his voice.

"Help me," she said.

And suddenly she was Mary again. He almost crossed to her. But he didn't. He remembered that one of the things that had landed him here, wherever this was, was his predilection for riding to the rescue. Or thinking he could.

"You know, that's what The Man said to me," Jimmy said. "*Help me*. He wanted me to get him on his feet, give him a last look at his dimming empire."

Mary turned her back on Jimmy and reached into the drapes and found the cord and yanked them open. She had her own anger. It was closer to the surface than either one of them thought.

It was the picture window.

It was the drawing room.

It was the house on Russian Hill.

Jimmy felt stupid for not figuring it out before now.

Still with her back to him, Mary said, "I'll explain it to you. He's gone. Crossed over. Released. The special exception for Sailors with years of service. The grace of God. A time and a place. That's all I know about it. That's all *he* knew, all he understood about it. That leaders sometimes are given a gift."

"Turn around, let me see you," Jimmy said.

She turned. She let him stare at her. She knew that right now she was two women to him. She was giving him a chance to try to fit one woman onto the other.

"I understand how you feel," she said.

"Do you?" he said.

She walked to him. Her hand rose to touch his face, but she stopped it on its way.

She said, "I remember standing in some trees in the middle of the night, in the clothes I had been sleeping in. I remember a man telling me, when he finally got around to it, that he was not what he seemed. That he was something that nobody was, that *couldn't be* as far as I knew."

"All right," Jimmy said.

"I remember six men in a semicircle on a deck, one of them with his face covered with a gray wool scarf, and it a warm night, too."

"All right, I get it."

"No, you don't. You only get part of it, Jimmy."

She didn't sound angry anymore.

"We're even," he said.

Her face fell. "Is that what you think this is? Something as small and as far away as that?"

The flywheel in his head was spinning so fast it felt like it could come apart. He was trying to *see* it, how this had happened, how he had come to be in this room. He was making lists in his head, drawing diagrams, schematics. He was trying to piece it together. He was trying to re-create the wiring, get it together to where, when he threw the switch, the circuit completed and the light came on.

The call to Lucy.

The stop in Saugus.

The trip north.

The Beatles in the glove box, the CD he never remembered buying.

The way the fake Lucy looked, dressed, cried. Died.

Mary walked past a table, brushed her fingers across what must have been a switch. All the lights in the room went out at once.

He couldn't see anything. He heard her walk away from him, toward the window.

His eyes adjusted. What he saw first was a dull red glow, her shoulders and the reflection of their line in the glass of the window.

Until that moment, he wasn't sure. Wasn't sure she was a Sailor. It pressed down on him, the knowledge. The fact of it.

He said, "Is that your house, in the Haight? The black house?"

"Yes."

"Why are you here, in The Man's house?" he said. "You seem right at home."

"For the last six years, I worked with Martin. One of the ones who worked for him, but one of his favorites. He never left this house. Everything came to him."

"Why did you marry a Sailor?"

"I want you to be with me," she said, there in the dark.

"Why did you marry a Sailor?" he said again.

"I want us to be together."

"Why did you marry a Sailor?"

This time, she let the clock in the other room play a little fill. "I didn't," she said. "Hesse is just someone I work with. I'm not married."

Jimmy's heart dropped another hundred floors.

"I knew me being married would draw you closer," she said, "not push you away. Would make you want me more. Especially with the kind of man Hesse is."

"What about *your boy*? Where'd you get him?"

"He's mine. Jamie. He's mine. He's *mine*. I'm his mommy, and that's where we live, Tiburon."

She found her softest voice. "Come here," she said.

He stayed where he was. He felt like the pile of sticks The Man was.

"Come here, Jimmy."

He crossed to her. There, behind her, was the City, the Bay. A ship was leaving, out under the Gate.

"How did you die?" Jimmy said, that question they alone can ask. And usually never do.

"I took pills."

"You always hated drugs."

"I know."

"Why did you do it? What made you? Why did you want to die?"

She took his hand. "To reach *you*," she said.

He pulled away his hand. "A girl died, Mary."

"I know," she said. "But that wasn't because of me."

"It wasn't?"

"That was part of someone else's plan," she said. "I didn't order it. I wouldn't have. I had what I wanted. You were here."

"She was a human being."

Mary could have stopped then. But she didn't stop. "Heartbroken girls die every day," she said.

The low clouds and high fog had cleared altogether. The City, the world, was all spread out before them, like a board game.

"Look at us," she said. She meant their reflection in the window, red by blue. Red. Blue. It was like there were four of them.

He was looking past them, at a judging sky.

"I want us to be together," she said again. "We'll do everything together." A sentence for each of the two Marys.

CHAPTER THIRTY-SIX

The last boat over.

Jimmy liked the idea of that. It matched what he was feeling. He was on one of the piers, leaning against the stub of a piling, smoking the last of the American Spirits. He had left Mary in the house on Russian Hill, blew off all of them up there, and the sense of purpose they rode in on. They didn't have to show him out. He knew the way. He walked over a block and came down to the waterfront on the cable car, on the Hyde Street line, the last run of the night. The car was almost empty, just Jimmy and a Chinese man who looked a hundred years old. It was after two by the time he made it back down to Fisherman's Wharf. The Sailors had had it to themselves all night and had trashed it good. The tourists were all still instinctively hanging back, waiting in their hotel rooms until this particular unearthly storm passed. Most of the Sailors had already cleared out, made the crossing to Alcatraz. The ones left milling around, asking questions of each other, of anyone who'd half listen, were the lost ones. The uncertain ones. The undecideds. The ones even more conflicted than Jimmy. Walkers, most of them, with the faintest red or blue auras of all.

He watched the coming and going. Whitehead's strange black ship made four trips over and back just while Jimmy was standing there, taking aboard anybody who wanted a ride over, north or south, friend or foe, before it was too late. The name was on the stern. *White Rose.*

He turned and looked at Alcatraz, the turtle shape of it, the sweep of the light. *In Time.* Wasn't that the name of the painting in Hesse's office? The sailboat making it into port just ahead of the black storm, just in time. If Hesse *was* a doctor.

How could you hope to be with someone if you started with a lie? With a host of lies, interlaced, one feeding off another after a while. As soon as he thought it, he heard Mary's answer: *You started with a lie. You started us with a lie.* She was right, he had lied to her from the first minute. The first word he spoke to her was probably a lie.

He remembered it. "Let's hear your clever first line," she had said, on the sidewalk on Sunset Strip.

"I don't have one," he had said. *I . . . I* was a lie. He didn't exist, not in the way she knew.

"I don't have a clever *last* line, either," he had said. At least that wasn't a lie.

He threw away the tailings of the cigarette and got on board the black ship. Jimmy was the only passenger, the last of the night to go over.

ALCATRAZ.

Every city, every society of Sailors had its place. The Place. When they met all together, for whatever ceremonial necessities, they met there. In L.A., it was aboard the *Queen Mary.* Here, it was Alcatraz. There were always enough Sailors in high places in any city to give their brothers and sisters some space. To facilitate. Sailor cops and Sailor firemen would be there to direct Norms away, to declare the glare of lights or the cars or the lines of people filing into a pubic place hours past midnight "nothing" or "a private party."

Sailors covered the island. As the black ship angled in to bump against the dock, Jimmy saw them. Everywhere. The hundreds, the overflow from the main gathering inside the prison. Whoever was in charge had sure enough fired up the place with blazing lights. It was so bright, so *alive*, there were bound to be calls in the morning to the *Chronicle*. Groner would probably take them.

The local Sailors still thought Jimmy was somebody. As he came off the ship, they stepped out of his way, cleared a path across the dock and up the Z of the ramp, to the big prison buildings on the cap of the rock.

Up top, there was really only one big building. It was two or three hundred feet long, two-thirds as wide, tall, with thick walls angling in. Like a fort. Like a prison. Like a structure used to test bombs. The walls were a cream color in the daytime, and peeling under the almost constant salt wind, but at night they just looked gray. There were support buildings down the slope and out on the point, but they didn't matter, just the big building. There was a concrete and grass yard in front, the front facing San Francisco, and another, all concrete, on the back corner, facing Tiburon.

The light of the lighthouse swept around like a scythe.

Jimmy ducked it, went through the crowd and inside.

They called the main cell block Broadway. It was two tiers high, "oft-photographed." The factions of Sailors had divvied up the space the way they'd divided up the parking lots over at the Wharf. But most of them seemed to be thinking outside the box. Any box. Half were drunk, the other half high, high either from pills or pot (or acid, this being San Francisco), or just from the unsettling mix of order and chaos. Like a prison.

Or maybe it was the cold that had them jumping. It was freezing. Beyond the main cell block was the cafeteria, tables long ago ripped out, but not the clunky apparatus in the ceiling where they could spray out gas in the old days, "to quell a disturbance." Some of them spilled over into that.

On the back wall of the main cell block was the gunrail, a balcony of sorts on the dividing wall. One end of it was against a high, barred window. A man was posted there, looking out the window, looking up at the sky. At intervals, he would broadcast a number. And then repeat it. Wherever he'd started with it, he was down, or up, to thirteen.

Jimmy heard a few more repetitions of his Christian name.

Sailor men and women *dressed* for occasions like this, usually arch versions of whatever they wore living. Whatever that was. The parade down to the docks hours past midnight must have been a sight for any insomniac Kansans peeking around the hotel curtains. There were men in bowlers, men in stevedore caps, men in those slanted knit caps union organizers fancy. Men in oversized Vietnam cammies. Among the women, there were festive Mae Wests and Marilyns and Jackie O.'s. And too many hippie chicks, who probably still had daddies out there somewhere wondering what had happened. A couple walked around wearing real Mae Wests, inflated life vests, glow sticks glowing. Most of the Sailors wore black armbands, but it wasn't a grim scene. What it felt like was a nightclub, a disco minus the music, a meat market in some urban deconstructed space with a cynical name like Regrets. And a rope to keep the wrong ones out.

None of the principals were in sight, not on the floor. There was probably a VIP lounge somewhere.

Security wasn't perfect. A few Norms made it in. There was Les Paul, walking around wide-eyed, with his guitar case and his stingy-brim hat, with a bottle of beer in his hand.

Jimmy saw Angel. Angel had spotted Les Paul, too. He made it over to the kid even before Jimmy did.

"What are you doing here?" Jimmy said to Les.

"He thought it would be interesting," Angel said. "Maybe he'll write a paper about it for school."

"There's a boat out there, you should go get on it," Jimmy said to the boy. "You don't need to see this."

Les Paul put the beer on the floor and started away.

"I talked to him for a long time," Angel said. "I explained it. Sort of. You know how it is."

"She was his sister? For real?"

"Yeah. I just told him his sister was mixed up in something. He always wanted to come to San Francisco. It'll be hard to get him home." Angel scanned the heads. "Machine Shop is somewhere. With that Jeremy, in with those people. He's gone over or something."

"Yeah, he had a lot of back and forth in him," Jimmy said.

"Are you all right?" Angel said.

"I don't know what I am."

Angel was used to lines like that from Jimmy. "Did you find out what it was? Who wanted you here, why?"

"Yeah, I did," Jimmy said. And stopped right there.

They had found a small space next to a cell wall where there weren't others pressing in on them, but now somebody touched Jimmy.

Mary. Mary looking like Mary Magdalene in a hooded cloak, a cassock, though fashionistas probably called it something else. It was black, closed in around her face. One minute she was Mary Magdalene, the next Death in *The Seventh Seal*.

Angel saw her, saw the edge of red light.

It took a lot to surprise Angel. He wasn't surprised. He stepped away.

Jimmy dropped a little of his attitude. "Have you ever been to one of these?" he said. "A little of it goes a long way."

"Can we go somewhere, talk?" Mary said.

"No," Jimmy said. But then he said, "I'm going to go. I don't care about this. Look, when this is over, maybe—"

The man at the window said, "Nine. Nine."

"*Number Nine*," Jimmy quoted. He opened the curtains over Mary's face. "Turn me on, Deadman," he said.

"Jimmy . . ."

"Come with me," he said.

People around them began to recognize her.

"Mary! It's Mary . . ."

It drove her away.

Or maybe it was the Watcher at the window, whose excitement was growing.

"Eight. Eight!"

She looked at him, then went away. Jimmy watched her go, the way people crowded around her, reached out to touch her. He didn't know if he'd ever see her again. If he could. Or if he wanted to.

The clotting crowd pressed in around him. He might have waited too long to escape.

"Seven! Seven!"

"That's bullshit," a voice beside him said. Jimmy turned. It was somebody he didn't know. The man was looking up at the town crier on the gunrail. "He doesn't know shit," the man said. "You can't call phases of the moon by the minute. It's bullshit. *They'll* call it. When the time comes. Just like they'll call the results."

He wore black, head to toe. Right down to the motorcycle boots.

"But I guess some people like that hocus-pocus," he said.

He had a good blue glow on. He offered his hand to Jimmy. There was a studded leather band around it.

"Kingman," he said. "Like Arizona, only farther out."

Jimmy didn't think they looked at all alike.

Kingman had others behind him. They now moved in a pack around Jimmy, closed in intentionally. A semicircle. It was the junior members of the L.A. board of directors. Boney M, Perversito. Even the fat man.

Two industrial floodlights on stanchions popped on, aimed at the center of the gunrail.

"You need to remember who your friends are," Kingman leaned close and hissed into Jimmy's ear.

"You're not my friends," Jimmy said.

"Yeah, that's what I meant," Kingman said.

The door at the far end of the gunrail, the end away from the window, opened.

Whitehead was the first through it.

"Five," the window man said. *"Five!"*

"Shut up!" Kingman yelled at the window man. Some of the crowd laughed. The window man gripped the railing with both hands.

On they came. The candidates.

What followed the appearance of each man onto the gunrail, into the spotlights, shouldn't be called applause, certainly not cheering. But it had a sound, a Sailor-specific sound, something that came out of the back of the mouth, halfway down the throat. Like the huzzahs in the House of Commons. Affirmative grumbling. The vocals were accompanied by the sound of shuffling feet, like walking in place. It was how they registered their respect.

Whitehead got a good reception. Jeremy stood on a bench under the gunrail and scanned the crowd, mentally taking names of any who thought otherwise.

Then it was Steadman. He was so big he had to duck to come through the doorway.

The L.A. contingent responded. And a few of the reds.

There wasn't ever going to be a vote; that wasn't the way it worked. But for now it seemed even between the two men, Whitehead and Steadman.

"The Next!" Kingman shouted out. "Steadman!"

The feet shuffled louder. Then a rhythm came out of it. And the rhythm turned into stomping.

Led by the black motorcycle boots.

Jeremy glared at Kingman and the SoCal Sailors.

"What?" Kingman said, glaring back at Jeremy. *"What!"*

Jeremy seized one of the floodlights and turned it on Kingman. Jimmy was caught in the glare, too.

But the crowd's attention wasn't diverted for long.

Because now Whitehead turned toward the door.

To present Mary. In her hood.

Mary Magdalene. Death Mary. A surprise candidate.

"Queen Mary!" a woman shouted. Men joined her.

Jimmy fell the rest of the way. Face down.

He knew she was known. He knew she had her friends. He didn't know that she was poised to rule them, insofar as any of them allowed themselves to be ruled. He thought she had brought him here because she loved him.

She had brought him here to share a throne.

Christina Leonidas had seen Jimmy in the spotlight and now had squeezed in next to him.

"Can a woman be The Next?" she said.

The question was answered when Whitehead handed Mary a white rose.

"I yield," Whitehead said. And bowed at the waist.

The crowd grumbled their approval.

News joined in, lifting all-too-trusting eyes to the hooded figure on the balcony, the moment's Juliet.

"Your enemies watch you, learn from you," Kingman said to Jimmy. "Red Steadman taught me that. Look at all these News. Fresh dead. They got all this from us. From the Cut thing. Run up the numbers, freak everybody out. But it's not over yet."

Mary looked down at Jimmy, in the other spotlight.

Kingman leaned even closer to him, to make it personal, to make it like a dirty joke, and said into his ear, "I stood over her, man, up in that white house up in Benedict Canyon, had the bloody, dripping knife in my hand. And something stopped me." He laughed the ugliest laugh of all, an ugly breath blown in Jimmy's ear. "Now here we all are . . ."

"One," the now-chastised lookout said. "One."

But it wasn't over. Jeremy shifted the other spotlight from Mary and Whitehead to Steadman.

Steadman moved to the rail.

He looked like a king.

Battling rumbling began, a war of voices and marching feet. The prison seemed to quake with it. Maybe the walls of Alcatraz would crumble with the collective fear and anger and hunger.

Who would it be?

Steadman or Mary?

Jimmy had had enough. He wanted a door. He saw Angel. Angel waved him over. He was along the side. Jimmy started toward him.

"Wait," Mary called down. "Wait."

Her voice stilled the crowd. Completely. In a second.

The light was still on him. Jimmy Miles. The waning crescent moon was now in the frame of the barred window. The hour of decision. Steadman looked defeated, one way or another. A few voices called out Jimmy's name. A few more.

Mary dropped Whitehead's rose, held out her hand to him. To *him*.

Jimmy looked up at her and said, loud enough for any of them to hear, "Whose idea was all the killing?"

Just when it was starting to get romantic.

HE came down the Z to the docks, to where one of the red-and-white ferries idled. A crewman leaned on the rail with a hand spotlight, teasing the fish.

Jimmy stopped and turned before he got on board. He could hear them, up the hill, receiving their queen. In his head, he could see her there, and suspected he always would, for whatever years he had left to serve.

CHAPTER
THIRTY-SEVEN

They left the top down all the way, even when they ran through a little rain south of Salinas. The kid had his porkpie hat on. The guitar was covered.

Life was good.

"Where'd you get that hat?" Jimmy said over the wind.

"It was my dad's," Les Paul said. "It was in the closet."

"Where's he?"

"Down in L.A. someplace."

The kid wasn't in any hurry to get home. You could feel it coming from him. Going home felt like a sentence.

Jimmy came off the 101 into the middle of Paso Robles. Angel and Lucy were behind them in the Mercury. Jimmy slowed, let him come up alongside.

"Take the 46," Jimmy said. Angel nodded and sped ahead.

Jimmy turned off to the right. He knew where the kid lived, a few blocks ahead, a street over from the main drag where the little store was. But he didn't go there yet.

He drove up into the brown hills a mile off the highway. There was a hundred-year-old oak with free shade underneath it. Jimmy parked.

He popped the rear deck on the Porsche and checked the oil, to have something to do.

"All that stuff you saw, forget it," he said, his head over the engine. It crackled like a fire.

Les was looking to see if he could see the ocean from here.

"I never been up here," he said.

"It's nothing for you to think about the rest of your life," Jimmy said, standing, closing the hood. "It's not something a guy needs to know. It's not even real. A lot of it. They just make stuff up."

The kid turned. "I don't want to forget it. I want to use it. In my music."

It made Jimmy want to cry. Something did.

"What's your name, anyway?"

"Johnny," the kid said.

ANGEL had found his own shade tree, at the roadside twist of stainless steel memorializing James Dean. On 46 just before it meets 41. Lucy was just coming out of the little café with a Coke to go.

Jimmy was flying along at a hundred when he came up on them. He pulled it down into fourth and braked just enough to skid into the dirt lot in front of the memorial.

But Angel saw him coming. He already had the door of the Mercury open for Lucy, and she got in, and Angel roared out of there ahead of Jimmy, letting the speed slam the door closed.

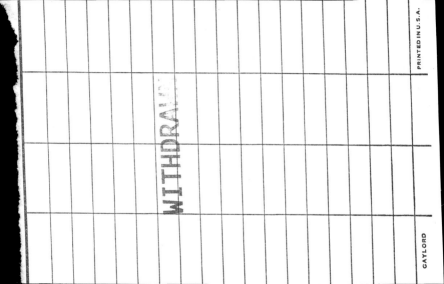

PRINTED IN U.S.A.

GAYLORD